THEMES IN DRAMA

An annual publication
Edited by James Redmond

2

DRAMA AND MIMESIS

CAMBRIDGE UNIVERSITY PRESS

CAMBRIDGE

LONDON · NEW YORK · NEW ROCHELLE

MELBOURNE · SYDNEY

Published by the Press Syndicate of the University of Cambridge
The Pitt Building, Trumpington Street, Cambridge CB2 1RP
32 East 57th Street, New York, NY 10022, U.S.A.
296 Beaconsfield Parade, Middle Park, Melbourne 3206, Australia

First published 1980

Printed in Great Britain at
the Alden Press, Oxford

Library of Congress cataloguing in publication data

Main entry under title:
Drama and mimesis.
(Themes in drama; no. 2)

Includes index
1. Drama–Addresses, essays, lectures.
2. Theater–Addresses, essays, lectures. I. Series.
PN1655.D66   809.2   79-9054

ISBN 0 521 22179 X

Contents

Contents

FORUM

Contributors

Michael Anderson, *Professor of Drama, University College of North Wales, Bangor*

Susan Bassnett-McGuire, *Graduate School of Comparative Literature, University of Warwick*

Victor Dixon, *Professor of Spanish, Trinity College Dublin*

Jonathan Dollimore, *School of English and American Studies, University of Sussex*

Charles J. Dunn, *Professor of Japanese, School of Oriental and African Studies, University of London*

John Fuegi, *Director of the Comparative Literature Program, University of Maryland*

Brian Gibbons, *Department of English and Related Literature, University of York*

Ronald Gray, *Fellow of Emmanuel College, Cambridge*

Tom Lawrenson, *Professor of Theatre Studies, University of Lancaster*

Charles Leland, *Professor of English, St Michael's College, University of Toronto*

John Pilling, *Department of English, University of Reading*

Richard Proudfoot, *Department of English, King's College, University of London*

Michael J. Sidnell, *Director of the Graduate Centre for the Study of Drama, University of Toronto*

E. G. Turner, *Professor of Papyrology, University College, University of London*

Illustrations

Editor's preface

This is the second volume of *Themes in Drama*, which is published annually. Each volume brings together reviews and articles on the dramatic and theatrical activity of a wide range of cultures and periods. The papers offer original contributions to their own specialised fields, but they are presented in such a way that their significance may be appreciated readily by non-specialists. The review section is unusually important, since reviewers have much more than customary scope to give detailed critical accounts of drama in performance, and to discuss in depth the most significant contributions to dramatic scholarship and criticism. Each volume indicates connections between the various national traditions of theatre by bringing together studies of a theme of central and continuing importance.

For much of the long European tradition the subject of the present volume – drama and mimesis – was discussed with a confident simplicity which we now gaze at in wonder. Plato in discrediting Athenian plays, and Aristotle in defending them, took it for granted that the purpose of drama was to imitate and that the value of drama was to be assessed with reference to its mimetic function. Aristotle begins the *Poetics* with the firm assertion that both tragedy and comedy, with other art forms, are modes of imitation: they vary in subject matter, in form, and in style, but each is mimetic of human experience. For two and a half millenniums we have spoken of verisimilitude, of holding the mirror up to nature, of slice-of-life realism, and dramatic excellence has commonly been equated with a minute fidelity of imitation. The Greek dramatist whose name was most revered in this respect, Menander, was the obvious choice for the initial paper in the present volume. 'Menander and life, which of you imitated which?'[1] is the exclamatory question Aristophanes of Byzantium sent ringing through the centuries, to reinforce the supposition that drama ought to be related in a very direct way with actuality.

The nature of the language spoken on stage is at the centre of the issue and is discussed regularly in the following papers. E. G. Turner offers a detailed consideration of Menander's use of a set of rhetorical devices. In dramatic dialogue of high quality, however close it may seem to contemporary conversation, there is always a heightened deployment of conventions: the raw imitative function is modified by the desire to achieve effects of emphasis, surprise, concision, or pattern. This is true of Menander and it is true of television and the cinema, where we find the most extreme modern forms of dramatic vraisemblance. When we say that art is mimetic, we are – far from closing the subject – implicitly raising many subtle questions about the nature of the process. The papers in the present volume make some of those questions explicit, and hold them for scrutiny. E. G. Turner's analysis of Menander's mastery of rhetorical technique leads him to offer reconstructions of mutilated texts, and to question the relationship between Menandrian dialogue and the common speech of his plays' first audiences.

In the second paper Jonathan Dollimore looks at the greatest age of English drama and considers a question which was to be of recurrent interest: what is the nature of the reality that drama is to imitate? The Elizabethan play is a curiously mixed art form, and at the heart of the confusion of purposes, of conventions, of styles, there is the conflict between idealist and empiricist approaches to mimesis: the conflict, that is, between the impulse to portray an ideal universe controlled and ordered by divine providence and the contrary impulse to imitate the puzzling disorder of observed actuality.

The issue of poetic justice and the recurring wish to define the literary arts in terms of their opposition to 'history' expose in broad, clear terms a factor which is often at work with such subtlety that its presence is not detected: one of the strands in the complex weave of purposes when any work of art is created or appreciated is the desire to find an *alternative* to actuality. The process of mimesis can never be passive, and the active element is felt to involve some kind of victory over the material being imitated. Aristotle confronted the truth that we derive pleasure from works of art which portray unpleasant subjects – an ugly animal, to take a surface example, or the fact that death is unavoidable, to take a deep one – and the imitation of such aspects of reality involves not only a rubbing of our noses in the mire but also a sense of achieved superiority. In art, however 'realistic' we may suppose it to be, we have the wild raw materials of actuality made tame, or at least held in chains. When those chains become too obtrusive, of course, they must be replaced with new ones. Jonathan Dollimore's discussion of *The Revenger's Tragedy* dwells on an aspect of that play which has many analogues: the playwright deliberately invites the audience to remark the contrast between his own tactful good sense and the crudity of older plays which accepted some foolishly clumsy convention – in this case that stage thunder can lend metaphysical point to the action. In a similar way Aeschylus is made fun of by Euripides in the *Electra*, early Elizabethan tragedy is ridiculed by Shakespeare in *Hamlet*, and by Ben Jonson in *Cynthia's Revels*.[2] One way for an artist to claim our approval is for him to invite our contempt for some particular artificiality he has decided to eschew. In the many innovatory movements in the literary and in the fine arts there is commonly a plea to nature or reality and a vigorous rejection of some tired convention. There is a demand for what seems to be a closer imitation of actuality; but often what is apparently a call for extreme vraisemblance is really an invitation for us to accept uncritically a different set of conventions.

Eric Bentley may not seem unfair in his commentary on a section of the *Poetics*:

> Art mirrors life. Aristotle's word is *mimesis*. We are too sophisticated if we do not allow the word to carry its literal denotation: sheer reproduction . . . a raw slice of life may be served up as art. It is not any deviation from life that we are enjoying. The fact of imitation is sufficient to turn pain to delight.[3]

But Aristotle is writing in admiration of *Oedipus Rex* and, far from advocating anything like 'sheer reproduction' or 'a raw slice of life', the *Poetics* emphasises the paramount importance of a carefully structured plot, stresses the need for organisation and a proper proportion of one part with another, admires dramatic effects that are elaborately contrived. Something like sheer reproduction can be achieved in filmed drama; but Aristotle asks for gesture and language which will be convincingly appropriate when enacted out of doors by heavily masked actors to an audience of as many as seventeen thousand Athenians. Every Athenian play was a *Gesamtkunstwerk* where music and dancing were of central importance, and Aristotle liked Athenian plays as they were. If he had wanted to denigrate the highly stylised art of Aeschylus, Sophocles, and Euripides and to demand that the more conversational mime with its domestic interest should be developed as an extremely realistic form, the *Poetics* would be quite different.

And so it is with other cases. Hamlet's advice to the players could be paraphrased as a demand for a simple and close imitation of human manners, but the advice comes in a play which makes full-blooded use of a wide range of contrasting styles and conventions. So too with Ben Jonson's claim to be concerned with 'deedes, and language, such as men doe vse':[4] it is a comparative not a categorical statement. So too with Vindice's parody of stage thunder (see p. 39): he is rejecting one very ancient, very important, recently discredited stage convention, but he and his author retain many more. And so too with Ibsen's discussion of the very carefully structured *Ghosts*:

> The language must sound natural, and each individual person in the play must have a characteristic mode of expression; no one person speaks like another, of course. Much can be corrected in this respect during rehearsals; one can easily hear then what does not sound natural and unforced, and thus what must be altered and realtered until the dialogue is completely faithful and realistic. The effect of the play depends to a large extent on the audience imagining it is sitting and listening and watching something actually going on in real life.[5]

That last sentence is crucial to the whole issue of mimesis, and the formulation offered by Arthur Miller is representative of a theoretical position shared by many dramatists influenced by Ibsen's middle plays:

> I wanted . . . to write so that people of common sense would mistake my play for life itself.[6]

An extreme theory of mimesis serving an extreme theory of dramatic delusion is to be found almost everywhere one looks. It is not surprising that Brecht should speak as if the whole of European drama were an empire ruled over by a tyrannical delusion by means of a rigorous mimesis. But the emperor of that empire has no clothes, as Dr Johnson made very clear in his logical demolition of seventeenth-century mimetic theory in France. Johnson was defending Shakespeare against French strictures that his plays have a range of time and geography that prevents the audience's believing in their actuality:

> The necessity of observing the unities of time and place arises from the supposed necessity of making the drama credible. . . . It is false, that any representation is mistaken for reality; that any dramatick fable in its materiality was ever credible, or, for a single moment, was ever credited.

Johnson is right, of course, but he is right within limits; what he says of the actor–audience relationship is true but not complete:

> The truth is, that the spectators are always in their senses, and know, from the first to the last, that the stage is only a stage, and that the players are only players. They come to hear a certain number of lines recited with just gesture and elegant modulation. The lines relate to some action, and an action must be in some place; but the different actions that compleat a story may be in places very remote from each other; and where is the absurdity of allowing that space to represent first Athens, and then Sicily, which was always known to be neither Sicily nor Athens, but a modern theatre.[7]

This is part of the truth, but it does not allow for Johnson's own vulnerably sensitive response to drama – he tells us that his shock at the death of Cordelia lasted for many years.[8] We do not in fact sit through every performance with our eyes dispassionately evaluating the actors' gestures and our ears giving marks out of ten for modulation. And yet in his central point Johnson's contribution is necessary. The talk of mass delusion in a theatre has no reference to any actual or possible event, and we may be reluctant to be told about 'life' by playwrights who seem to be so ill-informed about their own profession. The disguised truth is that the host of men who have spoken of a mimesis so direct, simple and complete that 'people of common sense' should mistake a 'play for life itself' were speaking figuratively.

Coleridge shifted the discussion into its proper sphere, where it is recognised that art is on a plane other than that of actuality, and that very familiar words – such as 'believe' and 'disbelieve' – operate on that plane with quite different force. Response to drama, he argued, is analogous to dreaming:

> It is laxly said that during sleep we take our dreams for realities, but this is irreconcilable with the nature of sleep, which consists in a suspension of the voluntary and, therefore, of the comparative power. The fact is that we pass no judgement either way: we simply do not judge them to be unreal, in consequence of which the images act on our minds, as far as they act at all, by their own force as images.

The playwright's function is not to reproduce actuality, but to elicit the audience's aesthetic acquiescence:

> We *choose* to be deceived. The rule, therefore, may be easily inferred. Whatever tends to prevent the mind from placing it[self] or from being gradually placed in a state in which the images have a negative reality must be a defect, and consequently anything that must force itself on the auditor's mind as improbable, not because it *is* improbable (for that the whole play is foreknown to be) but because it cannot but *appear* as such.[9]

And in a more famous formulation he spoke of the writer's task as being to create 'a human interest and a semblance of truth sufficient to procure for these shadows of imagination that willing suspension of disbelief for the moment, which constitutes poetic faith'.[10]

The process of imitation is not simple in its purposes or in its effects. If in a successful theatrical experience the stage images act on our minds to some extent like images in a dream, the analogy operates on various levels: in the third paper Tom Lawrenson examines some theatre buildings that men have dreamed of, and pointedly takes our minds away from aesthetic theory to the architectural and sociological practicalities of the theatre as they were in France and Italy in the eighteenth century. This paper reveals with special force a truth about most ages of the drama: that theatres have usually been designed and built in accordance with some demands which are unrelated to dramatic art. There have had to be rows of boxes, because the ladies wanted to see one another and to be seen by the gentlemen. The play must not prevent private conversation, so in a theatre in seventeenth-century Holland there were boxes that had curtains with which the occupants could shut the play out altogether. In any theatrical event there will be a constant flux in performance and in audience reaction. There are times when sensitive individuals are caught up in aesthetic conviction by the mimesis, and there are moments that wonderfully move the mind with images that will haunt it for decades. There are hours when the performers are going through their paces with professional skill, and the audience watches them with approval and appreciation. There are some bad times when everyone is waiting with little patience for it all to stop.

Since the most important process is not one of sights and sounds being perceived by our eyes and ears but rather of visual, aural and tactile images being received creatively by our imaginations, it is not surprising that the greatest dramatic intensity can sometimes be achieved when the mimesis is not in the least like 'life itself', but is very highly stylised. The development of modern bourgeois realism in Europe and America has regularly been opposed by demands for a theatre which would strive to reattain the power of the *Gesamtkunstwerk*, and oriental drama has often been a source of inspiration. In the fourth paper Charles Dunn gives an appreciative account of the Japanese puppet tradition. With visibly manipulated dolls representing the characters, this dramatic form can work on the imagination with extreme force so that one play, *The Love Suicides at Sonezaki* (see p. 70), drove many of its audience to emulative self-destruction. Coleridge in conversation made the relevant point:

> It is a poor compliment to pay to a painter to tell him that his figure stands out of the canvas, or that you start at the likeness of a portrait. . . . Look at that flower vase of Van Huysum, and at these wax or stone peaches or apricots! The last are likest to their original, but what pleasures do they give? None, except to children.[11]

The concept of mimesis must not be limited to a close and direct imitation of human contexts and manners: most of the plays we greatly admire are concerned with other things.

If a play is in some ways like life, it has always been clear that life is in some ways like a play. The simile was so common in Greek and Latin literature and so overworked in Elizabethan and Jacobean drama it is surprising that Pirandello could dwell on it to such effect in his great trilogy *Six Characters in Search of an Author, Each in His Own Way*, and *Tonight We Improvise*, the last of which Susan Bassnett-McGuire analyses in the fifth paper. How in a performance can a sense of spontaneity be reconciled with dramatic form? How in actuality can the conviction that human behaviour has a strong element of free will be reconciled with any concept of an orderly universe? How is our exhilaration at the representative man's seemingly unfettered act to be reconciled with the consoling belief that every action is tied to its place in a coherent system? The problems have always preoccupied our serious playwrights. Oedipus's crimes were predicted, but were they therefore preordained? In the end the murder of Hamlet's father is revenged, but how much of the revealed Hamlet is involved in the sword-fighting? Playwrights have always explored the maze of difficulties in the conflicting claims of free will and determinism, and in the problematic relationship between 'character' and action. Pirandello developed a strikingly personal form of the ancient allegorical use of theatrical situations and metaphors to make complex, confused, passionate statements about life and drama. The question had always been implicit in the theatre and Pirandello in play after play makes it violently explicit: what is there in life for art to imitate?

John Fuegi, in the sixth paper, discusses three of Brecht's productions to show in detail the mixed nature of his approach to the question of mimesis. Brecht's actors meticulously imitating the details of a real hanging but wearing clownish 'whiteface', a grotesquely exaggerated model of a man being so convincingly dismembered that spectators fainted, a stage pursuit which mixed admirable dexterity of movement with pathos and terror – this mixture aligns Brecht with the mimesis of Greek, medieval, Elizabethan and oriental dramatists. Brecht often spoke as if his plays were outside the broad European tradition of serious drama, and in *Schriften zum Theater* he offers to define his work as *nichtaristotelisch,* meaning that he rejected the mimesis, delusion, and empathy associated with Aristotle's view of the relationship between a play and its audience. Partly because of the influence of Lessing, the tradition of bourgeois realism was especially strong in German theory and practice in the nineteenth century. One of Lessing's many purposes was to turn German dramatists away from Racine and Corneille towards the prose play with a modern subject. In the course of *Hamburgische Dramaturgie* Lessing builds up an interpretation of the *Poetics* which is in some ways similar to that offered by Eric Bentley – Aristotle talks of fear, he means the spectator's fear on his own behalf, the spectator will identify and empathise most easily with stage figures who are most similar to himself in circumstance, so Aristotle would prefer a bourgeois prose play (for example, George Lillo's *The London Merchant*) to a verse drama embodying myth. In Germany it was Lessing who established this extraordinarily improbable interpretation of Aristotle, and it is Lessing's Aristotle that Brecht felt obliged to reject. Lessing's argument is that drama should above all evoke the spectator's empathy and that contemporary life closely observed will be the most effective dramatic mode. Brecht had no taste for bourgeois realism, and he was led to reverse Lessing's argument. The *Verfremdungseffekt,* whereby the audience was to be made emotionally distant from the characters, plays a key role in Brecht's theoretical rejection of bourgeois realism, but how would audiences be emotionally distant from his Grusche, Kattrin, or Shen Te, when they have deeply cared for Antigone in a fixed mask, for a boy actor Ophelia, for Phèdre in Racine's Alexandrines, and for those lovers of Sonezaki, who were sticks and cloth and paper?

In the seventh article Victor Dixon gives an appreciative account of the plays of Antonio Buero Vallejo, a dramatist not as familiar as he deserves to be with international audiences; and in discussing the theory and practice of 'immersion-effects' he explores important aspects of the question of what we mean when we speak of audiences 'identifying' with characters. In the eighth paper Michael Anderson analyses some contemporary British plays and indicates the most interesting approaches to the crucial issue of the 'language' of drama – a term as complex as 'mimesis' itself.

The review section of the present volume discusses theatre practice as well as dramatic history, criticism, and theory. Richard Proudfoot surveys the

Shakespearian productions directed by Peter Brook; the articles by Brian
Gibbons, Charles Leland, Michael J. Sidnell, and John Pilling were
prompted by recent books on a range of periods and cultures.

The section entitled Forum offers a platform where controversial issues are
debated. In this, the first Forum, the subject is the critical reputation of
Ibsen. In *Themes in Drama*, volume 1, *Drama and Society* James McFarlane
reviewed Ronald Gray's book *Ibsen – a dissenting view*, remaining unper-
suaded by the dissent but stimulated by the argument:

> . . . that there *is* a body of opinion that shares Gray's views is undeniable; that
> it has traditionally found expression either in polite though eloquent disregard
> (as with Leavis) or in brief dismissive phrases (as with Eliot) makes it all the
> more welcome that Gray should now put it with all the forcefulness and
> passionate conviction of which he is known to be capable. He brings to the task
> a brisk impiety and a spirited iconoclastic zeal which the continuing debate
> requires from time to time if a merely stultifying cosiness or a regressive
> in-breeding is to be prevented from totally taking over. At the very least this
> book raises legitimate doubts about a whole range of matters relating to
> Ibsen's achievement which will now have to be squarely faced and – thanks to
> his forthright definition of them – can now be vigorously debated.[12]

Ronald Gray, in the present volume, makes use of the opportunity offered
by Forum to contribute further to a controversy that demands extensive and
direct examination. Ibsen's contemporary reception was so complicated by
social and political issues that the question of his dramatic genius was often
left insufficiently examined.

The editor invites contributions to Forum, on any major dramatic or
theatrical issue which calls for debate.

The third volume in the series *Themes in Drama* will be *Drama, Dance and
Music*, and the fourth will be *Drama and Symbolism*. Contributions are invited
for the fifth volume, *Drama and Religion*, and should be submitted in final form
before the first day of March 1981. Potential contributors should write to the
editor for further information and a copy of the series' style sheet (enclosing a
stamped, addressed envelope, or international reply coupons).

The editor will be pleased to receive books on all aspects of drama and
theatre to be considered for review.

JAMES REDMOND
Editor, *Themes in Drama*

Department of Drama,
Westfield College,
University of London,
London NW3 7ST

N.B. Correspondence sent before June 1980 should be addressed to the
Editor at
Department of English, University of California, Riverside,
California 92521, U.S.A.

NOTES

1. Menander, *Reliquiae,* ed. A. Koerte and A. Thierfelder, 2 vols (Leipzig: Teubner, 1959), II, 7.

2. In Euripides' treatment of Electra's recognition of Orestes there is obvious ridicule of Aeschylus' use of the lock of hair and the footprints as factors in the same recognition in *The Choephori.* Hamlet's dismissive 'the croaking raven doth bellow for revenge' at III, ii, 248 points to the gap between the crude exaggeration of early Elizabethan tragedy (the specific reference is to the Queen's Company's *The True Tragedy of Richard III*) and the psychological delicacy of his own play. In the induction of *Cynthia's Revels* Jonson lashes out in many directions, and *The Spanish Tragedy* itself is not spared his contempt: 'Another (whom it hath pleas'd nature to furnish with more beard, than braine) prunes his mustaccio, lisps, and (with some score of affected othes) sweares downe all that sit about him; *That the old Hieronimo* (as it was first acted) *was the onely best, and iudiciously pend play of Europe.'* *Ben Jonson,* ed. C. H. Herford and Percy Simpson, 11 vols (Oxford: The Clarendon Press, 1925–52), IV, 42.

3. Eric Bentley, *The Life of the Drama* (London: Methuen, 1965), pp. 9, 10.

4. *Ben Jonson,* III, 303.

5. *The Oxford Ibsen,* ed. James Walter McFarlane, 8 vols (London: Oxford University Press, 1960–77), V, 477–8.

6. Arthur Miller, *Collected Plays* (London: Cresset Press, 1958), p. 19.

7. *The Yale Edition of the Works of Samuel Johnson,* 10 vols (New Haven and London: Yale University Press, 1958–77), VII, 76–7.

8. *Ibid,* VIII, 704.

9. *Coleridge's Shakespearian Criticism,* ed. T. M. Raysor, 2 vols (London: Constable, 1930), I, 129–30.

10. *Biographia Literaria,* ed. George Watson, (London: J. M. Dent & Sons Ltd, revised 1960), pp. 16–89.

11. *The Table Talk and Omniana of Samuel Taylor Coleridge,* ed. T. Ashe (London: George Bell & Sons, 1903), p. 240.

12. *Themes in Drama,* vol. I, *Drama and Society,* ed. James Redmond (Cambridge University Press, 1979), p. 302.

Themes in Drama Conferences

The 1980 Conference on the subject of the fourth volume of *Themes in Drama*, 'Drama and Symbolism', will be held in California and will be sponsored by the University of California, Riverside, for which generous hospitality the Editor and Cambridge University Press wish to express their gratitude. A wide range of drama and theatre will be considered, and the term 'symbolism' will be taken to include functions of stage design, costume, and movement as well as symbolic elements in dramatic texts. The Conference will take place on May 16th, 17th, and 18th. Further details may be obtained from

> James Redmond,
> Editor, *Themes in Drama*,
> Department of English,
> University of California,
> Riverside,
> California 92521

The 1981 Conference will be held in London and the subject, as of the fifth volume of *Themes in Drama*, will be 'Drama and Religion'. The Editor invites the submission of papers to be considered for inclusion in this Conference, further details of which will be available from February 1981. All correspondence after June 1980 should be sent to the Editor at

> Department of Drama,
> Westfield College,
> University of London,
> London NW3 7ST

The rhetoric of
question and answer in Menander

E. G. TURNER

There is an often quoted anecdote of Menander narrated by Plutarch, *Moralia*, 347E. Professor Handley[1] has discussed it illuminatingly. I borrow his translation: 'Well, Menander, the festival's nearly here and you haven't composed your comedy, have you?' 'Composed my comedy', replied Menander, 'I most certainly have: I have my treatment of the theme worked out – I just have to set the lines to it' (δεῖ δ᾽ αὐτῇ τὰ στιχίδια ἐπᾶσαι). 'The point is not that the dialogue is of no consequence (one need only read some to discover that that is not the case)', writes Professor Handley, 'But that it is secondary to the design.' I am very happy with this note, provided it does not draw attention away from the *stichidia*. For a very great deal of art has gone into their composition – the apparently effortless composition of a Mozart. Professor Sandbach, in his paper at the *Entretiens sur Ménandre* at the Fondation Hardt in 1969[2] has called attention to some aspects of that art. He himself emphasised at the end of his paper that there was much more work to be done and suggested ways in which it might be carried further.

A very few scholars have availed themselves of his invitation. There is a thoughtful paper by John Feneron entitled 'Some Elements of Menander's Style'.[3] In a dissertation for the London Ph.D. submitted in 1977,[4] Nick Bozanic has some suggestive observations, especially in his chapter five: 'Language as action – narrative, interruptions, dialogue'. I shall come back to some of his points.

These remarks might suggest that what I am going to deal with is 'dialogue' in general. I am not. To discuss Menandrian dialogue I should need to take systematic account of a multitude of topics: for instance, the use of different types of metre (the iambic trimeter, the trochaic and iambic tetrameter, the occasional resort to lyric verse) and the suitability of each for differing dramatic situations; the special suitability for the stage of various types of syntax (for instance, asyndeta, nouns and verbs without connections); the way vocatives (or oaths, or proverbial expressions) contribute to the whole and may be used to give an individual stamp to a stereotyped stage *persona*; the convention of asides, appeal outside the stage to a statue of Apollo or Pan, mockery of public figures, address to the audience (all that we sum up under the heading of 'dramatic illusion'); an important aspect would be the 'cutting-in' of quotations (that is, the mimicry in a reported speech of the actual words and tones of the first speaker); the theory of 'interruptions' propounded by Nick Bozanic. Some of these points will come up incidentally, for my paper certainly concerns the dramatic art of Menander as expressed in the words he chooses to put into the mouths of his *personae*.

But what I want above all to address myself to is his use of question and answer. For I am convinced that this is a specialised form of dramatic technique. Indeed I found it difficult to choose an appropriate title for my inquiry. In speaking of 'the *rhetoric* of question and answer' I do not use the word rhetoric in any derogatory sense. I mean by it the literary, stylistic art of using question and answer to achieve a particular desired effect. For a public speaker *to pithanon* is that which persuades and convinces his audience; to a writer for the comic stage *to pithanon* means something different. It means not convincing a body of listeners of the truth of a case, but carrying them with you. The comic writer does not necessarily have a case to get across. It is the continuous attention of the audience that he wants. Bozanic[5] pointedly cites Aristotle, *Rhetoric*, 1408a, 19–23, πιθανοῖ δὲ τὸ πρᾶγμα καὶ ἡ οἰκεία λέξις (action and the appropriate diction is the persuading agent) and notes Demeas' self-questioning, ἦ 'στὶ πιθανόν (can it be acceptable for . . .?), *Samia*, 216.[6] The comic writer will use different means from those of the speech writer: the *techne* of his rhetoric will utilise some of the devices appropriate to a man on a platform or speaking into a microphone, but he will have other tricks up his sleeve. In ancient Greece the writer is likely to have worked inside a long tradition, handed down from master to apprentice, from Alexis to Menander for instance.

It is this aspect of the use of question and answer that I should like to spend some time upon. It has struck me as an important stylistic feature of writing for the stage, and I have been astonished not to find it already thoroughly discussed by others. When I framed some queries on the subject, expecting to find the answers in the writings of others, I discovered the greatest difficulty in eliciting any answers at all. Grammarians prescribe the norms for interrogative sentences, how they are phrased, their introductory particles, the order of words in such sentences; but it is not for them to discuss why ideas are framed as questions in the first place. Usually this is taken to be self-evident: except in J. D. Denniston's great book, *The Greek Particles*.[7] His work is one of the few conspicuously helpful works I have found. A philosopher of language or linguistic philosopher – a Chomsky, a John Lyons – may spend time ferreting out this aspect of things. But he will usually be interested in the questions in isolation, not set in a context of action and characterisation, while themselves contributing to the fun and laughter. I hope to draw on the resources of grammar, linguistics, stylistics and literary criticism: but no single one of these disciplines in isolation offers me what I am looking for.

Rhetoric, the art of self-expression so as to elicit a given response, is sovereign over them all. This is why the Lady figures in my title.

In the ancient literature[7a] I have found only one explicit discussion, namely in Demetrius, *On Style*, § 279. He is talking of oratory, and sets the use of a question inside the context of *elenchos*, a cross-examination. The following is Rhys-Roberts's translation:

> In speaking it is sometimes forcible to address questions to the audience without disclosing one's own view. For instance: 'Nay, he was appropriating Euboea and establishing a fortress to command Attica; and in so doing was he wronging us and violating the peace, or was he not?' The orator forces his hearer into a sort of corner, so that he seems to be brought to task and to have no answer. If the positive statement 'he was wronging us and violating the peace' were substituted, the effect would be that of precise information rather than of cross-examination.

In passing, let us note that in this example the answer expected by the orator was 'Yes'. When I was first taught about them, attention was concentrated on the negative aspect of rhetorical questions, and the favourite type of question was 'Are we down-hearted?' But such questions are of much greater complexity than this, as we shall see. And they are susceptible equally of positive or negative intention.[8] A type example in Menander of the first sort is offered by the apostrophe to Night by Thrasonides at the beginning of *Misoumenos*:

Thrasonides.   Have you ever seen any other man more
                          wretched,
                      a more star-crossed lover than me?

(*Mis.*, A 4–5)

In modern criticism, too, I have found little. No stylistic or literary implications seem to be discerned in the asking of questions. There is no section on them in J. D. Denniston's *Greek Prose Style*,[9] admittedly only a torso of a book, put together from fragmentary notes. But there is a helpful starting point in H. Weir-Smyth's *Greek Grammar*,[10] § 2640. He draws a distinction between 'questions asked for information and questions asked for effect'. The latter are usually termed rhetorical questions. 'In rhetorical questions the speaker knows the answers in advance, and either does not wait for the answer or himself gives it.' In a new section he continues: 'Rhetorical questions awaken attention and express various shades of emotion; and are often used in passing to a new subject. Such questions are very rare in Lysias, somewhat frequent in Plato, common in Isaeus, highly developed in Demosthenes. The rhetorical question is much more favoured in Greek than in English.' You will notice he makes no mention of drama or comedy. And yet comedy offers a particularly rich field for an investigation of this kind. For it concerns an area of human life in which the conduct of human beings towards each other is exposed in full view: how can X over-reach Y? how shall Z gently reprove X? how shall A tactfully remind B of an obligation? how shall C win over D? – all this before our eyes, in a way which we accept as plausible and related to the life we ourselves know, and yet which also moves our laughter and excites our sympathy.

But the distinction between questions asked for information and questions asked for effect is a very useful starting point here too. And it is complicated by a consideration which will at once occur to you: is the information for the other *personae* in the play or for the audience? Is the effect on the other *personae* or the audience? Often enough the answer will be: both. But the reaction of the other *personae* may not be the same as that of the audience. In exploiting this counterpoint the dramatist shows his skill; we in analysing it can penetrate to the very essence of drama.

But first we must face what may appear to be a prime difficulty. In a discussion of this topic the 64,000-dollar question is: when is an utterance a question? The mark of interrogation as a form of punctuation did not, I think, come into use till Palaeologan times; it is unknown in antiquity. Yet, as we shall see, the difficulty is an unreal one.

Let us consider the case of *Dyskolos*, 472–3. The cook for the picnic at Phyle discovers he has forgotten to bring a stew-pot. He sends the slave to ask a cottager to lend him one. That cottager is Knemon the misanthrope. When Getas trips up to him with his request, the dialogue runs:

> (Γε.)   . . . ἀλλ' αἰτησόμενος λεβήτιον
> (Κν.)   λεβήτιον;
> (Γε.)   λεβήτιον.

> Getas.   . . . I've come to ask for a stew-pot.
> Knemon.   Stew-pot?
> Getas.   Stew-pot.

The important word is picked up and repeated as a question. This is paralleled by a passage from a story by P. G. Wodehouse – alas, I do not remember the title and would like to know – which has been known to reduce my wife to helplessness, but left younger members of the family with stonily straight faces. The dialogue runs like this:

> Wasp.
> Wasp?
> Wasp.
> Wasp.
> Wasp.

The context is a rather strict gentleman's club, in a room where silence is usually observed. One member observes the insect in question crawling on another member's collar (he does not know him personally) and takes a swipe at it – misses, I think, but catches his fellow member a good buffet. Explanatorily he murmurs his excuse: Wasp. The rejoinder comes from incomprehension – and indignation: Wasp? The third utterance is an emphatic reassurance: Wasp. The other gets the point: WASP. Member number one repeats it to show that he understands he is forgiven for breaking the normal rules.

In Menandrian questions that have no special introductory word, the first word may be a noun (or a name), a pronoun, an adjective, an adverb (e.g. ἐνθάδ';), a verb, whether in a finite tense or participle or even 'cut in' – see, e.g., 'οἴει' λέγεις; ('Is that what you think', you say?) *Aspis*, 274, a preposition, a vocative, an oath (such as πρὸς θεῶν),[11] a negative (οὐ very commonly, but also μή).

What may be laid down as a principle is this: if an utterance is to be made by a *persona* in comedy – an utterance that may be important to the development of the action, or may illustrate character – that utterance will gain immeasurably in vivacity if it can be put as a question, or as a series of questions. Since liveliness and buoyancy are vital to creating that atmosphere for a play in which it shall swim straight into the audience's hearts and affections as well as propel the action forward, we may make it a canon of interpretation that if a piece of Greek can be taken as a question, it *should* be taken as a question.[12] This canon is implicit in a number of suggestive interpretations by Professor F. H. Sandbach.[13]

This proposition can be supported by looking at its converse – those passages from which questions are notably absent. For instance, when the old Curmudgeon, Knemon, in *Dyskolos*, hauled up dripping and shocked from the cistern into which he had fallen, holds forth in continuous speech to a stage crowded by the whole cast. Between verses 708 and 753 – more than forty lines of continuous trochaic tetrameters – he asks only one question (at 729 – no doubt in response to some movement among the actors). The remainder is statement: serious and grave, a chance to let the old misanthrope raise the curtain on his motives and justify himself. The case is similar in Demeas' long monologue in act III of *Samia*. Unlike Knemon, Demeas is alone on the stage. In this monologue he tells us how he had been led to think that Moschion must be father of the child represented to him as his. After an early question (to the audience as much as to himself, 'is it acceptable to reason' ἢ 'στ[ι] πιθανόν, v. 216) more than sixty verses follow which do not include a single question, except those 'cut in' from the reported words of the nurse. The mood is serious, questions are out of place.

If a piece of Greek can be taken as a question, it should be so taken, I asserted. But there can of course be good reasons why it should not be so taken, as in the following example, from a soliloquy:

(Χαρ.)   αὐτὸν δὲ δείξω σ' εἰς ὅμοι' ἐπταικότα·
        καὶ χρήσετ' αὐτή σοι τοτ' ἠπίως, σὺ δὲ
        ταύτην ἀτιμάζεις· ἐπιδείχθησει θ' ἅμα
        ἀτυχὴς γεγονὼς καὶ σκαιὸς ἀγνώμων τ' ἀνήρ.

Charisios.   I'll convict you yourself of the self-same
                 Error; and she will treat you lightly, while
                 You scorn her; men will point fingers at you
                 As hapless, heartless, clumsy all at once.

(Epitrepontes, 915–19)

The second and third verses could be taken as questions to himself by
Charisios – except that the whole passage is perhaps itself to be thought of as
a declaration to Charisios by some divine power (τὸ δαιμόνιον) – to compare
farce with Menander, like the supposed St Thérèse in Feydeau's *The Girl
From Maxim's* addressing her devotee. In Menander undoubtedly the intention is serious, not farcical.

It must be recognised that the gradations between question, exclamation,
order and wish are very fine indeed.[14] A question may contain a courteous
order, like the following:

  (Kν.)   θυγάτριον,
             βούλει μ' ἀναστῆσαι λαβοῦσα;

  Knemon.   Daughter,
             Are you willing to take my arm and help me stand?

(Dyskolos, 700–1)

I recollect an American physician who said to a patient suffering from a
wrenched tendon 'Do you want to jump up and down a bit?' (he meant:
please jump up and down). We say 'How do you do?' – τί πράττεις; (e.g.
Georgos, 43). It is quite embarrassing if the question is taken seriously and
answered with deliberation.

The interrogative cluster πῶς ἄν (how might it . . .) may easily precede a
wish (so at *Samia*, 102 in an apostrophe to Athens). But I must admit to
finding this interrogative πῶς ἄν awkward at *Samia*, 151–2:

  (Mo.)   [πῶς ἄν, π]υθόμενος μηδὲ ἕν τοῦ πράγματος,
             ἐσπουδακότα μ' αἴσθοιο συλλάβοις τε μοι;

  Moschion.   [How would it be if], calling for no details,
               You would only learn I'm serious and help?

For the restoration at verse 151 I would prefer [εἰ γάρ] for the interrogative
πῶς ἄν, even if εἰ γάρ seems to belong to the high style.

But before we embark on examination of detailed examples and scenes, it
will be helpful to propose some general principles of classification. I have
already drawn attention to Weir-Smyth's distinction (*Grammar*, § 2640.2)
between questions put for information and for effect. This we must always
have at the back of our minds. Regarding 'effect' I have up to now done no
more than mention *vivacity* or *emphasis*. There will be more to say on both
these headings and on effect generally. Meantime we should observe that the

results evoked will be very different according to the types of speech in which the questions are placed. Here I would suggest a four-part framework:

(1) Longish utterances, whether 'monologues' (when only one *persona* is visible on the stage), or speeches, such as that of Knemon in *Dyskolos* already alluded to. There may be an eavesdropper; there is always the audience, who are from time to time explicitly taken into the speaker's confidence.

(2) The short question which is in the nature of an interruption.

(3) The rapid alternation of questions, in which the *personae* are constantly hitting the ball to each other. I shall call this the 'rally' type of question and answer. The dramatist hopes to produce a protracted exchange, in which our attention moves rapidly from one side of the net to the other. Neither side must gain a service-ace (for instance, by an outright conversation-stopper), but they must continue to return each other's forehand, backhand and lob until there is a particularly clever and decisive retort. Another passage from *Dyskolos* will serve as type example:

(Σμ.)   ὦ Γοργία, ποῦ γῆς ποτ᾽ εἶ;
(Γο.)   ποῦ γῆς ἐγώ;
        τί ἐστί, Σιμίχη;
(Σμ.)   τί γάρ; πάλιν λέγω·
        ὁ δεσπότης ἐν τῶι φρέατι

Simiche.   Gorgias, where in the world are you?
Gorgias.   Where
           In the world am I? What's wrong, Simiche?
Simiche.   How can you ask 'what's wrong'? I'll tell you again,
           Master's in the well.

(*Dyskolos*, 635–7)

Dyskolos, 552–3 could serve as another example; so could *Dyskolos*, 402–14 (translated on pp. 15–16).

(4) Alternations in which the parties speak at greater length and may finish with a question. These are still to be counted as true dialogue (except that the participants may number three, not two), in the sense that the comeback arises out of the provocation. I shall treat examples of this: first, those in which only one of the participants knows the answers; secondly, where the exchanges themselves produce an answer in the form of a completely transformed dramatic situation; thirdly – a special form of the foregoing, in which the dramatist keeps up the tension by making his *personae* talk at cross purposes in their questioning.

Behind these classifications, and as it were subtly altered by them, we must also take account of the many different types of emotion that can be displayed by the tone of a question; the ways in which it can be utilised to present traits of character; the contributions it can and does make to the structure of a drama; and the utility of questions as mere matters of technique.

Mere matters of technique – detailed analysis can usefully begin by noting how technical problems can be met by use of question and answer. A 'tag' question,[15] to adopt the terminology of Quirk *et al.*, not only obtains the agreement of the person to whom it is addressed, it also carries the audience along with it:

   (Σω.)   ἔνδον περιμενεῖς, οὐ γάρ;

   Sostratos [to Gorgias].   You will wait for me indoors, won't you?

                                       (Dyskolos, 782)

Such a 'tag' performs the function of the schoolmaster's 'Do you follow me?', French 'n'est ce pas', or modern slang O.K.[16] Equivalent phrases in Menander's Greek are πῶς (how do you mean, please explain, *passim*), πῶς ἂν οὖν (e.g. *Aspis,* 315), matched pairs of interrogatives in dialogue, e.g. τηλικοῦτος . . . πηλίκος (at your age . . . of what age . . .,? *Aspis,* 258–9), repetition in dialogue by correlative, as it were an echo (τίνα τρόπον, . . . ὄντινα τρόπον, in what way? . . . in what way do you say? *Dyskolos,* 362–3; πῶς . . . ὅπως, *Dyskolos,* 625 *Sikon.* What do you mean? . . . *Simiche.* You ask me what I mean?). A Greek theatre audience sat in the open air, and it was much larger than the audience in any modern play-house. It was essential that all present should understand the finer points of the action, and repetition in dialogue was a well understood way to make sure that it would. No doubt this accounts for the frequent repetition of a single word, preceded by an interrogative τί (why do I say . . .? e.g. at *Dyskolos,* 321). Sometimes the interrogative repetition calls attention to an emotional conflict in the first speaker (*Chrysis.* τί 'καί' (what do you mean, 'and'? *Samia,* 374, to Demeas who had broken short at καί (and), had almost given away his inner feelings). Sometimes τί οὖν λέγεις or λέγω (what does all this amount to?, i.e. 'to come to the point') not only allows a résumé for the audience's benefit (*Aspis,* 328, with λέγεις), but may be an admission by a speaker trying to explain a delicate matter that he has become confused in his own verbiage (*Dyskolos,* 284, with λέγω).

Unless he has reached a moment that calls out for monologue (whether heroic or mock-heroic), Menander shies away from long unbroken speeches. An auditor on stage can effectively interrupt a long utterance with a rapidfire question τί οὖν (what follows from that?), e.g. *Aspis,* 342. What would have been continuous narrative from Daos at the opening of *Aspis* is effectively punctuated by intermittent questions from Smicrines (e.g. at 19–20). An interruption can, however, do more than offer variety and forestall possible tedium. Nick Bozanic has developed an interesting theory of its deliberate use by the dramatist to 'alter the direction of the dialogue', taking as his first example:

(Πα.) ἔστι δέσποτ᾽, ἀλλὰ λανθάνειν –
(Δη.) τί 'λανθάνειν'; ἵμαντα παίδων τις δότω

Parmenon.   That's how the case stands, but to keep secret –
Demeas.   What do you mean 'keep secret'? A whip, someone . . .

(*Samia*, 320–1)

'Instead of an explanation from Parmenon', writes Bozanic, 'which would disabuse Demeas of his suspicions regarding Moschion and Chrysis, we have Demeas confirmed in his suspicions. This dramatically significant event is confirmed precisely by the interruption.' Undoubtedly an important point of dialogue technique is involved, though I am not sure that I should describe it as a technique of interruption. At this point (and elsewhere) it is not a monologue that is interrupted. In this case Demeas is cross-examining a previously trusted slave. The dramatist makes the slave falter in his explanations, and Demeas pounces on the slip. The remainder of Bozanic's exposition holds good: the event is dramatically significant.[17]

Another technical service performed by questions is that they are thrifty of precious dramatic time. Resumptive τί φήις; (what's that you say?) may occur at the opening of a play (*Dyskolos*, 50 – we are to suppose the characters enter in earnest conversation) or the opening of an act. (*Misoumenos*, 276 – Kleinias is talking from the street through the open house door to his housekeeper inside, and the audience learns that he has only just discovered, what it has suspected, indeed probably knew, that his house has been made the place of safe-keeping of his neighbour's armoury of swords. We may contrast the opening of act II of *Dyskolos* (verses 233–4) which has incurred the just censure of Professor Sandbach; note that on this occasion Menander has abandoned the resumptive question in favour of an imperatival εἰπέ μοι (tell me).)[18] The fact that a character may be supposed to have been reasoning a matter out before entry makes it natural for him to shape his opening line as a conclusion stated interrogatively, as Knemon does in *Dyskolos*:

(Κν.) εἶτ᾽ οὐ μακάριος ἦν ὁ Περσεὺς κατὰ δύο
       τρόπους ἐκεῖνος . . .;

Knemon. Doesn't it follow that Perseus in the story
         Was lucky on two counts . . .?

(*Dyskolos*, 153–4)[19]

Menander has much to compress into the thousand odd verses which constitute his play, and space-savers are welcome. As such we may classify the little cluster (A) τί οὖν; (B) τί γάρ; (in that order, *Aspis*, 171, where A = Daos, B = Smicrines; cf. *Dyskolos*, 553, 636). Very difficult these phrases are to translate, too, especially τί γάρ;[20] Professor Sandbach translates 'you ask me "what?" ?', Professor Handley, 'What are we doing, you ask?' A similar cluster is τί δέ; e.g. at *Aspis*, 376 Chaereas τί δέ τοῦτο (what about this?).

Another technical use of a question is to call attention to the presence of a bystander on stage[21] by addressing a question to him. So the dripping wet Knemon, emerging from the well, notes the presence of Sostratos:

> (*Κν.*)   τί παρέστηκας ἐνταῦθ' ἄθλιε;

> *Knemon.*   What are you up to, standing by, wretch?
>
> (Dyskolos, 702)

An 'extra' – that is, a non-speaking character – may sometimes be singled out as the object of such a question. Here is one case, which may stand for several, where there is no agreement among scholars about who is addressed or who is the speaker:

> ποῖ κέχηνας, ἐμβρόντητε σύ;

> What are you gaping at, you lunatic?
>
> (Dyskolos, 441)

A similarly phrased question at *Samia*, 105 is almost certainly addressed to a porter.

This last example touches on the convention of 'asides'. They are defined thus by David Bain in his recent book:[22] 'when X and Y are on the stage together, an aside is any utterance by either speaker not intended to be heard by the other, and not in fact heard or properly heard by him'. Given the fragmentary state of Menander's surviving text, it is often difficult on this definition to assert that a particular remark must be an aside. But some clear examples there undoubtedly are, discussed by Bain, who indeed comments on Menander's natural handling of the convention.[23] Asides which reveal the speaker's emotion very naturally fall into question-form. Such is Demeas' outburst when he catches sight of his long-lost daughter:

> (*Δη.*)   ὦ Ζεῦ, τίν' ὄψιν οὐδὲ προσδοκωμένην
>   ὁρῶ;
> *Demeas.*   O Zeus, what unexpected vision do I see?
>
> (Misoumenos, 210–11)

Bain does not discuss the difficult case of *Dyskolos*, 441 (what are you gaping at, you lunatic?). It draws no answer or comment, but this fact alone does not make it an aside. There are not many unanswered or ignored questions in Menander's dialogue, but there are some. Leaving aside the uncertain cases of Sostratos' questions at *Dyskolos*, 168, 171 or 378, we may note Gorgias' apparent address to empty air:

> (*Γο.*)   τί κακοπαθεῖν σαυτὸν βιάζῃ;

Gorgias.   Why force yourself to hard physical toil?

(Dyskolos, 371)

Of a different order, of course, are the questions with which at *Misoumenos*, 286, 289, 311, 312 Kleinias plies a peripatetic Getas, who does not answer because anger prevents his noticing. That the effect is farcical may be conceded to Bain.[24] But overt farce on stage hides intense emotion indoors.

This last scene is a reminder that technique is more than a matter of the conventions; the technique of a master will also secure dramatic effectiveness. Undoubtedly Menander uses question and answer in a dramatically effective way. We may look at this from two sides – first the interaction with the audience. An action will be effectively developed if it contains just enough that is mystifying for the audience to begin to feel the need for certain questions to be answered. Then, it is easy in dialogue for one *persona* to put this question to another. Seventy verses go by before this moment is reached in the exposition scene of the *Aspis*. How, the audience begins to want to know, is the slave Daos so sure that his master was killed on the battlefield when all the casualties had been buried in a common grave? Smicrines puts the question for them *(Aspis, 72)*, to be answered by Daos in words and by display of his visibly battered abandoned shield. As Bozanic has observed,[25] the effect of pathos on the audience is different from that on Smicrines; the latter now has proof that he is heir to the dead soldier's spoils. Questions in the first person (true rhetorical questions) are also used frequently for the purpose just discussed. They may occur in monologue also. Who is the mysterious, knowledgeable and prophetic figure who speaks the postponed prologue of the *Aspis*? The audience has been forming conjectures, and at the end the figure herself pops the question:

> Who am I, this universal umpire,
> And administratrix? My name is Chance (Τύχη).

> *(Aspis, 147–8)*

Daos' exit line towards the end of act I of this play is an apostrophe to her that is almost a punch-line:

Daos.   O Chance, what a change of masters have you
         Effected! What great wrong have I done you?

> *(Aspis, 213–15)*

At times the question may smack of the tragic chorus introducing a new character with a καὶ μήν (look now . . .). So Getas in *Dyskolos* (to himself) seeing his master introduce his new companions to the party:

Getas.   What's he up to bringing these guests here now?
          How did he make friends with them?

> *(Dyskolos, 610–11)*

In a monologue the speaker may take the audience into his confidence:

Sostratos is lost in admiration of his girl while Gorgias is in the well rescuing her father:

> The girl and I at ground level did nothing
> At all. What else was to be expected of us?
>
> (*Dyskolos*, 671–3)

Similarly a cook may question the audience about the menu he should serve (*Dyskolos*, 518). The audience is still a participant in Menandrian comedy.[26]

Rhetorical questions have, however, a much greater value for their impact on the other *personae* on the stage. By a rhetorical question (in the sense of a question asked to create an effect) the questioner, unlike a man merely making a statement, corners the person he addresses and implicitly expects his agreement or disagreement. He throws the whole force of his personality at him and demands an answer. This man-to-man confrontation is the starting-point of real drama. Menander makes a *persona* use questions to carry threats (*Dyskolos*, 114, 115, 'cut-in'), self-justification (*Aspis*, 205, cf. 260 and *Dyskolos*, 288), annoyance (*Dyskolos*, 817, an upper-class speaker; *Aspis*, 221, one slave to another – similarly *Dyskolos*, 546–7, like the English 'do you think I have ten pairs of hands?') and anger:

> *(Κν.)*   ποῦ 'στιν ἡ τοιχωρύχος;

> Knemon.   Where's the thief?
>
> (*Dyskolos*, 588)[27]

Contempt can effectively be thrown into question form (*Aspis*, 241, one slave to another); so can astonishment (*Aspis*, 167, 310), apologetic admission (*Dyskolos*, 152), or a brush-off:

> Daos.   Why take any notice of me? Your head
> Of course is better than mine.
>
> (*Aspis*, 208)

This is a slave addressing his new master. Sarcasm, too, goes well into a question (*Dyskolos*, 53, friend, or parasite, to friend; 568–9, one slave to another). So does reproof (*Dyskolos*, 401–2), and even despair (*Dyskolos*, 576).

A specially effective way of employing question and answer is to use them to illustrate *ethos*, the dramatic type and quality of a *persona*. A passage in *Aspis*, act II does so with real virtuosity. The soldier-hero has apparently died abroad, at the very moment of successfully collecting spoils as dowry for his sister. The first need is for a funeral. The villainous aged Smicrines peremptorily takes charge (verse 252). He further asserts his undoubted right according to Attic law to marry his niece, now enriched, thereby overriding the moral claims of Chaereas already betrothed to her and disregarding the differences of age. How can there be effective protest from his younger brother (I suppose the speaker at 256 and 258 to be *Chaerestratos*, not *Chaereas*)? The protest is put as a question:

(*Χα.*)   Σμικρίνη,
          οὐδὲν μέλει σοι μετριότητος;
(*Σμ.*)   διὰ τί, παῖ;
(*Χα.*)   ὢν τηλικοῦτος παῖδα μέλλεις λαμβάνειν;
(*Σμ.*)   πηλίκος;
(*Χα.*)   ἐμοὶ μὲν παντελῶς δοκεῖς γέρων.
(*Σμ.*)   μόνος γεγάμηκα πρεσβύτερος;

Chaerestratos.   Smicrines,
          Have you no thought for keeping the decencies?
Smicrines.   Why do you say that, boy?
Chaerestratos.   At your age are you going to take a lassie?
Smicrines.   How old do you think I am?
Chaerestratos.   One foot in the grave, I'd say.
Smicrines.   Am I the only old man to have taken a wife?
                         (*Aspis*, 256–60)

The delicate matter is put by way of a tentative question; it is answered (evaded rather) by counter-questions, which reveal the full shiftiness of Smicrines. Chaerestratos tries again. Chaereas, the girl's childhood friend, is to marry her. τί οὖν λέγω; (What am I trying to say?, verse 263) shows Chaerestratos searching for the right words. Smicrines, he suggests, will not be penalised; let him keep all the war booty, Chaerestratos will supply the dowry. The downright nastiness of Smicrines comes out in a further remarkable series of questions:

(*Σμ.*)   πρὸς θεῶν, Μελιτίδηι
          λαλεῖν ὑπείληφας; τί φήις; ἐγὼ λάβω
          τὴν οὐσίαν, τούτωι δὲ τὴν κόρην ἀφῶ
          ἵν', ἂν γένηται παιδίον, φεύγω δίκην
          ἔχων τὸ τούτου;
(*Χα.*)   τοῦτο δοῖεί; κατάβαλε.
(*Σμ.*)   "οἴει;" λέγεις; τὸν Δᾶον ὥς με πέμψατε
          ἵν' ἀπογραφὴν ὧν κεκόμικεν δή μοι –

Smicrines.   In heaven's name,
          Do you think you're talking to a Booby?
          What are you suggesting? *I* take the property
          And leave the girl to him, so that their child
          Shall sue me later for it?
Chaerestratos.   Is that what
          You think? Drop it.
Smicrines.   'Think', you say? Send Daos
          Over with a list of all the booty –
                         (*Aspis*, 269–75)

I shall now proceed to analyse two longer passages in which the questions are arranged 'structurally' – i.e. they contribute to the development of the dramatic action. First, an example of question and answer in a passage where the aim is simply to inform the audience of what is going on. Incidentally, I think we shall be able to mend the text at this passage. At the end of act II of *Dyskolos*, the town-bred rich dandy Sostratos has persuaded Gorgias, neighbour to the Curmudgeon, the name-character of the play, to allow him to put on a leather apron, pick up a two-pronged mattock and pretend to be a peasant hard at work on the rough ground at Phyle, the barren precipitous rocks that grow little more than sage-brush. In that guise he may have a chance once again to see the Curmudgeon's daughter, with whom he has fallen instantly in love. Having set the scene in front of the cliff at Phyle where is the cave of the Nymphs, Menander has to transplant Sostratos' family there. His solution is a picnic. In thirty-four verses the cook Sikon and household slave Getas amusingly tell us of the coming picnic (attended, of course, by sacrifice) and the expected invasion of country peace by a party on a day's outing from Athens. The cook has to struggle with the sheep (at once sacrifice and main dish for the picnickers). He is followed by Getas loaded down with as much as four donkeys could carry. (Text and translation are given on pp. 15–16 below.) Why are they suddenly appearing on the scene? We, the audience, want to know. And so does Sikon the cook. He is as much in the dark as we are. It is he who puts the questions (verses 409, 411 twice, 412, 413) and Getas who knows the answers every time, summing it up neatly at 417–18: 'That's why we are sacrificing, to divert alarm to good.' But the questions and answers are made amusing in their own right; the information comes to us slowly, bit by bit, two steps backward for every one forward. Menander is like a musician, proceeding by a series of complicated modulations, from G♭ to G major. The slow-witted (but shrewd) Getas can only get one thing out at a time. Realisation of this design of question and answer will now help us to a restoration of verses 405–6.[28] At verse 405 the cook Sikon says: 'There is a large company to come it seems.' This verse is written at the top of a page in the Bodmer manuscript, and there is a tear. ὡς ἔοι[κε, itself, implies a slight tone of uncertainty, akin to a question. The first editor, followed by everyone, then made him answer his own question: στρ]ώματ' ἀδιήγηθ' ὅσα / φέρεις. It's an indescribable amount of bedding you're carrying. The Bodmer papyrus then continues after a dicolon (i.e. change of speaker) τί δ'ἐγώ[a tear which will hold, I think, five to six letters, as in the preceding verse]ερεισον ταυτα δευρο' ἰδου: this, it is to be noted, is both unmetrical and marks no change of speaker till after ἰδού. The reason why no satisfactory reading has been found (not for want of trying, see the apparatus of all editions at this point) is that editors have not observed the planned alternation of questioner and answerer: the questions belong to Sikon, the answers to Getas. We must give τί δ'ἐγώ[κτλ. to Sikon: it is as if, in a stereo speaker system, we needed to reverse left and right-hand channels. This can be done quite easily by supposing that in B what is lost in 405 is a dicolon followed by βρ]ώματ' (this will occupy exactly the same space): Getas replies to the cook's implied query 'You are carrying an indescribable quantity of ingredients.' The next question is then the cook's: 'What on earth am I doing here at all?' (τί δ'ἐγω[γε δεῦρ';) to which Getas answers 'Put these things down. Now look at it like this. (ἔρεισον ταῦτ'· ἰδού.) If a person has a dream about Pan of Paeania even, to him we shall go straight off and sacrifice, that's for certain.' The producer would invent some business for tumbling the loads on the ground. Getas would plant himself foursquare before beginning his explanation. And even then he doesn't offer a subject to the verb 'has a dream': it is the content of a supplementary question.[29] An emended translation of this passage follows, but I print the old text.

(Γετας.)	τεττάρων γὰρ φορ[τίον
	ὄνων συνέδησαν αἱ κάκιστ' ἀπολο[ύμεναι
	φέρειν γυναῖκές μοι.
(Σικ.)	πολύς τις ἔρ[χεται
	ὄχλος, ὡς ἔοι[κε. στρ]ώματ' ἀδιήγηθ' ὅσα 405
	φέρεις.
(Γε)	τί δ' ἐγω[γε;]
(Σικ.)	ταῦτ' ἐπέρεισον δεῦρ'.
(Γε.)	ἰδού.
	ἐὰν ἴδῃ γὰρ ἐνύ[πνιο]ν τὸν Πᾶνα τὸν
	Παιανιοῖ, τού[τ]ῳ βαδιούμεθ', οἶδ' ὅτι,
	θύσοντες εὐθύς.
(Σικ.)	[τ]ίς δ' ἑόρακεν ἐνύπνιον;
(Γε.)	ἄνθρωπε, μή με κόφθ'. 410
(Σικ.)	ὅμως εἶπον, Γέτα·
	τίς εἶδεν;
(Γε.)	ἡ κεκτημένη.
(Σικ.)	τί πρὸς θεῶν;
(Γε.)	ἀπολεῖς· ἐδόκει τὸν Πᾶνα –
(Σικ.)	τουτονὶ λέγεις;
(Γε.)	τοῦτον.
(Σικ.)	τί ποιεῖν;
(Γε.)	τῷ τροφίμῳ τῷ Σωστράτῳ –
(Σικ.)	κομψῷ νεανίσκῳ γε –
(Γε.)	περικρούειν πέδας.
Getas.	A load for four donkeys
	Was what those damned women piled on my back.
Sikon.	There's to be a real crowd, it seems.
Getas.	An infinity
	Of ingredients you're carrying.
Sikon.	What am I
	Doing here at all?
Getas.	Put them down. Now look. If
	A person has a dream about Pan of Paeania,
	We'll be off there instanter, that's certain.

Sikon.   Who had a dream?
Getas.   Man, don't bore me.
Sikon.   Still, tell.
        Who dreamed?
Getas.   The mistress.
Sikon.   What about, for heaven's sake
Getas.   You'll kill me. She thought she saw Pan –
Sikon.   the god
        Of this shrine?
Getas.   This one.
Sikon.   Doing what?
Getas.   Sostratos
        My master
Sikon.   – A fine young man –
Getas.   being clapped in irons.
                            (*Dyskolos*, 402–14)

                                        401–5 ed. pr.
403 -σαν ακακιστ᾽απολ.[P (fort. απολυ[)   406 ἐπέρεισον Bingen, Quincey;
cetera ed. pr.: φερεισ:τιδ᾽εγω [4–5] ερεισονταυταδευροϊδου:P   407–8 ed.
pr.: ανιδη—τονπανατε | τονπαιανιοι—βαδιουμεθ᾽ P   409 ed. pr.:
θυσοντοσευθυσ[. .]ιδ᾽εωρακεν P (scil. [:τ]ιδ᾽)

This, then, we regard as a specimen of structural question and answer,
between two persons only and emotionally neutral. In my early classification
I suggested that a more subtle type was that in which two or three participants, by mutual exchange of question and answer in each other's presence,
helped to elicit the truth concerning an event important to the action. As
illustration of what I believe to be a brilliant piece of cross-questioning *à trois*
protracted to add to the suspense, I choose a passage (alas, much mutilated)
from the end of act IV of Menander's *Epitrepontes*. It is that in which Charisios
is at last convinced not only that he is the father of the foundling child, but
that Pamphile, his own wife, is its mother, and that it was conceived in that
moment of passion at the festival of the Tauropolia when he violated an
unknown girl. We have most of acts II, III and V of this play: the fragmentary
infillings leave a number of questions unanswered about a dramatic creation
which for human sympathy, riveting theatre and delicate sympathy must
rank as a masterpiece. In act III the flute-girl Habrotonon had brilliantly
sketched to Onesimos, her accomplice, how she was to exploit her opportunity: she will take the ring of the foundling child, held in trust by a scared
Onesimos, go into Charisios and use all her artfulness to make him draw the
deduction that he is its father and she its mother. The anticipation of this
scene which she communicates to the theatre is itself a little lesson in the
composition of dialogue, and Nick Bozanic has dwelt on its interest[30] as a
statement by Menander himself of how dialogue should be written: 516–34S
ἀνακρινεῖ . . . φήσω . . . ἥξει φερόμενος ἐπὶ τὸν ἔλεγχον . . . ἐρεῖ . . . λέγῃ . . .

προσομολογήσω . . . λέγουσα . . . ἀκκιοῦμαι τῷ λόγῳ, ἐρωτᾶν (he'll ask me . . . I shall say . . . he'll rush into cross-examination and say . . . I shall confirm his words, but shan't speak first . . . I shall be arch . . . I shall find out . . .). But Menander is too much of a master to repeat himself by narrating how it actually turned out; it is only by hints that we learn that she carried off her role and convinced Charisios. One is the rumour the suspicious Smicrines picks up that one of the hard drinkers indoors (he means Charisios) has had a child by a woman of the streets. From what source could this have got around, except from Habrotonon herself, or from Onesimos, or from Charisios? The second is from Habrotonon's own statement made sincerely and affectionately to Pamphile, the child's mother, that she (Habrotonon) only *pretended* to be its mother in order to trace the identity of the real mother: ironically she is carrying her pretended, Pamphile's real, baby at the moment of this meeting. The revelation of the truth to Pamphile precedes the revelation to the baby's father Charisios. He has overheard Pamphile refusing to obey a tyrannical father Smicrines and desert her husband ('I came to him as a partner for life'), and cannot but contrast her constancy and his own arrogant assumption of moral superiority. It is just after he has steeled himself to refuse to let her father take her away that he becomes aware of the presence of his man Onesimos in the company of Habrotonon. The scene which follows is an exchange so managed as completely to convince him (we may note it is an asset that Pamphile cannot be present, too. A modern playwright would probably have made her participate, but Menander could draw on the services of only three speaking players, so she is excluded from the stage).

Analysis of a tattered text will not make easy reading. But I should like to look more closely at this splendid climactic scene. The text I print is only a provisional one. Up to verse 949, it is taken from Del Corno's edition[31] (with some doctoring, and some additions to the apparatus). From 950–8 I give Professor Sandbach's Oxford Classical Text.

The Cairo papyrus is much damaged here; portion β1↓ gives us the beginnings of verses 934–51S; P. Oxy. 1236 back gives us nearly complete verses from 923–34S and then a few beginnings; and we have longer pieces of verse from the Cairo codex fr. Q2↓, 950–8S.

> . .]ω διαρρήδην· ᾽ἐμοὶ σύ, Σμικρίνη,
> μὴ] πάρεχε πράγματ᾽, οὐκ ἀπολείπει μ᾽ ἡ γυνή·   610 [930S]
> τ]ί οὖν ταράττεις καὶ βιάζῃ Παμφίλην;᾽
> τ]ί σ᾽ αὖ βλέπω ᾽γώ;
> (Ον.)   πάνυ κακῶς ἔχω σφόδρα.
> ο]ἴμοι τάλας. καὶ σο[ῦ δ]έομαι τούτοις [∪ ‿
> μή μ᾽ ἐγκαταλίπῃς.
> (Χαρ.)   οὗτος ἐπακροώμε[νος
> ἕστηκας, ἱερόσυλε, μου[;
> (Ον.)   μ]ὰ τοὺς θεούς,   615 [935S]

ἀλλ' ἀρτίως ἐξῆλθον· ạ[. . . . .] λαθεῖν
ἔσται σε πρα[. .]μια[. . . . . . .]ησ[
πάντ' ἐπακροάσει: πọτ[. . . .] οὐ̣ θ[
ἐγώ σε λανθάνειν̣ ποιν[
<u>βροντῶντα</u>: διạ .ε[620 [940S]

ABPOTONON

          <u>ἀλλ' οὐθὲν ὀφθησε</u>[
(*Χαρ.*)   <u>τίς</u> εισ[. . .]αν̣.εἰ̣ς̣[
(*Ον.*)   <u>οὐκ αἰσ</u>[. . .]ν[
(*'Αβρ.*) <u>οὐκ ἦν ἐ̣</u>[μὸν
(*Χαρ.*)   <u>οὐκ</u> ἦν σό[ν;   625 [945S]
(*'Αβρ.*) <u>βο̣ύ</u>λει μ' ἀπ[
          <u>ἀλλ</u>' ἐξαπει[
          <u>ἐμ</u>' ἐπρ[
          ε[.]εισ[
(*Χαρ.*)   τί φῄς, 'Ον[ήσιμ'], ἐξεπειράθη[950
(*Ον.*)   αὔ]τη μ' [ἔπε]ισε, νὴ τὸν 'Απόλλω [[631]
(*Χαρ.*)   καὶ σύ μ]ε περισπᾶις, ἱερόσυλε·
(*'Αβρ.*)   μὴ μάχου,
    γλυκύτ]ατε· τῆς γαμετῆς γυναικός ἐστί σου
    τέκνον] γάρ, οὐκ ἀλλότριον,
(*Χαρ.*)   εἰ γὰρ ὤφελεν.
(*'Αβρ.*) νὴ τὴν φίλην Δήμητρα.
(*Χαρ.*)   τίνα λόγον λέγεις;   955
(*'Αβρ.*) τίνα; τὸν] ἀληθῆ.
(*Χαρ.*)   Παμφίλης τὸ παιδίον;
    ἀλλ' ἦν ἐμ]όν.
(*'Αβρ.*)   καὶ σόν γ' ὁμοίως.
(*Χαρ.*)   Παμφίλης;
    'Αβρότο]νον ἱκετεύω σε, μή μ' ἀναπτεροῦ
              (desunt uersus fere x)

      p. n. *Ονη*/ supra πάνυ D   **613** [**933S**] in fine versus .ε̣..ạ leg. Hunt.
621 [**941S**] ὀφθησε[Wilamowitz   **622**[**942S**] τίς εἰ σ[ύ:] Sudhaus   **623**
[**943S**] οὐκ αἰσ[, Cairensis, teste E.G.T.   **624–5** [**944–5S**] suppl. Kö.   **629**
[**949S**] unam ι. ante priorem ε fuisse censet Gué.   **630** [**950S**]suppl. Sudhaus   **631** [**951S**] suppl. Jensen   **950** ἐξεπειράθης ἐμοῦ Sudhaus:?
ἐξεπειράθητέ μου   **951** αὕτη μ' ἔπεισε Sudhaus καὶ θεούς Jensen   **952** καὶ σύ
με Sudhaus: τί σύ με Jensen spatio brevius: alii alia   **953** suppl. Wilamowitz   **954** τέκνον Koerte: τουτὶ Wilamowitz: αὐτῆς Capps   **955** .....]φ C,
suppl. Headlam   **956** suppl. Coppola: ἐγώ; τὸν Jensen: πάντως
Robert   **957**]ιν: leg. Jensen, Koerte, sed hoc bene uti potuit nemo:]ọν in
imagine uideo et ita suppleui   Add **954** [ἴδιον] Arnott, *ZPE* 1978, 15

Charisios, then, has reached a firm decision (930–1). The opening of 932
could be apostrophe of the absent Smicrines. Less probably it might mean
that he now catches sight of Onesimos. Certainly from the middle of the
verse, C names the latter as speaker and the probable second person singular

genitive in 933 coupled with the second person imperative in 934 makes it likely that he has come on stage together with Habrotonon. I translate to show how I think the passage ran:

Onesimos.   I really am in a fix,
    Oh, lordie! Lady, please, don't abandon
    Me to this mess.
Charisios.   Vandal, you've been standing
    Eavesdropping?
Onesimos.   I swear by high heaven
    I've only just come out.

The part-distribution is uncertain. Sudhaus thought he could read character names in C, but no one else has been able to.

In C, from 941S = 621 Kö., there seems to be a paragraphus under the beginning of each verse; with a possible exception between 944 and 945, where there are big holes in the papyrus. In the new photographs of the Cairo codex[32] neither I nor Dr Cockle could see a paragraphus after verse 944; but the possibility that there was one must be admitted. But this does not mean that the eleven verses from 941 to 951 inclusive must be assigned each as a complete verse to a single character, as if this passage were somehow imitating the *stichomythia* of tragedy because it is solemn. The only verse which there is any manuscript evidence to treat as a unit is 951S, where C closes with a dicolon; perhaps this makes it likely that all of 950S goes to Charisios. Professor Sandbach in his commentary has already drawn attention to the improbability of hieratic *stichomythia*.

Some other will o' the wisps should now be thrown overboard: one is that 942 is to be restored $\tau i s \; \epsilon \hat{\iota} \; \sigma [\acute{\upsilon};$ and perhaps that 944 and 945 have a matched $o \grave{\upsilon} \kappa \; \mathring{\eta} \nu \; \acute{\epsilon} [\mu \acute{o} \nu$ and $o \grave{\upsilon} \kappa \; \mathring{\eta} \nu \; \sigma \acute{o} [\nu.$ Let us observe further that 943 should be read $o \upsilon \kappa \; \alpha \iota \sigma [$ (not $\epsilon \iota \sigma [$ or $o \iota \sigma [$ – this I offer you from the new photographs, and confirmed by Dr Cockle).

The essential starting point is the observation that at 952–4 Habrotonon is treated as having complete authority (the authority almost of a *dea ex machina*) – and as also possessing the trust of Charisios. It is therefore unthinkable that at 943 he could address her so insensitively as Gomme's conjecture $o \grave{\upsilon} \kappa \; \grave{\epsilon} s \; [\kappa \acute{o} \rho \alpha \kappa \alpha s \; \sigma \grave{\upsilon} \; \kappa \alpha \grave{\iota} \; \tau \grave{o} \; \pi \alpha \iota \delta \acute{\iota} o \nu \; \tau \grave{o} \; \sigma \acute{o} \nu;$ (To the devil with you and your baby) would suggest. The conjecture was improbable even when Gomme made it, since the papyrus was thought to have $\epsilon \iota \sigma [,$ not $\epsilon \sigma [;$ we now know it to have had $\alpha \iota \sigma [\quad].$ Charisios in fact behaves quite differently towards Onesimos and towards Habrotonon. It is the former who is addressed twice (verse 936; verse 952) as $\acute{\iota} \epsilon \rho o \sigma \acute{\upsilon} \lambda \epsilon$ (committer of sacrilege): the choice of word for vocative (as in Plato, e.g. with $\mu \alpha \kappa \acute{\alpha} \rho \iota \epsilon$) is not otiose. Onesimos is regarded by his master as one who tramples clumsily on sacred ground, those inner feelings which should be respected. But towards Habrotonon Charisios' manner is different: he has the recollection of (he supposes) a sentimental *tête-à-tête* and the obligations of paternity following a chance encounter: the passage has almost no significance unless he continues right to the end to think of her as mother of his son. Onesimos' excuses continue to ἐπακροάσει in the middle of 938 (after 936 there is no paragraphus in the Cairo codex, no dicolon in that from Oxyrhynchus). Charisios begins a threat at πότ᾽[and continues to βροντῶντα (940). This is where Habrotonon chips in (some form of διατελεῖν or διὰ τέλους ?).

(Ἀβρ.)	διὰ τέ[λους ἁμαρτάνεις σκόπου·]
	ἀλλ᾽ οὐθὲν ὀφθήσε[ι σύ γ᾽ εἰδὼς ὧν δοκεῖς.]
(Χαρ.)	τίς εἶσ[ετ᾽;] αὐλεῖς [δητ᾽ ἄριστα· νῦν λέγε.]
(Ἀβρ.)	οὐκ αἰσ[χῦ]ν[–

Habrotonon.	Right to the end you miss the mark.
	But you'll be proved to know nothing of what you fancy.
Charisios.	Who *will* know? You're a good flute player. Now use words.
Habrotonon.	No shame . . .

(verses 940–3)

In 943 with αισ[there are four possibilities, at least: if it is part of αἰσχύνω, verb, it may be future first person (as question or statement) οὐκ αἰσ[χῦ]ν[ῶ σ᾽; or it may be passive αἰσ[χυ]ν[οῦμαι first person, αἰσ[χυ]ν[εῖ second person, also future followed by participle, or it may be part of αἰσ[χρό]ν. Since we have no more of the verse, there is *no* check available. But the (perhaps falsely) enticing idea of οὐκ ἦν ἐ[μόν in 944 (which can only be spoken by Habrotonon) means there must be at least one change of speaker after οὐκ αἰσ[χυ]ν –. Verse 943 might end τὸ παιδίον; but there are alternatives. If 944 is given to Habrotonon, it is the *surprise* line for Charisios ('It wasn't *mine*, this baby') and it bewilders him. The whole line given to her might run οὐκ ἦν ἐ[μὸν τὸ παιδίον τοὐκκείμενον] (then the child exposed wasn't mine?). But if there is no paragraphus, we could give the rest of the verse plus run-over to Charisios [πῶς; οἶσθας οὖν σαφῶς ὅτι] / οὐκ ἦν σόν;

Verses 946–9 offer no firm foothold, and I pass over them. But I suppose that the frustration and tension bottled up inside Charisios can break now on the unfortunate Onesimos, and that it is corroboration that is sought from him. In 950, as Professor Sandbach notes, we may write τί φήσ᾽ (third person, with elided iota) (what does X say?) and even ἐξεπειράθη[γ᾽ ἐμοῦ (did *she* try it out on me?) as well as ἐξεπειράθ[ητ᾽ἐμοῦ or ἐξεπειράθη[ς. Onesimos' confirmation is that of Adam in Genesis, feeble fellow that he is: 'the woman persuaded me'. Charisios is on the rack, and the denigratory epithet ἱερόσυλε (vandal) shows his feelings even better than [καὶ σὺ μ]ε περισπᾷς; (And you are also leading me this dance? Is nothing sacred to you?). Now for five verses all is plain sailing:

Habrotonon.	No sparring!
	Darling man, it's your own wedded wife's
	Baby, no one else's.

Charisios.	If only it were.
Habrotonon.	It is, by blessed Demeter.
Charisios.	What story's this?
Habrotonon.	Story? The truth
Charisios.	Pamphile's? The baby?
	The baby?
Habrotonon.	And yours too.
Charisios.	Pamphile's?
	Habrotonon, I beg you, don't raise me up
	(To disappoint me)

(verses 951–7)

From 950 I am content to follow Professor Sandbach until we reach the beginning of 957. There ἀλλ' ἦν ἐμ]όν (a rewriting, to suit the traces of Wilamowitz's earlier ἐμὸν γὰρ] ἦν) is meaningless to me. In the historical sense '(I was told) it was mine' – i.e. some 400 verses two acts earlier. It has no zip. If it is to be translated 'but (as I now see) that makes it mine', it is odd Greek: I should have expected [ἦν ἄρ' ἐμ]όν. Professor Handley has suggested (quoted by John Feneron)[33] that we should restore simply [τὸ παιδί]ον. The noun has already been used in an astonished question. It is repeated as an astonished question. It is the right length. It offers the repetition in inversion ABBA. I remember Professor Handley saying in comment: 'it prolongs the growing excitement by a graduated and formalised realisation for which the rhetoric offers a natural expression' (noted at the time in my copy of the Oxford Classical Text). The form is that of Μοσχίων ἔα μ'· ἔα με Μοσχίων (Moschion, let me be; let me be, Moschion), *Samia*, 465.

I am aware that I have adumbrated problems, not solved them and have confined myself to a limited field. In the first place I have restricted myself to Menander. Dear reader, you will immediately want to know how his manner differs from that of Aristophanes? from other Greek comic writers? from the tragedians? from Plato? How far is the asking of questions, where the corresponding thought would in English be a statement or a command, a function of the Greek language itself? and if it is, within what limits does Menander heighten them in expressive force, so that they cease to be imitative of common speech?

NOTES

1. E. W. Handley, *The Dyskolos of Menander* (London: Methuen, 1965), p. 10 and n. 4.
2. *Entretiens sur l'antiquité classique: Tome XVI Ménandre* (Geneva, 1970), pp. 113–43.
3. J. Feneron, 'Some Elements of Menander's Style', *Bulletin of the Institute of Classical Studies*, 21 (1974), pp. 81 ff.
4. Nick Bozanic, 'Structure, Language and Action in the Comedies of Menander', London Ph.D. dissertation, 1977.

5. *Ibid.*, p. 73.
6. The Greek text used in quotations from Menander, together with line nume-ration, is that of F. H. Sandbach's Oxford Classical Text *Menandri Reliquiae Selectae* (Oxford: Clarendon Press, 1972), unless I specify otherwise. The trans-lations into English are my own. When no point of Greek interpretation is involved, I have given the example in English only.
7. J. D. Denniston, *The Greek Particles* (Oxford: Clarendon Press, 1934; second edition revised by K. J. Dover, 1954).
7a. There *are* two other ancient critics I should have quoted. Dr Vicky Stafford of Stanford and Berkeley has called attention to Pseudo-Longinus, *On the Sublime* §18 Russell, and Professor George Kennedy of Chapel Hill to Quintilian IX 2.8. 'Emotion' writes Pseudo-Longinus (translated by D.A. Russell) 'carries us away more easily when it seems to be generated by the occasion rather than delibera-tely assumed by the speaker, and the self-directed question and its answer represent precisely this momentary quality of emotion. Just as people who are unexpectedly plied with questions become annoyed and reply to the point with vigour and exact truth, so the figure of question and answer arrrests the hearer and cheats him into believing that all the points made were raised and are being put into words on the spur of the moment.' Quintilian takes as example the beginning of Cicero's First Catilinarian Oration and exclaims 'quanto magis ardet quam si diceretur "diu abuteris patientia nostra" '. Both critics operate in the context of oratory, not drama.
8. R. Quirk, S. Greenbaum, G. Leech and J. Svartvik, *A Grammar of Contemporary English* (London: Longmans, 1972), § 7.71, p. 401: 'A *positive* rhetorical question is like a strong *negative* assertion, while a *negative* question is like a strong *positive* one.'
9. J. D. Denniston, *Greek Prose Style* (Oxford: Clarendon Press, 1952; second impres-sion, 1959). A posthumous book seen through the press by H. Lloyd-Jones.
10. H. Weir-Smyth, *Greek Grammar* (Cambridge, Mass.: Havard University Press, 1920, revised edition by Gordon M. Messing, 1956), § 2640, p. 196.
11. After an oath, e.g. *Aspis*, 269.
12. The single word picked up and treated interrogatively, as already seen at *Dyskolos*, 473, must imply some difference of spoken intonation, presumably differing stress, in order to be intelligible as a question.
13. F. H. Sandbach and A. W. Gomme, *Menander: a Commentary* (Oxford: Oxford University Press, 1973). Here is an example taken at random: on *Dyskolos*, 785, 'to place the question mark not after συγκεχώρηκα, but after λαμβάνειν (ed. pr.) gives a less lively speech'.
14. Quirk *et al.*, *A Grammar of Contemporary English*, p. 400 use the phrase 'an exclamatory question' (e.g. Hasn't she grown! Am I hungry!).
15. *Ibid.*, § 7.59, p. 390.
16. For instance, a banner stretched across the Euston Road in May 1978 lettered 'EGA stays, O.K.' (EGA = Elizabeth Garret Anderson Hospital).
17. Bozanic, 'Structure, Language and Action', pp. 86–7. This discussion of a single passage does not give a fair representation of Bozanic's well-argued chapter. He offers a lengthy treatment of *Aspis*, 34, 45, 48, 49, 52, 68–9, 72, etc., as well as of *Dyskolos*, 81–123. On *Aspis* he makes the telling comment, with which I am in full

agreement: 'One should think of narratives and interruptions as a single expressive unit.'

18. Sandbach and Gomme, *Menander*, p. 173, n. 13: 'It is hard to believe that the talk
between Gorgias and Daos had only just reached the point where the former
utters his remonstrance.'

19. Sandbach and Gomme *ad loc.* offers parallels.

20. Denniston, *The Greek Particles* spends three pages (pp. 77, 81, 85) on it. Sandbach
and Gomme, *Menander*, on *Dyskolos*, 553; Handley, *The Dyskolos of Menander* on
the same passage. Often enough 'what else?' will give the sense, but not here.

21. Raymond Raikes, who produced my translation of Menander's *Girl From Samos*
on the radio, advised me to add a line or two here and there to be spoken by a
character who had been silent for a spell, to remind listeners that he was still
present.

22. David Bain, *Actors and Audience: a Study of Asides and Related Conventions in Greek
Drama* (Oxford University Press, 1977), p. 17.

23. *Ibid.*, chapters 6 and 7; the comment is at p. 150.

24. *Ibid.*, p. 141.

25. Bozanic, 'Structure, Language and Action', pp. 68–9.

26. On the notion of dramatic illusion, see most recently Bain, *Actors and Audience*,
chapters 11 and 12.

27. One of the few examples of a rhetorical question in Greek cast in a *who*/*which* form
instead of a *yes*/*no* form.

28. I use Professor E. W. Handley's text. This is one of the places where Professor
Sandbach's discarding of square brackets [ ], and assumption of certainty in
restoration does Menander a disservice.

29. On the palaeographical mechanics of the change: I would suppose that from τί δ'
ἔγωγε δεῦρο, δεῦρο was shifted early towards the end of the verse (put the baggage
down *here*) and what would have been found in B (had there not been a tear)
would have been, e.g., δῆτ'. For an example of elided δευρ' at this point in the
verse in this very play see verse 610; and for βρώματα compare as parallel verse
776 ⟨οἱ δὲ⟩ καταβεβρωκότες κτλ. (they've already fed and . . .). In support of this
reconstruction I would point out that (with a dicolon) the number of letters
supposed lost at 405 remains five; that verse 406 needs fairly radical surgery
anyway; that a load of food-stuffs βρώματα (the cook's raw material) is a much
more likely load to carry than mattresses to sit on; and that I do not regard φέρεις
(you are carrying) addressed to the cook who already has his arms full with the
sheep as disqualifying this reconstruction. He might be carrying spices in a sort of
knapsack; or φέρεις might mean 'you are bringing', not physically carrying.

30. Bozanic, 'Structure, Language and Action', pp. 80–1.

31. Dario del Corno, *Menandro, Le Commedie*, 1 (Milan, n.d. [1966]), pp. 260–3. Line
numeration followed by Capital S is the new numeration introduced by Professor Sandbach.

32. Published in 1978 as a Supplement to the *Bulletin of the Institute of Classical Studies*
of the University of London.

33. Feneron, 'Some Elements of Menander's Style', p. 93, n. 27.

Two concepts of mimesis:
Renaissance literary theory and
The Revenger's Tragedy

JONATHAN DOLLIMORE

In the Renaissance, says Panofsky,

> art theory lifted from a thousand years of oblivion the notion – self-evident in
> classical antiquity, purged away by Neoplatonism and hardly ever considered
> in medieval thought – that the work of art is a faithful reproduction of reality.[1]

This revival of the theory of art as imitation (mimesis) is crucial for understanding the literary consciousness of the Elizabethan period, especially the
rapid growth of its drama.[2] Although it refers to Renaissance art generally,
the following observation from Arnold Hauser also indicates what was
happening in the Elizabethan theatre:

> The real change brought about by the Renaissance is that metaphysical
> symbolism loses its strength and the artist's aim is limited more and more
> definitely and consciously to the representation of the empirical world. The
> more society and economic life emancipate themselves from the fetters of
> ecclesiastical dogma the more freely does art turn to the consideration of
> immediate reality.[3]

In the *Poetics* Aristotle used the concept of mimesis in several senses, some
of which are complex. For present purposes they can be reduced to two: 'the
representation of reality . . . and its free expression'.[4] Moreover, there are
strong arguments in favour of representation as the more important of the
two: 'primarily the term mimesis in the *Poetics* must be taken as referring not
to some kind of aid or parallel to nature but to the making of a likeness or
image of nature'.[5] In the Renaissance, however, Aristotle was, notoriously,
given free interpretation and there have always been differing views on the
nature of the reality which art imitates.

Put somewhat simplistically, there were those who interpreted that reality
idealistically, and therefore to be represented through the 'metaphysical
symbolism' of which Hauser speaks, and those who interpreted it empirically
– and, correspondingly, to be represented in terms of 'immediate reality'.
Growing from the first of these two views is the additional conception of art
as didactic: typically, art represents an ideal moral order which improves
those capable of apprehending it. When idealist mimesis takes on this
didactic dimension its conflict with empiricist mimesis is most acute. The

period in question, and its drama, was particularly susceptible to this conflict. Initially, the problem was this: how can the artist at once represent the ideal order and an actuality which seems to contradict it? This question generates others: what is the ontological status of the ideal? How, if at all, does it relate to the actual? In short, a revival of mimetic realism in art coincided with new-found anxiety over the very nature of reality itself.

T. S. Eliot disapproved of the Elizabethans' 'impure art', their attempt 'to attain complete realism without surrendering . . . unrealistic conventions'.[6] Bertolt Brecht, on the other hand, approved of this impurity, particularly its elements of 'experiment' and 'sacrilege', and its dialectic potential.[7] I shall argue that this controversial aspect of Elizabethan theatre stems in part from a dynamic conflict between idealist and empiricist mimesis. The issue can be summarised in this way: on the one hand didacticism, ossified as a dramatic convention inherited from the Morality tradition, demanded that the universe be seen to be divinely controlled; justice and order were eventually affirmed, conflict resolved, and man re-established within, or expelled from, the providential design. On the other hand, drama was rapidly progressing as an art form with empirical, historical and contemporary emphases – all of which were in potential conflict with this didacticism. I submit too, that an important way of understanding this underlying tension is to approach it through the literary theory of the period.

I

In the sixteenth century the attack on literature, especially drama, gained new force with the growth of puritanism. During what Spingarn has termed the third stage of English criticism – 'the period of philosophical and apologetic criticism'[8] – literature was most persistently defended against the new wave of hostility. To the charge that literature, as fiction, involves falsity the apologists responded by stressing (under the influence of Aristotle) its mimetic function; the further charge that such literature inevitably inclined towards obscenity and blasphemy was met by advancing its didactic purpose.

In some instances this didactic justification was explicitly ideological:

> playes are writ with this ayme, and carryed with this methode, to teach their subjects obedience to their king, to show the people the untimely ends of such as have moved tumults, commotions, and insurrections, to present them with the flourishing estate of such as live in obedience, exhorting them to allegeance, dehorting them from all trayterous and fellonious stratagems.[9]

But it was also an integral part of a complex theological and ethical world view. As such, it was embedded in the literary consciousness of the sixteenth century, particularly the Morality drama.

Central to literary didacticism has been the notion of poetic justice. We find the idea in the literary theory of both Sidney and Bacon.[10] But before examining their work I propose to move forward in time and see what happened to poetic justice during the period when it was most vigorously expounded. The idea refers, of course, to the rewarding of the virtuous and the punishing of the vicious, usually in a proportional and appropriate way. Moreover, almost always this just distribution of deserts is portrayed as evidence of providential intervention. Stated thus crudely the theory seems to merit the scorn that it has often attracted. Thomas Rymer, who coined the expression and advocated, though he did not invent, the idea,[11] has been particularly open to attack. But the idea is not, necessarily, either crudely didactic or naive. For the Elizabethans, and Rymer, the idea was protected from this charge because it was actually a part of a sophisticated (though problematic) distinction between poetry and history – a distinction which also goes back to Aristotle. Sophocles and Euripides, says Rymer, found in history.

> the same *end* happen to the *righteous* and to the *unjust, vertue* often *opprest*, and *wickedness* on the Throne: they saw these particular *yesterday-truths* were imperfect and unproper to illustrate the *universal* and *eternal truths* by them intended. Finding also that this *unequal* distribution of rewards and punishments did perplex the *wisest*, and by the *Atheist* was made a scandal to the *Divine Providence*. They concluded, that a *Poet* must of necessity see *justice* exactly administered, if he intended to please . . .   (p. 22)

History, then, contradicts poetic justice and even provides evidence for questioning providence. There is no pretence that in life itself justice is seen to be done; poetic justice is administered by the artist as a result of a rather uneasy alliance between aesthetic and didactic interests: in tragedy, says Rymer,

> Something must stick by observing that constant order, that harmony and beauty of Providence, that necessary relation and chain, whereby the causes and the effects, the vertues and rewards, the vices and their punishments are proportion'd and link'd together . . .   (p. 75)

Here, however, the precept is showing signs of strain since Rymer's idea of 'harmony and beauty' is ambiguously poised between being a substitute for reality on the one hand, and a revelation of a more ultimate reality on the other. Moreover, Rymer's aesthetic delight in the 'harmony and beauty of Providence' is at odds with his reference elsewhere to 'God Almighty, whose holy will and purposes are not to be *comprehended* . . .' (p. 22).

Samuel Johnson, in preferring Tate's *King Lear* (in which the ending is altered and Cordelia rewarded) makes the same alignment between poetic justice and aesthetic pleasure:

> A play in which the wicked prosper and the virtuous miscarry may doubtless be good, because it is a just representation of the common events of human life.

> But since all reasonable beings naturally love justice, I cannot easily be
> persuaded that the observation of justice makes a play worse.[12]

Again, the crucial question poses itself: is this 'justice' – which, it is conceded,
does not exist in life – simply a pleasing illusion or a revelation of a more
ultimate (i.e. providential) order? David Daiches has highlighted the inconsistency in Johnson's position: 'Johnson . . . at the same time praised Shakespeare for knowing and imitating human nature and blamed him for not
having sufficient poetic justice in his plays. You cannot have it both ways.
. . .'[13] No literary form can have poetic justice grafted onto it as a moral–
aesthetic-embellishment which pleases, yet does not alter the fundamental
sense. This is especially so with drama: in an elementary sense, both drama
and poetic justice are concerned with actions and their consequences, events
and their eventual import; hence, a play which incorporates poetic justice
does so at a structural, and therefore very meaningful, level.

Amusingly, but significantly, another advocate of poetic justice, John
Dennis, interpreted the lack of such justice in Shakespeare's plays in this
way:

> the Good and the Bad . . . perishing promiscuously in the best of Shakespear's
> Tragedies, there can be either none or very weak Instruction in them: For such
> promiscuous Events call the Government of Providence into Question, and by
> Scepticks and Libertines are resolv'd into Chance.[14]

Exactly so! Empiricist mimesis portrays the actual world which, quite
obviously, differs from the providential order. Now it is not this difference *per
se* which disturbs Dennis – it is, after all, a difference presupposed in the very
distinction between secular and divine – but, rather, its *dramatic* representation; drama depicts, perhaps more acutely than any other literary genre,
the problematic relationship between the two realms.

Dennis's anxiety was not in any sense new. William R. Elton, in an
important study, has demonstrated at length how in the latter half of the
sixteenth century it was felt, increasingly, 'first, that providence, if it existed,
had little or no relation to the particular affairs of individual men; and,
second, that it operated in ways bafflingly inscrutable and hidden to human
reason'.[15] He explains these attitudes with reeference to the Epicurean revival, the influence of Montaigne, Calvin, Bacon and others. It would seem
to be just this problematic relationship between secular and divine which
underlies the equivocal status of poetic justice in literary didacticism. On the
one hand it is a fictive construct which pleases, whilst on the other it is a
metaphysical construct which reveals the providential design – Rymer's
'universal and eternal truths'. Perhaps Rymer is poised between these two
positions because neither was satisfactory. Certainly an unsympathetic critic
might claim that the first explanation is inadequate because it involves an
escapist idealism, and the second simply implausible. Addison, in fact,

argued against Rymer for largely these reasons: he found the notion of poetic justice 'contrary to the experience of life . . . nature and reason'.[16]

II

I now revert to the Elizabethan period and desire to show how the ambiguity in question was apparent in the most considerable work of literary theory of that time, Sidney's *Apology for Poetry*. Sidney, like Rymer, and also following Aristotle, advocates poetry in preference to history. Discussing their relative merits in terms of what they depict (respectively the ideal and the actual) Sidney says:

> if the question be for your own use and learning, whether it be better to have it set down as it should be, or as it was, then certainly is more doctrinable the feigned Cyrus of Xenophon than the true Cyrus in Justin . . .[17]

Sidney repeatedly stresses this point; the poet, with his 'feigned example' (p. 110) can instruct, whereas the historian 'being captivated to the truth of a foolish world, is many times a terror from well-doing, and an encouragement to unbridled wickedness' (p. 111). Moreover, poetry instructs pleasurably, even though this pleasure is achieved through radical deception: 'those things which in themselves are horrible, as cruel battles, unnatural monsters, are made in poetical imitation delightful' (p. 114). For Sidney poetic justice is the instructive principle of poetry generally: 'Poetry . . . not content with earthly plagues, deviseth new punishments in hell for tyrants' (p. 112). And, indeed, of drama specifically: 'if evil men come to the stage, they ever go out (as the tragedy writer answered to one that misliked the show of such persons) so manacled as they little animate folks to follow them' (p. 111). The emphasis is strongly prescriptive; 'right poets' he says,

> imitate to teach and delight, and to imitate borrow nothing of what is, hath been, or shall be; but range, only reined with learned discretion, into the divine consideration of what may be and *should* be.   (p. 102, italics added)

But if this didacticism is achieved by completely disdaining 'what is, hath been, or shall be' what, finally, is the ontological status of that which is imitated? Sidney implies that it is wholly fictive. The poet ranges 'only within the zodiac of his own wit' (p. 100). Apparently, then, the poet is not imitating a pre-existent eternal ideal, but one which he himself creates.[18]

Elsewhere, however, Sidney seems to realise the implications of such a theory and affirms the contrary. Of the different kinds of mimesis he says: 'The chief, both in antiquity and excellency, were they that did imitate the inconceivable excellencies of God' (p. 101). Also, and with Aristotelian and Platonic emphasis, he speaks of poetry's 'universal consideration' and 'perfect pattern'.[19]

The ambiguity remains unresolved in the *Apology*. Critics, inclining one

way or another in their commentary on the work, have offered incompatible
interpretations. Thus Geoffrey Shepherd, a recent editor of the *Apology*, sees
Sidney's ideal as metaphysical:

> [Sidney's] religious faith and his poetic theory rest on the belief that intelligent
> design, not chance, is inherent in nature itself. It is from this position that
> Sidney urges that poetry can provide what history cannot guarantee, a grasp
> of the universal design and order.[20]

Daiches, on the other hand, concludes that it is fictive: for Sidney, says
Daiches,

> *imagination does not give us insight into reality, but an alternative to reality.* . . . He
> almost proceeds to develop a theory of 'ideal imitation', the notion that the
> poet imitates not the mere appearances of actuality but the hidden reality
> behind them, but stops short of this to maintain the more naive theory that the
> poet creates a better world than the one we actually live in.
> (*Critical Approaches to Literature*, p. 58)

But why stress this ambiguity? It is of the first importance in that it
concerns the ontological status of what poetry represents and, therefore, its
didactic function. In the context of Christian theology morality depends,
ultimately, on a metaphysical sanction for its prescriptive force; if it is
accepted that what is being apprehended (and imitated) is a metaphysical
ideal with real ontological status, then the prescriptive force of poetry is
considerable; conversely, if the object of imitation is ideal in a fictive sense
only, it cannot thus prescribe.

Now, Francis Bacon in his account of poetry in *The Advancement of Learning*[21] argues that the ideal world represented by poetry *is* entirely fictive. He
thereby completely undermines its didactic function. Bacon divides human
learning into three groups: History, Poesy and Philosophy. Each stems from
a corresponding faculty of understanding – respectively, Memory, Imagination and Reason. The difference between History and Poesy is defined
unambiguously: 'History is properly concerned with individuals, which are
circumscribed by place and time . . . *I consider history and experience to be the same
thing* . . .' (*De Augmentis Scientiarium*, p. 426, italics added). Poesy is 'nothing
else but Feigned History' (*Advancement*, p. 87); Memory and History are
concerned with empirical reality; Poesy and Imagination are confined to the
world of fiction. Poesy 'commonly exceeds the measure of nature, joining at
pleasure things which in nature would never have come together, and
introducing things which in nature would never have come to pass' (*De
Augmentis*, p. 426).

Bacon goes on to describe precisely the interrelationship between poesy,
poetic justice and providence:

> The use of this Feigned History [i.e. poetry] hath been to give some shadow of
> satisfaction to the mind of man in those points wherein the nature of things

doth deny it; the world being in proportion inferior to the soul; by reason whereof there is agreeable to the spirit of man a more ample greatness, a more exact goodness . . . than can be found in the nature of things . . . because *true history* propoundeth the successes and issues of actions not so agreeable to the merits of virtue and vice, therefore poesy feigns them more just in retribution, and more according to revealed providence.

(*Advancement*, p. 88, italics added)

In *De Augmentis* this suggestion that poetry is agreeable illusion is even stronger: 'Poesy seems to bestow upon human nature those things which history denies to it; and to satisfy the mind with the shadows of things when the substance cannot be obtained' (p. 440). Consequently the fictive and ideal elements of poetry are inferior by comparison with those branches of knowledge which engage, albeit painfully, with empirical reality:

So as it *appeareth* that poesy serveth and conferreth to magnanimity, morality, and to delectation. And therefore it was ever thought to have some participation of divineness, because it doth raise and erect the mind, by submitting the shews of things to the desires of the mind; whereas reason *doth bow and buckle the mind unto the nature of things.* (*Advancement*, p. 88, italics added)

Note how reason, and by implication its corresponding category of learning, philosophy, are now aligned with history and memory on the side of reality.[22] By organising categories of knowledge in this way Bacon retains The Aristotelian categories of poetry and history, but effectively *reverses* their priority.

Sidney concurs with Aristotle's judgement that poetry 'is more philosophical and more studiously serious than history' (Sidney, *Apology*, p. 109). Bacon asserts the contrary, and the reversal results from the different ontological status accorded to the ideal world of poetry.

Aristotle rejected the Platonic theory of two worlds – that is, the world of sense experience, and the ultimate world of Forms, apprehended intellectually. The 'universal truths' that Aristotle substituted for Platonic Forms, though still metaphysical, refer much more closely to particular things and events in the world: 'By "universal truths" we mean the kinds of thing a certain type of person will say or do according to probability or necessity, which is what poetry aims at. . . .'[23] Plato's Forms are *transcendent*, beyond the empirical world and existing independently of it; Aristotle's universals are *immanent*, dependent upon this world and revealed through it. For Plato the particular things 'imitated' or 'reflected' their Form. One weakness in this dualism is the inability to explain the relationship between Form and particular in terms more precise than metaphors of imitation. Further, the ontological status of this purely transcendent Form has, from the outset, been difficult to define.

The distinction between the metaphysical reality which is transcendent, and that which is immanent, remains at the centre of Western theology and philosophy, especially in the period under discussion. It is, for example, apparent in the Anglican–Puritan debate over the issue of exactly how divine and secular are related. And the same issue is being disputed, implicitly or explicitly, in the aesthetic theory. Predictably, theology and aesthetics relate closely. Thus, for Richard Hooker the providential design was still immanent in the empirical world, and this despite the Fall. But Fulke Greville pessimistically thought the contrary; the deviation of the actual world from the divine plan increased with the distance in time from the Fall. He termed the process 'declination'. Sidney is closer to Greville than to Hooker; he endorses Aristotle's conception of the 'universal consideration' which poetry imitates. But, with his repeated insistence that the poet borrows 'nothing of what is' (p. 102), that he creates 'another nature' (p. 100), Sidney's ideal, in so far as it is metaphysical at all, is transcendent rather than immanent, more Neoplatonic than Aristotelian. Significantly, he uses the metaphor of the 'erected wit' knowing what perfection is but being prevented from '*reaching* unto it' by the 'infected will' (p. 101, italics added). Bacon effectively denies the poetic ideal any real ontological status whatever – immanent or transcendent. It is an ideal which is pleasing, gratifying, possibly useful, but ultimately illusory.

Bacon's priorities are clear; moving from poetry to the other branches of knowledge he declares: 'It is not good to stay too long in the theatre. Let us now pass on to the judicial place or palace of the mind, which we are to approach and view with more reverence and attention' (*Advancement*, p. 89). Bacon gives poetry an idealist function only to undercut idealism itself. Moreover, a brief re-examination of the foregoing quotations will indicate the extent to which providentialism generally, and poetic justice specifically, are steered into the fictive world of poetry and imagination (see especially pp. 30–1 above). In this connection Bacon makes a fascinating remark on the contemporary theatre:

> Dramatic Poesy, which has the theatre for its world, would be of excellent use if well directed. For the stage is capable of no small influence both of discipline and corruption, Now of corruptions in this kind we have enough; but the discipline in our times has been plainly neglected. And though in modern states play-acting is esteemed but as a toy, except when it is too satirical and biting; yet among the ancients it was used as a means of educating men's minds to virtue.   (*De Augmentis*, p. 440)

One might add that the neglect of this 'discipline' on the contemporary stage, the reluctance to use the theatre as a means of 'educating men's minds to virtue' was in part due to a distrust of poetic justice and providentialism similar to Bacon's own! Much of the didactic drama of the sixteenth century conformed to Bacon's view of what the theatre should do.[24] Clearly, however, contemporary drama, with its 'corruptions' and capacity to be 'too satirical and biting' was not conforming to this pattern. Significantly, satire was one of the manifestations of a new dramatic realism, both in tragedy and comedy. Given his own assertion that history and experience are identical (see p. 30 above), and his remarkable classification of drama as 'History made visible' (*De Augmentis*, p. 439), Bacon should have realised that the theatre could not easily be incorporated in his aesthetic. Drama in this period was fulfilling increasingly the function of 'History' rather than 'Poesy'.

Fulke Greville makes this point. Like Bacon, he classifies knowledge within the categories of the ideal and the actual. In *A Treatise of Human Learning*[25] he asserts that the function of the 'arts' in general, and poetry in particular, is the truthful portrayal of reality. Moreover, analysing the relationship between word and object, Greville strongly implies that this reality is empirical. Greville rejects intellectual speculation which fails to produce concrete results (stanza 28). He attacks arts like philosophy which are 'Farre more delightfull than they fruitfull be' (stanza 29). Those who engage in linguistic sophistry he calls '*Word-sellers*' and '*Verbalists*' (stanzas 30, 31) adding, in one of many conclusions to the same effect:

> *What then are all these humane Arts, and lights,*
> *But Seas of errors? In whose depths who sound,*
> *Of truth finde onely shadowes, and no ground.*   (stanza 34)

Greville prefers the usefully active life to the idly contemplative, and argues for general truths, gathered from experience and nature and applied to present circumstances. He distrusts language and rejects

> . . . termes, distinctions, axioms, lawes,
> Such as depend either in whole, or part,
> Vpon this stained sense of words, or sawes:
> Onely admitting precepts of such kinde,
> As without words may be conceiu'd in minde.   (stanza 106)

'*Grammar*', '*Logike*', 'the *Schooles*', '*Rhetorike*' – all come under scathing attack. For Greville linguistic structures constantly carry the danger of obscuring reality or, worse, actually becoming a substitute reality. He condemns such fabrications as 'the painted skinne / Of many words' (stanza 107). It is to empirical reality that he wants language to refer, and therefore advocates uses of language which

> . . . most properly expresse the thought;
> For as of pictures, which should manifest
> The life, we say not that is fineliest wrought,
> Which fairest simply showes, but faire and like.[26]

The essential point is made in stanza 112:

> *if the matter be in Nature vile,*
> *How can it be made pretious by a stile?*

So far Greville's theory is wholly in accordance with his preference, expressed in the *Life of Sir Philip Sidney*, for 'images of life' in literature rather than 'images of wit'.[27] Greville sees his own images of life appealing 'to those only, that are weather-beaten in the Sea of the World' (p. 224). Such images engage with the reality of experience and the imperfection of the world whereas 'images of wit' do not. These latter images he associates with

> witty fictions; in which the affections, or imagination, may perchance find exercise, and entertainment, but the memory and judgement no enriching at all.   (p. 223)

If Greville is here echoing Bacon's classification of the faculties and their corresponding categories of knowledge, there is an implied preference for history as the subject of literature. Actually, it is contemporary society as well as 'life' and history in the wider sense which Greville saw his own drama as representing. He destroyed one of his tragedies because he believed it politically dangerous; it could, he said, have been construed as 'personating . . . vices in the present Governors, and government' (p. 156). Moreover, the 'true Stage' for his plays, says Greville, is not the theatre but the reader's own life and times –

> even the state he lives in . . . the vices of former Ages being so like to these of this Age, as it will be easie to find out some affinity.   (p. 225)

Thus Greville expresses a strong preference for a form of empiricist mimesis, both in the *Life* and the early sections of *Human Learning*. Yet, when giving a specific account of poetry later on in *Human Learning* he suddenly switches tack, investing the art with an idealist function. It has, he says, the potential for showing a disordered fallen nature 'how to fashion / Her selfe againe' by reference to the ideal – the '*Ideas*' of 'Goodnesse, or God'. Further, poetry '. . . like a Maker, her creations raise / On lines of truth' and 'Teacheth vs order vnder pleasures name' (*Human Learning*, stanza 114). Here Greville embraces a Platonic conception of the artistic function at odds with the earlier renunciation:

> *These Arts, moulds, workes can but express the sinne,*
> *Whence by mans follie, his fall did beginne.*   (stanza 47)

H. N. Maclean has argued that Greville discounted the fictive element in poetic creation to the extent of considering himself one of the 'meaner sort of Painters' disparaged by Sidney in the *Apology*.[28] These are painters who represent what they actually see rather than its idealisation. But despite embracing empiricist mimesis, Greville retains the didactic function of art even though his 'images of life' reveal a world so ineradicably corrupt that little moral instruction of a positive kind can be extracted from it. It is an instance of the conflict between the absolute and the relative which characterises his work and, according to a recent account, his life.[29] Underlying the conflict is uncertainty about the final relationship of secular and divine. The desired relationship is for the empirical reality to reveal the absolute order, yet this is what the Calvinist will usually deny: the secular realm is corrupt and his transcendent God can only be known through faith and scriptural authority. Furthermore, if the Calvinist accepts the doctrine of the decay of nature (as did Greville), then, through 'declination', the disjunction between the mundane and the divine increases with time. As the possibility of experiencing divine order through secular experience decreases, it becomes increasingly necessary to affirm its existence through faith.

The distinction in stanza 18 of *Human Learning*, between 'apprehension' and 'comprehension' reflects the dilemma (perhaps, too, its tortuous, obscure syntax is a way of registering the paradoxical strain which the dilemma involves):

> Besides; these faculties of apprehension;
> Admit they were, as in the soules creation,
> All perfect here, (which blessed large dimension
> As none denies, so but by imagination
> Onely, none knowes) yet in that comprehension,
> Euen through those instruments whereby she works,
> Debility, misprison, imperfection lurks.

The 'faculties of apprehension' are wit, will and understanding. 'Comprehension' is the successful exercise of those faculties with regard to true knowledge. Essentially it is a distinction which points to a gap between awareness and understanding:

> . . . our capacity;
> How much more sharpe, the more it apprehends,
> Still to distract, the lesse truth comprehends.
>
> (*Human Learning*, stanza 20)

'Apprehension' becomes the acute, anxious awareness of the 'comprehension' which is desired but denied.

To recapitulate: Sidney equivocates on what, as Tatarkiewicz reminds us, was one of the central problems of Renaissance aesthetics: 'What is the object, the material cause of poetry: reality or fiction?'[30] Sidney retains the didactic function of literature but comes dangerously close to dispensing with the providential sanction which, in the late sixteenth century, it presupposed and depended upon. Once it is denied that the source of the didactic scheme is a reality both ultimate and more real than the phenomenal world, the scheme itself withers in the face of a world which contradicts it. And, of course, this is what Bacon, by implication, does deny. He answers the question 'reality or fiction?' by opting firmly for the latter. As such his illusionist account of poetry has little application for the contemporary theatre. Yet he also argues that the ideal order which literature has traditionally portrayed, together with the vehicle of that portrayal, poetic justice, are fictions. In this respect Bacon concurs with some contemporary dramatists: intentionally or otherwise both he and they subvert the didactic function of art together with the metaphysical categories which it presupposed.

Thus, the ambiguity found in Sidney's *Apology* can be seen as preparing the way for Bacon's subversion of idealist mimesis. Bacon, in turn, leads writers like Greville to a profound distrust of illusion as an aesthetic objective; Greville felt that if literature is to be prevented from becoming mere escapism it must confront reality without any 'formalist' misrepresentation: '*if the matter be in Nature vile, | How can it be made pretious by a stile?*' But he cannot press the theory to its conclusion since the portrayal of this vile matter threatens both the metaphysical absolute and the didactic scheme. Eventually, and nowhere is this more apparent than in Greville's own play, *Mustapha*, a moral commitment to confront the world in all its vileness undermines a moral commitment to represent the providential design. And this, surely, is the most important respect in which Greville made explicit the profound intellectual conflicts latent in the theatre of his day.[31] Aristotle and Sidney affirm the superiority of poetry to history; Bacon reverses this priority; for Greville the old distinction between poetry and history collapses into an outright contradiction between absolute and relative, ideal and empirical. Metaphysical categories became susceptible to experiential disconfirmation and especially so in the contemporary theatre. As David Bevington has shown: 'The diversity of aim between realistic expression of factual occurrence and the traditional rendering of a moral pattern inevitably produced an irresolution in the English popular theatre at a time when Marlowe was its leader.'[32]

I have argued here that this irresolution is not merely a technical issue, or the lapse in dramatic propriety reprimanded by Eliot as 'faults of inconsistency, faults of incoherency, faults of taste . . . faults of carelessness' (Eliot, 'Four Elizabethan Dramatists', p. 111). Rather, it is manifestation of a deep conflict in the consciousness of the age, the conflict involved in attempting to reconcile providentialism with empirical reality. Further, the literary theory of the period brings that conflict into a particular focus, especially the debates over poetic versus actual justice, 'poesy' versus 'history', the fictive representation versus the actual representation – in short: idealist mimesis versus empiricist mimesis. Thus, additionally, I have argued against the received view that Renaissance literary theory has little relevance to Renaissance literary practice. It has little direct critical application, certainly, but considerable relevance.

Although the conflict in question was especially acute in the Renaissance it was by no means limited to it. Nor, indeed, was the desire for a resolution of that conflict; as Maynard Mack once observed:

the metaphor of harmony from discord . . . has influenced Western thinking for more than twenty centuries ... it has the special virtue for theodicy of recognising the fact of evil while restricting its significance. It enabled one to take account of the observed heterogeneity and conflict of things but reconcile them.[33]

Playwrights of the late sixteenth and early seventeenth centuries inherited a morality structure, a form of idealist mimesis, with exactly this potential for reconciliation; however, those of them who took seriously the social and metaphysical dislocation of the age, and who could envisage no easy solutions, repudiated both morality structure and its harmonising potential. The coherence of their plays resides in the sharpness of definition given to that dislocation, not in an aesthetic, religious or didactic resolution of it. Thus the alternative to such resolution is not necessarily 'irresolution' in the sense of intending, yet failing, to dispose of contradictions. On the contrary, it may be that contradictory accounts of experience are deliberately forced into an open disjunction, and the tension which this generates is a way of getting us to confront the problematic nature of reality itself.

Some such account as this would, I suggest, explain the considerable difficulties which critics have encountered with plays like Marlowe's *Dr Faustus*. One reason why this play in particular has caused so many interpretative difficulties is that, for many critics, to acknowledge that a work of literature not only confronts conflict and contradiction, but incorporates them within its very structure, is to admit that work as an aesthetic failure. This attitude, though it still prevails, is less common than it was; under the influence of very different fields of literary criticism (in England now one dare, almost, speak of theory as well as criticism) there is less concern with organic form, reconciliation, integration, equilibrium, and so on, as criteria of aesthetic success. Writers like Brecht, Walter Benjamin, Pierre Macherey, and, from a different quarter, John Bayley,[34] show us how literature may reveal its most important meaning precisely where it is most discordant. Unfortunately, criticism of some of Shakespeare's contemporaries is still largely dominated by an aesthetic orthodoxy which sees resolution and transcendence of conflict as major indications of aesthetic success. Not surprisingly, this critical orthodoxy identifies sympathetically with orthodox providentialist dogma in the Elizabethan period: a preoccupation with aesthetic harmony finds its counterpart in a preoccupation with metaphysical harmony. The result is that dramatists who were actually challenging providentialist orthodoxy, are interpreted as conforming to it. In order to do justice to the plays of these dramatists we need to disentangle them from such criticism.

I wish to pursue my argument in a close analysis of one such play, Tourneur's[35] *The Revenger's Tragedy*. I have chosen it, first, because it is an outstanding Jacobean tragedy, secondly, because it is still largely in the grip of the criticism in question.

III

Many critics have felt that if *The Revenger's Tragedy* is not fundamentally orthodox, then it cannot help being hopelessly decadent. If, for example, it can be shown to be rooted in orthodox morality (in the sense of affirming Morality-play didacticism and its corresponding metaphysical categories) then an otherwise very disturbing play is rendered respectable. Moreover, the embarrassing accusation of a critic like Archer – who described the play as 'the product either of sheer barbarism, or of some pitiable psychopathic perversion'[36] – can be countered with the alternative view that it is a 'late morality' where 'the moral scheme is everything'.[37]

This moral scheme demonstrates, allegedly, the workings of a severe retributive justice which inexorably destroys the sinful and attests to the existence of a providential reality controlling human affairs. Accordingly, there is a precise alignment between morality and providentialism, the former deriving from, and being sanctioned by, the latter. In short, what is attributed to this play is a form of idealist mimesis. Actually, this is a view of the universe and of human existence which *The Revenger's Tragedy* precisely denies. Through parody Tourneur subverts the dramatic conventions which embody the didactic and metaphysical preoccupations of idealist mimesis. Simultaneously he offers his own version of empiricist mimesis: a realism which sees the social aberration of court life as rooted in the prior fact of an aberrant nature, ungoverned by any kind of law – social, natural or supernatural. For Tourneur there is no ideal metaphysical order, transcendent, or immanent.

In a highly influential book, M. C. Bradbrook asserts that *The Revenger's Tragedy* 'might almost be called a *drame à thèse* on the contrasts between earthly and heavenly vengeance, and earthly and heavenly justice'. And, regarding its protagonist, Vindice, 'Heaven is responsible for his fall, and Heaven alone'.[38] Robert Ornstein believes that 'even as Vindice's character disintegrates, the incorruptible, remorseless moral order that governs his abandoned world reveals itself'.[39] These and many other critics[40] have substantiated this interpretation by pointing to (i) the orthodox moral perspective which is, allegedly, implicit in characters' responses to heaven, hell, sin and damnation, and (ii) the extensive use of ironic peripeteia which allegedly destroys evil according to a principle of poetic justice. I propose to challenge, in turn, each of these arguments.

It is instructive to begin with the following, characteristic, utterance from Vindice: 'Were't not for gold and women, there would be no damnation; Hell would look like a lord's great kitchen without fire in't' (II, i, 257–9). Here, one appreciates the simile while recognising that its sense ends with the wit. 'Hell' and 'damnation' serve as expletives, carrying expressive force without pointing to a potential or threatening reality (cf. II, ii, 155–6: *Vindice*

[*Aside*]. Heart, and hell! *Hippolito* [*Aside*]. Damned Villain!). In act v the contemporary concern for truly damning one's enemy at the point of death[41] is treated as mere superstition and an incidental opportunity for one of the play's most spirited 'jests'; about to stab the already dead Duke, Vindice asks:

> Shall we kill him now he's drunk?
> *Lussurioso.* Ay, best of all.
> *Vindice.* Why, then he will ne'er live to be sober.
> *Lussurioso.* No matter, let him reel to hell.
> *Vindice.* But being so full of liquor, I fear he will put out all the fire.
> *Lussurioso.* Thou art a mad beast.
> *Vindice* [*Aside*]. And leave none to warm your lordship's golls withal, – for he that dies drunk falls into hellfire like a bucket o' water, qush, qush.
>
> (v, i, 46–55)

But it is in Vindice's rhetorical invocations to heaven that the underlying mockery of the supernatural surfaces most distinctly:

> Why does not heaven turn black, or with a frown
> Undo the world? – why does not earth start up,
> And strike the sins that tread upon't? (II, i, 254–6)

The implied parody of the providential viewpoint, and the *caricature* of the vengeful god, could not be more obvious:

> *Vindice.* O, thou almighty patience! 'Tis my wonder
> That such a fellow, impudent and wicked,
> Should not be cloven as he stood, or with
> A secret wind burst open.
> Is there no thunder left, or is't kept up
> In stock for heavier vengeance? [*Thunder sounds*] There it goes!
>
> (IV, ii, 194–9)

Here the traditional invocation to heaven becomes a kind of public stage-prompt ('is there no thunder left . . .?') and God's wrath an undisguised excuse for ostentatious effect. In performance such lines beg for a facetious Vindice[42] half turned towards the audience and deliberately directing its attention to the crudity of the stage convention involved. In effect, the conception of a heavenly, retributive justice is being reduced to a parody of stage effects. In the following pun on 'claps' heaven is brought down to the level of a passive audience applauding the melodrama:

> When thunder claps, heaven likes the tragedy.
>
> (v, iii, 47)

As the above quotations suggest, Tourneur makes Vindice the agent of the parody, investing him with a theatrical sense resembling the dramatist's own:

> *Vindice.* Mark, thunder! Dost know thy *cue*, thou big-voic'd cryer?
>   Duke's groans are thunder's *watchwords.*
>
>   (v, iii, 42–3, italics added)

> When the bad bleeds, then is the tragedy good.
>
>   (III, v, 205)

It gives an intriguing flexibility to Vindice's role, with the actor momentarily stepping through the part and taking on – without abandoning the part – a playwright's identity. This identity shift is instrumental to the parody: at precisely the moments when, if the providential references are to convince, the dramatic illusion needs to be strongest, Vindice (as 'playwright') shatters it. He does so by prompting for thunder from the stage, by representing thunder as a participant in a melodrama waiting for its 'cue', and by re-casting the traditionally 'frowning' heaven as a spectator clapping the action. The convention linking 'heaven', 'thunder' and 'tragedy' is, together with its related stage effects, rendered facile; providentialism is obliquely[43] but conclusively discredited.

Peter Lisca, in seeing the references to thunder and heaven as eliminating any doubt as to the play's 'sincere moral framework' (Lisca, p. 250) seems to miss an irony in tone and delivery which, in performance, would actually contradict the kind of moral conclusions he draws. Discussions of the extent to which a play is indebted to older dramatic forms are often marred in this way by an inadequate discrimination between the dramatic use of a convention and wholesale acceptance of the world view that goes (or *went*) with it. Obviously, the distinction becomes more than usually crucial when, as is the case here, the convention in question is being subjected to parody.

Tourneur also exposes the hypocritical moral appeals which characters make to the providential order. An audience will, for example, simply *hear* the sermonising rhetoric of the Duchess's attack on illegitimacy:

> O what a grief 'tis, that a man should live
> But once i' th' world, and then to live a bastard,
> The curse o' the womb, the thief of nature,
> Begot against the seventh commandment,
> Half-damn'd in the conception, by the justice
> Of that unbribed everlasting law.
>
>   (I, ii, 159–64)

The hollowness of this rhetoric is, of course, compounded by the sheer hypocrisy of its delivery: the Duchess is seen speaking not from the pulpit, but while in the act of seducing her stepson and inciting him to murder his own father. Nevertheless, it has often been argued that this orthodox link between providence and morality ('the justice / Of that unbribed everlasting law') once suggested, no matter by whom or how hypocritically, remains as an implicit norm by which the dramatist structures his play and evaluates characters within it. In some instances of the drama of the period this may be true, but Tourneur's attitude is different. He saw that this 'law' was simply inoperative. He further saw that moral behaviour, though by no means the same thing as morality itself, is a necessary condition for the latter's viable existence. Action which violates moral ideals on a sufficiently extensive scale is seen to corrode the ideals themselves in the end. This becomes increasingly clear as the play progresses. Still in act I, for example, there is a moral posturing more insidious even than that of the Duchess. Antonio, celebrating publicly his wife's chastity (she has committed suicide after being raped) is seen to value that chastity much above her life. 'Chastity' and 'honour' emerge, in fact, as wholly distorted ethics – little more than the wilful impositions of the male ego in a male-dominated world. Discovering his wife's dead body to 'certain lords' Antonio exclaims:

> be sad witnesses
> Of a fair, comely building newly fall'n . . .
> *Piero.*   That virtuous lady!
> *Antonio.*   Precedent for wives!   (I, iv, 1–7)

What is being celebrated, and in a language of artificial grandeur that reeks of affected grief, is not her innate virtue but her *dutiful* suicide, her obedience to male-imposed terms of honour:

> *Antonio.*   I joy
> In this one happiness above the rest . . .
> That, being an old man, I'd a wife so chaste. (I, iv, 74–7)

Chastity in this court involves a life-denying insularity dictated by male vanity rather than disinterested virtue. Again, it involves a hypocrisy masked by an appeal to the providential order: 'Virginity is paradise, lock'd up. / You cannot come by yourselves without fee, / And 'twas *decreed* that man should keep the key' (II, i, 157–9).

Peripeteia allegedly constitute the structural evidence for the providential interpretation. Thus Bradbrook argues that the scene in which the Duke is murdered 'illustrates how, if earthly law is corrupt there is an "unbribed everlasting law" which is inescapable' and which manifests itself through 'an enlarged series of peripeteia' (pp. 165, 172). Lisca offers the most extreme recent account, arguing that 'the moral attitude expressed in *The Revenger's Tragedy* proceeds from a Christian point of view (the Puritan) . . .' and that the peripeteia become 'the intestinal division of evil itself, a division which while seeming to lead to multiplication ironically ends in cross cancellation' (pp. 242, 245). Behind the view of these and other critics seems to be the assumption that peripeteia possess an inherently providential significance. This is not necessarily the case; at one level these ironic reversals are more intimately bound up with Vindice's (and Tourneur's) sense of artistry than anything else:

> *Vindice.* That's a good lay, for I must kill myself. Brother, that's I; that sits for

me. . . . Here was the *sweetest occasion*, the *fittest hour*, to have made my revenge
familiar with him; shown him the body of the duke his father, and how *quaintly*
he died . . . and *in catastrophe*, slain him over his father's breast; and O, I'm mad
to lose such a sweet opportunity.   (v, i, 4–21, italics added)

This delight in the 'fittest hour' and the 'quainter fallacy' (IV, ii, 5) involves a
dramatic irony and wit where characters either have their expectations
thwarted, suffering sudden and extreme reversals of fortune, or where the art
of revenge depends for its success on a vicious appropriateness. Vindice's
advice to Lussurioso on how to kill the Duchess and Spurio (whom they
expect to find in bed together) is an extreme instance of the latter point;
Vindice's delighted anticipation of the proposed execution here amounts to
a mode of aesthetic villainy: 'Take 'em finely, finely now . . . Softly, my lord,
and you may take 'em twisted . . . O 'twill be glorious / To kill 'em doubled,
when they're heap'd. Be soft, / My lord' (II, ii, 169–iii, 4). As J. M. R.
Margeson has observed, in the Italian *novelle* and many of the later comedies
and tragedies influenced by them, 'ironic reversals flourished mightily,
aiming at no more than a special kind of theatrical pleasure'. He also notes
the absence of providential intervention in the tragic stories of the *novelle*,
although translators of the stories often made (albeit with some difficulty)
their own didactic additions. Clearly Jacobean dramatists also used the
ironic reversal for more than theatrical pleasure, but the serious purpose to
which it was put was very different from the blinkered orthodoxy of the
translators.[44] In *The Revenger's Tragedy* the ironic reversal is the expression of
sophisticated malice devised and executed by characters against each other.
That malice epitomises the assimilation of the barbaric and sophisticated
extremes inherent in the Italianate court setting. In acknowledging this
there is no need to feel compromised (as did Archer) by the vision of a
'psychopath'. Through the peripeteia Tourneur also demonstrates beyond
doubt that, for almost all its inhabitants, this sexually obsessed and violent
world becomes self-stultifying. Assertion of will meets with counter-assertion
and survival is of the fittest but, even for them, only temporary. This is not
proof of a controlling providential order, but the consequence of human
extremes – extremes of avarice, hate and lust – being too closely confined and
ungoverned by *any* kind of law. Here, as with, for example, *The White Devil*
the final sense we are left with is that no one can survive a world so
treacherous and insecure, partly because no one adheres even minimally to
the moral law that would make survival possible. But – and this is the crucial
point – it is the total absence of law, not the intervention of supernatural law,
that accounts for the destruction.[45] At the widest level the ironic reversals
are a dramatic way of pointing a secular fact: there is a random but
eventually inevitable collision of wills and hence a repeated thwarting of
individual effort. As such these reversals, in their cumulative effect, suggest a
barely relieved futility. Yet, the theatrical sense informing these reversals,

and the self-consciousness of those initiating them, testify to something more complex than a simple acknowledgment of, or surrender to, this futility. 'Just is the law above!' remarks Antonio with orthodox solemnity after the series of murders in the last act; "twas somewhat witty carried, though we say it' replies Vindice, referring to one of the same. In that reply, as elsewhere, Tourneur's mocking intelligence and acute sense of parody – the kind that 'hits / Past the apprehension of indifferent wits' (v, i, 134) – converge in a 'witty' and decisive rejection of Antonio's crude, providential rationalisation.

IV

I have been arguing for a view of *The Revenger's Tragedy* as a play dealing not with a world informed by a divinely ordained justice, but a human reality at once barbaric, sophisticated and self-stultifying. Tourneur, while probing this world, simultaneously repudiates one conventional way (the providential) of giving point and coherence to it; the idea of a retributive justice is reduced, consciously, to a parody of theatrical convention. But Tourneur's own direct probing of 'this luxurious day wherein we breath' (i, iii, 110) becomes an equally effective repudiation, and it is to this that I now want to turn.

The play centres on the frenetic activity of an introverted society encompassed by shadows and ultimately darkness – the 'heedless fury' and 'Wildfire at midnight' which Hippolito describes (ii, ii, 172). The Court, 'this luxurious circle', is a closed world where energy feeds back on itself perpetuating the unnatural act in unnatural surroundings: the location of the Duke's death is an unsunned lodge, 'Wherein 'tis night at noon'. Decay and impermanence stress the futility of man's obsessive struggle for fulfilment. Yet there is no anticipation of other-worldly compensation, Junior's cynical rejection of the relevance of heaven to his impending death (iii, iv, 70–4) being typical. The play's view of mortality is reminiscent of Schopenhauer; I quote briefly from his *Parerga and Paralipomena* simply to emphasise that it is not necessarily a view which entails a conception of man as inherently sinful or governed by divine law. The experience Schopenhauer describes is a contingent one with secular boundaries:

> The vanity of existence is revealed in the whole form existence assumes . . . in the fleeting present as the sole form in which actuality exists; in the contingency and relativity of all things . . . in continual desire without satisfaction; in the continual frustration of striving of which life consists. . . . Thus its form is essentially unceasing *motion* without any possibility of that repose which we continually strive after . . . existence is typified by unrest. . . . Yet what a difference there is between our beginning and our end! We begin in the madness of carnal desire and the transport of voluptuousness, we end in the dissolution of all our parts and the musty stench of corpses.[46]

One is reminded too of the more restrained, yet somehow almost as pessimistic, account of London by Tourneur (or whoever that 'C.T.' was)[47] at
the opening of 'Laugh and Lie Downe: Or, the Worldes Folly':

> Now in this Towne were many sundrie sorts of people of all ages; as Old, and
> young, and middle age: men, women and children: which did eate, and drinke,
> and make a noyse, and die . . . they were Creatures that serued the time,
> followed Shaddowes, fitted humours, hoped of Fortune, and found, what? I
> cannot tell you.[48]

In *The Revenger's Tragedy* this sense of urban life as futile striving is
intensified by the dramatist's insistence that here there is no alternative:
activity occupying the immediate dramatic focus – 'this present minute' – is
made, through graphic 'off-stage' description, to appear as just a bolder
representation of that which pervades the rest of life:

> My lord, after long search, wary inquiries,
> And politic siftings, I made choice of yon fellow,
> Whom I guess rare for many deep employments;
> This our age swims within him . . .
> He is so near kin to this present minute.   (i, iii, 21–6)

Moreover, characters move into the line of vision already 'charged' with a
common motivating energy – sexual, aggressive or otherwise – which varies
in intensity only depending on whether it is the dramatic foreground or
background that they occupy. It is, consequently, a world whose sense ends
with its activity – a world, that is, whose senselessness becomes instantly
apparent when activity culminates in death. Vindice highlights this through
a detached awareness which Tourneur exploits to full effect as part of a
structural interplay between movement and stasis.

Movement illustrates, repeatedly, the forces that impel, but simultaneously constrain and destroy, man; forces inherent in the human, but also
the social, condition. Of the first kind, the human or inborn condition, the
most extreme is obviously the sexual – the 'riot' of the blood (i, i, 11). 'I am
past my depth in lust, / And I must swim or drown' says Lussurioso (i, iii,
88–9), testifying to the destructive yet compulsive nature of that lust. The
other kind of condition, the social, is powerfully realised as either a grinding
poverty or thwarted ambition – both of which render the individual vulnerable to court exploitation. Thus we see Hippolito being sent from court –

> To seek some strange-digested fellow forth,
> Of ill-contented nature, either disgrac'd
> In former times, or by new grooms displac'd   (i, i, 76–8)

while for Lussurioso 'slaves are but nails, to drive out one another'. For his
second slave he demands one who,

> being of black condition, suitable
> To want and ill content, hope of preferment
> Will grind him to an edge.   (iv, i, 69–71)

Both Machiavellian intrigue and lust are depicted as inherent aspects of the frenetic movement and become inextricably linked with it in imagination:

> *Vindice.*   my brain
> Shall swell with strange invention; I will move it
> Till I expire with speaking, and drop down
> Without a word to save me; but I'll work –
> *Lussurioso.* We thank thee, and will raise thee.   (I, iii, 119–23)

The point is stressed throughout with the recurrence of that word 'swell' in imagery of tumescence:

> . . . drunken adultery.
> I feel it swell me   (I, ii, 190–1)

> I would embrace thee for a near employment,
> And thou shouldst swell in money   (I, iii, 76–7)

> Thy veins are swell'd with lust, this shall unfill 'em
>   (II, ii, 94)

(see also I, ii, 113 and IV, i, 63).

Movement, for the main characters, is this incessant drive for self-fulfilment through domination of others.[49] Movement is also presented as a process of inevitable disintegration; it is as if the dissolution of death works from *within* the most frantic of life's activities:

> O, she was able to ha' made a usurer's son
> *Melt* all his patrimony in a kiss[50]   (I, i, 26–7, italics added)

> I have seen patrimonies *washed a-pieces*, fruit fields turned into bastards, and, in a world of acres, not so much dust due to the heir 'twas left to, as would well gravel a petition.
>   (I, iii, 50–3, italics added)

So, the assertion of life energy does not stand in simple contrast to the process of dissolution but rather seems to feed – to become – the very process itself. Yet, because the contrast is still presupposed in the very vigour of that assertion, there is a shocked realisation that much more is involved than just an attentuated life force, or a death-in-life cliché. Tourneur uses a perspective that discovers, rather than fabricates, the contradictions in experience.

Vindice's silk-worm image makes for the same kind of emphasis at a point immediately prior to the height of the dramatic action:

> Does the silk-worm expend her yellow labours
> For thee? for thee does she undo herself?   (III, v, 72–3)

Dissolution, the sense of helpless movement and a lack of purpose, are all concentrated in this image. The depiction of an uncontrollable movement towards dissolution also recalls Vindice's earlier lines where drunkenness is seen to release the barely conscious, the sub-human inclination:

> Some father dreads not (gone to bed in wine)
> To slide from the mother, and cling the daughter-in-law.
>
> (I, iii, 58–9)

Here, in lines whose meaning is reinforced by the natural stress falling on 'slide' and 'cling', the involuntary action of a human being is reduced (casually yet startlingly) to the reflex action typical of an insentient being. In all these ways the futility and destructiveness of man's social life are shown to have their source in some deeper condition of existence; at the very heart of life itself there moves a principle of self-stultification.

Contrary to this use of movement, the stasis with which it contrasts involves a form of detachment, the medium of insight and a limited foresight. Whereas to be caught up in the temporal process is to be blindly preoccupied with the 'minute' (a recurring expression – see especially I, ii, 168; I, iii, 26; I, iv, 39; III, v, 75), the brief moments of inaction allow for a full realisation of just how self-destructive is this world's expenditure of energy, of just how poor is the benefit of the 'bewitching minute'. It is reflected, initially, in the way Vindice's opening commentary is delivered from a point of detached awareness – a detachment represented spatially with him withdrawn into the shadowed region of the stage and directing attention at the procession. And at III, v, 50 ff., just before the (by now) anticipated climax, his own contemplative state directs attention to the lifelessness of the skull, a wholly static, tangible representation of death and a striking visual contrast to the frenetic activity of life in this court. Insight of this kind is limited to Vindice; by others it is actually evaded. Thus whereas Vindice realises that 'man's happiest when he forgets himself' (IV, iv, 84) but cannot in fact forget himself for very long, Ambitioso checks his realisation that 'there is nothing sure in mortality, but mortality' with a resolve to action: 'Come, throw off clouds now, brother, think of vengeance, / And deeper settled hate' (III, vi, 89–90; 92–3).

Given a world of dislocated energy as its dramatic subject, what kind of formal unity is such a play likely to possess? The answer is suggested by Vindice. He is a character who elicits the sympathy accorded to one who displays an acute and disturbing awareness of a corrupt world he is inescapably confined to, and of which he therefore, inevitably, becomes a victim. It is as such that, at the play's close, he surrenders life with comparative indifference, a surrender which recalls his earlier 'My life's unnatural to me, e'en compell'd / As if I liv'd now when I should be dead' (I, i, 120–1). Internalising the tensions and contradictions of his world, Vindice becomes the focal point for those aspects of the play which, though inextricably linked, will not – indeed, cannot – be finally resolved into a single coherent vision. In the famous fifth scene of act III for example, he is in turn exhilarated, deeply pessimistic and viciously vindictive. To say this, however, is not to support the view of Vindice (or Tourneur) as neurotic, or of the play as a structural failure. The important point is that a vital irony and a deep pessimism are held together dramatically without thereby being neatly integrated, and the reason for this is that Tourneur is not aiming to give a cohesive view of the world, but a view which retains a hold, albeit a precarious one, on an incohesive world. This is also why the elements of the play exist in discordant relationships: it incorporates in its structure the dislocation inherent in its subject. Additionally, it is why the element of parody should not be excused by critics or underplayed by performers for the sake of a simplifying unity; to the extent that it is undermining idealist mimesis – subverting one, *conventional*, way of investing a chaotic world with significance – the parody is of central importance.

Tourneur refrains from replacing the providential account of experience with an alternative, ordering scheme; he does not, for example, formally pattern and balance the conflicts of the play in a way which allows them to cancel each other out at an aesthetic level. Rather, he aims to thrust into dramatic life the view that life itself works its own destruction. Nor does he mitigate the stultification of his 'accursed palace' by allowing its inhabitants the role of splendid despair. In fact, it is a play where human suffering is never seen to vindicate human existence. To that extent *The Revenger's Tragedy* is beyond tragedy.

NOTES

1. E. Panofsky, *Idea: A Concept in Art Theory*, tr. Joseph J. S. Peake (Columbia: University of South Carolina Press, 1968), p. 47.
2. For the sake of brevity, and unless otherwise indicated by the context, I follow the convention of using 'Elizabethan' to refer to drama of both the Elizabethan and Jacobean periods.
3. Arnold Hauser, *The Social History of Art: Renaissance, Mannerism and Baroque*, 4 vols (London: Routledge & Kegan Paul, 1962), II, 2.
4. W. Tatarkiewicz, *History of Aesthetics*, 3 vols (The Hague: Mouton; Warsaw: PWN–Polish Scientific Publishers, 1970), I, 144.
5. William K. Wimsatt and Cleanth Brooks, *Literary Criticism: A Short History* (New York: Alfred A. Knopf, 1959), p. 26. For a full account of the development of the concept in classical times see Göran Sorbom, *Mimesis and Art: Studies in the Origin and Early Development of an Aesthetic Vocabulary* (Stockholm: Svenska Bokförlaget, 1966).
6. T. S. Eliot, 'Four Elizabethan Dramatists', in *Selected Essays* (London: Faber, 1932), pp. 114, 116.
7. Bertolt Brecht, *The Messingkauf Dialogues*, tr. John Willett (London: Methuen, 1965), p. 60.

8. J. E. Spingarn, *A History of Literary Criticism in the Renaissance* (New York and London: Columbia University Press, 1908), p. 256.

9. Thomas Heywood, *An Apology for Actors* (reprinted for the Shakespeare Society, London, 1841), p. 53.

10. And even in the work of earlier writers; M. A. Quinlan, *Poetic Justice in the Drama* (Notre Dame, Indiana: University Press, 1912) lists, among others, Ascham, Gascoine and Whetstone as being aware of, and sympathetic to, the idea. Quinlan rightly observes that because of the growing opposition to drama, especially in the form of censorship, 'it was far more necessary for the defenders to justify the drama on the grounds of morality than to show that its chief end was to please' (p. 30).

11. Thomas Rymer, *The Critical Works*, ed. Curt A. Zimansky (New Haven: Yale University Press, 1956), especially pp. xxvii–xxix.

12. Samuel Johnson, *Selected Writings*, ed. R. T. Davies (London: Faber, 1965), pp. 294–5.

13. David Daiches, *Critical Approaches to Literature* (London: Longmans, 1956), p. 68.

14. Quoted in Clarence C. Green, *The Neo-Classic Theory of Tragedy in England during the Eighteenth Century* (New York: Blom, 1966), p. 141.

15. William R. Elton, *King Lear and the Gods* (San Marino, California: The Huntington Library, 1968), p. 9.

16. Joseph Addison, *The Spectator*, no. 40 (16 April 1711).

17. Sir Philip Sidney, *An Apology for Poetry*, ed. Geoffrey Shepherd (Manchester University Press, 1973), pp. 109–10.

18. Compare F. Patrizi: 'the poet similarly [to the painter] can either paint a likeness, or express fantasies of his own devising, which have no counterpart in the world of art or nature, nor in God's universe'. *Della Poetica* (1586), p. 91.

19. Sidney, *Apology*, pp. 109 and 110. The same emphasis is apparent in Sidney's reference to 'the *idea* or fore-conceit of the work' (p. 101).

20. *Ibid.*, Introduction, p. 53; see also p. 55. J. W. H. Watkins offers a similar interpretation in *English Literary Criticism: the Renaissance* (London: Methuen, 1947), p. 120.

21. *The Philosophical Works of Francis Bacon* (reprinted from the texts and translations of Ellis and Spedding) ed. John M. Robertson (London: Routledge, 1905). All page references are to this one-volume edition.

22. In *Descriptio Globi Intellectualis* this alignment of philosophy is even more explicit: 'In philosophy the mind is bound to things' (p. 677).

23. Aristotle, *On the Art of Poetry*, ch. 9.

24. That Bacon had this kind of drama in mind is suggested by his remark in *Novum Organum* to the effect that 'stories invented for the stage are more compact and elegant, and more as one would wish them to be, than true stories out of history' (p. 270).

25. In Geoffrey Bullough, *Poems and Dramas of Fulke Greville*, 2 vols (Edinburgh and London: Oliver and Boyd, 1939), I.

26. Stanza 109; compare stanzas 103 and 110. Greville's view of the painter differs from Sidney's: see the *Apology*, p. 102.

27. Fulke Greville, *Life of Sir Philip Sidney*, ed. Nowell Smith (Oxford: Clarendon Press, 1907), p. 224. In fact, Greville's 'images of life' closely resemble the 'images

of true matters' which Sidney sees as the historian's concern, not the poet's (*Apology*, p. 109).

28. Hugh N. Maclean, 'Greville's Poetic', *Studies in Philology*, LXI (1964), 170–91, and Sidney, *Apology*, p. 102.

29. Ronald A. Rebholz, *The Life of Fulke Greville* (Oxford: Clarendon Press, 1971), p. xxiv.

30. Tatarkiewicz, *History of Aesthetics*, III, 167.

31. Una Ellis-Fermor, *The Jacobean Drama*, (London: Methuen, fifth edition, 1965), ch. 10. See also Paula Bennett, 'Recent Studies in Greville', *English Literary Renaissance*, II (1972), 379.

32. David Bevington, *From Mankind to Marlowe* (Cambridge, Mass.: Harvard University Press, 1962), p. 261.

33. Alexander Pope, *An Essay on Man*, ed. Maynard Mack (London: Methuen, 1950), Introduction, p. xxxiv.

34. *Brecht on Theatre*, tr. John Willett (London: Methuen, 1964); Walter Benjamin, *The Origin of German Tragic Drama*, tr. John Osborne (London: NLB, 1977); for a brief but suggestive application of Benjamin's ideas to Elizabethan drama, see Charles Rosen's review article, 'The Ruins of Walter Benjamin', *The New York Review of Books*, vol. XXIV, no. 17, pp. 31–40; Pierre Macherey, *Pour une théorie de la production littéraire* (Paris: Maspero, 1971), translated as *A Theory of Literary Production* by Geoffrey Wall (London: Routledge, 1978); John Bayley: *The Uses of Division: Unity and Disharmony in Literature* (London: Chatto, 1976).

35. I am assuming nothing about, nor contributing to the debate about, the authorship of this play; 'Tourneur' must, therefore, be taken to simply denote whoever wrote *The Revenger's Tragedy*. All quotations from the play are from R. A. Foakes's edition in The Revels Plays series (London: Methuen, 1966).

36. William Archer, *The Old Drama and the New: An Essay in Re-Valuation* (London: Heinemann, 1923), p. 74.

37. John Peter, *Complaint and Satire in Early English Literature* (Oxford: Clarendon Press, 1956), p. 268.

38. M. C. Bradbrook, *Themes and Conventions of Elizabethan Tragedy* (Cambridge University Press, 1935) pp. 165–6, 174.

39. Robert Ornstein, 'The Ethical Design of *The Revenger's Tragedy*', *English Literary History*, XXI (1954), 87. But see also Ornstein's later discussion of the play in *The Moral Vision of Jacobean Tragedy* (Madison: University of Wisconsin Press, 1960).

40. For other views of the play as being either a vindication of divine justice, or structured in such a way as to demonstrate orthodox morality – with divine justice implied – see L. G. Salingar, '*The Revenger's Tragedy* and the Morality Tradition', *Scrutiny*, 6 (1938); H. H. Adams, 'Cyril Tourneur on Revenge', *Journal of English and Germanic Philology (JEGP)*, 48 (1949); Peter, *Complaint and Satire;* P. Lisca, '*The Revenger's Tragedy:* A Study in Irony', *Philological Quarterly*, 38 (1959); I. Ribner, *Jacobean Tragedy: The Quest for Moral Order* (London: Methuen, 1962); A. L. and M. L. Kistner, 'Morality and Inevitability in *The Revenger's Tragedy*', *JEGP*, 71 (1972); P. B. Murray, in *A Study of Cyril Tourneur* (Philadelphia: University of Pennsylvania Press, 1964) offers an interesting development of this argument: 'it is not God who . . . deals out the ghastly reprisals of the *lex talionis*, but Satan' (p. 233).

41. Compare Thomas Nashe's *The Unfortunate Traveller* in *Works*, ed. R. B. McKerrow, 5 vols (Oxford: Blackwell, 1965), II, 325–6. Eleanor Prossor, *Hamlet and Revenge* (Stanford University Press, 1967), pp. 255–75, discusses more than twenty instances of this kind of revenge in the literature of the period.

42. This is, perhaps, the 'pose of indignant morality' that Archer detected (p. 74) but misunderstood. But Archer had misgivings: 'One cannot, indeed, quite repress a suspicion that Tourneur wrote with his tongue in his cheek . . .' (p. 75). Indeed one cannot!

43. If, as seems likely, *The Revenger's Tragedy* was written after May 1606 such obliquity may, apart from anything else, have been an effective way of avoiding a tangle with the statute of that month to restrain 'Abuses of Players'. This act not only forbade the player to 'jestingly or profanely speak or use the holy name of God or of Christ Jesus, or of the Holy Ghost or of the Trinity' but also commanded that the same were not to be spoken of at all 'but with *feare and reverence*' (italics added). It is precisely this kind of 'feare and reference' that is being parodied. The statute is reprinted in W. C. Hazlitt, *The English Drama and Stage* (London: Roxburghe, 1869), p. 42.

44. J. M. R. Margeson, *The Origins of English Tragedy* (Oxford: Clarendon Press, 1967), p. 136. G. Boklund has demonstrated how Webster uses repeated ironic reversals to demonstrate that it is 'chance, independent of good and evil' which governs events in *The Duchess of Malfi*. See *The Duchess of Malfi: Sources, Themes, Characters* (Cambridge, Mass.: Harvard University Press, 1962), pp. 129–30.

45. This is also Thomas Hobbes's view of man when ungoverned by *human* law. Man's nature, he says, leads to 'a condition of war of everyone against everyone'. Thus, without strong government restraining him, man lives in 'continual fear, and danger of violent death; and the life of man [is] solitary, poor, nasty, brutish, and short'. *Leviathan*, ed. Michael Oakeshott (Oxford: Blackwell, 1946), pp. 85, 82.

46. From R. J. Hollingdale's selection, *Essays and Aphorisms* (Harmondsworth: Penguin, 1970), pp. 51–4. For a complete edition of *Parerga and Paralipomena* see E. F. J. Payne's translation, 2 vols (Oxford: Clarendon Press, 1974).

47. See *The Works of Cyril Tourneur*, ed. A. Nicoll (London: Fanfrolico Press, 1929), pp. 16–18.

48. *Ibid.*, p. 275.

49. Compare Hobbes: 'I put for a general inclination of all mankind, a perpetual and restless desire of power after power, that ceaseth only in death.' *Leviathan*, p. 64.

50. Compare Shakespeare's Timon: '. . . thou wouldst have plunged thyself / In general riot, *melted* down thy youth / In different beds of lust . . .' (IV, iii, 256–8).

The ideal theatre in the eighteenth century: Paris and Venice

TOM LAWRENSON

The evolving shapes of theatres, the comparison of moments in that evolution as between one country and another, are not the normal concern of the student of dramatic literature, and might be thought, at first blush, to have little *droit de cité* in a work devoted to drama and mimesis. Even more might this appear to be the case when it comes to a comparative study of projects for theatres which were not actually built.

Yet the shape of the theatre does sporadically influence dramatic literature, and very rarely does the reverse obtain in the modern era (although opera provides one outstanding example at least, that of Wagner's Bayreuth Festspielhaus). As the great French actor–director Louis Jouvet put it: 'Dans la "ressuscitation" d'une esthétique dramatique, le verbe peut nous égarer, non l'édifice.' (In the 'ressuscitation' of a dramatic aesthetic, the Word can lead us astray, not the edifice.) [1] If, furthermore, we accept the imitation of the Ancients quite simply as a form of mimesis we must needs accept the imitation of the form of the ancient theatre too. For the search for that San Graal of men of the Renaissance, the melopoeia (that perfect blending of music into the drama attributed to the ancient Greeks), the five-act tradition, the distinction of the genres, the unities and the shape of the theatre itself are all objects of imitation. Here, however, a significant difference supervenes. The written word is considerably easier to manipulate than stone, or bricks and mortar, or even wood. Vitruvius, whom, for the purposes of the argument we may describe as the Aristotle of theatre shape, is not followed in French (at least) theatre architecture as is Aristotle in French dramatic literature: the treatment of Vitruvius' *Ten Books on Architecture* by individuals and academies alike manifests a line of negative scholarship which interests itself mostly in the superficialities of decoration: the orders of columns and the like. [2] In Italy, during the period of the Renaissance, it is not easy to find a theatre other than the Olympic Theatre at Vicenza where there is a conscious attempt to put Vitruvian theory into practice, by an Academy founded for the study of that precept, and in France throughout the seventeenth century the theatre simply is not an autonomous feature of the urban scene: it is normally housed in a pre-existing rectangle of some sort or other, usually an indoor tennis court. We may indeed say that the attempted renaissance (if by renaissance we mean a rebirth of ancient lore) does not come in Italy or France, where theatre form is concerned, until the eighteenth century and that then it is not a renaissance in reality but merely in fancy.[3] The only remote approach to a rebirth of the shape of the ancient theatre is to be found in Victor Louis' Grand Théâtre de Bordeaux.

It is precisely because it is easier to plan than to build that the unbuilt project frequently tells us more of what was in the architectural air than can the product in three dimensions on the ground, subject as it is to the constraints that the architect in his study pays little heed to. He dreams on the drawing board. Particularly is this the case with the opera. As a relative latecomer to the theatrical field, it finds itself saddled with pre-existing houses in France in particular, and with the burning of the Paris Opera in 1763 the great dream of the ideal theatre begins. It is here that a comparative (if limited) juxtaposition of plans as between Italy and France can be illuminating. It is, after all, the dream that gives expression to subconscious desires, that delivers from the contingent, from the constraining nexus of reality. One might even speak, in respect of the plans we are to examine, of dreams of varying depth. There are dreams so close to the surface of consciousness that they could in truth have been built as theatres; and there are others so profoundly rooted in their liberation from conscious reality that these theatres, meant as vehicles for illusion, are themselves pure illusion.

The dream of the ideal theatre exists in a number of forms, and has a number of awakenings. The general dream is of an aesthetic nature: the awakening is, naturally, an inrush of commercial considerations. There is the dream of the ideal acoustic, doubtless with flat walls for reverberation. Indeed, both dream and awakening are to be found in what is probably the most widespread treatise on theatre form of the European eighteenth century, Patte's *Essai sur l'architecture théâtrale* of 1782.[4] He is aware of sound as vibration, though he regards it as a series of vibrations in the air rather than of the air. He is aware of the phenomenon of reverberation, which he regards as the science of acoustics.

The real awakening of these dreams of the perfect acoustic is the commercial viability of wall space. There is the dream, too, of perfect visibility and here again the awakening is what might be called the income-bearing wall and its exploitation, with, this time, an additional dimension of great socio-theatrical importance: the desire for *intervisibility* in the auditorium considered as a social autonomy: the ladies in particular wish to see each other, and to be seen by the men. Intervisibility and the privacy of the theatre boxes, in superposed rows around the walls, destined for activities other than watching the stage, seal off the audience from the stage more than the proscenium arch and its curtain. The dream is Epidauros. The awakening is the Fenice in Venice.[5]

A most interesting work appears in 1762, the year before the first burning of the Paris Opera. It is Eneo Arnaldi's *Idea di un teatro nelle principali sue parti simile a teatri antichi, all'uso moderno accomodato.* (The idea of a theatre similar in its principal parts to the ancient theatres, adapted to modern usage.)[6] The reference back to the Ancients has begun, consecrated in the title: the compromise between ancient and modern still seems possible. This is an early example of that dialectic between then and now which will face subsequent planners in their dream of the ideal theatre, and is reminiscent of the Quarrel of Ancients and Moderns which had already taken place in France, in the literary sphere. Vitruvius is one authority, the paying public another, in the Venetian Republic at least, and no man can serve two masters.

The fire risk in the European theatres of the seventeenth and eighteenth centuries was staggering, and this is not the last occasion on which we shall find the burning down of a theatre house giving rise to a spate of dreaming on the drawing board. Arnaldi's remarks themselves were inspired by the burning of the theatre at Verona. In his preface, after a customary and ritual genuflexion before the altar of Vitruvius, he denounces the insufficiency of the modern theatres relatively to the ancient (Roman), especially the material of which they are constructed: wood is inadequate. Semi-circular, amphitheatrical seating (he goes on) was a necessity for the ancient theatre: it is impossible, he claims, to imagine the auditorium of the theatre of Marcellus in Rome arranged in boxes. Yet the modern public requires them, so Arnaldi gives his house boxes, and this will scandalise Milizia later.[7]

Curiously enough, Arnaldi rejects what he calls the recent innovation of rows of boxes in retreat the one above the other, claiming that it detracts from the visibility, and that it offends against the principal rules of architecture.[8]

The simple fact is that, despite the superficial appearance of his semi-circular auditorium, Arnaldi leans decidedly towards the moderns. He enumerates the differences: the moderns have boxes instead of open amphitheatrical seating. They cannot have a portico walk-way round the upper periphery, precisely because of the boxes. The orchestra is of necessity reduced, as it now contains the musicians and not the senators. Instead of the three doors of the Roman *frons scenae* (stage building façade) there is only one opening. There is, he suggests, a natural and proper difference between ancient and modern theatre architecture.

Let us note immediately that in using the Ancients as example Arnaldi had yet contrived to preserve important elements of the contemporary playhouse: boxes, the 'orchestral' orchestra, and the single Italian proscenium arch. There remains the semi-circle of Arnaldi's auditorium, and it is in fact his main tribute to Vitruvius: the ovoid form of auditorium, he remarks, is currently preferred to the Vitruvian semi-circle, or the truncated ellipse of Palladio's Teatro Olimpico. Yet with the oval form, spectators at the back of the house are farther from the stage than with a semi-circle. They cannot hear as well; moreover, the oval ensures that those boxes nearest the stage virtually face away from it, forming what the French were shortly to call 'places de souffrance'. This we shall hear of again, from Milizia. All their current auditoria, he tells the Italians, are deeper than they are wide. His prescriptions for the site of the theatre echo those of Vitruvius: it must be healthy, unencumbered, with the addition of a piazza for vehicles.

Still claiming to base himself on Vitruvius, he demands a rectangular scenic space (*pulpitum*) which, he declares, Vitruvius recommends as the best form for projecting the sound.

To find the nearest French analogy to Arnaldi we have to break the chronological line and turn to a master-carpenter called André-Jacob Roubo[9] (see plate 1). 1777, the year of Roubo's publication, is the year before the Paris Opera was burned down for the second time. Like Arnaldi, he claims authority from the Ancients: 'Réunir sous un même point de vue la connaissance historique et locale des théâtres anciens et modernes.' (To unite under a single scrutiny the historical and local knowledge of ancient and modern theatres.) Like Arnaldi again, and unlike Cochin, whom we shall consider later, he favours the semi-circular auditorium. 'Il n'y a qu'à changer la forme de l'éllipse tronquée de la poire ou du soufflet (qui sont les formes des salles italiennes) en un demi-cercle parfait.' (All that is to be done is to change the form of the truncated ellipse, the pear shape, or the bellows shape, which are the Italian auditorium shapes, into a perfect semi-circle.) His ideal site is the same as Arnaldi's: autonomous, free-standing, preferably in the middle of a square. He envisages the major part of the action as taking place on the forestage, the stage rectangle behind being reserved largely for decoration. The sight-lines for the perspective set are inferior to the·truncated ellipse of the Olimpico, but superior to those of Soufflot's (real) Grand Théâtre de Lyon of 1754. There are stage boxes (*loges d'avant-scène*), that is to say, *places de souffrance*, or at least their occupants would 'suffer' where visibility was concerned. Let us add that his amphitheatre is more 'Roman' than that of Arnaldi; however, he does add boxes to his auditorium, but only two rows, and there are no seats in the amphitheatre below the 'first floor' created by the first row of boxes; yet again, this is to facilitate that 'inter-visibility' of which we have spoken.

The first publication of Charles-Nicholas Cochin is of 1765, after the first fire at the Paris Opera.[10] He himself says, with disarming frankness: 'C'est, proprement parlant, le théâtre de Palladio.' (It is, strictly speaking, Palladio's theatre.) The reality, as we shall see, is Italian, of 1585; and in 1765, a Parisian dreams of it. However, according to Filippi[11] Cochin was equally inspired by the theatre at Imola (see plate 2).[12] Morelli, in 1780, speaks of this theatre.[13] One sees immediately that the acting area and the area for

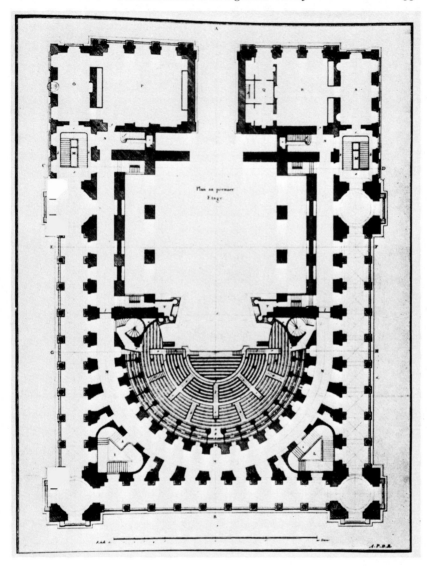

1 Plan of Roubo's Theatre. From *Traité de la construction des théâtres et des machines théâtrales* (Paris 1777)

décors is the exploded and modernised form of the Olympic *proscenio*. Morelli himself explains that relatively to his two preceding theatres, this is a wider stage, virtually abolishing the proscenium arch, with an enlarged acting area, and, with its three groupings of stage decoration, an optimum view of the stage picture for everybody. (That is to say, an uneasy compromise

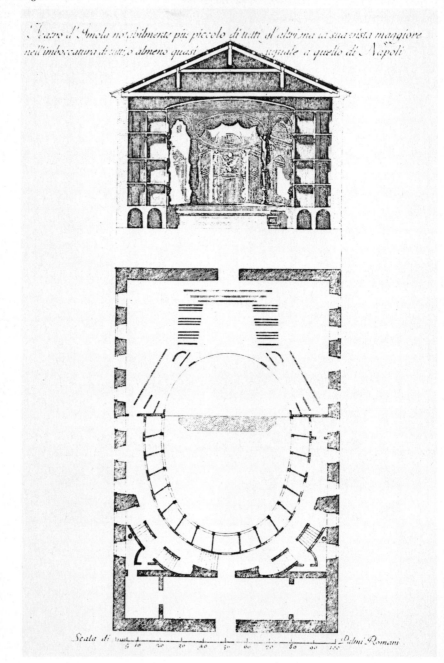

2　The theatre at Imola. From Cosimo Morelli, *Pianta e spaccato del nuovo teatro di Imola*
(Rome 1780)

between a monolinear perspective set and an amphitheatrical auditorium!)
Cochin's unbuilt theatre plan displays three groupings of perspective wings,
like Morelli's, but more flattened. Inasmuch as his stage decorations are not
as deep as Morelli's he may be said to be closer to the Olympic Theatre; what
are, in the Olympic, doors in the manner of the Roman *frons scenae* have
become, under the modernising vision of Cochin, three rather small proscenium arches. Even so, Cochin may be said to have progressed a long way
compared to his French predecessors, though the inspiration of the Olympic
Theatre (which he freely admits) and of Imola (which he does not) is clear
enough. Indeed, the distance traversed is best demonstrated by superimpos-
ing his plan over that of François d'Orbay's first Comédie Française of 1689.
This Cochin obligingly does for us himself (see plate 3).

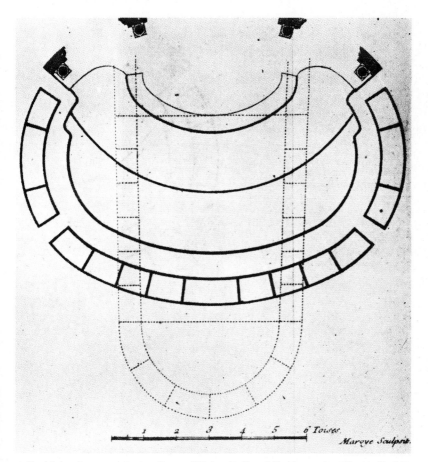

3 Cochin's plan superimposed on d'Orbay's Comédie Française. From Cochin,
Projet d'une salle de spectacle pour un théâtre de comédie (Paris 1765)

In a very real, if somewhat gnomic sense, the history of European theatre architecture is that of the squaring of a circle. Only in the deepest unencumbered dream does one find the interior circle of an auditorium matched by the line of an outer circle: only rarely, in other words, is the total theatre building conceived of as circular in the ancient manner.

The reason for the failure to build a modern amphitheatre is not far to seek. Boxes cannot be accommodated in an amphitheatre of rising tiers of united seating. The French architect Patte[14] reviews the social and economic reasons for the use of boxes: the Ancients had their amphitheatre:

> ... mais cette disposition ... paroît trop contraire à nos étiquettes, à nos usages. Nous sommes habitués depuis long-tems à des loges: elles facilitent à chacun d'assister au Spectacle, suivant son rang ou ses moyens, & de s'y rassembler avec ses compagnies ou ses sociétés ordinaires. Les femmes, accoutumées depuis long-tems à faire le principal ornement de cet objet de nos plaisirs, ne trouveroient pas leur compte à ces gradins sur lesquels elles paroîtroient isolées et confondues: la propreté des habits même répugne à cette distribution; outre cela, c'est la location des loges à l'année qui produit le revenu le plus assuré des Théâtres permanens dans les grandes Villes ... [15]

> ... but this arrangement ... seems too contrary to our etiquette, our customs. We have been long accustomed to theatre boxes; they help everybody to participate in the Spectacle according to rank or means & to meet with their normal company or society. The Ladies, long used to being the principal ornament of this object of our pleasures, would not be satisfied with these steps on which they would appear isolated in a single mass: considerations of vestimentary hygiene, even, seem to exclude such a distribution; apart from this, it is the letting of boxes by the year which produces the surest income for the permanent Theatres of the large Towns.

Here at least is rude, waking reality. Patte concludes that the modern theatre world is saddled with boxes.

So it is with a Venetian counterpart, Francesco Riccati (1718–97).[16] This is hardly surprising as the author is not speaking particularly of the ideal theatre but of the typical Italian theatre, though not without a critical outlook. The arguments against the ancient amphitheatre adapted to modern usage are the same: for social and economic reasons, boxes are essential. He is less gallant towards the Italian women than is Patte towards the French: they like the closed boxes which permit them to indulge in their interminable conversation.[17]

We come to our final pairing. One of the writers (the Italian) is certainly amusing to read; the other (the Frenchman) produces plans which are certainly amusing to look at.[18]

With these two writers, we do for once seem to be on the way to the total circle, periphery matching the inner lines of the house. Milizia is the sworn enemy of the *palchetti* (boxes) and this leads him to consider in detail and with pungency every one of their deleterious effects. In this he sharply distinguishes himself from Boullée. The exteriors of the modern theatres, he avers, in no way announce their internal function. The material is wrong: they are made of wood, so much so that the maximum life of a theatre is scarcely fifty years.[19] All features of its internal shape conspire to ensure that everyone sees and hears as little as possible: the *palchetti* ensure that in a theatre with a capacity of two thousand only a fifth of the spectators can be seated so as to see and hear adequately. He gives examples of stone buildings: Turin, Naples, Bologna, Berlin, but again the interiors are spoiled by the *palchetti*. Only the Olimpico is a good theatre, and even the auditorium of that, he implies, should have been a semi-circle, the truncated ellipse being accounted for merely by the limitations of the site. Venice, we are told, has seven theatres, casually erected by patrician families on top of burnt houses or on the foundations of older buildings. Only one of them, the San Grisostomo, does not stray far from the principle of the semi-circle, but the large public attracted by the opera created a desire for more boxes: three were added on either side of the proscenium and the consequent elongation of the house spoilt the semi-circle. The same mania affects the other theatres.

In his confrontation between ancient and modern he has based himself on three factors: the solidarity of the edifice, the accessibility of the site, and convenience. In terms of visibility he regards the forestage as an error, because the people in the boxes near the stage (we are back to our *places de souffrance*) see the actors either from the side or from the back. The filled boxes of the theatre house he describes as 'un caos di teste e di mezzi busti' (a chaos of heads and half-bosoms). The attack on the dove-cote auditorium mounts in intensity. He even claims that it affects the quality of dramatic writing. The corridors behind the boxes are good for turning about, standing about, showing off, withdrawing, hiding, and acting generally exactly as though you were at home. Is it surprising (he cries) if the operas are worthless? Nobody goes for the purpose of listening. The result simply is not theatre. After dealing with the effect of the boxes on visibility and audibility, Milizia indicts them as leading to bad behaviour and concludes that to reform the theatre you must reform the *mores* of the city.

In his hatred of theatre boxes, in his sociology of the theatre, he is a puritan of theatre structure. What would he have said of the small boxes in the Dutch theatre of the early seventeenth century, which were each equipped with individual curtains which could conceal the occupants from the rest of the audience, and the disappearance of which was so regretted by the dramatist Tengnagel:

> In the old days young lovers liked the theatre. If they wanted to frolic a little, quick, they closed the curtains. But today all is open. Nothing more to be done.[20]

The plan of the theatre is not in fact Milizia's but is that of Vincenzo

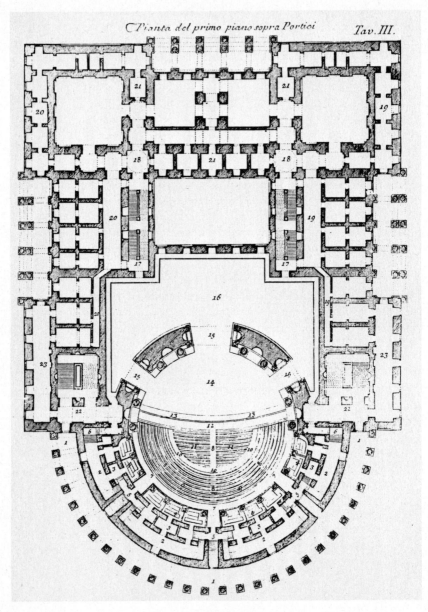

4 Milizia/Ferrarese theatre plan. From Milizia, *Del teatro* (Venice 1773)

Ferrarese: a complete circle, half of which is stage, half auditorium (see plate 4) and on every plane it is conceived as a sphere. Milizia even becomes completely formalistic in saying that Roman theatres erred in so far as stage (*pulpitum*) and stage-building façade (*frons scenae*) clashed by their rectangular shape with the semi-circle of the auditorium. Yet he preserves, as will Boullée, a perspective setting with a single line of sight and a single vanishing point and this gives him a deep stage which is at total variance with the overall lines of his building. He tries vaguely to face up to this by varying the columns which he places upstage, but without conspicuous success. However, what he has succeeded in creating, like Arnaldi, like Cochin, like Morelli, Roubo and Boullée, is a vastly enhanced stage width, a width which he defends vigorously: you can see more, hear more; the actors have greater freedom of movement.

When he comes to the cost of the theatre he evinces all the advantages enjoyed by the dreamer over the real builder. The price? (he exclaims) – what was the price of the Diocletian Baths, the Vatican piazza, Versailles? In any case, he continues, you can use the theatre for all sorts of gymnastic games and others, and he enters into detail on this topic. This is interesting and rare, for it shows us a Milizia moving, well ahead of his time, towards the theatre–cultural-centre recreation-centre.

In conclusion (and it is almost a dream become nightmare) we pass from the puritan to the megalomaniac. What is truly intriguing as between Boullée and Milizia is that, using as points of departure totally different ethical, social, and other bases, they reach such surprisingly similar forms.

Boullée's plan (see plate 5) is the fruit of the excessive imagination not of a man who, like Milizia, abominated the auto-spectacular, the narcissistic theatre house which looked in upon itself, but of one who, judging from recurrent remarks in his manuscript, saw only that in the theatre. Boullée the megalomaniac is precisely the archetype of that member of the public reviled by Milizia: he represents a paroxysm of narcissism in the audience. For him (and here he becomes distinctly comic) the theatrical occasion is as much as anything else an exhibition of women. Paradoxically, his enthusiasm for this amenity of spectacle is virtually Italian, and the opposite of Milizia's attitude.

Je vois le sexe le plus aimable se rendre dans nos Salles de Spectacles, et ne paraître s'y rassembler que pour rivaliser d'attraits, charmer nos cœurs, manifester son empire, et y recevoir aussi les hommages du génie qui, inspiré par l'amour et les Grâces, se plaît souvent à y célébrer les attraits de ce Sexe enchanteur. Oh! qu'il est donc bien vrai qu'une salle de spectacle doit être considérée comme le Temple du Goût.

I see the most adorable sex coming to our Theatre Houses, seeming to assemble there only to rival each other in attraction, charm our hearts, manifest their empire, and to receive there too the homage of genius which, inspired by love

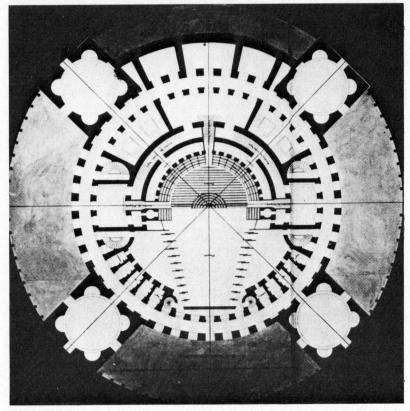

5 Plan of Boullée's Opera House. From Boullée, *Architecture, Essai sur l'art*

and the Graces, is oft pleased to celebrate the attractions of this bewitching Sex. Ah! how true it is, then, that a theatre house must be considered the Temple of Taste.

The most curious thing about this unique project, at least as far as its circular periphery goes, is that Boullée has invented it without reference to the Ancients. He has chosen it simply because it is beautiful.

As regards the number of places, his megalomania runs riot: 'Assuré par les dimensions que je lui ai données et par mes autres dispositions, qu'elle serait commode, favorable, et suffisante; je n'ai pas voulu avilir l'art en calculant les places que je pourrais y avoir de plus.' (Assured by the dimensions I have given it, and by my other dispositions, that it would be commodious, favourable and adequate, I have not chosen to debase art by calculating how many more places I could get in.)

What then may we conclude from this admittedly random series of juxtapositions? Two things, I think, at least. First, no one in the European eighteenth century, even upon the drawing board alone, resolved the existing tension between a theatre set in linear perspective and the amphitheatrical form of a theatre house. Secondly, our 'dreamers' are all, and already, in search of that enhanced, wider, front of contact between spectator and spectacle which is such a modern preoccupation.

NOTES

1. *Témoignage* to Henri Goutier, *L'essence du théâtre* (Paris, 1943), p. vi.
2. Cf. chapter 4 of my *French Stage in the Seventeenth Century* (University Press, Manchester, 1957).
3. Cf., for France, my two successive articles: 'The Shape of the Eighteenth-century French Theatre and the Drawing Board Renaissance', *Theatre Research/Recherches Théâtrales*, vol. VII, nos. 1/2 and 3.
4. Pierre Patte, *Essai sur l'architecture théâtrale, ou de l'ordonnance la plus avantageuse à une salle de spectacles, relativement aux principes de l'optique et de l'acoustique* . . . (Paris, 1782).
5. See, for example, Nicola Mangini, *I teatri di Venezia* (Milan, 1974), plates 46–50.
6. Eneo Arnaldi, *Idea di un teatro nelle principali sue parti simile a teatri antichi, all'uso moderno accomodato* (Venice, 1762).
7. See p. 59.
8. The French architect Jean-François Blondel, *Architecture françoise* (Paris, 1752–6), 11, 33, had already advocated the boxes *en retraite* one upon the other: 'ce qui donneroit à nos spectacles un tout autre coup d'oeil pour l'assemblée et une forme pyramidale et amphithéâtrale *convenable à ces sortes d'édifices*' (which would give to our spectacles a completely different view for the audience and a pyramidal and amphitheatrical shape *suitable to this sort of building*) (italics added).
9. André-Jacob Roubo, *Traité de la construction des théâtres et des machines théâtrales* (Treatise on the construction of theatres and theatre machines) part 1 (Paris, 1777).
10. Charles-Nicholas Cochin, *Projet d'une salle de spectacle pour un théâtre de comédie* (Paris, 1765).
11. Joseph de Filippi, *Parallèle des principaux théâtre modernes de l'Europe et des machines théâtrales françaises, allemandes et anglaises* . . . (Paris, 1860).
12. Cosimo Morelli, *Pianta e spaccato del nuovo teatro di Imola* (Rome, 1780).
13. This now gives us three major European attempts to reconcile the irreconcilable: perspective set, and amphitheatre house, namely, the Olympic Theatre, Imola, and Cochin's project.
14. See note 3 above.
15. Pp. 165–6. Nevertheless, in the account left to us by Filippo Pigafetta of *Oedipus Rex* which opened the Olimpico in 1585, we are still told that (in an auditorium built after the Roman manner) the sight of the ladies taking their seats in the orchestra was one of the pleasures of the earlier stages of the night.

16. Francesco Riccati, *Della costruzione de teatri secondo il costume dell Italia* (Bassano, 1790).

17. See Harold Zielske, 'Box House and Illusion Stage – Problem Topic in Modern Theatre Construction. Observations and Contemplations concerning its Genesis', in *Theatre Space. An Examination of the Interaction between Space, Technology, Performance and Society*. (International Federation for Theatre Research. Eighth World Congress, Munich, 1977). Zielske propounds a new and important theory in the development of the Italian *loggia*, namely that they did not spring to birth fully formed in Venice to accommodate a newly fragmented society (he has no difficulty in demonstrating that the Roman-type *cavea* auditorium could do *that*) but that they existed long before the Venetian opera in Italy and elsewhere in Europe as a natural architectural feature (e.g. surrounding houses with windows) where a central spectacle *of any sort* was contemplated. '. . . the development of the box system form took place outside the theatre and was a procedure originating purely in the history of architecture by which theatre and theatre construction have simply profited . . .'

18. Francesco Milizia, *Del teatro* (Venice, 1773, and Rome, 1771). Etienne-Louis Boullée, 1728–99. See Helen Rosenau, *Boullée's Treatise on Architecture* (London, 1953).

19. It is not for nothing that so many theatres are called 'The Phoenix.' They continually rise from their own ashes.

20. J. Fransen, *Les comédiens français en Hollande au XVIIe et au XVIIIe siècles* (Paris, 1925), p. 18. Fransen translates into French, and this I have translated into English.

The Japanese puppet theatre

CHARLES J. DUNN

INTRODUCTION

The purpose of this article is to provide an historical and descriptive foundation upon which comparative or more detailed and advanced studies can be
built. The material under observation will be what may be described as the
indigenous puppet theatre of Japan, by which is meant that which has not
derived from the West during this century. I do not propose to enter the
speculative field of the possible derivation from continental Asia in the
millennium before 1600, but to describe development entirely within Japan,
and to take in the physical history of theatre, puppets, plays, music and so on,
and finish with a more extended and, I hope, more penetrating treatment of
the present-day position.

Another remark which seems worth making in this preliminary statement
is that all aspects of Japanese art have traditionally been constructed upon
an artistic family or artistic school, with the result that there is a lack of
interplay and interconnection between forms. Thus, while the various types
of puppet drama have not shown reluctance to mix between themselves, they
nevertheless have generally kept quite separate from that other theatre
which uses an artificial face, that of the masked actor, the tradition of which
in Japan is as rich and varied as that of the dolls.

Since 1875 most Japanese have been called by two names, family and
given name (in that order), and this is the practice that will be followed here.
In the period before this date, how one was named depended upon many
factors, such as one's class or rank and whether one had chosen a *gō* (artistic
name) for any particular art or performance. However, tradition has normally by now determined by what name a person is known in relation to any
one form, in this case the puppet theatre, and for the pre-modern period this
traditional name will be used, with a fuller form given if necessary for
reference at first occurrence. Finally, a note is perhaps necessary on the term
bunraku, now widely used for the three-man puppets and their theatre;
strictly speaking this can be employed for this theatre only after 1872, when
the Bunraku-za (Bunraku Theatre) was founded in Osaka, taking its name

from a family of theatre-owners who had set up their first puppet theatre there in 1805; *bunraku* is thus used sometimes for this form of drama from the beginning of the nineteenth century. Before then some appellations in use were *ningyō-shibai* (doll theatre), *ayatsuri* (manipulation – often, but not always, referring to string puppets), and *jōruri,* which will be explained later.

PUPPETS BEFORE 1600

The first references to puppets for entertainment in Japan date from about 900, in an early glossary, and a rather fuller mention in about 1100, in an essay by Ōe Masafusa (1041–1111) on *kairaishi,* who were wandering entertainers, the men being jugglers, conjurers and puppeteers, and the women adorning themselves with the earnings of whoredom. Occasional references over the next four centuries indicate that puppet manipulation did not die out, even though their name, *kugutsu,* was applied far more often to female entertainers who did not use puppets. It is thought, without a great deal of evidence, that Buddhist temples and Shinto shrines used puppets in religious propaganda, and courtiers' diaries occasionally mention entertainments which may have used dolls. In the sixteenth century, however, references become more frequent and one can be certain that a group of puppeteers worked from the shrine of the god Ebisu at Nishinomiya, on the Inland Sea to the west of Osaka. Their religious duty was to go round the neighbouring fishing villages and show the god catching a giant sea-bream, thereby ensuring good catches of this delicious fish, but they clearly had the free time to go off and give entertainments as far as Kyoto, the then capital of Japan, about forty miles away. Their entertainment repertory seems to have been copies of the dances that were given by human entertainers – lion dances, excerpts from *nō* plays (which were already more than two centuries old) and folk-dances. They were to be the ancestors of *bunraku* performers.

THE DEVELOPMENT OF PUPPETS FROM 1600 TO THE PRESENT DAY

Social conditions in Japan have always had a strong influence on the arts and entertainments, and second only to the great upheaval of the Meiji Restoration of 1868, when the country finally emerged from its feudal isolation, was the time about 1600, when the civil wars that had raged across the countryside and through the cities finally came to an end, and the merchants of Osaka in particular began to acquire power and affluence. The theatre arts had already begun to develop. *Nō* plays have already been mentioned; there was also increasing interest in popular song and dance, and the presence in Nagasaki in the west of Japan of Jesuit missionaries and their importation of some elements of Western culture had acted as a stimulus towards the quest for pleasure. Military rulers and the imperial court did little to discourage these developments, and the last years of the sixteenth century were gay with dancing in the streets, extravagant costume and elaborate pageantry. This was not to last long, for the Tokugawa family were soon to take over the rule in their new capital of Edo (modern Tokyo), and to impose a puritanical, Confucius-based, regime of control and restriction. However, the lowest of the four classes of society, the merchants (the others being warriors, farmers, and craftsmen) were beginning to acquire wealth and were looking for ways of spending it, and in the three major cities of Kyoto, Osaka and, later, Edo, there emerged a popular audience eager for entertainment. *Nō* plays had already opened the way to commercial performance with their 'fund-raising' programmes that supplemented their normal role of taking part in religious ceremonial, but *nō* was soon to become the special property of the warriors and no longer generally available to the public. The way was thus open to other forms.

The puppet theatre was one of those to benefit from these conditions. Japanese dramatic historians rightly place its origin at the moment when the various elements of puppet with its manipulator, chanter and accompanying instrument were brought together in a performance in Kyoto, thus establishing from the first moment the typical pattern of the Japanese doll theatre, in which the puppet is worked by a silent operator, with the words, both conversation and narrative, recited and chanted by another performer, with musical accompaniment. Ever since the thirteenth century, if not before, there had been chanters, not unlike minstrels in the West, who had recited warlike tales, especially *Tales of the Heike (Heike-monogatari)*, to the accompaniment of the *biwa*, an instrument like a lute, or the rhythm of a scratched or tapped fan. These performers, who are not completely extinct even today, for no form of art ever seems entirely to disappear in Japan, gradually extended their repertory to include, among other items, a new story involving the pathetic hero of *Tales of the Heike*, the great general Yoshitsune of the Genji line who had defeated the enemy clan of the Heike, only to incur the enmity of his brother Yoritomo and die a miserable fugitive. This new story was of a night which the youthful Yoshitsune spent with a talented young beauty, Lady Jōruri, who later cared for him and nursed him back to health after he had been abandoned sick in a sand dune. Some more down-to-earth commentators think that she was a star performer in a high-class brothel, but, be that as it may, the story became very popular and when in the latter half of the sixteenth century there was imported from the Ryūkyū Islands south of Japan a new musical instrument, the three stringed *shamisen*, much more manageable and more capable of sentiment than the more percussive *biwa*, some progressive members of the chanters' guild are said to have taken it up to use to accompany the story of Jōruri. And when the first performance of the puppet theatre was put on, by legend has it, a sword-decorator named Chōzaburō, who had learned chanting and accompaniment from a blind performer, the *shamisen* was used. Chōzaburō chanted the text and played his own accompaniment, and also brought in from Nishinomiya a puppeteer named Hikita (or Hitta). In their first programme was a performance of the story of Jōruri, and from then on it became usual to call puppet theatre, and especially the chanted text, *jōruri*, a name which persists until today. The first contemporary account of these early performances is in diary entries dated 1614,[1] with the play *Amida's Riven Breast (Amida no munewari)* and adaptations of *nō* plays, performed by Nishinomiya puppets who hung a curtain in the garden for the purpose. It is easy to infer from slightly later illustrations, and the surviving practice with portable equipment in local puppet performances, in the island of Sado and in the mountain area of Chichibu, that the puppets were of the type known as *sashikomi*, that is dolls without feet, somewhat like glove puppets, into which the hands were inserted from below. The curtain was stretched to cover the manipulator, who held his hands over his head, so that the dolls appeared to move on an imaginary surface at the level of the top of the curtain. There may or may not have been a higher curtain, so arranged that the action took place in a horizontal rectangle. The play *Amida's Riven Breast* has a typically Buddhistic plot, in which Amida (Amithaba, a Buddha who lives in a paradise in the west, and is prayed to as protector of mankind, particularly in Pure Land sects) gives up his liver, in place of that of the heroine, to make a remedy to cure a young prince in India.

The *sashikomi* dolls persisted as the principal form until the end of the century, and were the ancestors of modern *bunraku* dolls, but there were other types used, including mechanical devices and automata, and string puppets. The latter became associated with a theatre which specialised in plays with a Buddhist content (like *Amida's Riven Breast*), and are known as *sekkyō* ('expounding the sutras'). This theatre has persisted, in more or less obscurity, until the present, and still gives performances with string puppets of pieces some of which are traditional and others newly devised, mainly nowadays on television.

It was not long before the puppets joined other forms of entertainment in more or less permanent theatres in Kyoto, on the banks of the Kamō river. River banks had traditionally been areas in which outcaste populations, which included almost all entertainers, lived. A rival theatre with living actors, the *kabuki*, was also established at about the same time, but brought on itself official bans because of the licentiousness of its early performances with female actors (prohibited in 1629) and then the bad influence of boy actors (restricted in 1652). Truly dramatic staging of plays with adult male actors was not to be established till later in the century, and the puppets, who seemed to have been looked on favourably by the authorities, were able to develop freely. The plays began to be published as 'certified texts' by the chanters; many of these survive, and, along with other evidence, enable a reasonably well documented account of the history of puppet drama of the seventeenth century to be written. The plays, consisting as they do of the chanted text, are in the form of stories, for the chanter not only gives the dialogue, but announces who is speaking, and sets the scenes. Some are illustrated, not with scenes as played by the puppets but as they would be with human, or occasionally holy or monstrous, participants.

The puppet theatre spread rapidly from Kyoto to Osaka and Edo. In Kyoto where a sort of *fainéant* imperial court remained, and in Osaka, plays with religious or traditional themes remained popular, but in Edo, where the audiences included a large number of low-ranking warriors, violent plays with a superhuman warrior, Kinpira, as their hero, flourished, narrated robustly, with puppets on occasion dismembered by the chanter laying about him with an iron stave.[2] Influenced by these *kinpira* plays the Edo *kabuki* actor Ichikawa Danjūrō I initiated a style of acting called *aragoto* ('rough stuff') which has remained a characteristic type of performance of his family. A somewhat softened form of *kinpira* plays also became popular in Kyoto and Osaka, and formed part of the repertory of the two last great chanters of what has come to be called 'old *jōruri*', Inoue Harima-no-jō (1632(?)–1685) and Uji Kaga-no-jō (1635–1711). The second components of their names, the literal translation of which would be 'Governor of Harima' and 'Governor of Kaga', are purely formal titles accorded to them for performing at the imperial court. The conferment of this sort of title on chanters was quite common, as was also the adding of the suffix -*dayū* (derived ultimately from an old court rank, but degraded to become applicable to any entertainers) to another element to form a stage name. Satsuma-dayū, for example, had been an early chanter in Edo, and Takemoto Gidayū (1651–1714) was to succeed Harima and Kaga as top chanters. They themselves had done something towards the refinement of *jōruri* by introducing, for example, in the case of Uji, elements from *nō* plays; both were also publishing collections of purple passages from their plays, with some assistance, in the form of notation, for amateur performers. Kaga employed a farmer turned chanter, who had studied under a pupil of Harima, to sing secondary roles, and this man established his own theatre in Osaka in 1684, and adopted the name of Takemoto Gidayū.

During this period there had still been no noticeable development of the puppets themselves, but the plays were showing increasing complication, and the chanting had clearly been improving all the time. One development which had taken place had been the separation of the chanting from the accompaniment, so that in the top-ranking theatres at least, there were now *shamisen* players to partner the chanters, and development from the old style, in which voice and instrument tended to alternate, to a new, in which accompaniment could if necessary be continuous. The custom of having one person perform both the chanting and the accompaniment is still to be found in local theatres. Authorship of plays had been anonymous, apart from a shadowy writer of some *kinpira* plays, Oka Seibei, and they were probably normally written by the chanter himself. Harima is in fact known to have employed a young man of *samurai* stock, who had recently moved to Kyoto, to write for him. This was the first step in the career of Chikamatsu Monzaemon (1653–1724), who went on to write *kabuki* plays, then *jōruri* under Kaga, and finally, in 1684, joined Gidayū in his new enterprise, along with another student of Harima, Takezawa Gon'emon, a blind *shamisen* player. Together they wrote and performed the so-called 'new *jōruri*', among the characteristics of which was the replacement by a team of experts of the old jack-of-all-trades chanter, who had also been accompanist, author and choreographer, leading to excellence in all fields. Chikamatsu's abilities in taking old plots and tricking them out with imaginative detail and characterisation, and Gidayū's skill in charming audiences with his expressive voice, and in borrowing the best elements from other performers, were used first in historical and traditional plots, but from 1703, when Chikamatsu wrote his first 'domestic play', their range was extended. *The Love Suicides at Sonezaki (Sonezaki shinjū)*, like many others that were to follow, was the dramatisation of an actual incident of a love-affair between a young merchant and a high-ranking courtesan which led to a double suicide. Their tragic realism and immediacy drew large audiences and their popularity caused a wave of love suicides which disturbed the authorities so much that they made double suicides a crime.

Up to this period, except for a frequent use of automata, usually, apparently, in special set pieces or interludes, the puppets in the mainstream theatre had seen hardly any development from the one-man *sashikomi* dolls worked from behind a curtain or screen which concealed the manipulator. Now, the Takemoto Theatre began to consider improving the overall spectacle. The final switch to three-man puppets was not to be until 1734, but in 1705 there was the first use of *degatari*, that is, having the chanter visible to the audience, in full ceremonial garb, and having the manipulators too show themselves. By these means what had up to now, in spite of the chanter's audible pre-eminence, been visually a pure puppet theatre, became the complex performance that it has remained until today.

The next generation of plays after Chikamatsu's death included within a single drama the two styles of historical and domestic plays which he had written, and were of great length, enough to fill by themselves the day-long programmes which had formerly been (and, indeed, were later to become once more) a selection of shorter pieces, historical plays being longer than domestic ones. These new plays were often written by a group, not to say committee, of authors, who had acts and episodes allotted to them, but the obvious dangers of this method seem to have been avoided, for the majority of these plays have remained popular to the present day. Perhaps the best known is *The Loyal League (Kanadehon Chūshingura)*, written by three authors, in eleven acts, and elaborating and only thinly disguising an actual incident in which a young lord goaded into drawing his sword in the ruler's palace was condemned to self-immolation; his retainers, reduced to masterless men by his death and confiscation of his property, secretly planned revenge against the villain of the piece, which they exact in a final scene of attack on his mansion. Plays written at this time are, in practice, the earliest that remain in the normal repertory. This is partly because Chikamatsu was writing for the simpler, more manageable *sashikomi* puppets, the new more elaborate, three-man ones, while capable of more expression, being less handy about the stage, and partly because his style was more narrative, more literary and more allusive than the direct, dramatic plays that came later. Already in the eighteenth century audiences could not be expected fully to appreciate his work in the form in which he wrote it, and it was much adapted for performance.

The live *kabuki* theatre in the early eighteenth century, well-established now after its early difficulties, took over puppet plays as fast as they were produced. The technique was to continue the use of the chanters for scene-setting, narrative and comment, but to have the actors deliver their own dialogue. This led to a stylised action, with the actors depending on the pace of the chanter, and displaying feelings as they were mentioned by him and using rhythmic movement, a form of dance, in their expression. The development of *kabuki* brought a decline in the Osaka puppet theatre, so that from about 1750 to 1850 there were only occasional performances, and its full revival, under the name of *bunraku,* only took place in 1872, with the support of the prefectural authorities. There had been enough activity in Edo and other cities, in companies touring in rural areas, in private and amateur performances of chanting without puppets, for there to be the performers available to staff the Bunraku Theatre when it was established, but only one new play was to be adopted into the repertory, along with some borrowings from comic interludes in the *nō* theatre.

This historical account can be concluded with some remarks on the local groups and puppets of the *bunraku* and other types. In many places distributed throughout Japan there are local amateur groups using *bunraku* dolls and *gidayū* chanters. It is often said by these performers that such and such a puppeteer was in the district at the time of the opening-up of Japan to the world (1850–70) and that, thinking that this would be the end of traditional Japanese performing arts, he had abandoned his equipment and gone away. Local inhabitants thought it would be a pity not to use it, so puppet performances had continued. In some parts, like the islands of Shikoku and Awaji, dolls manipulated in the *bunraku* way had been given larger heads. In some remote areas, like the Chichibu Mountains and the island of Sado, small dolls, like those of the early eighteenth century in Osaka, had continued to be used, with some development, but not necessarily with *gidayū* chanting. Very often local performances are connected with festivals of the local Shinto shrines; the performances are conceived of as being given to entertain the local gods, in theatres sited in the shrine precincts.

THE PUPPET THEATRE TODAY

The two ingredients of chant and music on one hand and the puppets and their manipulators on the other are still the basis of *bunraku*. The typical theatre is rectangular in form, the auditorium having either no gallery or one that is set far back, so that it is impossible to look down on the action. Between the audience and the stage is a low platform divided by a transverse gangway from a screen or partition rising about three feet from the floor. This is known as the *tesuri* (hand rail) and its top forms the notional height of the ground upon which the puppets move. Behind this is another gangway in which the manipulators work, and behind this again is set any building which the play requires, with its floor more or less at the same level as the *tesuri*. Entrances and exits are normally made through curtained approaches to the right and left, but if the circumstances demand, they can be made from the back. To the left (I use 'left' and 'right' from the audience point of view) is also placed the *geza* or effects room, which is not a traditional component of the puppet stage but borrowed from *kabuki*.

To the right, cutting off the corner of the stage and auditorium, is a diagonally placed partition, the lower part of which incorporates a small revolving platform, on which sits the chanter with his accompanying *shamisen* player on his left. Above this is another chamber, screened from the audience by semi-obscuring bamboo curtains, for chanter and accompanist when they do not appear in full view. It will be remembered that *degatari* was a later development. Although normally two persons only (chanter and accompanist) appear on the revolving platform, room may be made for a second chanter, and sometimes, when a whole band of chanters and instrumentalists appear in some spectacular piece, provision is made for them to be accommodated. Most pieces have only chanter and instrumentalist, however, and they make their entrance already seated, and can be relieved by a second pair by a half turn of the platform. An essential part of the chanter's equipment is his book of the play, which is placed on a decorated reading desk placed before him. At the beginning and end of his stint, the chanter raises this book over his bowed head in the traditional gesture of gratitude expressing thanks to his teachers and forebears for the tradition handed down to him. The *shamisen*, a three-stringed instrument played with a heavy ivory plectrum, is the largest and has the thickest column of any of the types of this instrument, for it has to produce enough sound to fill the theatre. This large *shamisen*, and the shape of the reading desk, are typical of the *gidayū* style; in others, for example those that play for dance pieces in the *kabuki* theatre, each has its own set sizes and shapes of equipment, apart from artistic particularities of the performance itself.

Chanter and musician both wear formal attire, with *hakama* (divided skirt) and *kataginu* (stiffened winged shoulders), when they appear before the public.

A variety of curtains can be used to hide the stage. In intervals between pieces an elaborately embroidered drop curtain is lowered. Between scenes, a draw curtain can be pulled across to make a scene shift, but this may be done without a curtain, on a dark stage. Modern puppet theatres have a revolving stage, and trap doors. The characteristic gangway *(hanamichi)* of the *kabuki* stage is hardly ever used with the puppets; when it is it is under *kabuki* influence, and is not very successful, since the dolls are made to walk in mid-air, and have not the *tesuri* to provide a notional floor.

Each principal puppet has three men to manipulate it (see plate 6). The leading puppeteer is on the left, and works the head with his left hand, and the puppet's right hand with his own right. The second is on the right, works the puppet's left hand with his right, and has his own left free for any emergencies or adjustments. The third man is responsible for the feet, and crouches, usually on the right of the second man. The costume of the three manipulators varies with the piece to be played and the puppet to be worked. At the least spectacular end of the scale, all three wear black clothes, with their heads in black hoods, or the principal manipulator of the main doll may show his face, still with black clothes; or next, he may wear colourful costumes, and so on through several stages until, very rarely, all three have uncovered faces and ornamental clothes. The topmost level may see the principal in a quick-change costume, matching that of his puppet, to achieve a picturesque effect, with stage hands pulling out tacking threads to remove an outer layer, or allow panels to fall down and show a new costume. These more striking effects are nowadays reserved for dance pieces and other derivatives of the *nō* drama.

The general construction of the puppets is an assembly of detachable parts. The body is a mere framework, with a certain amount of applied padding, and is given shape by the clothes. Arms and, in the case of male puppets and young girls, legs, are loosely tied on, and rely for their articulation upon the way they are worked. Feet have as much leg attached to them as will be shown by the costume. A staid man will always wear his *kimono* long, and thus will not show his legs; a bully will be constantly tucking his skirts up into his girdle, and will thus show a good deal of leg, maybe with a jointed knee. There is a handle behind the heel for the foot-manipulator to get a grip. Puppets representing women after the age of childhood do not have legs and feet, and the bottom of the skirt of their *kimono* is moved to imitate walking or running. Arms, like legs, are as long as the circumstances

74

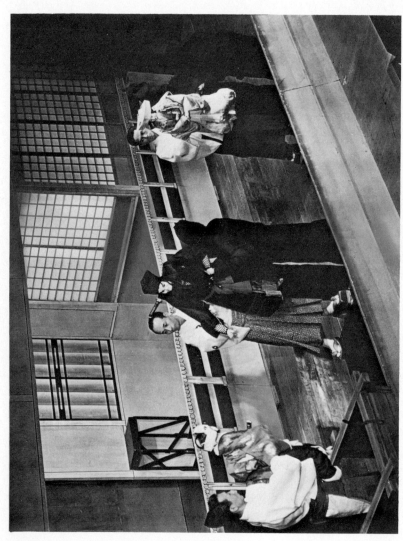

6 The *bunraku* stage viewed from above to show its arrangement. Each main puppet is manipulated by three men, two with black clothes and hoods

require, and come in many varieties of hand, from an unjointed five fingers, sometimes incorporating something held in the hand, but carved solid, such as a hand holding a plectrum, to the technical masterpiece of a fully jointed, string-worked hand used for plucking the strings of a musical instrument, manipulated from a frame which protrudes from about the elbow position. However, such a complicated device as this hand is only used when necessary to achieve a special effect; normally simplicity is preferred, and there is no objection to a manipulator slipping his white-gloved fingers out to hold whatever is required at the moment. If a male puppet has to show a bare chest (or a female appear topless, which is very rare), a papier-mâché torso is fitted.

The head is what gives the puppet its individuality, and the rest of the equipment and clothing follows the pattern set by the head. Leaving aside some specialised examples, there are ranges of male and female heads to suit various ages and characters, with different permanent colouring, from the dead white of young women (to match women's white make-up), lovers and priests, to rubicund warriors. Additional colouring could also be applied. Women's heads normally have no eye or mouth movements (except for one or two middle-aged villainesses), and are named for their type of role, e.g. 'young woman'. Men are sometimes named for the original role for which they were made, and may have opening mouths, closing eyes, eyes which turn to left and right, and even eyes which cross, for use in the *mie* or pose-striking, representing strong emotion, grief or triumph, which is common to *bunraku* and *kabuki*. These are all worked by levers on the handle which extends downwards from the neck, and also has a control for raising the head from a nodding position. The head can have either a permanent wig, or one fitted for the occasion, with various women's styles, including the young princess with silvery decorations or the courtesan's massive coiffure bristling with tortoise-shell and coral.

Special heads are used for women-into-fox roles, with a human head on one side and a fox's on the other, the change being made with a twist and a flick to bring the hair over to expose the new face. Another has a beautiful girl transformed into a demon by a control which sends out horns, turns the eyes round to golden orbs, and shows dreadful fangs. One of the great number of single-man comic smallish puppets used for crowds and common soldiers is called 'split pear' and has a face which can drop down to show a bloody shapelessness as he is struck with a sword. A similar effect can be obtained with a mask of a normal face that can be whipped off to show wounds painted on the features below.[3] All heads, except one, are of wood painted white or with reddish tinge, the surface reflecting the lighting very strongly. The one exception is a fabric covered face for the blinded warrior Kagekiyo.

When the puppet theatre started in the seventeenth century, its programmes consisted of a series of relatively short pieces. By the time of

Chikamatsu at the beginning of the eighteenth, a theatre's day might last
from dawn to dusk, staging a series of items of increasing importance and
artistry, with the best reserved for the afternoon. It seems that the theatres
closed as darkness fell, and in the evening the most popular performers
would often go to the town houses of high officials and play there. Chikamatsu's 'historical' dramas, like *The Battles of Coxinga (Kokusen'ya-kassen)*[4]
were very long and full of fantastic episodes, such as a fight with a tiger. His
'domestic pieces' were considerably shorter. The joint-authorship plays were
also very long and with their mixture of scenes and styles virtually consti-
tuted a whole day's varied programme in themselves.

The present-day trend is for the Asahi-za in Osaka, which is the head-
quarters of the *bunraku* company, and the National Theatre, which has a
small theatre and stage specially equipped for the puppets and acts as their
Tokyo centre, to put on programmes of about four hours with normally three
pieces. In Osaka it is usual to give two different programmes in one day,
starting, say, at 11.30 a.m. and 5 p.m. Ocasionally one programme will
consist entirely of excerpts from one long play, but more often there are
completely separate pieces, perhaps two excerpts from long plays, and one
interlude, which may be an adaptation of a comic interlude (*kyōgen*) from the
nō theatre. Such interludes constitute the only new puppet pieces in the
bunraku stage, and are given in an untraditional formalised style, very much
under the influence of the live *kabuki* theatre.

One popular excerpt chosen from the many that are in the current
repertory is from *The Loyal League*,[5] mentioned earlier. It is described here to
give an example of typical complication of plot and intricacy of action. In
this one of eleven acts the head of the conspiracy is leading a life of
debauchery in order to deceive the followers of his planned victim into
thinking that the vendetta has been abandoned. Among the incidents are
some drunken reeling about the stage, the delivery of a long letter from two
other conspirators, a spy coming and hiding under the floor, the appearance
at a window of an adjacent room of a woman, who, in one of the climaxes of
the scene, reads with the aid of her mirror the letter in the hands of the
pretended drunkard (see plate 7). It being a long letter in the form of a
lengthy scroll, the under-floor spy is also able to start to examine it as it
unrolls over the edge of the floor. The spy is eventually detected and killed by
a sword-thrust through the floor. The woman is discovered and is on the
point of being bought out by the chief conspirator so that he can kill her to
prevent her disclosing the secret, when her brother saves her by revealing
that she is the wife of a retainer who was admitted to the conspiracy as he
died, signing the bond in the blood of his slit belly. Unlike the audience, she
had not known till then of the suicide of her husband, for she had been sold
into prostitution earlier on the day of his death by her father, who was killed
by a robber who stole the money thus obtained which he was bringing home

7 The restaurant scene from *The Loyal League*. The lady reads the letter in her mirror, while the spy under the floor also begins to read it

with him. His son-in-law accidentally shot the robber and finding the money
on him, was joyfully taking it back with him as a gift of providence, only to
find his wife already gone, and himself suspected of the murder when his
father-in-law's body is brought in. It was only in the interval between his
disembowelling and his actual death that it was discovered that the old man
had died of a sword-thrust, and not a shot from the musket that the young
man was hunting with at the time; so he is allowed to join the conspiracy and
his wife's life is spared.

It is apparent that the audiences of the past enjoyed this sort of complication of plot, all carefully explained to them by the chanter, who is able to
point out the dramatic ironies and implications of all the incidents as they
unfold, as well as giving the dialogue as it is uttered, and in the appropriate
voices. The scene contains instances of the conflict of loyalty and human
affection which are a constant theme of puppet plays. Present-day audiences
tend not to be so conversant with the details of the story when only one
excerpt is played, and are less dazzled by the fantastic devices than their
predecessors were, but among the older spectators, especially in Osaka, are
still women who are reduced to tears by the tragedy of it all. The style of
playing of the scenes in such plays tends towards great movement and
activity, and the climax of them is often a passage in which one gets an
impression that the three manipulators have the greatest difficulty in maintaining control of the puppet, which is trying to escape from them.

While *bunraku* thus performs violent action with great effect, it is also
superb in the portrayal of greater emotion. A typical piece of this sort, an
adaptation of a play originally by Chikamatsu entitled *The Love Suicides at
Amijima (Shinjū Ten-no-Amijima)*,[6] is still often performed. It portrays the
cruel dilemma that was to lead so many to suicide, in which, in this
dramatisation of a real incident, a young paper-merchant squanders money
on pleasures in a brothel, only to fall in love with one of the inmates. Having
wasted the family finances on thus becoming a favoured client, he has no
longer the resources to buy her out (i.e. to refund to the proprietor the money
that the latter had paid to the girl's father for her services). His wife offers to
sell her clothes to obtain the money for him, but her father prevents this act of
marital loyalty. The courtesan is persuaded to reject him for the sake of his
family, and suffers in silence when he attacks her for fickleness. His wife goes
into a nunnery and he and his lover seem free to marry, but at the last
moment he gets into a quarrel with one of her clients and kills him. All hope
of happiness lost, they go off to suicide, buoyed up by the hope of being
together throughout eternity in the Western Paradise of the Buddha Amida.
The querulous weakness of the paper-merchant's character, one of the most
delicately written by the master, and the staunch sweetness and virtue of the
women, are portrayed in a realistic style. The wife and sweetheart are dolls
with calm white faces and gentle gestures, and their manipulators demon-

strate a loving skill. In moments of stress there is a subtle heaving of the breast, or effects of shadow play across the features, and a projecting hook on the lower lip catches the towel to simulate the choking back of tears. Children are cared for with loving attention, final union is shown with discreet gestures as the lovers go off together. In *bunraku* more subtle delicacy and refinement go into the portrayal of loving women than into any other character, and the older the manipulator becomes the more skilled is his performance, often with virtuoso movements as his doll chops vegetables or sews a seam, threading the needle, rubbing it on her hair for lubrication, and stitching swiftly and regularly, to the applause of the audience.

Female roles play an important part in *bunraku*, for not only do they require great skill in manipulation, they also constitute an area in which merchant-class audiences, among whom there were more women than men, could have direct access to the conflict between loyalty and human sentiment. A wife's loyalty to her husband, whereby she might support him in his desire to be with his beloved courtesan, made impossible any overt jealousy on her part. The tragedy of a mother forced to watch uncomplaining as her son is beheaded to save her husband's lord's son was something that could be felt by all the mothers present.

CONCLUSION

Bunraku thus puts on complicated and serious plays, with a wide range of characters played by casts of puppets which take the place of actors in the live theatre, and have an identity separate from that on the stage when they are in the dressing room. It is not a company of performers taking only one part, but a troupe of doll actors ready to play their roles in accordance with their particular skills and characteristics. But at the same time they are not the sole and unassisted performers of the role. It can indeed be argued that they are there only to illustrate what the chanter is reciting. They depend on his words to carry out their actions and show their feelings, and their acting is dotted with tiny pauses as they wait for the cues which he gives them. Having limited facial expression of their own, they depend on the chanter and sometimes the manipulator, with their human features, to use them in their stead. Sometimes, when they are male puppets, they can open their mouths, but the voice is at the side of the stage and belongs to the chanter, who does most of their laughing and crying, their whispering and shouting, for them; flashes of emotion sometimes pass over the manipulator's eyes, too, but, knowing that his doll cannot speak, he does not allow his mouth to move, except when it tenses in concentration at some exacting movement or utters a grunting cry to co-ordinate a quick change of costume simultaneously for himself and his puppet.

Perhaps the early puppets, with their hidden vocal performers, seemed to be speaking for themselves. If so, television has turned back the clock, for *bunraku* is frequently to be seen on its screen, often as a doll theatre with the chanter not in sight, but only in hearing, and the effect, while fine entertainment and superb puppetry, somehow lacks the richness of the *bunraku* in the theatre.

NOTES

1. A detailed account of this early period is in Charles J. Dunn, *The Early Japanese Puppet Drama* (London: Luzac and Co., 1966), which also includes translations of two versions of *Amida's Riven Breast*.
2. A typical play *Kinpira and the Goblin* is translated in Dunn, *The Early Japanese Puppet Drama* appendix III.
3. For further details on puppet heads, see Tsuruo Andō, *Bunraku: The Puppet Theatre* (New York and Tokyo: Walker/Weatherhill, 1970) and Donald Keene, *Bunraku* (Tokyo: Kōdansha International, 1965).
4. Translated in Donald Keene, *Major Plays of Chikamatsu* (New York and London: Columbia University Press, 1961), pp. 195–269.
5. See Donald Keene, *Chūshingura* (New York and London: Columbia University Press, 1971) for a complete translation.
6. Translation in Keene, *Major Plays*, pp. 387–425.

Select reading list of works in English

Andō Tsuruo, *Bunraku: The Puppet Theatre*, tr. Don Kenny. Performing Arts of Japan, no. 1 (New York and Tokyo: Walker/Weatherhill, 1970), 222 pp.

Arnott, Peter D., *The Theatres of Japan* (New York: St Martin's Press, 1969), 391 pp.

Dunn, Charles J., *The Early Japanese Puppet Drama* (London: Luzac and Co., 1966), 154 pp.

Dunn, Charles J., 'Introduction to the Study of Japanese Puppets', *Art and Archaeology Research Papers*, (June 1975), pp. 22–35.

Ernst, Earle, *The Kabuki Theatre* (London: Secker & Warburg, 1956), 296 pp.

Ernst Earle (ed.), *Three Japanese Plays from the Traditional Theatre* (London: Oxford University Press, 1959), 200 pp.

Keene, Donald, *Bunraku: The Art of the Japanese Puppet Theatre* (Tokyo: Kōdansha International, 1965), 293 pp.

Keene, Donald (tr.), *Major Plays of Chikamatsu* (New York and London: Columbia University Press, 1961), 485 pp.

Keene, Donald (tr.). *Chūshingura: The Treasury of Loyal Retainers* (New York and London: Columbia University Press, 1971), 183 pp.

Scott, Adolphe C., *The Puppet Theatre of Japan* (Rutland, Vermont and Tokyo: Charles E. Tuttle Co., 1963), 173 pp.

Art and life in Luigi Pirandello's
Questa sera si recita a soggetto

SUSAN BASSNETT-McGUIRE

The parallels between the collapse of rationalist concepts of form and structure within the work of art and the 'fragmentary' universe uncovered by the implications of the ideas of Freud and Einstein have been widely discussed. Problems such as the inadequacy of language as a means of contacting others, the impossibility of defining 'reality', the existence of man in relation to his fellows' perceptions of him, the Sartrian dilemma of the *Être-en-soi* and the *Être-pour-soi* recur through the works of twentieth-century dramatists, enclosed within the formal problem of the presentation of those ideas in theatre terms. The struggle to express the concept of a fluid, formless universe through the formal medium of the play has continued through the century, from the attempts of the Italian Futurist playwrights, through the stages of what may loosely be termed German Expressionist theatre and on into the age of Absurd Theatre and the Happening; and the role that Pirandello has played in that struggle is continually attested to by critics who claim him as a seminal twentieth-century dramatist. Martin Esslin, for example, declares that 'Pirandello more than any other playwright has been responsible for a revolution in man's attitude to the world that is comparable to the revolution caused by Einstein's discovery of the concept of relativity in physics'[1], and that 'Pirandello's influence pervades all contemporary drama';[2] Robert Brustein[3] presents a vision of Pirandello as a kind of prophet, an anticipator of major trends in drama from Beckett to Pinter, from O'Neill to Genet; and Nicola Chiaromonte states that

> the main characteristic of Pirandello's plays, namely, the presence of the intellect as the prime mover of the dramatic action, is to be found at the basis of every important development in the contemporary theatre;[4]

and adds Brecht to the list of French and Italian playwrights influenced by Pirandello's work.

Such claims for the importance of a single dramatist are wide-reaching in implication and although direct influence of Pirandello on later playwrights should largely be discounted, the myth of Pirandello as a seminal figure in the theatre still remains and presents a major problem for anyone attempting to 'place' his significance in historical terms. In his editorial in *Theatre Quarterly*[5] Clive Barker quotes an anecdote about a student who asks why, if Pirandello is so important, does no one produce his plays nowadays. And indeed, after the great Pirandello boom of the 1920s in Europe and the United States, performances of Pirandello's work have declined considerably. There was a brief revival of interest in Britain in the 1950s, due largely to the one-man campaign mounted by Frederick May at the University of Leeds, but Pirandello does not translate well and British acting styles are unsuited for the blend of melodrama, irony and anger intrinsic to the plays. In Italy, Pirandello has become a 'classic', the shock techniques of his works have long since faded into respectability and, perhaps because his lesson was so well learned by later generations of writers, his experiments in form appear mainly dated and unexciting. Whereas the works of Chekhov, Ibsen and Strindberg, the other seminal dramatists of popular mythology are performed today fairly regularly, anyone wishing to approach Pirandello must do so most frequently as a reader and not as a spectator.

That Pirandello was aware of the potential readership of a playtext as distinct from the audience attending a performance of his work is apparent from his stage directions, which often have a narrative function of their own quite distinct from the scripted narrative and from the movement towards 'unplayableness' in his later years. Steen Jansen in his paper on 'Struttura narrativa e struttura drammatica in *Questa sera si recita a soggetto*'[6] analyses the stage directions and concludes that in this play, the third of the 'trilogy of the theatre in the theatre', Pirandello has attempted to destroy the boundaries between fiction and reality in textual terms as well as in stage terms; by this analysis Jansen has opened the way forward to a new reading of Pirandello that might compensate for the lack of productions.

Questa sera si recita a soggetto (Tonight We Improvise) is a play that presents the contemporary reader/audience with a number of problems, and an analysis of the text offers an ideal starting point for an examination of Pirandello's theatre. First, it is Pirandello's most radically experimental play in terms of theatre form, and the complexities of staging it make productions very rare indeed. Moreover, as Jansen points out, the stage directions are presented in such a way that the reader has to confront the problem of whether to treat the text as a work of dramatic or narrative structure. And then, in terms of content, the ideas seem to prefigure the work of any number of later playwrights who might be considered, to use a loosely conceived and applied term, Absurdists. In *Questa sera si recita a soggetto*, existence itself is perceived as a kind of imprisonment and this vision is presented through the metaphor of the play – just as actors are doomed to the confines of the stage in order to have any being, so man is doomed to the spatial and temporal limits of his own existence. Freedom is impossible and the escape routes of dreams, imagination and illusion all lead to dead ends.

In *L'umorismo*, Pirandello discusses the fallacy that logic can lead man to security and happiness:

> L'uomo non ha della vita un'idea, una nozione assoluta, bensì un sentimento mutabile e vario, secondo i tempi, i casi, la fortuna. Ora la logica, astraendo dai sentimenti le idee, tende appunto a fissare quel che è mobile, mutabile, fluido; tende a dare un valore assoluto a ciò che è relativo. E aggrava un male già grave per se stesso. Perchè la prima radice del nostro male è appunto in questo sentimento che noi abbiamo della vita.[7]

> (We do not have absolute notions about life; in reality we only have fluctuating impressions which vary according to circumstances, chance, the seasons and the times. By abstracting ideas from feelings and impressions, logic aims to freeze in a fixed form what is essentially fluid and changeable. It strives to evaluate as absolute what is relative. In so doing it merely aggravates the spiritual malaise, because the root source of our illness lies in this awareness we have of life.)

Questa sera si recita a soggetto is an illustration, both in content and form, of that clash between fluidity and fixity, between the freedom of changing impressions and the binding limitations of absolute aims. Through this play Pirandello investigates the concept of freedom on a number of levels – within the context of the play itself, in society, in the mind of individuals, in the form of dramatic art, and the conclusion is that freedom is illusory. Man must coexist with others and can never escape from what he is. His imagination may allow him to move beyond the limits of his daily life, but it also traps him forever by forcing him to remember moments of time past that he would prefer to forget. The final message of the play is that freedom is relative, and one man's notion of freedom may be perceived to be entrapment by another.

In the first scene, Hinkfuss, the director, explains to the audience what the improvisation advertised in the title of the play will mean. The actors, *my* actors as he calls them, have been given a basic story outline and will work from that. As he talks, it becomes clear that by 'improvisation' he means unscripted dialogue. He has provided scene changes, lighting effects and other technical aids and has determined the order of events. At the start of his address, he declares that he has eliminated the author, but as the speech progresses he increasingly emphasises his own importance. He begins by stating that he is in charge and goes on to explain how he directs actors, technicians and stage hands. Towards the end of his address he again rejects the author and states that he alone is responsible for the performance.

The 'freedom' of improvised dialogue is just a sham, because the existence of a story outline is already a limitation. Moreover, Hinkfuss takes pains to reiterate over and over again that he is in control. Nothing can happen that he does not know about and therefore the actors are not free and must follow the plan laid down by their director, who is himself bound by the story outline on which his plans are based.

When the actors try to rebel against the limitations imposed by Hinkfuss,

he attempts to manipulate the reality of their protests to convince the
audience that he is still in charge:

> [*con un lampo di malizia, trovando lì per lì la via di scampo per salvare il suo prestigio*]:
> Come il pubblico avrà capito, questa ribellione degli attori ai miei ordini è
> finta, concertata avanti tra me e loro per far più spontanea e vivace la
> presentazione.
> [*A questa uscita mancina, gli attori restano di colpo come tanti fantocci atteggiati di
> sbalordimento. Il Dottor Hinkfuss lo avverte subito: si volta a guardarli e li mostra al
> pubblico*]:
> Finto anche questo loro sbalordimento.   (p. 218)

> ([*with sudden malice, unexpectedly finding the way to save his face*]:
> As the public will have gathered, this revolt on the part of the actors against my
> orders is fake and was arranged beforehand between them and me so as to
> make the introduction livelier and more spontaneous.
> [*At this underhand speech, the actors are dumbstruck in attitudes of astonishment like so
> many puppets. Doctor Hinkfuss recognises this at once: he turns to look at them and points
> them out to the audience*]:
> This astonishment of theirs is fake, too.

This speech follows the argument between Hinkfuss and the actors that
begins as soon as he tries to introduce them to the audience at the start of act
I. He introduces the Leading Man first, by his real name. The actor objects
and accuses Hinkfuss of insulting him because, he claims, he is so well known
to the audience that introductions are superfluous. He asserts his own
independence, using the puppet image that recurs throughout the play and
then explains a second reason for feeling insulted by Hinkfuss. Dressed as
Rico Verri, he claims that his own personality no longer exists. He has
agreed to participate in the improvised performance, but the words he
speaks must come from the character he has assumed:

> . . . le parole che debbono nascere, nascere dal personaggio che rappresento, e
> spontanea l'azione, e naturale ogni gesto; il signor——— deve vivere il
> personaggio di *Rico Verri*, essere *Rico Verri*: ed è, è, già.   (p. 216)

(The words must be born, born from the character I play, the action must be
spontaneous and every gesture must be natural; Mr ——— must live the part
of *Rico Verri*, he must be *Rico Verri*; and he is, he is already.)

The Leading Man claims that, if he is to act a part spontaneously, he must
become the character, he must eliminate his own personality and take on
another. His argument is exemplified immediately after this speech when the
Character Actress slaps the Old Comic Actor because she has already
become Signora Ignazia. In this comic scene the two actors argue about
spontaneity and improvisation, with the Comic Actor maintaining that he
had no chance to defend himself against the unexpected attack and the
Character Actress arguing that if he had known in advance there would have
been no spontaneous reaction at all.

The first stage of rebellion against the director introduces a number of issues that are dealt with further as the play proceeds. The most obvious is the clash of roles, between the omnipotent director and the actors. In his address in scene i, Hinkfuss explained that the theatre relies on coexistence – the director needs actors, technicians, the living tools to make his play and the actors need the framework the theatre creates for them. However, Hinkfuss makes the mistake of seeing these people as instruments to serve his own ends. The actors claim the freedom to lose themselves in other personalities and resent being subordinate to Hinkfuss's commands. The order that he would impose conflicts with their desire for spontaneity and they rebel. The second stage of their revolt comes in the final section of the play, following Hinkfuss's speech to the audience in which he recognises that his vision of Mommina differs from that of the actress portraying her. As in his first address, Hinkfuss has touched a level of awareness that he has failed to understand. Throughout the play this is his chief defect; he verbalises a series of issues that he ignores in his ensuing actions. He is a satirical figure, a pedant who mouths what he cannot practise or comprehend.

In this second stage of revolt the actors first declare that they will leave the stage. Then they give Hinkfuss an ultimatum: either he goes, or they do. Hinkfuss is outraged and protests demanding an explanation. The actors give him their idea of theatre – if they are in a play, they should have been given written parts, careful details of position, all pre-ordered and nothing unexpected. The Leading Lady accuses Hinkfuss of having created something other than a play: 'First you unleash life in us.' By allowing the actors to improvise and take over the personalities of the characters he wanted them to represent, Hinkfuss has given life to a whole new group of persons and his 'control' becomes superfluous. The Leading Man admits that they are trapped by the existence of an audience, 'here is the public that can't be sent away', but goes on to say that they will continue not as actors, but as characters presenting their story for the judgement of others. The freedom to do this can only be gained by sending Hinkfuss away. The director is unnecessary, since the actors will live out the story *as* the characters. The Character Actress explains 'When you live a passion, that is true theatre.' The Leading Man reiterates this statement – 'Once a life is born, no one controls it.'

In the clash between Hinkfuss and the actors, we see exemplified the clash between the absolute and the relative. Hinkfuss wants to impose order even on improvisation, everything must be defined and conform to his vision. The actors demand the freedom to allow chance impressions and unprogrammed action to happen without a predetermined pattern, i.e. they demand to bring characters to life.

But after Mommina's death, in the final moments of the play, Hinkfuss reappears, unsubdued, claiming credit for the ending: 'You did as I said.

That wasn't in the story.' The Old Comic Actor explains that Hinkfuss never left the theatre, and although banished from the stage he has been working with the electricians secretly controlling the lighting effects. The actors have only had a very limited kind of freedom, restricted by the stage, the audience and above all by the fact that they are imitating other lives. Mommina dies, but the Leading Lady does not. The play is limited in time but the actors' lives go on after the play has ended. The Old Comic Actor sums up the vital difference between acting, even improvised acting, and living. Acting can only exist up to a point, and reality on stage is limited: 'no one can expect an actor "to kick the bucket" every night'. Guildenstern in *Rosencrantz and Guildenstern Are Dead* touches the heart of the problem:

> I'm talking about death – and you've never experienced *that*. And you cannot *act* it. You die a thousand casual deaths – with none of that intensity which squeezes out life . . . and no blood runs cold anywhere. Because even as you die you know that you will come back in a different hat. But no one gets up after *death* – there is no applause – there is only silence and some second-hand clothes, and that's – *death*.[8]

The actors can only reproduce reality within set limits. Once an actor feels pain or actually dies he is no longer acting. The actors are doomed to failure in their revolt because they are demanding the freedom of life within the constrictions of theatre and this is an impossibility.

Oscar Büdel feels that *Questa sera* is one of Pirandello's most important plays, which 'more than any other, embodies the quintessence of Pirandello's attempts at analytically dissecting, as it were, the art of theatre'.[9] Unquestionably the play does explore the question of the meaning of theatre and examines the roles of playwright, director, actors and audience but Pirandello uses this exploration as a metaphor for considering the function of art in life and the tension that exists between the refining process of the one and the limitless motion of the other. *Questa sera* is above all a play about the relativity of freedom in art and in life. One level of this investigation is freedom as it is conceived in terms of theatre.

Hinkfuss's position demonstrates the problem of the director's freedom. He is limited by the existence of a story outline and by the physical aids he has at his disposal. The actors are further restricted by the existence of the director and by the presence of an audience who watch their every movement. In act I the Leading Lady expresses her fears about improvised acting and claims that she needs the comfort of a script and a rehearsed set of actions that she can follow.

On a more universal level, her fear is man's fear of chance and disorder. Just as she needs the comfort of a script, and ordered frame in which to operate, so man needs the illustory comfort of belief in absolutes. He needs to believe that what is fluid and changeable *can* be fixed and defined. In formlessness is insecurity and fear, both for the world of life and the world of the stage. The stage directions for the Intermission scenes return to the limited freedom of the actor:

> Nel ridotto del teatro le attrici e gli attori figureranno con la massima libertà e naturalezza (ciascuno s'intende, nella sua parte) da spettatori tra gli spetta-
> tori.   (p. 237)

> (In the theatre lobby the actors and actresses will conduct themselves with the utmost freedom and naturalness each one, of course, in his part as members of the audience.)

The actors are also restricted by the characters they have to represent, and must try to wipe out their own personalities in order to assume new ones. Similarly, the characters are imprisoned by being able to exist on stage only through the actors. *Questa sera* examines the freedom of the characters to exist beyond the actors and the conclusion is that they can only come to life if the actors' personalities are totally subordinated.

The play opens with a discussion on defining limits as the 'audience' argue about when the play begins. The lights in the theatre go out, the bell for the commencement of the performance rings, but the curtain does not go up and raised voices are heard coming from behind it. The Spectators' reactions to this confused non-beginning divide into three stages. The first line of the play 'Che avviene?' (What's happening?) leads to speculation – perhaps there is a fight on stage, perhaps it is all part of the performance. After speculation comes outrage. The Old Gentleman who later walks out, protests loudly that this is an outrage, he has never heard of such a thing. The third stage after indignation is fear, and a woman asks anxiously whether there might be a fire backstage. This threefold process, speculation, anger and fear is reminis-cent of the reactions of the Neighbours in *Cosi è, se vi pare* to the Ponza–Frola situation. These are the stages in man's response to the unknown and the unexpected. Like the Leading Lady who wants the security of a script, the audience want the security of what they believe a play ought to be.

This first scene presents the audience's reactions in comic terms. The Spectator in the Stalls keeps asking himself when the play begins and three times we hear his voice anxiously trying to convince himself that all is in order and the unexpected noises are under control. When he first hears the sounds he speculates – 'Maybe this is part of the performance.' Then, when Hinkfuss appears and apologises for the delay, suggesting that the audience might consider it an involuntary prologue, the Spectator expresses his delight at having guessed that the noises were part of the play. Finally, when Hinkfuss has requested the audience not to ask questions and interrupt, the Spectator decides that the performance has *not* yet begun. Hinkfuss replies with an assertion that he is wrong – the performance has begun: 'La rappresentazione è cominciata, se io sono qua davanti a voi' (p. 207) (If I'm here in front of you, the play has begun). The irony here is that Hinkfuss and the Spectator are each thinking in totally different terms. Hinkfuss maintains that the performance is to be improvised, in which case anything that happens is part of that performance, whereas the Spectator is still thinking in terms of the conventional play structure. The irony becomes even more pointed later in the play, when Hinkfuss is told to leave the stage and protests because this unexpected event cannot be manipulated by him and brought under seeming control.

The question of defining limits is also present in the play in physical terms. *Questa sera* is not tied to a stage; it moves round the theatre. Action takes place on the stage, in the lobby, in a box in the auditorium and among the audience. Scene i consists of an exchange between Hinkfuss and some Spectators who are, of course, actors carefully placed around the auditorium. In this way the barrier between audience and actors on the stage is broken down and as Hinkfuss squabbles with the public the line of separation between stage and auditorium becomes increasingly blurred. With this technique of confusing levels of reality by placing actors representing spectators among the real audience, Pirandello anticipates a number of similar experiments by later dramatists. At the same time, the whole scene is part of a scripted play that Pirandello, the playwright has composed and ordered in every detail.

Throughout this play, various technical aids make the stage itself far more flexible than it is in, for example, *Così è* or *Enrico IV*, plays which conform to the traditional three-act pattern. In act I lighting effects enable the audience to see through an exterior wall into the Cabaret. Later, in act III, there is a dark, empty stage with three bare walls giving a sense of closeness and imprisonment (the stage directions refer to the 'three bare walls of her prison'). The Leading Lady touches all three walls with her forehead, intoning 'This is a wall!' to emphasise the fact that she is trapped within their boundaries, and the stage directions call for particular lighting effects to reinforce her words. Moreover, the actors have the freedom to move in a kind of dream world, beyond the limits of time or place. Anything is possible in the realm of the play where the rules governing life do not exist. Bergson describes life as 'evolution in time and complexity in space . . . it never goes backwards and never repeats itself'.[10] The world of the play is in complete contrast to this, for any evolution is strictly preordered, and repetition and movement backwards and forwards in time are not uncommon. In act III, Mommina and Rico Verri quarrel bitterly and her relatives interrupt, defying the 'reality' of the room she is imprisoned in:

> *Nene* [*dal buio, insorgendo*]. Oh vile! Adesso le parla di noi!
> *Verri* [*gridando, terribile*]. Silenzio! Voi qua non ci siete!
> *La signora Ignazia* [*venendo verso la parete, dal buio*]. Belva, belva, te la tieni
>   addentata, lì dentro la gabbia, a dilaniarla.

Verri [*toccando la parete due volte con la mano, e due volte, al tocco, rendendola visibile*].
   Questo è muro! Questo è muro! – Voi non ci siete!   (p. 280)

(*Nene* [*coming up out of the darkness*]. The pig! He's talking about us now!
Verri [*shouting furiously*]. Silence! You aren't here!
Signora Ignazia [*coming towards the wall, in the darkness*]. You wild animal, wild
   animal, you're keeping her there in that cage to be gnawed at and torn to
   pieces.
Verri [*touching the wall twice with his hand and both times, at his touch, the wall becomes
   visible*]. This is a wall! This is a wall! You are not here!)

Actors can move through walls, they can deny the existence of other
characters, they can adjust reality to their own ends and in this respect they
have unlimited freedom. But the play must end, and then the rules of life and
time take over again when the dream world no longer exists. The exchange
between Verri and Mommina's relations also points to the fact that actors
must coexist and the reality of the individual must fit in with the others
around him. Verri can protest that the others do not exist, that they are not
present, but he is outnumbered four to one by the women who insist that they
have a right to speak and intervene. Stage reality is flexible and not the
property of any one individual.

   The diffusion of the performance around the theatre, the breakdown of
the audience–actors barrier and the freedom of the actors within the play to
transcend limits of time and place, along with the use of lighting for emphasis
and effect, show that the playwright has himself broken out of the confines of
traditional theatre form. The notion of the fourth wall has gone completely,
along with the idea that the function of the play is to reproduce real life
incident as faithfully as possible. Pirandello's stage directions call for elaborate deliberately unrealistic lighting effects and in act II the actors move out
into the auditorium and a film is projected on stage. (The parallels between
this play and the work of German Expressionist playwrights are striking but
are outside the scope of this study.)

   The first scene flouts convention in several ways – by the device of not
raising the curtain immediately, the intervention of the Spectators, the
argument between Hinkfuss on stage and members of the public in the
auditorium and Hinkfuss's long speech. The scene also examines the freedom
of the audience. That the spectators can come and go as they please is
illustrated by the outraged exit of the Old Gentleman and Hinkfuss's retort
that anyone can go if they feel like it. But if they choose to remain, the
audience find that they cannot escape the play, which continues to happen
even during the Intermission when they go out into the theatre lobby and
simultaneously on the stage for those who remain in their seats. Moreover,
the first scene introduces the doubt in the minds of the real audience as to
whether the person sitting next to them is an actor or not. Attempts are also
made to blur even this distinction. In act I, for example, the stage directions

call for the Spectators in all parts of the house to start clapping, with the proviso '*smetteranno subito, se il pubblico vero non seguirà per contagio l'esempio*' (p. 219) (they will stop at once if the real audience don't catch on and do the same).

The pace of the play varies enormously, which serves further to confuse the audience and to contrast with the canons of a 'well-made' play. The Intermission scenes are played simultaneously and move so fast that the audience must inevitably miss much of what is going on. In contrast, Hinkfuss's address to the audience is a violation of theatre rules regarding audience attention span. It is long, didactic and requires careful listening, because it outlines the theme of the play. One of Pirandello's most common techniques is to present didactic points in speeches by certain 'knowing' characters, such as Diego Cinci, Laudisi or Leone Gala. In this play he breaks the pattern in two ways. First, Hinkfuss is not a 'knowing' character, he is stupid, wordy and less aware than the actors he tries to direct. Secondly, Hinkfuss's speech is exceptionally long and much of it is bound to be lost. Pirandello presents a series of sophisticated concepts through a stupid character and in a form that fails to emphasise them sufficiently.

Hinkfuss claims that his speech is based on solid reasoning and then goes on to argue out his point. There is no attempt now or later in the play to build up sympathy for Hinkfuss, although his speech is so crucial. He uses a series of words relating to freedom: *la liberazione* occurs three times, *libera* occurs once and the verb *liberare* occurs twice. All these words continue to recur through the rest of the play at frequent intervals. In this speech, Hinkfuss discusses types of freedom, in art and in life, that he cannot later put into practice. He begins by trying to define the roles of author and producer. First he declares that the author's contribution ends as soon as he writes the last word of his play. After this point, his function is superfluous because the play must pass to the director and the actors so that it can be presented on stage. There is a distinction between the written work of art and the play that we see, because the former is the product of a single effort and the latter is the result of many individuals' concerted efforts. Today, Hinkfuss announces, he has gone even further and by refusing to use a script he has eliminated the author completely. He fails to realise that he is restricted by the existence of the story he has decided to use as his basic guide, even though he has freed himself from the limitations of a script.

He explains further that in the theatre what matters is the *creazione scenica* which he alone controls. He uses actors and technicians to fulfil the effect he wants to create. But he admits that his creation is not absolute – in another theatre, with other actors and other staging, it would be completely different. The only way for the play to remain the same eternally is 'se l'opera potesse rappresentarsi da sè, non più con gli attori, ma coi suoi stessi personaggi che, per prodigio, assumessero corpo e voce' (p. 209) (if the work could perform itself, without using actors, but with its own characters who, miraculously, come to life and speak). Since this kind of miracle cannot happen, the only way for the play to be transferred to the stage is through the *creazione scenica*. The play must depend on others to come alive and, ironically, since it is subject to interpretation and will be produced differently at different times, it will never be identical when performed. By 'coming alive', i.e. by becoming more than words on a page, the play becomes subject to the relativity of life and can never be consistent.

Later in the speech, Hinkfuss uses the favourite Pirandellian metaphor of the statue as a work of art that is free from time and motion, but which must move and speak if its creator is to truly believe that he has endowed it with *vita per sempre*. For this to happen, it must cease to be a work of art and become alive:

> Ma a questo patto soltanto, signori, può tradursi in vita e tornare a muoversi ciò che l'arte fissa nell'immutabilità d'una forma; a patto che questa forma riabbia movimento da noi, una vita varia e diversa e momentanea; quella che ciascuno di noi sarà capace di darle.   (p. 211)

> (But only on one condition, ladies and gentlemen, may that which art has fixed on the changelessness of form be translated into life and once more acquire movement: on condition that this form regain motion from us, with variable, diverse, transitory life: that which each one of us is able to bestow.)

The statue is fixed forever in the immutability of its form, but the play enjoys a freedom the statue cannot have. The play exists as a work of art in an unchanging form only so long as it is on the page, for once it is taken over by actors it acquires a new dimension. The theatre is midway between the fixity of art and the inconstancy of life, because it is conceived as the one and takes shape as the other. It is freer than the unmoveable statue and freer also than life which is subject to limitations of time, but at the same time it can never be free from the necessity of living actors who alone can make it live.

The author, says Hinkfuss, sees the play as the liberation of his creative energy, the expression of his inner thoughts. By writing the play, he frees the ideas trapped in his head and believes that putting those ideas in the fixed frame of the written play will save them from disappearance and grant them the immortality of the statue. So the play is a paradox: it is free in so far as it is able to escape from fixity and yet endure in time, and it is an expression of freedom in that it represents the liberation of the author's thoughts. But it is also restricted by needing actors to bring it to life and by existing also as a work of art conceived and expressed in a set form. Hinkfuss puts this paradox on a wider scale by describing the problem of duality in life. Motion and consistency together are both necessary and impossible:

> La vita deve obbedire a due necessità che, per essere opposte tra loro, non le consentono nè di consistere durevolmente nè di muoversi sempre. Se la vita si

movesse sempre, non consisterebbe mai: se consistesse per sempre, non si
moverebbe più. E la vita bisogna che consista e si muova.   (p. 210)

(Life must obey two necessities, both opposites, which prevent it from either
lasting consistency or constant motion. If life were always in motion, it would
never be consistent: if it were always consistent, it would no longer move. And
life must be consistent and in motion.)

This tension between consistency and motion exists in life and in the world of
the play, but art is free from it, fixed as it is in an unalterable form. There is
no tension in the statue – it cannot move, it can only consist. Hinkfuss
outlines the human situation, man's quest for a similar permanence, for the
security of unchangingness:

Ciascuno di noi cerca di crear se stesso e la propria vita con quelle stesse facoltà
dello spirito con le quali il poeta la sua opera d'arte.   (p. 210)

(Each one of us seeks to create himself and his own life by those same spiritual
faculties the poet uses to create his work of art.)

This effort is doomed to failure, because life, unlike the statue, is trapped in
time. Nor can the attempt to create a life and a personality to defy change
ever succeed; man may delude himself that he has succeeded but he can
never achieve such security and consolation. Moreover, such a creation
exists to fulfil certain aims, and is therefore limited by its own ends. Both the
freedom the artist believes he has won by producing a work of art and the
freedom that man tries to gain by building himself an individual existence
are illusions, and the only real freedom is death.

This is the ultimate step – freedom from the tension and struggle against
that tension can only mean death and an end to being. There can be no real
freedom in this life. Ironically the play can only survive because it can still be
'removed from the fixity of its form' and subjected to the infinity of varied
interpretations. As a work of art, the play is fixed in the form devised by the
author, but it can only come to life in performance. The statue may be
immortal, but it has its constant immortality only because it is not live.
Death and art are, therefore, aspects of the same fixity.

After this discussion of freedom, Hinkfuss acts in a manner that belies all
he has said. He starts by explaining what he is going to do, even pointing out
the empty box in the auditorium where the actors will play one scene and
telling the audience that they will have no respite during the Intermission.
He explains the background to the plot they are about to see and names the
members of the La Croce family. By giving this kind of detail, Hinkfuss takes
away the audience's freedom to be surprised by the action that is to follow
and proves that the 'improvisation' he talks about is nonsensical. Everything
is preplanned, even the surprises, and he assures the audience that he is in
complete control. At the end of act I, after the quarrel with the actors,

Hinkfuss announces that the play will begin in five minutes and at the end of act II he interrupts the action to call a halt. He tries to control the time of events and put the improvised scenes into a limited time context. Nor is his desire to organise and restrict the action confined to ordering the actors about and imposing a schedule. In the Intermission he tells the audience that he appears before them freely and uses that freedom to produce ridiculous stage effects, such as the airfield scene or the 'synthetic representation' of a typical Sicilian religious procession to add 'a bit of colour' to the play.

In his preface to *Sei personaggi in cerca d'autore* Pirandello expresses his contempt for the kind of theatre Hinkfuss tries to emulate, and the stage directions of *Questa sera* mock him also. In act II, Pirandello tells us that Hinkfuss starts to beat about the bush and the stage directions to the Intermission scenes continue to make fun of him. The irony here is that Pirandello both uses Expressionist techniques and satirises them in the same play.

Hinkfuss abuses his freedom as a director by interrupting the action whenever he thinks it is getting out of his control, a logical course of behaviour in a scripted play, but one which has no place in an improvised happening. In act I he interrupts the action to warn the actors about keeping to the plot and not getting too far ahead. He wants to introduce them and nothing more. In act II, he again interrupts to call for a scene change as the actors go up to the box. His interruptions continue until the actors rebel and force him to leave and throughout the play there is a clash between the order he wants to impose and the actors' freedom in bringing the characters to life without a script. This clash exemplifies the tension between consistency and motion – Hinkfuss wants a single order, imposed by himself and the actors want to let the action develop at its own pace.

Within the Sicilian plot the question of relative freedom is presented in other forms. Mommina's physical imprisonment, trapped within the walls of her husband's house is the most immediately striking instance of curtailment of liberty. This situation is made even more horrifying when the children appear and we learn that they too are never allowed to experience more of the outside world than the view they have from the only open window. Mommina recognises that their situation is worse than hers, since she at least had freedom of movement before marrying Verri, but at the same time she has to acknowledge that the children are unaware of their plight. Mommina feels trapped because she was once free, but her daughters have no know-ledge of the 'freedom' which has been taken from her. Awareness of freedom is also relative. The children may be said objectively to be deprived of the liberty enjoyed by other human beings, that of movement in the world outside their house, but since they do not know this they have greater freedom, the freedom of innocence, unconfined and unprejudiced. To Mom-mina the room is her prison, but to the children it is home. What is daily life to them is a denial of life to her and it finally kills her. As the Character Actress introduces the scene, describing how Mommina was imprisoned in the tallest house in the town, she describes the impression of the world gained from looking out on it through the tiny window. Rooftops, the superficial covering of a house, under which life goes on in all its variety, are all the prisoners in the house on the hill may see of the world. The only signs of life to reach them are sounds – footsteps, a barking dog, an occasional voice and the striking of the church clock. The Character Actress tells of Mommina's sense of despair at hearing the clock strike the passing of time, bringing her life inexorably towards an end and reminding her of her imprisonment:

> Ma perchè seguita a misurare il tempo, quell'orologio?
> A chi segna le ore?
> Tutto è morto e vano. (p. 276)

> (Why does that clock keep on telling the time?
> For whom does it strike the hours?
> All is dead and in vain.)

Time reminds the prisoner of the movement of life outside that she cannot share and increases her sufferings by making her remember the limits of her own existence. As a prisoner in the house she is trapped in spatial terms, and as a human being she is trapped in terms of time. Her sole means of escape is through her own mind, into the world of illusion, memory and imagination.

It is this escape that torments Rico Verri. He can lock doors and bar up windows, he acknowledges that he could put out her eyes to stop her looking out of the one window, but he is powerless to control what goes on in her mind. Mommina's intangible thoughts, hidden from Verri forever, torture him with recognition of his own helplessness. He can impose physical constraints, but he can never reach inside her thoughts. Only death can put an end to Mommina's dreams and his own mad jealousy and anguish because he cannot possess her completely. Verri's anguish is the anguish of man frustrated in his attempts to be in absolute control, and the whole Sicilian plot is an illustration of Hinkfuss's statement that touches the heart of the play: 'La liberazione e la quiete non si hanno se non a costo di finire di vivere' (p. 210) (Freedom and peace can only be had at the price of ceasing to live). Only death can end Mommina's imprisonment and Verri's obsessive jealousy that holds him in a trap more terrible than her physical one, because he has not even got the temporary solace of illusion. In his mind, what he imagines only intensifies his torment. Whilst Mommina's thoughts bring relief and escape, Verri's thoughts only entrap him further. Again, freedom is a paradox – escape for Mommina increases the anguish imprisoning Verri. The idea of mental suffering preventing escape reaches its peak with the Verri–Mommina quarrel in act III, but is introduced earlier in the play through the enigmatic figure of the Chanteuse, who although she feels a sympathy for Sampognetta cannot overcome her inner pain. The stage directions describe her as *strana* and she is deathly pale, dressed all in black, a figure almost from a nightmare, symbolising grief.

The notion of pain as imprisonment is presented in comic terms early in act III, when Signora Ignazia tries to get rid of her toothache. Her family persuade her to say an Ave Maria, reminding her that in a similar situation previously, the pain had gone during the prayer. Before she can say the Ave Maria, a set of preparations have to be made – the room must be darkened, there has to be a candle, a statue of the Madonna, a small table to serve as an altar. Once the scene has been set, Hinkfuss bathes it in surreal green light, 'miracle-working light', and Donna Ignazia can begin to pray. Almost immediately there is an interruption, as Totina enters wearing Manzini's uniform and singing. Hinkfuss capitalises on the interruption to introduce a clap of thunder and a violent flash of lightning to break the mood of prayer.

On one level this interruption is a comic anticlimax and the lightning emphasises this, but at the same time the scene illustrates what is happening in the whole play. The props are improvised and the decision to stage the prayer is quite impromptu. Totina's interruption with an irrelevance that shatters the mood set up by the others, reflects Hinkfuss's continued interruptions, the one important distinction being that he interrupts to keep control over the actors and Totina's interruption is because she has a performance of her own to present. The reason for the elaborate prayer scene is to help Signora Ignazia forget her pain and one of the functions of the traditional theatre is to make the audience temporarily forget the pain of being alive while they watch the play. Pirandello mocks both this kind of escapist theatre and the ritual of setting up the prayer scene.

After his Intermission scene, Hinkfuss describes the theatre as a great, hungry machine that has been undernourished by the poor food supplied by playwrights, a reference to the type of theatre, that is popular but has no substance – the theatre of show and no meaning. Pirandello's theatre carries a message and a warning about the fleeting nature of illusion, the play and life itself. The theatre, Hinkfuss says, in the same speech, is spectacle – 'Arte sì, ma anche vita! Creazione sì, ma non durevole, momentanea!' (p. 247) (Art yes, but also life! Creation yes, but not lasting, momentary!). The theatre must not be considered as escape from life, it must *be* life, a fleeting, transitory experience that cannot be fixed in time.

Following Totina's interruption and her sisters' protests, Signora Ignazia cries out suddenly that perhaps her toothache has gone. She is not sure at first, but gradually becomes more confident until the pain returns and destroys all illusion. The prayer ritual has been unsuccessful; it merely provided a temporary distraction and the reality of the pain is still there. Signora Ignazia's response is the response of man to the ever-present pain of life: she will continue the struggle and will create a new performance to help her forget. This time she wants her daughters to sing part of the opera *Il Trovatore* and when Mommina tries to refuse, she urges her with a kind of desperation. She needs the performance, needs the illusion acted by her daughters to take her mind away from her immediate pain. At the same time, Mommina suffers from having to comply with her mother's wishes. Signora Ignazia needs others to help create her analgesic illusion, but ignores the fact that others might be reluctant to act for her. Mommina is persuaded and sings *Stride la vampa!* while her mother chants a kind of litany, using the words of the song to describe her own situation:

> Si, *dàgli, martella*, addosso a me . . . *La vampa*, si. Ah! . . . ce l'ho in bocca, la vampa . . . *Lieta*, si, *lieta in sembianza* . . .   (p. 255)

> (Yes, *take each his hammer*, bear on me . . . *The fire*, yes, . . . Oh, I've got that fire in my mouth . . . *happy*, yes, *happy in appearance* . . .)

Here she touches on the idea of outer appearance contrasting with inner feelings. '*Lieta in sembianza*' sums up both the role of the actor, who is to appear as his part demands regardless of his own personality and the position of man in his daily life, where he constantly tries to mask the confining forces that trouble him. In this immediate scene, '*lieta in sembianza*' describes what is happening on stage – Signora Ignazia is trying to pretend that her toothache is lessening, and Mommina is singing the part of Azucena unwillingly. These levels of meaning are consistent features of many of Pirandello's plays, and much of the irony comes from recognising that actions or words have a function on more than one level.

Later it is again significantly *Il Trovatore* that Mommina uses as the play to show her children what theatre is. *Il Trovatore* has a melodramatic plot based on a series of tragic misundersandings and is a story of deluded hope. The *Trovatore* himself is symbolic of the artist and the searcher, as the term indicates. As singer and poet, the troubadour has one role, but as wanderer he represents man moving uncertainly through life. Again various levels of meaning are at work, and in terms of the plot the *Trovatore* has the two freedoms Mommina is denied – freedom to sing and freedom of movement.

Pain as imprisonment, from which the only escape is through diversion, a temporary solution that does nothing to solve the problem, is given practical illustration in the final scene, with less comic overtones than in the toothache scene. Signora Ignazia's pain is physical, Mommina's is spiritual, but both seek the same way out. Mommina's imagination that enables her to dream is one form of escape and has the same function as the illusion of the theatre tries to create for her children. She describes the physical appearance of a gala night at the theatre and moves on to recount the plot of *Il Trovatore*, singing snatches from the opera and occasionally recalling events from her own past. This speech ties the idea of free-ranging imagination as escape with the notion of escape through the world of the theatre. The limitless world of imagination and the constructed world of the theatre serve the same purpose. Man can escape from immediate pain through the formlessness of imaginative illusion and through the order of the play.

Throughout the play Signora Ignazia uses images of cages and wild animals. In act II she insults the Customers from the Cabaret, saying they should be put in cages like wild beasts. Later, in the Intermission, she refers to the Sicilians among whom she lives as creatures with *occhi di lupo* and in act III she accuses Verri of keeping Mommina in a cage so that he can savage her and tear her to pieces. These three images tie up with the idea of masking, keeping hidden the forces of unreason that Pirandello describes in *L'umorismo* as the flux of life which undermines man's constructed world of protection. Passion, the moment when the flux surges up and overflows can be kept in check, in custody as it were, until it breaks out and the individual becomes its prisoner. Rico Verri is a slave to his exaggerated jealousy, a passion that he cannot keep under control. After Mommina's death, Signora Ignazia refers to her as a bird in a cage, another image of imprisonment, but with different implications. Mommina has been trapped in a cage and the imprisonment has broken her spirit and killed her. Verri and the Sicilians, Signora Ignazia feels, are too wild and untamed *not* to be restrained. Her fear of the strong, uncontrollable passions that lurk behind the façade of socialised man may be paralleled to man's fear of what is irrational. To create some kind of ordered context, man establishes and lives in organised societies, deluding himself that he has successfully suppressed irrational passions. The Sicilian plot illustrates the fallacy of that illusion – Sampognetta cannot restrain his feelings for the Chanteuse and dies as a result. The Chanteuse in act II breaks off her song and rushes to Sampognetta's defence when the clients make fun of him. Later in the same act, Signora Ignazia is overcome with fury against the same clients. In act III, Rico Verri interrupts Mommina's song and cannot control his anger. Outbreaks of anger recur through the play, on various levels: among the characters of the Sicilian plot, among the audience, among the actors, but probably the clearest example comes in the final scenes of the Mommina–Verri story. Verri's anger and frustration almost drive him mad and Mommina's desperate longing for the life that has been denied her overwhelms and finally kills her. Passion has taken over; the forces of instinct have swept reason away.

The notion of man also imprisoned by society is another motif in the play. Rico Verri's jealousy is made more terrible because he believes that the townspeople mock him. When Mommina's mother and sisters become wealthy and famous, due to Totina's success as an opera singer, Verri claims that his torment is increased. Earlier in act II, the cruel joke played on Sampognetta happens because the townspeople are critical of his relation-ship with his own wife. When Signora Ignazia and her daughters, accompanied by the young men, meet the jokers with Sampognetta, who is innocently wearing the horns they fixed to his head, they turn and accuse her of outraging public decency.

Society imposes limits on the individual who must conform to them, or be ostracised by his fellows. The irony of this is apparent in the final scenes, when Verri bows to public acclaim of the La Croce sisters and returns to release Mommina, only to find that she is already dead. The behaviour of the mother and sisters is condemned by the whole town and leads ultimately to Mommina's imprisonment and destruction. But the rules of society are flexible, and when they become famous, the pattern changes and they become admired, allowed liberty in their private lives that they could not have as unknown members of a community. Different social codes apply in different situations, illustrating the fallacy of believing in the security of any one man-made order.

Freedom from struggle only comes with non-being, and the words from *Il Trovatore* repeat the notion of death as release:

> La morte ognora
> è tarda nel venir
> a chi desia
> a chi desia morir! (p. 288)

> (How death delayeth
> lingers, or seems to fly
> from him who longeth,
> longeth to die!)

Earlier, in act III the death of Sampognetta illustrates the same point. In the plot established by Hinkfuss, he is supposed to enter, fatally wounded and die pathetically on the bosom of the Chanteuse, surrounded by his family. What happens is a comic anticlimax. The actors on stage break out of their roles and quarrel over the Leading Lady's improvisation, forgetting to give Sampognetta his cue. He comes on stage in a rage, demanding an explanation. Hinkfuss's answer is to organise the scene as he planned it and get the actors to take up where they left off. They play an exaggerated scene of grief and distress, until Sampognetta, who has refused to speak during their act, declares that he cannot fulfil his role:

> Non riesco a morire, signor Direttore; mi viene da ridere, vedendo come tutti son bravi, e non riesco a morire. (p. 263)

> (I can't die, dear fellow; I just want to laugh when I see how good all these actors are, and I can't die.)

Hinkfuss argues with him, but he remains intransigent. If Hinkfuss wants him dead, he will just declare himself dead and not waste any time. He illustrates this by falling 'dead' onto the sofa – 'Ecco fatto la scena: sono morto!' (p. 264) (There's the scene for you: I'm dead!). He feels that his scene has been ruined – 'Per me, l'entrata era tutto' (p. 264) (For me, that entrance was everything) and now that the entrance never took place because his cue was missed, he feels that there is nothing left for him to do. The absurdity of this scene contrasts strongly with the subject matter – to the actor, the finality of death means nothing. What matters is the effectiveness with which he arouses emotions in his audience. Sampognetta describes the scene that should have taken place:

> . . . dovevo dir queste cose da ubriaco, in delirio; e passarmi le mani insan-
> guinate sulla faccia – così e sporcarmela di sangue
>   [*domanda ai compagni*]
> s'è sporcata?
>   [*e come quelli gli fanno cenno di sì*]
> – bene –
>   [*e riattacca*]
> – e atterrirvi e farvi piangere – (p. 265)

> (. . . I was supposed to say all this in drunken delirium; running my bloody
> hands over my face – like this – befouling myself with blood
>   [*asking his comrades*]
> is it befouled?
>   [*and as they nod*]
> – good –
>   [*continuing*]
> – I was supposed to terrify you and make you weep.)

After this speech he falls dead, the Leading Lady in her role as Mommina bursts into tears and so affects the other actresses that they all start crying '*sinceramente*'. At this point Hinkfuss interrupts, turns off the lights and ends the scene. Sampognetta's stage death illustrates the fine line between pre-planned art and spontaneous gesture and feeling in the theatre. He refuses to play this scene because his dramatic entrance has been left out and he mockingly summarises what he should have done. In spite of this mockery, his 'death' is given reality by the distress of the Chanteuse and Mommina. What began as an angry take-off ends with the result the original scene intended: pathos. No matter how Sampognetta 'dies', once he is dead, the play can proceed as planned.

After concluding the scene, Hinkfuss tells the audience a little about stage deaths. The author, he claims, would have favoured an unobtrusive heart attack for the character, but Hinkfuss wants theatrical effect and so planned a highly melodramatic murder and death scene. Death, which for the living man means an end to struggle and liberation from the imprisonment of existence, is another example of the limited freedom of the character who can be killed off by actor, director or author in any way they like. Death for the living is a finality, but for the characters it is an action to be repeated as often as the play is performed. The actor, however, can only produce an objective view of death, reproducing the visual moment of dying. Each time he dies on stage he is reproducing an unknown experience and it is of little importance whether he is 'living' his role or not. Hinkfuss proposes the view of death as a stage effect, a dramatic moment to be portrayed as forcefully as possible. The author, whom Hinkfuss derides, would have been satisfied with an unspectacular fact of death, but in the world of the play, where real death cannot be performed, the illusion of dying is the only answer.

The paradox of death as escape and as final, irrevocable limitation is a major aspect of the play, which seeks to examine the notion of freedom on different levels. Life is seen as trapped by time, and man is trapped by his unending search for security in a world of chance and change. Art can move beyond those limits of time and place, it can rearrange reality in any way the artist chooses, but at the same time it is confined by its very form and by the fact that it is fixed and not subject to variation. In *L'umorismo,* Pirandello discusses the clash between imprisonment and liberty, between fixity and motion, again using the statue image. The statue is beyond time and change and is fixed in a niche for generations past and yet to come, whereas man's body is subject to the process of living and ageing, and inside that body is a mind or soul that can 'melt into all forms and dissove into motion'. The statue reproduces only the body, the outer shell, and fixes it forever in a single gesture in a unique moment of time. The moving spirit inside the body can never be reproduced in a form that aims to fix and define. Likewise the play can only present the gestures and actions of the characters, it can give an objective representation of pain and death, but it can never actually give us pain and death without going beyond its limits. If the actors begin to feel the emotions or griefs they are portraying they can no longer be said to be acting. But the play does not crystallise and hold gestures in the same way as the statue. Drama is an art form and yet it is an art form with great flexibility. The play may be fixed on the page, but once it is taken over by the actors and presented in the theatre it assumes another dimension. It is both freer than life and more confined than life, freer than art and likewise more restricted.

Questa sera si recita a soggetto presents a great range of angles to the problem of the existence and definition of freedom, and deals with this problem both in theoretical terms and in terms of the structure of the play. The whole is constructed around a philosophical debate that can never be resolved – perceptions of freedom change from person to person, from moment to moment and man is only free in so far as he exists, which, since liberation can only come with death, as Hinkfuss tells us, means nothing. Freedom is just one more illusion which man seeks to stabilise in order to make his life more meaningful, but like all illusions it is relative and indefinable.

It is not difficult to understand why, when discussing Beckett's *Waiting for Godot,* Raymond Williams talks about the characters being caught in a 'Pirandellian' situation where human beings are 'mutually destructive and frustrating'.[11] The barren landscape that Beckett uses so consistently, the prison settings used by Sartre, Pinter's closed rooms, Ionesco's device of using multiple sets to show that there is no way out may be compared to Pirandello's use of the actor trapped on a stage in *Questa sera si recita a soggetto* as a metaphor for the physical and spiritual limitations of man's existence, and in this sense Pirandello may be said to be the 'anticipator' of later developments in theatre. Certainly the adjective deriving from his name has become an acceptable critical term, although the looseness of its usage is yet another illustration of the way in which his contribution to theatre is assumed rather than analysed historically.

Many of Pirandello's plays have all but disappeared from repertoire both in Italy and abroad, perhaps because so many of them are consciously literary, reworkings in three-act fourth-wall form of short stories that centre on issues of social role-playing and fragmentation of personality. Of the 'trilogy of the theatre in the theatre', only *Sei personaggi in cerca d'autore* (1921) (Six Characters in Search of an Author) the first of the three is performed regularly, while the infinitely more ambitious *Ciascuno a suo modo* (1924) (Each in His Own Way) and *Questa sera si recita a soggetto* (1930) (Tonight We Improvise),[12] the most revolutionary piece of all, are rarely produced. And yet it is these three plays that must be considered primarily in any investigation of Pirandello as a seminal figure in twentieth-century drama, for here Pirandello attempted to find a form that would contain his philosophical concept of personality and experimented in ways that still appear daring and innovative today. Wylie Sypher, in discussing *Sei personaggi in cerca d'autore,* relates the play to the work of Picasso and comments that

> Pirandello 'destroys' drama much as the cubists destroyed conventional things. He will not accept as authentic 'real' people or the cliché of the theatre any more than the cubist accepts as authentic the 'real' object, the cliché of deep perspective, – the contour of volumes seen in the light of the studio – or under the sunlight either.[13]

How much more applicable might this analysis be when considering *Questa sera si recita a soggetto,* where Pirandello attempts his major investigation of the structures of a dramatic text, the dynamics of performance, the concept of the relativity of existence and the relationship between life and art in theatre terms. Surely any attempt to place Pirandello's importance in twentieth-century drama should begin with an examination of *Questa sera si recita a soggetto,* possibly the most unjustly neglected major play of modern times.

NOTES

Edition used: L. Pirandello, *Maschere nude,* vol. 1 (Milan: Mondadori, 1958). English translation consulted: S. Putnam, *Tonight We Improvise* (New York: Dutton, 1932).

The play is divided into several numbered sections which I have called acts I, II and III. In addition, there is an opening scene, which I have called scene i and the Intermission scenes. S Putnam, in his translation, includes the Intermission scenes in act II.

1. Martin Esslin, *Reflections, Essays on Modern Theatre* (New York: Doubleday & Co., Anchor Books, 1971), p. 47.

2. Esslin, *Reflections*, p. 52.

3. Robert Brustein, *The Theatre of Revolt* (Boston, Atlantic: Little, Brown & Co., 1964), p. 316.

4. Nicola Chiaromonte, 'Pirandello and the Contemporary Theatre', *World Theatre*, vol. XVI, no. 3 (1967), p. 224.

5. Clive Barker, 'New Paths for Performance Research', *Theatre Quarterly*, no. 31 (1978).

6. Steen Jansen, 'Struttura narrativa e struttura drammatica in *Questa sera si recita a soggetto*', *Rivista italiana di drammaturgia*, 6 (Rome, 1977).

7. L. Pirandello, *L'umorismo* (Florence, 1920), pp. 218–19. English translation consulted: J. O'Malley, 'The Art of the Humorist', *Atlantis*, nos. 2 and 3 (1971).

8. Tom Stoppard, *Rosencrantz and Guildenstern Are Dead* (London: Faber & Faber, 1968), p. 89.

9. Oscar Büdel, *Pirandello* (London: Bowes, 1966), p. 98.

10. Henri Bergson, *Laughter* (New York: Peter Smith, 1956), p. 18.

11. Raymond Williams, *Modern Tragedy* (London: Chatto & Windus, 1966), p. 154.

12. The dates given here refer to the first Italian productions. It should be noted that *Questa sera si recita a soggetto* was first produced outside Italy, at the Neues Schauspielhaus, Koenigsberg, on 25 January 1930. The first Italian production took place at the Teatro di Torino on 14 April 1930.

13. Wylie Sypher, 'Cubist Drama', *Rococo to Cubism in Art and Literature* (New York: Random House, Inc., 1960), p. 294.

Meditations on mimesis:
the case of Brecht

JOHN FUEGI

> No one seriously concerned with the theatre can by-pass Brecht. Brecht is the
> key figure of our time, and all theatre work today at some point starts or
> returns to his statements and achievement.[1]

Very deliberately the title of the present essay is intended to suggest that it
is fruitful to link Brecht's theory and practice of stage mimesis with E. H.
Gombrich's seminal essay, 'Meditations on a Hobby Horse'.[2] Though Gombrich, to the best of my knowledge, has never examined Brecht, and I know
of no evidence that Brecht was familiar with Gombrich, I nevertheless feel
that Gombrich's aesthetics can significantly contribute to a deepened understanding of Brecht. In moving away from the detailed *trompe-l'œil* style of
'realism' that we associate with the names of David Belasco and Konstantin
Sergeivich Stanislavski, and in his moving towards a theatre which resolutely stressed its own theatricality (the theatre of the Elizabethans and
several strands of the theatre of the Far East come immediately to mind),
Brecht[3] created a practical stage aesthetic with striking parallels to Gombrich's deceptively simple 'hobby horse' theory of mimesis.

Those familiar with Gombrich's hypothesis will recall that he presents an
aesthetic theory almost completely at odds not only with classical Greek
mimetic theory but also with the major tenets of nineteenth-century theories
of 'realism' and that contemporary holdover from nineteenth-century
theory, the politico-aesthetic mode we refer to as socialist realism.[4] Keenly
aware of modern advances in the psychology of visual perception, Gombrich
brilliantly applies modern scientific discoveries to too long unchallenged
classical theories both of mimesis and of perception of objects imitated. In a
long passage which justifies complete citation, Gombrich observes:

> There is one sphere in which the investigation of the 'representational' func-
> tion of forms has made considerable progress of late, that of animal psychology.
> Pliny, and innumerable writers after him, have regarded it as the greatest
> triumph of naturalistic art for a painter to have deceived sparrows or horses.
> The implication of these anecdotes is that a human beholder easily recognizes
> a bunch of grapes in a painting because for him recognition is an intellectual
> act. But for the birds to fly at the painting is a sign of a complete 'objective'

8 Japanese lady with horse puppet in New Year celebration dance: artist Gyokusen

illusion. It is a plausible idea, but a wrong one. The merest outline of a cow seems sufficient for a tsetse trap, for somehow it sets the apparatus of attraction in motion and 'deceives' the fly. To the fly, we might say, the crude trap has the 'significant' form – biologically significant, that is. It appears that visual stimuli of this kind play an important part in the animal world. By varying the shapes of 'dummies' to which animals were seen to respond, the 'minimum image' that still sufficed to release a specific reaction has been ascertained. Thus little birds will open their beaks when they see the feeding parent approaching the nest, but they will also do so when they are shown two darkish roundels of different size, the silhouette of the head and body of the bird 'represented' in its most 'generalized' form. Certain young fishes can even be deceived by two simple dots arranged horizontally, which they take to be the eyes of the mother fish, in whose mouth they are accustomed to shelter against danger. The fame of Zeuxis will have to rest on other achievements than his deception of birds.

An 'image' in this biological sense is not an imitation of an object's external form but an imitation of certain privileged or relevant aspects. It is here that a wide field of investigation would seem to open. For man is not exempt from this type of reaction. The artist who goes out to represent the visible form is not simply faced with a neutral medley of forms he seeks to 'imitate'. Ours is a structured universe whose main lines of force are still bent and fashioned by our biological and psychological needs, however much they may be overlaid by cultural influences.[5]

This generic theory of 'audience response' to 'certain privileged or relevant aspects' of an object rather than to the object itself or to a full mimetic representation of that object is then given dramatic specificity in Gombrich's application of his theory to a child's 'hobby horse'. In another crucial passage in his brief but brilliant essay, Gombrich writes:

The 'first' hobby horse (to use eighteenth-century language) was probably no image at all. Just a stick which qualified as a horse because one could ride on it. The *tertium comparationis*, the common factor, was function rather than form. Or, more precisely, that formal aspect which fulfilled the minimum requirement for the performance of the function – for any 'ridable' object could serve as a horse. If that is true we may be enabled to cross a boundary which is usually regarded as closed and sealed. For in this sense 'substitutes' reach deep into biological functions that are common to man and animal. The cat runs after the ball as if it were a mouse. The baby sucks its thumb as if it were the breast. In a sense the ball 'represents' a mouse to the cat, the thumb a breast to the baby. But here too 'representation' does not depend on formal similarities, beyond *the minimum requirements of function*. [italics added] The ball has nothing in common with the mouse except that it is chasable. The thumb nothing with the breast except that it is suckable. As 'substitutes' they fulfil certain demands of the organism. They are keys which happen to fit into biological or psychological locks, or counterfeit coins which make the machine work when dropped into the slot.

In the language of the nursery the psychological function of 'representation' is still recognized. The child will reject a perfectly naturalistic doll in favour of some monstrously 'abstract' dummy which is 'cuddly'. It may even dispose of the element of 'form' altogether and take to a blanket or an eiderdown as its favourite 'comforter' – a substitute on which to bestow its love.[6]

If we can accept Gombrich's hypothesis that it is function rather than form that guides our responses to visual stimuli both in 'the real world' and in the world of art objects or 'representations' of a real world then we can apply the hypothesis to the long and distinguished history of the non-realist or non-naturalist theatre. We can postulate that *in terms of psychological function* it has mattered but little to the theatre spectator whether he viewed either a full mimetic stage representation, the triumphant *trompe-l'œil* realism of a Stanislavski or a Belasco, or the highly stylised representations of the classical Greek theatre, the medieval European theatre, the Elizabethan theatre, or the theatre of the Far East. However stylised the language of the play might become and however stylised might be the setting, the costuming, and the acting of the stylised text, nevertheless it would appear that such mimetic 'substitutes' satisfied, at some deep level, biological and psychological needs. In Gombrich's terms, the 'hobby horse' of the Elizabethan theatre or the Punch and Judy show or the Javanese shadow play can be satisfactorily 'ridden', though the staging be at a very considerable remove from the detailed mimesis of a Stanislavski. It is abundantly clear, for instance, that highly emotional audience response was an everyday occurrence in the highly stylised Greek theatre. It seems to have mattered not one whit to classical audiences that a *male* actor played the female roles of Clytemnestra, Medea, or Antigone and that this actor on platform shoes and in stylised mask played in a setting devoid of all realistic detail. It would seem that this presentational style of playing[7] satisfied, at a deep level, 'the minimum requirements of function'. The counterfeit, though by no means exact, was enough 'to make the machine work when dropped into the slot'. Likewise, to name but one other example from the long, long history of 'presentational theatre', it is very clear that Shakespeare was fully aware of the fact that he was not working in a fully mimetic or representational mode. Consider if you will the well-known prologue to *Henry V*:

> But pardon, gentles all,
> The flat unraised spirits that have dared
> On this unworthy scaffold to bring forth
> So great an object: can this cockpit hold
> The vasty fields of France? or may we cram
> Within this wooden O the very casques
> That did afright the air at Agincourt?

Fully aware that mimesis in any full and direct representational sense is quite impossible under such conditions, Shakespeare has the Chorus tell the audience that it will have 'to piece out our imperfections with your thoughts'. And, speaking specifically of the lack of real horses on his stage he recommends:

> Think, when we talk of horses, that you
>   see them
> Printing their proud hoofs i' th' receiving earth.

Reduced to the linguistic echo of 'the horse itself', may we imagine that these mere shades of horses yet 'serve the minimum requirement of function' and trigger an audience's response and cause the audience 'to piece out these imperfections', in a psychologically satisfying way? In fact may we go so far as to postulate that the human response (as distinct from the response of fish or of birds as in Gombrich's examples) is more complex and potentially more satisfying? May we not suppose that, for an adult member of Shakespeare's audience (then and now), there is the psychological pleasure of responding to Shakespeare's linguistic shades of horses and also another level of appreciation in the conscious participation in such pleasurable deception? This pleasure in deceit *as* deceit is not, we may assume, accessible to other members of the animal kingdom, but is directly relevant to a 'theatre theatrical', a theatre pleasurably self-conscious in the presence of the interplay of 'reality' and of the 'depiction of reality'.

Once we have freed ourselves from the tyranny of the ill-founded assumption that only full mimetic representation can generate profound emotional responses in theatre audiences, we are ready to look closely at Brecht's theory and practice of stage mimesis with its complex mixture of 'realism' in the Stanislavskian sense and its self-conscious, non-realistic 'theatre theatrical' elements reminiscent of the Chorus's initial speech in *Henry V*. In order to see the consistency of Brecht's use of this complex blend of elements, let us look at three major and representative productions, one each from the various stages of his thirty-two years of work as a stage director (1924–56).[8]

The first play actually directed by Brecht was the adaptation which he and Lion Feuchtwanger made in 1924 of Marlowe's play, *Edward the Second*. In rehearsing the adapted Elizabethan text, Brecht insisted on something that could well have been taken verbatim from Stanislavski. Brecht's associate on the 1924 production, Bernhard Reich, recalls as follows Brecht's rehearsing the scene in which Gaveston, the king's favourite was to be hanged:

> Those playing the soldiers who were to hang the king's favourite made, initially, a few gestures that might have indicated a hanging for those with a willing imagination. Every other German director would simply have gone on. Brecht interrupted [the scene] and demanded that the actors do it properly: tie the Hangman's knot and fasten the rope to the beam above. Shrugging their shoulders, the actors tried to follow the unexpected instructions of the director. Brecht stopped them again and demanded grimly and unswervingly that they repeat the hanging. He then set them the task of hanging Gaveston as virtuosos of the gallows. The public should enjoy [he said] watching how they actually hanged the young man.[9]

Though Brecht did not, of course, actually hang the young man, he seems very close here to stage mimesis in the Stanislavskian sense. Yet, at precisely the same moment in the production, we must also note, the actors played the scene in 'whiteface', so stark as to suggest the makeup worn by a clown in the circus. The *simultaneous* use of the ostentatiously non-realistic 'whiteface' and the carefully detailed 'realism' of the preparations for the hanging constitute a typically complex Brechtian stage statement. We are, at one and the same time, 'inside' and 'outside' a 'real' event. As we analyse this complex stage construct, we might ask ourselves whether, from the point of view of the 1924 German spectator, Brecht created an event meeting Gombrich's criterion: 'the minimum requirement of function'. To return to the 'hobby horse', has Brecht not created here, an eminently 'ridable' object? Is the scene sufficient to 'transport' a spectator? What are the minimum requirements of such 'transportation' and do they have very much to do with literal mimesis? From eye-witness accounts of the production, it is clear that the introduction of ostentatiously theatrical elements such as 'whiteface' did not undercut the emotional impact of the play in any way whatsoever.[10]

When we turn to a later stage of Brecht's career and look closely at the 1929 production of his play, *The Didactic Play of Baden: On Consent*, we find an even more striking example of what constitutes a sufficient 'minimum image' in terms of spectator responsiveness. There was built into this production an extraordinary example of what we can surely now call 'hobbyhorseness'. In order to demonstrate how inhuman people are to one another, Brecht constructed a clown figure with monstrously extended wooden legs and arms and a very large and very obviously false head. The patently false extremeties of the first clown were then sawn off in a way which exaggerated the act of sawing. Despite the patently 'hobby horse' character of the first clown figure, it is reported by Martin Esslin that the grotesque sawing of the clown's wooden limbs and head caused members of the audience to faint because of the gruesomeness of the scene.[11] If we may correctly consider that the stick figure of the clown in the Baden play had more in common with Gombrich's hobby horse than with Stanislavski's meticulous stage realism, and if we believe that audience members did in fact find the scene to be profoundly shocking, then we can surely see in the scene an exemplary illustration of Gombrich's thesis that we can be moved by art objects whose representational level only fills 'the minimum requirements of function'. The stick figure or 'image' of a man was apparently quite sufficient as a 'minimum image' to 'release a specific reaction' akin to that which we might assume would have been released had a 'maximum image' with a high degree of representational verisimilitude been employed in the *Baden* play.

If the logic we have employed thus far is sound and if Gombrich's theory of functional substitutes or 'dummies' can be applied correctly to stage 'representation', then we can suggest as a general principle that it is possible that once one crosses a minimum threshold of 'representation', one will trigger an emotional response whether or not one fleshes out the 'minimum image' with a greater level of verisimilitude. In crass metaphorical terms, we might say that a certain trap-door has been arranged to open when a minimum of ten pounds of pressure is placed on the door. The trap will not spring with amounts less than ten pounds but will always spring with pressure of ten pounds or more. In this metaphorical example 'the minimum image' is ten pounds. If this basic principle be deemed sound, then we may suggest that almost all the talk of whether audiences become more emotionally involved with 'fully representational' than with 'minimally representational' theatre is largely a question of hair-splitting. As in the trap-door example, reactions will be triggered by both images as long as both reach 'the minimum image' level. We do not inhibit emotional involvement if we maintain a sufficient 'minimum image' of an object or person 'represented'. Applied directly to each stage of Brecht's career as a playwright/director, as he continuously engaged in formal experiments which carried him away from the literal mimesis of a Stanislavski, we can see that we should *not* expect that audiences must have remained cool and distant just because Brecht deliberately departed from literal realism. Though Brecht himself consistently expressed discomfiture[12] when audiences responded in an emotional way to his plays, we may suggest that it would have been very surprising had audiences *not* responded to stage images that more than met the Gombrich standard of 'minimum image'.

When we turn to another Brecht play/production and look at his stage version of *The Caucasian Chalk Circle* we can see again that departures from literal mimesis do not necessarily (if at all) inhibit response to the images presented on stage. When Brecht staged Grusche's 'Flight into the Northern Mountains' in the play,[13] he organised the scene in ways strikingly akin to 'chase sequences' in the old American films that he loved. Grusche's escape (as the text of the play never allows us to forget), is a nip and tuck affair. What is true of the text, however, is even truer of Brecht's staging of that text. For instance, instead of completely stylising the crossing of the 2,000-feet-deep chasm (a scene that would probably be done in the traditional Chinese theatre solely with stylised gestures and with virtually no props), Brecht had built on the stage an actual rickety bridge, only some six feet off the ground to be sure, but a bridge nevertheless. In the production we find Grusche approaching the makeshift bridge at a point in the play where she is obviously exhausted and the pursuing soldiers are obviously closing fast. Other characters in the play have reached the bridge before Grusche and have already decided that the bridge is too unsafe to cross. When Grusche arrives and proposes to not only cross the bridge herself but to increase the danger by carrying the baby across as well, the bystanders urge her not to make such a suicidal gesture. Laden as she is with her bundle and her child, the bridge will, they assure her, collapse under the combined weight. But we are also told by the text of the play that for her to stand and wait for the soldiers is equally suicidal. The soldiers, one of whom she has physically assaulted in the previous scene, can be heard approaching and they will, as one bystander assures Grusche, 'make hamburger out of her' if she is caught. Under these tense circumstances she is willing to attempt to cross the bridge. May we assume that tension mounted for the theatre audience as the Grusche of Brecht's own production decided to cross with the added burden of the child? As Grusche crossed that bridge, swaying above the stage, clutching the child, and urged on by the gasps and prayers of the bystanders, with the pursuing soldiers now coming into view, might we ask whether Gombrich's 'minimum image' standard was met for that audience?

Whether we turn to early play/productions or to ones from the thirties or the famous Berliner Ensemble productions of the fifties, we consistently find in Brecht that, though he eschewed the use of detailed 'mimesis' as a guiding principle for a whole production, he nevertheless always maintained a substantial portion of 'literal representation' in each production. I know of no production of Brecht from any period of his life where he did not use the mixed mimetic style[14] exemplified by that 'whiteface' hanging scene. As with *Edward the Second*, he would simultaneously draw attention to the theatricality of a production while providing a substantial portion of 'realistic detail'. If we assume that only literal realism/mimesis will trigger strong audience responses, we will be led to try to believe that Brecht's audiences were left largely unmoved. If we grant, however, that Brecht consistently provided a highly representational 'minimum image' then we can see why audiences were in fact very deeply moved by his productions.[15] With Gombrich's thesis of the 'minimum image' as a guide, we can avoid the oversimplification of attempting to classify Brecht's work as being *either* 'realistic' *or* 'formalistic',[16] or *either* emotional *or* non-emotional (intellectual) in its impact.

For people seriously concerned with the theatre today, it continues to be fruitful to look both at Brecht's theoretical statements and at his actual stage productions. What we will find there, I think, is a highly modern and sophisticated 'self-reflexive' mimetic mode well-suited to twentieth-century experimentation both in the arts and in the sciences. I would hope that we can live comfortably with the paradox that such a modern stance is wholly consistent with several main strands of the history of the theatre. It is clear that Brecht was never more modern than when he was borrowing formal, structural and stylistic elements from Shakespeare or returning to the richly stylised theatre of the Far East. The 'hobby horse' which Aeschylus rode and which served Shakespeare so well has galloped into the modern theatre with Brecht astride and shows no signs of being ready to be put out to pasture. Though Gombrich's beast is but a crude creature of the nursery, perhaps we can never be too sophisticated to be 'transported' by it. Whatever it may lack in 'formal mimetic completeness' is surely of less importance than its demonstrable functionality. Is it possible that this ungainly wooden creation of the nursery can outrun the 'real' horses of Stanislavski and Belasco? Contemporary stage practice would seem to suggest such an unlikely conclusion.

NOTES

1. Peter Brook, *The Empty Space* (London: Macgibbon & Kee, 1968), pp. 71–2.
2. E. H. Gombrich, 'Meditations on a Hobby Horse or the Roots of Artistic Form', *Meditations on a Hobby Horse and Other Essays on the Theory of Art* (London and New York: Phaidon, second edition, 1971).
3. I do not wish to suggest here that Brecht worked alone in creating this stage aesthetic in the twentieth century. Parallels and possible sources abound in the Soviet and pre-Soviet avant-garde theatre in the work of Meyerhold, Tairov, Tretiakov and Eisenstein. For a discussion of Russian anticipations of 'Brechtian' theory and practice please see: John Fuegi, 'Russian "Epic Theatre" Experiments and the American Stage', *The Minnesota Review*, new series, no. 1 (Fall 1973), 102–12.
4. For an explicit discussion of Brecht's attitude towards the worst excesses of socialist realism, please see: John Fuegi, 'The Soviet Union and Brecht: The Exile's Choice', *Brecht Heute/Brecht Today*, II, ed. Eric Bentley, John Fuegi *et al.*, (Frankfurt am Main: Athenäum Verlag, 1972), 209–21.
5. Gombrich, 'Meditations on a Hobby Horse', pp. 5, 6.
6. *Ibid*, p. 4.
7. By 'presentational style' I mean a style where the actor does not 'become the part' but instead suggests or presents the part to an audience while retaining his own character as a human being who is an actor.
8. The examples chosen are not isolated ones. Dozens of other examples come readily to mind in plays such as *Mahagonny*, *The Threepenny Opera*, *The Measures Taken*, *The Horatians and the Curations*, *Saint-Joan of the Stockyards*, *In the Jungle of Cities*, *The Caucasian Chalk Circle*.
9. Bernhard Reich, *Im Wettlauf mit der Zeit* (Berlin, GDR: Aufbau-Verlag, 1970), pp. 253–4.
10. For confirmation of this contention please see not only Bernhard Reich (cited above) but also Marieluise Fleisser's account: 'Aus der Augustenstrasse', *50 Jahre Schauspielhaus, 25 Jahre Kammerspiele im Schauspielhaus* (Munich, 1951), pp. 52 ff.
11. Martin Esslin, *Brecht: A Choice of Evils* (London: Eyre & Spottiswoode, 1959), p. 42.
12. Of *Mother Courage* for instance Brecht noted ruefully: 'The success of the play, that is to say the impression it made, was, without doubt, enormous. People pointed to Weigel [Brecht's wife who played Courage in the production. J.F.], on the street and said: "There's Courage". But I don't believe now and did not believe then, that Berlin and all the other cities that saw it, understood the play', Brecht, *Schriften zum Theater*, VI, 161 (Frankfurt am Main: Suhrkamp Verlag, 1964).
13. For a close discussion of this play in performance in Brecht's own production, please see: John Fuegi, '*The Caucasian Chalk Circle* in Performance', *Brecht Heute/Brecht Today*, I, ed. Eric Bentley, John Fuegi *et al.* (Frankfurt am Main: Athenäum Verlag, 1971), pp. 137–49.
14. The phrase 'mixed mimetic style' is a conscious echo of Erich Auerbach's phrase in his *Mimesis* (Princeton University Press, 1953).

15. Please see note 12 above.
16. In the perennial discussion of 'realism' in Brecht, reference is often made to the fact that in the 1930s Lukacs numbered Brecht among the 'formalists' and 'bourgeois decadents' who had departed from the straight and narrow path of socialist realism.

The 'immersion-effect' in the plays of Antonio Buero Vallejo

VICTOR DIXON

A major concern in the discussion of dramatic mimesis this century has been to determine to what extent and to what purpose, by what means and in what respects – intellectual, emotional, or physical – the spectator should be *involved* in an imitated action. To that discussion Antonio Buero Vallejo, unquestionably Spain's most important dramatist since the Civil War, has made an original and practical contribution which deserves to be far more generally known. His most characteristic technique, and the subject of this study, has been the use of '*efectos de inmersión*' (immersion-effects).

The phrase was coined, by way of obvious contrast to Brecht's *Verfrem-dungs effekt* – or alienation-effect – by the author of the best of several recent studies of Buero's plays, Ricardo Doménech.[1] They were to be found, he pointed out, in *En la ardiente oscuridad* (1950), were partially used in *El concierto de San Ovidio* (1962) and *El tragaluz* (1967), and were more thoroughly exploited in *El sueño de la razón* (1970) and *Llegada de los dioses* (1971) – to which today he would presumably add *La fundación* (1974) and *La detonación* (1977).[2] For in recent years Buero has not only accepted Doménech's phrase and asserted his conviction of the validity of such effects;[3] he has made increasingly deliberate, systematic and obvious use of them. But as soon as one attempts a definition of *efectos de inmersión*, and in the light of it reviews Buero's twenty-one plays to date, one discovers – and this will be my main contention here – that he has been deploying these and analogous devices throughout his career.

My definition would be this: an immersion-effect occurs when the spectator is made to share a peculiar sensory perception (or lack of it), not with all the characters of a play but (normally) with only one, with whom he therefore feels a stronger sense of empathy or 'identification'. A moment's thought reveals, of course, that such effects are neither new nor exclusive to Buero: ghosts, dreams and fantasies, for instance, have long been familiar in the theatre and are common in the modern cinema. What distinguishes their appearance in Buero's plays is the consistency and yet the versatility, the inventiveness, the often striking originality with which he exploits them. It is often difficult, as a result, to establish the frontiers of our subject; but it is important to stress, I believe, that the sharing involved is of a sense-percept, not necessarily of an emotion and especially not of an intellectual attitude. For example, some of Buero's early plays include an 'oracle' or soothsayer, some of his later plays a narrator or intermediary, and his most recent plays a character more mature and shrewd though less visionary than their protagonist; such persons utter prophecies or judgements with which we may agree, intellectually, but in these cases we do not share abnormal perceptions. These are not *efectos de inmersión*.

Buero's interest in such effects can readily be related to his outstanding and consistent characteristics as a dramatist. In the first place, he is an intensely inventive practical playwright. His plays, though surprisingly diverse in style and setting, have always provided original and exciting theatre. They portray strong characters in extreme, explosive situations; well over half of them involve at least one violent death. Yet their impact has always been carefully calculated and so far as possible controlled. Every detail of their staging – unfashionably – is visualised and prescribed. Buero does his directors' and designers' work for them in advance, though he is always on hand also to make changes in rehearsal.[4] He has always taken pleasure and pride in his craft, in *el oficio*. In his early works, several of them *tours de force*, he deliberately courted technical difficulty as a challenge and a discipline;[5] and he has never ceased to essay new techniques. To quote Robert L. Nicholas: 'Buero has been the most sustained, innovative, refreshing theatrical force in Spain for over two decades primarily because of the constant experimental nature of his plays. For him, theatre is experimentation.'[6] The principal thrust of that experimentation, moreover, has always been to modify and intensify the impact of the play on the spectator. As Doménech puts it, 'en cada uno de sus textos dramáticos, Buero se ha planteado la relación entre el escenario y la sala de espectadores como un problema nunca resuelto, como un problema que hay que resolver *cada vez*'[7] (in each of his dramatic texts, Buero has tackled the relationship between the stage and the auditorium as a problem which is never solved, but which must be solved *each time*).

His writing has been influenced by a wide range of authors: Ibsen, Pirandello, Lorca, Valle-Inclán, Miller . . ., but since *Un soñador para un pueblo* (1958) it most obviously bears the imprint of the epic theatre of Bertolt Brecht, whose *Mother Courage* he faithfully translated for its first performance in Spain in 1966. Yet Buero rejects that stark distancing of the spectator by which Brecht supposedly sought to reduce the spectator to a dispassionate, intellectual analyst, and insists on the necessity that he be emotionally involved as well. Such a statement requires more careful amplification than I have room for here; for one thing, Buero makes the familiar point that Brecht, like Valle-Inclán, fortunately contradicted his own doctrines in practice (and even in theory) and has often been misunderstood;[8] for another, he far more emphatically rejects, as counter-productive and inartistic, crudely physical, uncalculated and uncontrolled techniques of audience participation, like those of Living Theatre.[9] And he claims to have been attempting for some years, with others, a new synthesis, a reconciliation of detachment and involvement, of – in the Nietzschean terminology he is fond of using – the Apollonian and Dionysiac aspects of drama.[10] Nevertheless it is apparent that his *dominant* concern has always been to involve the spectator, to induce his imaginative participation in the play, to persuade him towards emotional identification with the main characters.[11]

In the second place, Buero is a deeply serious, not to say solemn writer, with a strong sense of commitment. His mission as an artist, he has often said, is to 'open eyes', to provoke a 'removedora y eficaz inquietud' (a disturbing and effective unease), to pose fundamental questions. But he has always resolutely refused, to the exasperation of some younger radicals, to offer solutions, to put over in the theatre specific messages derived from other areas of inquiry – political or social science, philosophy or religion. Art for Buero is a means of knowing as well as of transforming reality, 'una especie de contemplación activa' (a kind of active contemplation). He parts company again from Brecht, therefore, in rejecting explicit didacticism in favour of the inexplicit, the problematical. He conceives his craft, as Ruiz Ramón has put it,

> como tarea de *puesta en drama* de la pregunta. Su teatro sería así una interrogación – siempre grave y fundamental – que se hace drama, esto es, acción, cuya respuesta compete al espectador, comprometido por el dramaturgo a ejercer el oficio de quien responde, a la vez testigo, actor y juez.[12]
>
> (as the task of presenting enquiry as drama. In this light Buero's theatre is a question – always a serious fundamental question – which becomes drama, that is, action, which it is for the spectator to answer; he is required by the dramatist to reply, at once witness, participant and judge.)

Yet it is not difficult to divine his own fundamental attitude and the message which he wants the spectator to take away. His plays stress the significance of the human individual, the need to assume individual responsibility, the possibility, through individual determination and commitment – though not without collective action – of fulfilling a universal urge to overcome Man's limitations, both socio-political and ontological.

He was seen at first, preposterously, as a pessimist – because then, as ever since, he was an implacable enemy of false, shallow optimism – by a public accustomed to look to the theatre for escapist entertainment. He has declared consistently that he is a tragic writer, but a hopeful one (*esperanzado*); that all tragic writers, whatever their conscious beliefs, are motivated by hope (*se escribe porque se espera*), are expressing a doubting faith (*una fe que duda*); that all true tragedies are characterised by an ultimate tension between hope and despair.[13] In his own case, it is in fact hard to resist the impression of a true optimist too cautious not to wear a tragic mask, but confident beneath it of the eventual triumph of freedom over necessity. His endings are almost always avowedly ambiguous; but they invariably imply, beyond the suffering and squalor of the present, not merely a faint hope but a firm faith in the future – not to say a nineteenth-century sense of the demonstrability of human progress.[14] His main characters it has become a critical commonplace to divide, as if into goodies and baddies, into *contemplativos* and *activos*.[15] This is a misleading simplification, but it has considerable validity. His *activos*, cynical and pragmatic (but often out of their depth) are *wrong*; his *contemplativos*, whom the others label idealistic *ilusos* (but who are by no means always impractical or inactive) are essentially *right*, and though usually defeated are always in some sense victorious. These visionaries, rather than their opponents, are plainly their author's surrogates, to a large extent (seventy per cent to thirty per cent, he has suggested, in the case of *El tragaluz*).[16] Fervently, but *not* despairingly, he wants the spectator to be inspired by them, to say *yes*, to and with them. For Buero, the tragic writer 'lanza con sus obras su anhelante pregunta al mundo, y espera, en lo profundo de su corazón, que la respuesta sea un sí lleno de luz' (. . . through his works hurls his eager question into the world, and hopes, in his innermost heart, that the answer will be a *yes* ablaze with light) – and in some plays the giving of that assent is shown on stage.[17] These dreamers are the bearers of Buero's message, and he urgently wants us to feel at one with them: intellectually to share their convictions and their visions, but also emotionally to identify with their sufferings and aspirations.

In the third place, these 'message-bearers' are often isolated from the other characters, and apparently from the spectator, not only by their nature but by a peculiarity of perception, both real and symbolic, which might seem to inhibit but can in fact facilitate identification. Some, like his Esquilache or his Velázquez, though superior to those around them in their idealism, integrity and sensitivity, are in other respects quite normal; but most of his *videntes*, by a paradox familiar in life and in literature, are individuals whose ordinary perceptions are defective, limited or distorted by blindness, deafness, madness. . . .[18] Buero's persistent preoccupation with those so afflicted is notorious; it relates, no doubt, not only to his genuinely compassionate nature, but also to the usefulness of their afflictions to his purposes as a playwright – as powerful devices for the creation of dramatic irony, but more fundamentally as symbols of the limitations which all men yearn to and will, surely, 'some day', overcome.[19] And above all, if the spectator can be induced – persuaded or forced – to *share* both the subnormal and the supernormal perceptions of such characters, by contrast with those of normal humans both on and off stage, his sense of empathy, of participation in their experience, will be unusually intense. This therefore has become the most characteristic (though not the only) way in which Buero has used *efectos de inmersión*.

Historia de una escalera, with which Buero leapt into prominence in 1949, cannot be said to contain any such effects; nor can *Las palabras en la arena* of the same year. 1950, however, saw the première of *En la ardiente oscuridad*, which was in fact the first play Buero wrote and which Doménech has rightly seen as 'un centro motor, del que parten – y al que regresan – las posteriores y sucesivas *exploraciones* del dramaturgo'[20] (a motive centre, from which the dramatist's subsequent and successive *explorations* set out – and to which they return). Characteristically, it contains his first immersion-effect. Set in a school for blind adolescents, the play concerns the disruption caused by a new pupil, Ignacio, who refuses to accept its naively optimistic philosophy of resignation to disability; eventually a 'loyal' pupil, Carlos, murders him and restores the initial *status quo* – with the sole difference that Carlos has himself been infected by Ignacio's anguished non-conformity, symbolic of 'Humanity's dissatisfaction in the face of our limitations'. Buero's technical brilliance is illustrated in his constant exploitation of the pupils' blindness as a source of dramatic irony; but for this very reason it may be that the spectator tends to feel detachedly superior, and akin instead to the somewhat oracular Doña Pepita, who apart from Ignacio's father is the only sighted character, whereas Buero is concerned that we should not merely sympathise but identify with Ignacio and Carlos. During a crucial conversation between them in the final act, therefore, when Ignacio is expressing the horror of being denied the perception of light, Buero directs that the stage lights and even the distant stars be gradually dimmed to total darkness, with the intention that we may briefly share their deprivation. In a commentary published with the play Buero mentioned that the effect had been intro-duced as one of several changes to a first version of 1946, but characterised it as essential. In a lecture given in 1970 he invited his hearers, disingenuously, to 'imagine' a play in which all or nearly all the characters were blind, and conceded that to communicate the horror of their blindness to the audience and involve it in their drama one might resort to crudely physical means; but alternatively, he added,

> si el supuesto autor de esta supuesta obra en un momento determinado . . . hace que todas las luces del teatro se apaguen lentamente, incluidas las luces-piloto de la sala, entonces es posible que se produzca una participación menos ostensible que la anterior, pero más profunda. Una participación más bien psíquica que física, con la cual al público se le ha venido a decir: Lo queráis o no, ahora sois ciegos.[21]

> (if the supposed author of this supposed work, at a particular moment. . . has all the lights in the theatre slowly extinguished, including the emergency lights in the auditorium, then it is possible that a participation may be produced which is

less obvious than the former, but more profound. A psychic rather than physical participation, whereby the audience has been told: 'Like it or not, now you are blind.')

Indeed he has often expressed a justifiable pride in having experimented with this effect so early:

> Esa reinteriorización del público en el espectáculo, por cuyos fueros se vuelve ahora, fue lo que yo intenté en solitario no ya en España, sino quizá en todo el teatro europeo de los años cincuenta.[22]

> (That reinclusion of the audience in the spectacle, which is championed today, was what I was alone in attempting, not just in Spain but perhaps in the whole of European theatre in the fifties.)

The impact of this slow blackout, moreover, is undeniable, especially in the context of the dialogue it accompanies; but to the fastidious spectator it may seem an 'artificial device'.[23] *En la ardiente oscuridad*, for all its metaphysical implications, adheres to the conventions of naturalistic illusionism; all its other light and sound effects are explained with careful regard for realism. By contrast, the blinding of the audience in act III is an alienating intrusion by the author. For superficially similar but aesthetically far superior effects we shall have to wait for *El concierto de San Ovidio* and *Llegada de los dioses*.

La tejedora de sueños (1952), a neo-classical tragedy in which Buero reinterprets the legend of the chaste Penelope, has no true immersion-effects; and the same may be said, in a very different sense, of his next play – his most mystical and least successful – *La señal que se espera* (1952). Set in a Galician country house, it concerns the owner Enrique and his wife Susana, two old servants, a philosopher friend Julián and Susana's former lover, Luis. The latter, a composer, is the first of Buero's many psychiatric cripples; but he has constructed an Aeolian harp in the hope that it will miraculously play a melody which he has forgotten and so cure him. At the end of act II, those on stage, and we in the audience, hear just such a mysterious melody, and it would seem that they and we are sharing either a miracle or a collective hallucination; but in act III we learn that the effect had been secretly contrived by Susana. At the end of the play, however, when all its characters have acquired new hope and a strange serenity, the audience hears a new and this time truly supernatural music, a species of 'harmony of the spheres'. We are presumably meant to accept this not merely as a symbol or as a Hollywood 'heavenly choir' but as a reality (within the context of the play); yet none of the characters, though they *sense* that the music is sounding, and Susana claims to *feel* it within herself, can *share* our perception of it. This is the reverse of an immersion-effect – but that very fact, of course, underlines Buero's interest in such devices and his eagerness to experiment.

Casi un cuento de hadas (1953), in which Buero retells a fairytale by Perrault, contains a curious series of immersion-effects. The spectator is made to share an ambiguity of perception, in this case with as many as five characters; to take by turns – and even simultaneously – both a normal and an abnormal view of the same reality: another of the characters. As act I ends, the ugly Prince Riquet, having won the love of the beautiful but initially stupid Princess Leticia, is transformed before her astonished eyes – and ours – into a handsome Prince Riquet; the double is played by a different actor. In act II it is this handsome Riquet whom she (and we) can see when they are alone together, although when other characters are present only the ugly Riquet is normally visible. In act III, when Leticia's love has wavered, she (and we) see first the ugly image, then both at once – and the images themselves wonder which is the true one. (There are further, confusing complications; the handsome prince is seen too by the clairvoyant Oriana, and also – immediately before he kills his rival Armando – both by Armando and by Leticia's sister, Laura.) Eventually Leticia comes to accept the ugly Riquet; but she and he (and we) have a final vision of his idealised image, which will continue to sustain their mutual love. Thus in Buero's sophisticated *quasi-* fairytale, the Beast becomes Prince Charming, but only by turns and in the eye of the beholder – especially the eye of Beauty. And what that eye sees, from one moment to another, Buero has used the pantomime devices of transformation and the second actor to make the spectator see. The choice is limited: ugliness, or beauty, or both at once; but this is an interesting early experiment with immersion-effects.

Madrugada (1953), a drama of suspense, has a real clock on stage. We share the heroine's secrets, and no doubt her anxiety to uncover those of the other characters, as with them we watch its hands approach the fateful hour of six in the morning; but there are no true immersion-effects. These reappear, however, in *Irene, o el tesoro* (1954). Phenomena experienced by the spectator and – for the most part – by the eponymous heroine may be interpreted either as 'real' or as hallucinations, for Irene may be mad. A widow whose baby was stillborn, she is befriended by a sprite, Juanito, whom she treats as if he were her child, but who is of course invisible to the other characters, her obsessively miserly brother-in-law Dimas and the members of his household. Juanito is instructed by a Voice whom he regards as God, in conversations at which Irene is not present; but these, like the strange light effects he produces and the tricks he plays on the others, in Buero's intention *may* have an objective 'reality' or *may* all be creations, in their different ways, of Irene's strange psyche. Eventually, when it is the brother-in-law, ironically, who has been removed to an asylum, we see Irene and her sprite leave by a balcony and ascend a pathway of light which he has shown her – although to the other characters it appears that she has fallen to her death in the street below. For most of us it may be harder than Buero intended to accept that the supernatural phenomena, and especially the Voice, can possibly be understood to exist except as fantasies in Irene's mind; but that is not material to our present purpose. The sharing by the spectator of experience, both visual and aural, which is perceived by no character other than the protagonist, is to prove prophetic in the development of Buero's drama.

Hoy es fiesta (1956), which was acclaimed as a return by Buero to the neo-naturalism of *Historia de una escalera,* seems at first sight to eschew immersion-effects. Pilar, the wife of the protagonist Silverio, has an abnormality of perception in that she is deaf. But the spectator is not made to share this peculiarity; he only tends, surely, to identify the more closely with the normal characters. This is especially true in the crucial scenes in which Silverio, alone on stage with Pilar and confident that she cannot hear him, pours out his feelings of guilt at having without her knowledge been responsible for the death of her daughter. Pilar's deafness is clearly more a symbolic than a real barrier to communication; Silverio could confess his secret in writing, though this, until too late, he lacks the courage to do. But it gives him the freedom to express his feelings, and the dramatist an opportunity, within the naturalistic convention, to resort to soliloquy, 'el vehículo revelador por excelencia del hombre interior'[24] (the vehicle *par excellence* for the revelation of the inward man). In these scenes, then, we identify with Silverio the more closely because we share with him a *normality* of perception which is denied to his partner by her disability. At one point, however, near the end of act I, Pilar envies his advantages, and so seeks to reverse their roles by playfully stopping his ears, as if to subject him, not the spectator, to an immersion-effect: '¡Es un capricho! Sordo por un momento, como yo. Ven.' (It's a whim! Deaf for a moment, like me. Come on.) Then she speaks words of love and gratitude which he, we suppose, cannot hear: but before the curtain falls he reveals (to us, not to her) that he has continued to hear, to share our perceptions, as we share his secrets, so that we feel an even closer identification with the normal character.

Las cartas boca abajo (1957) has similarly a series of crucial scenes between the protagonist, Adela, and a close relative, her sister Anita. Adela, like Silverio, though with more reason, is conscious of having wronged the other and longs for her forgiveness. But Anita is not deaf; she seems rather to be forever listening, and Adela often suspects, with good reason, that Anita may be lurking behind the curtain which conceals the door to her room. Nor is she physically dumb, though she never speaks; she may at any moment choose to break her brooding silence; it remains therefore a source of mystery and menace. In fact in reported encounters reminiscent of Strindberg's *The Stronger,* Adela feels forced – as Silverio is free – to pour out her inner feelings in a vain attempt to penetrate the other's unresponsiveness. In this way the spectator comes to know Adela, to feel contempt but also compassion for her, and to share her frustration at her inability to interpret the thoughts of the person who matters most to her. As in *Hoy es fiesta,* an abnormality which symbolises the breakdown of communication – a major theme of both plays – is used theatrically to induce the spectator to identify, not with the 'abnormal' character but with the 'normal' protagonist.

But *Las cartas boca abajo* contains another kind of immersion-effect. At the end of the first scene, we hear a 'twilight chorus' of birdsong, which Adela describes as joyous and hopeful. At the end of the fourth and last, we hear the identical sounds; but to Adela – thanks to a suggestion of her brother's, and her own conviction now that she is doomed to loneliness and remorse, at the mercy of Anita, a kite hovering over its prey – they are screams of fear and despair. As spectators, we may choose to hear what she (and we) heard before, or be induced to hear what she hears now.

Un soñador para un pueblo (1958), significant technically as the first of several historical dramas in which Buero makes much more fluid and flexible use of time and space, has no true immersion-effects. Yet it makes much play with Buero's favourite imagery of darkness and light, blindness and sight. Near the end of the first half, night draws in round the protagonist Esquilache and Fernandita, a young woman who symbolises the common people; they are 'como niños sumidos en la oscuridad' (like children plunged in darkness). But they are illuminated by the lighting of a street-lamp which is part of – and symbolises – the Enlightenment which Esquilache is trying to bring to eighteenth-century Madrid. Three are lit; but as he drives off into the night they are extinguished one by one by leaders of a reactionary mob. Before the curtain falls, the audience is made to share the prophetic darkness which the rebels mean shall await him on his return. The play has also the last of Buero's soothsayer-figures, in the person of a blind ballad-singer, who sells copies of an enigmatic almanack.[25] When its prophecies, at the end of the play, have proved unexpectedly true, his blindness, though there is no attempt to make us share it directly, becomes again a symbol of limitations common to us all: 'Ese ciego insignificante llevaba el destino en sus manos. Nada sabemos. Tan ciegos como él, todos.' (That insignificant blind man held our destiny in his hands. We know nothing. We are as blind as he, all of us.)

Las meninas (1960), Buero's play about Velázquez, has on the other hand, in a beggar called Martín, the first of the narrators or intermediaries I have mentioned, whose effect is inevitably to some extent to keep the spectator at a distance. He addresses us directly at the outset and continues to do so, although he explains, when his companion Pedro Briones calls him mad, that he is only *inventing* an audience. At the end, alone and wondering whether he may go wholly mad, he imagines himself begging bread by describing Velázquez's most famous picture to a fair-ground audience, with the aid of a copy, and a *tableau vivant* of *Las meninas* simultaneously appears behind him. Martín can be understood as an ironic figure of the author; but Pedro, who is nearly blind – and also therefore a character with whom we do not naturally identify – can paradoxically be seen as a figure of the spectator.

Shown Velázquez's sketch for his masterpiece, he is able to understand what the artist saw there:

> Un cuadro sereno; pero con toda la tristeza de España dentro . . . fantasmas vivos de personas vivas cuya verdad es la muerte.

> (A serene picture; but with all the sadness of Spain contained within it . . . living ghosts of people whose truth is death.)

He is able to feel, and to know that future spectators will feel, immersed in it:

> Quien los mire mañana, lo advertirá con espanto. . . . Sí, con espanto, pues llegará un momento, como a mí me sucede ahora, en que ya no sabrá si es él el fantasma ante las miradas de estas figuras. . . . Y querrá salvarse con ellas, embarcarse en el navío inmóvil de esta sala, puesto que ellas lo miran, puesto que él está ya en el cuadro cuando lo miran.

> (Whoever looks at it tomorrow will realise the fact in terror. . . . Yes, in terror, for there will come a moment, as is happening to me now, when he will not know whether he is the ghost before the gaze of these figures. . . . And he will want to be saved with them, to embark in the motionless ship of this room, because they are looking at him, because, as they look at him, he is in the picture already.)

In an article about the picture, Buero has suggested, similarly, that it is Velázquez's own intention there that

> nuestra deferente mirada se cruce con la suya en una suerte de 'participación' teatral que, sin recurrir a físicas provocaciones al estilo del más reciente teatro que puedan, por exceso, resultar inhibitorias . . . se constituya suavemente como partipación espontánea e inexorable [that we be convinced of] nuestra incorporación definitiva al momento fugaz y eterno que *Las meninas* nos regala.
>
> (*Tres maestros*, p. 93)

> (. . . our respectful gaze may encounter his in a kind of theatrical 'participation' which, without recourse to physical provocations in the manner of the most recent theatre, which may in their excess prove inhibiting, comes smoothly into being as a spontaneous and inevitable participation . . .our definitive incorporation in the fleeting and eternal moment which *Las meninas* presents to us.)

Velázquez himself, Buero is saying here, hoped for an immersion-effect. At the heart of his play, he shows it happening, for Pedro Briones. At the end, through the final *tableau*, he clearly hopes to produce the identical result in the theatre. By now Pedro is dead, to Velázquez's anguish; we cannot therefore exactly share, but Buero wants us to recapture, the way in which he saw and was immersed in *Las meninas*.

El concierto de San Ovidio (1962) has by contrast a narrator, Valentin Haüy, who is also, at the end of act II, both a spectator-figure and a participant. If Buero had not merely mentioned him, for the reader, in his introduction to act I, but had given him, like Martín, a kind of prologue, the distancing effect would have been increased and the irony inherent in his role diminished; but those crass critics who saw his epilogue as unnecessary might have realised that in a sense this 'excrescence' was the essence, and Haüy not peripheral but the protagonist. This is not to deny that Buero deliberately chooses as his central characters a group of unfortunates of whom history records almost nothing, that he involves the spectator deeply in their tragic if invented story, that in David especially he creates his perhaps most complex character and most satisfying role (*experto crede*); but the play shows also how these unknown individuals 'determinaron sin saberlo el destino de un gran hombre' (determined, without knowing it, the destiny of a great man). It tells obliquely the story of a vocation, and still more obliquely illustrates Buero's conception of his own.

Haüy was the first important pioneer in the education of the blind. The epilogue shows him reading to himself his *Troisième note* of 1800; the play 'proper' reconstructs, with the aid of a contemporary poster, the sort of incidents which could have led up to and followed the event which he said there had inspired him, in 1771, to take up his life's work: a grotesque performance, in a café run by one Valindin at the annual fair of St Ovid, by an orchestra of blind musicians. In an article of 1953, Buero recalled an analogous (though probably apocryphal) story, according to which Paul Ehrlich was inspired to undertake his search for a cure for syphilis by witnessing a performance of Ibsen's *Ghosts;*[26] in 1962, we find him seeking to show on stage the potentially inspiring effect of art – or in this case its degraded opposite – within a dramatic performance of his own, which itself, he might hope, as with all his plays, would inspire and ennoble some of its spectators. In that respect *El concierto de San Ovidio* is a play about spectator reactions – as indeed, in different ways, were *Las Meninas* before it, and after it *Dr Valmy*, *El tragaluz* and *Mito*. Its crucial and most striking scene is that of the orchestra's performance, which Valindin directly invites us to enjoy, in company with several on-stage spectators. To all of these but Haüy, who makes an historically undocumented but plausible protest, the blind musicians are hilariously funny. We are free to share their debased reactions and dehumanised behaviour; but if we do, if – to whatever degree – we see with their eyes rather than with Haüy's, we are included in the condemnation which he addresses to the performers: '. . . si vierais, el público sería otro espectáculo para vosotros' (. . . if you could see, the audience would be a spectacle for you too).

Clearly this is a further type of immersion-effect; but another which the play contains, though noted by Doménech and others, has been strangely misunderstood. Near the end, the blind David waylays Valindin in the café. As Buero makes sure that David and we are aware, it is a moonless night and the surrounding square is empty and unlit. David puts out Valindin's only light, and produces total darkness. Having long since sympathised with David, we exult, in the minute or two before he kills Valindin, at his turning the tables on his sighted tormentor. But Buero cannot by blinding us make us share his hero's perceptions at this point; David can still 'see', through hearing, touch and smell, as we and Valindin cannot. We share instead Valindin's sudden sense of impotence, his stark terror at finding himself the victim now. We share *his* sharing, as never till now, the helplessness of the blind, without their compensatory strengths. David's strategem produces a further play-within-the-play; within the immersion-effect to which Buero is subjecting us, the clown is subjecting his sighted ringmaster to an immersion-effect.

Buero's next *première*, in 1963, was the final version of a play first written in 1949, *Aventura en lo gris*. Thereafter, his first play to reach the public was *La doble historia del Dr Valmy*, which was published in the U.S.A. in 1967 and performed at Chester in 1968, but not presented in Spain till 1976. These two plays, then, span almost his whole career; yet they have some features in common. Each is set in a timeless present, in Surelia, a small police-state somewhere in Europe, and portrays individuals pitted against the machinery of political repression. From our present point of view, each uses, in an original way, a familiar type of immersion-effect – the dream sequence. *Aventura en lo gris* concerns eight refugees who arrive at a hostel near the frontier. One proves to be Alejandro Goldmann, the head of Surelia's totalitarian government, now in flight; another, Silvano, a professor of philosophy whom he had persecuted for 'defeatism'. The two acts take place one night and the following morning; between them, the set remains the same but is transformed into a dream-landscape and strangely lit; the actors reappear in expressionistic costumes and make-up; and for some ten to fifteen minutes we witness an 'adventure in the greyness', enacted and supposedly experienced by all the characters except one. The exception is Goldmann, the man of action who cannot dream or make others dream, but who, while they are dreaming, acts. During it, in fact, a young mother is killed, and Silvano is later able to prove that Goldmann was the murderer. By then all but Silvano have probably forgotten the dream; but he sees such 'collective dreaming' as Man's only hope for the future. Buero has attempted to make the spectator share an unusual shared experience; but *as* an experience, rather than merely a symbolic concept, it is unconvincing.

The central story of *La doble historia del Dr Valmy* might seem to explain its title, for it concerns a husband and wife both treated by the same psychiatrist. Daniel Barnes, a member of Surelia's secret police, has tortured a political dissident to the point of (in effect) castrating him, and as a psychological reaction has himself become impotent. He is anxious to abandon his grisly trade, but proves unable to and is eventually killed by his distracted wife Mary. To enable us to share Mary's state of mind just before this climax, Buero has her tell Dr Valmy of a recent nightmare, which is then enacted; she, the psychiatrist and the spectator see Daniel and his mother apparently about to mutilate her baby son. Both Valmy and the audience are not merely told of but made to witness, with horrific immediacy, an incident which took place only in Mary's mind.

Yet the story within which this occurs is itself in a sense taking place in the mind of the psychiatrist. Valmy throughout is dictating an account of the case to a secretary, and we share his recollections – although on three occasions he takes part in them; indeed he moves freely between the roles of narrator, spectator and participant. Two other characters, however, function both within this frame and outside it. At the outset, a lady and gentleman appear in the auditorium to tell us that the events we are about to witness are untrue, or exaggerated, or anyway couldn't happen *here*. At the climax of the Barnes's story, too, the action is 'frozen'; the houselights go up and these two reappear to invite us once more to share their incredulity and 'keep smiling'. But Valmy has by now made clear to us that these are two other patients of his, whose story he had narrated previously, and indeed that 'the present history is not totally intelligible . . . unless it is related to the previous one, and perhaps fundamentally they form a single history' – so that this is the true sense of *la doble historia*. Now the couple are led away by a nurse, and Valmy, continuing his dictation, relates that on one occasion, when he was telling the Barnes's story in an asylum, the subjects of his previous account, who were voluntary patients there, interrupted to call him a liar, although as neighbours of the Barnes's they knew he was telling the truth. That incident, we realise, is itself being enacted; we ourselves are the fellow-patients who were invited to share their simple-minded self-deception. In so far as we have done so and have rejected the central story as merely a theatrical fiction, we are as sick as they. The blackouts in *En la ardiente oscuridad* and *El concierto de San Ovidio* were intended to make us all blind; the sudden 'luz total en la sala' here makes us all clearsighted – and insane.[27]

El tragaluz (1967) has interesting similarities with *Dr Valmy*, but no less interesting differences. Designated an 'experiment', it is introduced by a pair of anonymous Researchers, who appear repeatedly in the auditorium and address the audience as if they and it were beings of a future age, who have met to witness the reconstruction, by means of detectors and computers, of an episode which occurred in the late twentieth century, 'in Madrid, once the capital of a former nation called Spain'. This frame, which was not part of Buero's original conception but which he later described as fundamental, must have in part a distancing effect, inimical to illusion and likely to encourage a detached, rational attitude in the spectator; yet Buero's intention is also, and preponderantly, to involve us emotionally, to produce what he has called 'a kind of historical shock'.[28] He wants us to share the supposed perceptions and outlook of an audience of the future, but also to identify with the fictional persons of the drama 'proper', and so to realise that we will be, *are being* observed and judged by a sort of historical conscience. He makes one Researcher insist:

> Si no os habéis sentido en algún instante verdaderos seres del siglo xx pero observados y juzgados por una especie de conciencia futura; si no os habéis sentido en algún otro momento como seres de un futuro hecho ya presente, que juzgan, con rigor y piedad, a gentes muy antiguas y acaso iguales a vosotros, el experimento ha fracasado.

> (If you have not at some moment felt like true beings of the twentieth century, yet observed and judged by a sort of future conscience; if you have not felt at some other moment like beings of a future which has now become present who are judging, sternly but compassionately, people of long ago who were perhaps just like yourselves, the experiment has failed.)

The play within the frame, however, contains a number of similar effects, which Buero employs with a new degree of complexity and ambiguity. It concerns a family – Father, Mother and two sons, Vicente and Mario – who came to Madrid as refugees at the end of the Civil War and have since lived in a basement flat. Sounds and movement from the world outside reach them via a street-level skylight (in the 'fourth wall') and the shadows it throws. To the boys as they grew up this afforded an amusing guessing-game, and it continues to constitute an enigmatic play within the play (within the frame) which we share with them. At one point, for instance, Vicente wonders whether a conversation he (and we) heard through it in fact took place only in his imagination. At another, when a stranger peers in (as the spectator is doing), Mario not only is conscious of being observed but speaks of a sense of identification with the observer. To the Father, the skylight appears to be a train, for he is insane or apparently so. His abnormality, it is gradually (and in Ibsenish fashion) revealed, is the legacy of an incident on their way to the capital. Vicente, then twelve, boarded a train alone with all the family's provisions, including tinned milk for his two-year-old sister Elvira, and so caused her death. Still 'aboard the train', still prospering by making victims, he has left the flat, become a self-seeking publisher and forced his secretary Encarna to become his mistress – although Mario, who wants to marry her, learns this only late in the play. At last, however, the Father prevents him from 'returning to the train' by killing him. Story and symbol are reinforced by a sound effect to which the Researchers specifically refer:

> Lo utilizamos para expresar escondidas inquietudes que, a nuestro juicio, deben destacarse. Oiréis, pues, un tren; o sea, un pensamiento.

> (We use it to express hidden troublings of the spirit which in our judgement should be stressed. You will hear, therefore, a train; that is, a thought.)

We hear this train-effect on four occasions when the Father is on stage; clearly it suggests the presence in his mind of his delusion or recollection. But nothing in the dialogue or directions tells us whether or not he or any other character shares with us the sensation of hearing it. Other things we hear and see, however, are no less deliberately mysterious. The playing area includes a number of other locations, and two actions often proceed simultaneously; but at times we cannot tell, as the Researchers point out, whether a scene is taking place in the 'real life' of the play, or in the imagination of a character in another scene, or in both. For their detectors – like the omniscient narrator in 'old-fashioned' fiction – can supposedly recapture both outward actions and inward thoughts. Thus on two occasions when Vicente is in his office, but lost in thought, we witness scenes in the basement but cannot know whether these are occurring only in his mind, or in 'reality', or in both. Similarly, in an early scene Encarna is in his office, but abstracted; and we see a prostitute at a café; we perhaps conclude that this person exists only in Encarna's mind as an image of her own degradation, present or future. But later, when visiting the same café with Mario, she sees and reacts to the prostitute in person; and near the end the Researchers announce to us that this person is to be the subject of their next historical reconstruction.

Mito, the libretto for an opera which was never composed, was published in 1968. Again the action is set in a police-state threatened by internal unrest and foreign intervention; but the immediate setting is an opera-house, identifiable with the one in which we are sitting. *Our* auditorium, however, has become backstage, because beyond the stage a new one has supposedly been built, from which at the outset another, unseen audience is witnessing the last scene of an opera: *Don Quixote*. Buero's protagonist, Eloy, is an ageing baritone who once sang the title-role, and is himself a contemporary Don Quixote. Mankind, he believes, will be saved by visitors from Mars; the prop-girl Marta is their emissary, and the barber's basin used in the current production, as its flying-saucer shape suggests, is a detector they have planted. These space-fiction fantasies seem absurd; but by a series of equivocal immersion-effects they are shared with Eloy by the spectator and in varying degrees by other characters. In the first act, Eloy and his 'Sancho', Simón, (and we with them) hear the basin, when struck, emit a sequence of musical notes. When Simón has left, in what may be a dream – but may *not* – six visitors from Mars appear to Eloy and 'marry' him to Marta. Near the end of the act, his voice is strangely amplified, to the surprise of the other characters; but they (and we) are further mystified by the arrival of two more visitors, who appear this time to be malevolent Venusians. These prove, however, to be two unpleasant hoaxers, who have practised a deception on us all – another play within the play – and who proceed to play a further Clavileño-type trick on Simón and Eloy. The latter, the last to be undeceived and scorned by all, sees his own audience-reaction (which we partly share) as symptomatic of Mankind's inability to distinguish fiction from fact. He broods on Man's naive self-deception, as 'Brechtian' images of atrocity are projected on a screen – images, we presume, which are passing through his mind and are visible to us, but to no other character. Near despair, he seems to fall asleep; we hear, with him, briefly, the consoling voices of his Martians and of Marta. Finally he makes an heroic attempt to save a fugitive dissident, and is killed; his body is carried off, but the basin is left on stage. Since act 1 it has given out when struck only a dull metallic sound; but now, and until the end of the opera, both before and after Marta removes it so that a new performance of *Don Quixote* may begin, the mysterious sequence of notes rings out again. It may be that, as in *La señal que se espera*, only we can hear this music; but several characters consider the basin with different degrees of wonderment. We cannot tell what each hears, just as we cannot be sure how seriously to take Eloy's apparent delusions. As in *El tragaluz*, Buero has used immersion-effects with deliberate and suggestive ambiguity.

Immersion-effects, we have been finding, have engaged Buero's interest throughout his career. But in the four plays which have appeared in the seventies their importance is even more apparent. Their duration has been increased, to extend to a high proportion of the playing-time. They have been shared exclusively, with tiny exceptions, by a single character and ourselves. When that character is on stage, we are denied those normal perceptions which he is denied, by deafness, blindness or mental unbalance, but we are given, in more than ample compensation, as he is given – by a phenomenally creative imagination or perceptive insight – a variety of 'alternative' sense-impressions of startling theatricality.

In *El sueño de la razón* (1970), the character is Goya. The play, set in December 1823, is an interpretation of the situation and state of mind which led him to petition the tyrannical Ferdinand VII for permission to leave Spain for France. The main setting is the Quinta del Sordo, a house across the Manzanares from the royal palace in Madrid which the 76-year-old artist was then inhabiting and decorating with his bizarre Black Paintings. Constantly changing projections of these provide the play's most important décor, and near its end, in a nightmare like the dreams in earlier plays, the stage is peopled by tormenting monsters from Goya's fantastic imagination, although these are soon replaced in 'real life' by the royalist soliders who are sent by Ferdinand to ransack the house and rape Goya's mistress Doña Leocadia. We are induced, therefore, to share Goya's grotesque visual perceptions of the world about him. But we are also forced to share, for the sixty per cent of the playing-time when Goya is on stage, the aural perceptions of a man who has been stone-deaf for over thirty years. We hear, that is, nothing which would normally be audible. A bell is shaken, a table thumped, soundlessly. The other characters are given lines to mouth but not to speak aloud; with Goya, we can only guess what they are saying. On the other hand we do hear, because he hears, a wide range of sounds not normally audible. Frequently the other actors are made to say what he imagines is being said, although in some cases they clearly *must* have been saying something different; thus a conversation between Leocadia and his daughter-in-law Doña Gumersinda becomes, hilariously, an altercation between a cackling hen and a braying donkey. Other Goyaesque noises, however, abound: the shrieks of owls, the howling of a dog, and especially the mewing of cats. More mysteriously, we hear repeatedly a whirring as of enormous wings, which may suggest on the one hand huge bats or predatory birds, or on the other the bird-men who for Goya (following Buero's inter-pretation of certain late works) represent possible saviours of mankind.[29] Repeatedly, too, we hear the voice of Mariquita, the daughter whom Goya can never expect to see again, as well as unidentified male and female voices and at times Goya's own disembodied voice, speaking enigmatic phrases he used as captions to late engravings. At moments of tension throughout, moreover, we hear, as Goya (but no other character) hears, a succession of dull thuds: his heartbeats. They vary in intensity and rapidity with the stress imposed by his situation, but his essential helplessness in the face of the odious ruler whose determination to crush him provides the play's tenuous plot. As it opens, we see the king, who is embroidering, with his creature Calomarde, who hands him an intercepted letter. He rises and looks through a telescope – towards us – at the Quinta del Sordo, then returns to his embroidery, outwardly calm; but he is disturbed by sounds which only he (and we) can hear, identical to those which later will represent Goya's quaking heartbeats. Clearly this is another immersion-effect, and one of several devices by which Buero compares and contrasts the painter and the embroiderer. Immediately, for instance, the king's place on stage is taken, after a blackout, by the ageing Goya; he too is looking through a telescope – towards us – but at the royal palace. We have moved through No Man's Land to near the camp of Ferdinand's defenceless but less fearful opponent. Near the play's end a disembodied voice asks: 'Who makes us fear?', and Goya can reply: 'He who has died of fear. A great fear in my belly. I am defeated. But he was defeated already.'

The main function of the immersion-effects in this play, however, is to reinforce the affinities between Goya and ourselves. He lives, he tells his friend Arrieta, 'in another world'; all those around him seem intangible ghosts, beyond the reach of his love. But this strangeness, he says, must signify something more. Arrieta agrees; he writes 'All deaf' – and Goya understands. His incapacity to make contact is only an aspect of the existen-tial isolation of all mankind. By Buero's technical innovations we are trans-ported to 'the island of his deafness', only to recognise there an alienation which we share with him and with all men.[30]

Llegada de los dioses (1971) represents a parallel development in the same line of experimentation.[31] Its blind protagonist – Buero's third – is a young

abstract painter, Julio, who has returned from Paris, with his girl-friend
Verónica, to the idyllic island home of his father Felipe, who is a water-
colourist, competent but shallow. Julio's blindness is recent, and psychological rather than organic; the play investigates its cause, but inconclusively. It
may be related to his having discovered that Felipe tortured prisoners during
World War II, or to a crisis of confidence in his own ability after the failure of
a recent exhibition and the success of one by his father, or to both. For some
seventy per cent of the playing-time, when he is on stage, we hear normally
but see what Julio sees or imagines. This at times is total darkness; by
contrast, for brief but increasingly longer periods he enjoys normal vision,
although for a long time he conceals this from the other characters (so that
we alone share the secret), and by the end these periods, and the likelihood of
a cure which they portended, seem to have gone for ever. For the rest, he
(and we) see fantastic images of two types. On the one hand, ironically and
for his own perverse amusement, he 'continues to paint', imagines his father's
bourgeois friends as ridiculous caricatures whose bland conversations are
accompanied by absurdly discrepant antics – performed by the actors with
the aid of grotesque masks or make-up. On the other hand, he is haunted by
illusions which though they too must emanate from his own psyche seem to
impose themselves upon him. Fears of sexual as well as artistic inferiority to
his father conjure up amorous behaviour between Felipe and Veronica
which is belied by their dialogue and the real situation, and other involuntary images include the whirling movements of a mobile, the crazing of
cracks which appears on the walls of the house, and the lurid, stormy
skyscapes we see beyond. These hint at a sombre, apocalyptic world-view;
but some are more directly horrific and menacing. At four points Julio is
confronted by the horribly mutilated spectre of a man whom, he has learnt,
his father caused to be tortured and blinded. In act I, his half-sister Nuria
serves him a glass she has filled with blood from her own arm; act II, the
trampolin-like toy which Felipe has bought her is seen as a coffin in which she
is carried off – prophetically, for she is to detonate an unexploded bomb left
behind after the war. After her death, her disfigured body appears beside
that of the tortured man, who proceeds to sink a dagger slowly into her
father's heart. Felipe dies of a heart-attack, in response presumably to the
death of his daughter and the behaviour of his son, or alternatively, as these
apparitions imply, by way of retribution for his atrocities. Blinded, Julio has
become involuntarily clairvoyant; sharing his blindness and his visions, we
share his suffering and his uncertain insights.[32]

La fundación (1974) represents a further advance in the exploitation of
immersion-effects. As the play opens, Tomás, a young writer, is gently
tidying a room, listening to music and contemplating, through a window, a
magnificent sunlit landscape. He talks to a companion who is ill in bed; he is
visited by his girl-friend Berta. The room belongs, it seems, to a well-

endowed Foundation for research in the arts and sciences. It has to accom-modate six, for the Foundation, we hear, it still under construction; but it is comfortably furnished, with armchairs, a refrigerator, a television set, a telephone, shelves laden with books and ornaments, elegant lamp-shades. . . . When Tomás's other room-mates appear, however, some of their words and actions seem inexplicable, and the furnishings begin to undergo a process of curious and gradual change. Not until the fourth and final scene is this change complete and the mystery fully explained. The 'ill' companion had been dead for six days; Berta – though she has reappeared three times – was never present. The room is now seen by Tomás and by us for what in reality it is: a bare, squalid prison cell. He and his companions are political dissidents who have been imprisoned and condemned to death because he, under torture, 'broke' and betrayed their secrets. To escape this reality, his mind has taken refuge in a schizophrenic delusion: the Foundation. During the few days covered by the play he recovers normal perceptions, though his return to normality is impeded by the fact that his cellmates, and especially their leader Asel, suspect that he may now be shamming insanity and continuing to betray them. By the end, another prisoner has been taken away to execution; Asel has committed suicide rather than risk 'breaking'; and the real informer has been killed. Tomás, now genuinely shamming, is taken off with the other survivor, perhaps to be executed. But there is a faint hope, thanks to Asel's cautious planning, that they may escape.

Tomás is on stage from start to finish. We are offered throughout no alternative to his perceptions, both visual and aural, and these are mostly abnormal. Like him, we are not at first aware of our abnormality but rather totally deceived; like him, we are only slowly enabled to comprehend the situation and replace false percepts with true, especially since some are illusions – misapprehensions of real phenomena – and others fantastic delu-sions. The fact that many of his words and actions, though natural and understandable to us, seem strange or suspicious to the other characters, intensifies both our involvement in the mystery and our identification with him. The stage picture, too, is a fundamental part of the process; for although in several of Buero's plays, from *Historia de una escalera* to *El tragaluz,* the setting is a permanent and potent visual metaphor, the ingenious set prescribed for *La fundación,* by virtue of its constant and unpredictable modifications, not only maintains our curiosity but invites us, with the protagonist, to absorb a message, to learn a lesson which is both socio-political and ontological. If he escapes, the 'free world' outside will prove to be another illusory 'Foundation', which he must recognise and seek to escape from . . . to another 'Foundation' . . . But ultimately he *may* reach that sunlit landscape which was the last of his fantasies to fade because in one sense it was real – an equivalent, as a stage-effect and as a symbol, of Leticia's

handsome Riquet or Irene's celestial skyway. This lesson Asel has learnt
from a life lived in and out of 'Foundations'; Tomás, and we perhaps with
him, has learnt it by being cured of a delusion. But for many people that
delusion persists. As Tomás and his lone companion leave, Buero's set-
changes are rapidly reversed, and as the curtain falls new occupants are
being invited to enter. We see again what they will presumably see, a
comfortable 'Foundation'; but we may choose to see what Tomás came to
see, and refuse to submit to this renewal of the immersion-effect.

Similarly, in *La detonación* (1977), a single immersion-effect persists almost
throughout. Again we are induced to enter a brilliant but distracted mind,
that of the satirist Mariano José de Larra, who committed suicide at the age
of twenty-seven on 13 February 1837. Described, like *Las meninas*, as a
fantasy, the play is partly history, partly imaginative interpretation. Its
time-span is at once a decade and a mere five minutes; for *La detonación*
affords a complex but intensely concentrated chronicle of Larra's life and
times, but this is presented as his turbulent 'stream of consciousness' immediately before – and by way of explanation of – his self-destruction. At the
outset, he is addressed by his servant Pedro and his daughter Adelita, who
continues to call to him from off stage throughout; but whereas their speech
is exaggeratedly slow, his is natural; we adjust therefore, to the tempo of a
mind which is feverishly racing and yet to us, as to its possessor, seems
normal. We share with him a sequence of recollections and imaginings,
mostly but not wholly in chronological order. Some are nightmarish dreams
and fantasies of the past which against his will he re-experiences in the
present. Some his servant, who acts as an apparently autonomous commen-
tator, seems to insist on his recalling; yet his own psyche is ultimately in
control and is re-enacting them before him. As well as author and protagonist, creating and living his last drama, he is 'the audience of his own
theatre', and we are his fellow-spectators. Almost all the other characters,
moreover, wear masks which fall as the satirist 'sees through' them, so that
with him we perceive both façade and true face, with an especially intense
effect when his mistress, deserting him, unmasks to reveal the features of his
deserted wife. Only in a brief but (says Buero) 'absolutely necessary' epilogue, after the explosion which destroys Larra's explosive personality, do
we stand aside as Pedro pronounces the author's comment. Pedro is the
protagonist's 'conscience', his maturer and shrewder though less visionary
friend, a symbol of the common man and the voice of history; he recalls many
of Buero's secondary characters. Larra, with whom Buero himself identifies
as clearly as with any of his protagonists, was a progressive, patriotic writer
determined to tell the truth as he saw it but impelled by a repressive
censorship to prudence, to *posibilismo*. Sadly, he never learned that one needs
an inexhaustible capacity to endure; and yet . . .

Aquella detonación que casi no oí, no se borra. . . . ¡Y se tiene que oír, y oír, aunque pasen los años! . . . ¡Como un trueno . . . que nos despierte!

(That explosion I scarcely heard never dies away. . . . And it must be heard, and heard again, though the years pass by. . . . Like a thunderclap . . . to awaken us!)

To Buero's Larra – and to Buero – as to Willy Loman, 'attention must be finally paid'.

It is difficult to predict, as Doménech wrote, what influence Buero's immersion-effects will have.[33] It could prove, but it seems unlikely, that he has essentially exhausted their usefulness, to himself and other dramatists, in the stimulation of audience involvement. Francisco Ruiz Ramón has warned that by exploiting them as single-mindedly as he has since *El sueño de la razón* he may run the risk of producing an imbalance between the form and content of his plays and so of restricting his own development.[34] But this fear was expressed before the appearance of *La detonación*, which does not bear it out; and it is diminished, surely, if we accept that the deployment of this and analogous devices has been central and productive throughout Buero's career as a dramatist – as the present study has been concerned to demonstrate.[35]

NOTES

1. R. Doménech, *El teatro de Buero Vallejo* (Madrid: Gredos, 1973), esp. pp. 49–51.
2. The dates in brackets are those of first performances; see esp. Doménech, *El teatro de Buero Vallejo*, pp. 302–9.
3. E.g. in an interview with José Monleón, *Primer Acto*, 167 (April 1974), 13.
4. Cf. 'Siempre intenté hacer obras que en el texto mismo ya revelaban su pretensión de ser escenificaciones y no simplemente textos dramáticos . . . yo he sido un autor que siempre he acotado muchísimo, hasta la saciedad, porque siempre vi el teatro en función de su representación. . . . Y yo entiendo que el autor dramático debe ser un hombre de teatro todo lo completo que pueda, pero creador, en virtud de ello mismo, de textos a los cuales no hay que retocar mucho, porque está casi todo previsto en ellos.' (I have always tried to write not merely dramatic texts but works which revealed in the text itself their aspiration to be staged . . . I have been an author who has always given a very great number, even an excess, of stage directions, because I have always seen theatre in terms of its performance. . . . And I conceive that the playwright should be as complete a man of the theatre as he can, but for that very reason should produce texts which do not need much retouching, because almost everything has been foreseen in them.) *Ibid.*, p. 10. It is sad to record, nevertheless, and though Buero's characteristic loyalty to his interpreters precludes him from admitting it, that by reason of the backwardness of dramatic practice in Spain his works have rarely enjoyed there the standard of presentation they deserve.
5. Comments like the following are characteristic: '*Hoy es fiesta* se desarrolla en construcción cerrada y atenida prácticamente a las tres unidades, buscando en ella dificultades que siempre me ha agradado idear y vencer, si podía. En

aquella, ya lejana, *Historia de una escalera*, me propuse resolver la acción en lugar de paso tan poco apto, al parecer, para ello y en absoluto de puertas afuera; dificultades similares he buscado en otras obras mías. Para situar la acción de *Hoy es fiesta* pensé en un conjunto de azoteas: como problema escénico, algo digno de ser abordado. Nunca he negado las posibilidades y excelencias de una construcción abierta, pero creía y sigo creyendo, que el autor debe dominar su oficio y que el ejercicio de la técnica cerrada es la única manera de dominarlo. Ninguna garantía mayor que ésa de su honestidad profesional, sobre todo cuando aún es novel.' (*Hoy es fiesta* develops within a closed structure, in accordance practically with the three unities, in quest of difficulties which I have always liked to create and overcome, if I could. Way back in *Historia de una escalera* I proposed to make the action take place and be resolved in a thoroughfare apparently quite unsuitable for the purpose, and completely 'out-of-doors'; I have sought out similar difficulties in other works of mine. As a setting for the action of *Hoy es fiesta*, I thought of a series of flat roofs; as a problem of staging, something worth attempting. I have never denied the possibilities and advantages of an open structure, but I believed and still do that the author should be master of his craft, and that to employ the closed technique is the only means of mastering it. There is no better guarantee of his professional integrity, especially when he is still a beginner.) *Negro sobre blanco*, 12 (Buenos Aires, April 1960), 1–2.

6. R. L. Nicholas, 'The Tragic Stages of Antonio Buero Vallejo', *Estudios de Hispanófila*, 23 (Department of Romance Languages, University of North Carolina, 1972), 14.

7. Doménech, *El teatro de Buero Vallejo*, p. 49.

8. Buero's position was most fully set out in his article 'A propósito de Brecht', *Insula*, 200–1 (July–August 1963), 1 and 14. See also esp. Emilio F. Bejel, 'Catarsis y distanciación en Buero Vallejo', *Hispanófila*, 48 (May 1973), 37–45. On Valle-Inclán, see Buero's study of 1966: 'De rodillas, en pie, en el aire', republished in *Tres maestros ante el público* (Madrid: Alianza Editorial, 1973).

9. See for instance Nicholas, 'The Tragic Stages', pp. 123–8; *Tres maestros*, pp. 16–27.

10. *Ibid.*; see also an interview in *Primer Acto*, 138 (November 1971), 38.

11. Writing of the tragedies of Lorca, for instance, he has said: 'Nuestra razón nos obliga a comprender que el modo de influir la obra de arte en el hombre no es sólo racional, y que su directa llamada a nuestros fondos más oscuros es, por lo menos, tan importante como su apelación al raciocinio.' (Our reason compels us to realise that the manner in which man is influenced by the work of art is not only rational, and that its direct call to our darkest depths is as least as important as its appeal to ratiocination.) And of his own: 'Hallar nuevas maneras de englobar al público en el espectáculo fue una de mis más tempranas preocupaciones y ha inquietado varias de mis obras.' (Finding new ways to include the audience within the spectacle was one of my earliest concerns and has been a preoccupation in several of my works.) *Tres maestros*, pp. 149, 19. Nicholas oversimplifies but is essentially correct when he states ('The Tragic Stages', p. 119): 'Regardless of the nature of his technical experimentation, each new production seeks to provoke in the audience an Aristotelian identification with

the various characters and their problems. In fact, the playwright's technical innovations are always calculated especially to evoke maximum empathy.'

12. F. Ruiz Ramón, *Historia del teatro español, 2: Siglo XX* (third edition, Madrid: Cátedra, 1977), p. 351. Cf. Buero's study 'Muñiz', in Carlos Muñiz, *Teatro* (Madrid: Taurus, 1963), pp. 53–70.

13. See esp. his study 'La tragedia', in G. Díaz-Plaja, *El Teatro: Enciclopedia del Arte Escénico* (Barcelona, 1958), pp. 63–87, and *Tres maestros*, pp. 133–44. Cf. K. Schwartz, 'Buero Vallejo and the Concept of Tragedy', *Hispania,* LI (1968), 817–24.

14. He reminds us, implicitly, for instance, that since 1771 the blind have been educated (*El concierto de San Ovidio*), that since 1823 the aeroplane has been invented (*El sueño de la razón*); similarly, he is clearly convinced that in the next few centuries mankind will recognise, rightly, 'the infinite importance of the particular case' (*El tragaluz*).

15. E.g. Doménech', *El teatro de Buero Vallejo*, pp. 66–9.

16. *Primer Acto,* 90 (November 1967), 12.

17. Cf. Silverio and Daniela in act III of *Hoy es fiesta,* or David and his companions in act I of *El concierto de San Ovidio.*

18. See Buero's own comments on *El tragaluz, Primer Acto,* 90 (November 1967), 12, and *Llegada de los dioses, Primer Acto,* 138 (November 1971), 37. A. C. Isasi Angulo, 'Hacia una nueva interpretación del teatro de Antonio Buero Vallejo', *Iberoromania,* 2 (1975), 131, writes, similarly: '*La fundación* es una variación de un tema caro a Buero: la realidad sólo es entrevista en toda su complejidad por personas deformadas física – o como en este caso – psíquicamente.' (*La fundación* is a variation on a theme dear to Buero; truth is only glimpsed in all its complexity by people who are physically – or, as in this case, mentally – abnormal.) Cf. Lucien Goldmann on Tiresias and Oedipus: 'Their physical blindness is an expression of the separation from the real world which inevitably accompanies a knowledge of the truth.' *The Hidden God,* trans. Philip Thody (London: Routledge & Kegan Paul, 1964), p. 44.

19. On his use of blindness, for instance, Buero has written: 'La ceguera es una limitación del hombre, algo que se opone a su libre desarrollo. Representa por ello, de modo muy claro, el fondo de cualquier problema dramático o trágico que es siempre . . . el de la lucha del hombre, con sus limitaciones, por la libertad.' (Blindness is a limitation of man, something which opposes his free development. For that reason it represents, in a very clear way, the basis of any dramatic or tragic problem, which is always . . . the problem of man's struggle, with his limitations, for freedom.) 'La ceguera en mi teatro', *La Carreta,* 12 (September 1963), 5.

20. Doménech, *El teatro de Buero Vallejo,* p. 54.

21. See Nicholas, 'The Tragic Stages', pp. 125–6.

22. From an interview with A.C. Isasi Angulo published in 1972 and reprinted in his *Diálogos del teatro español de la postguerra* (Madrid: Ayuso, 1974), p. 72.

23. Marion P. Holt, *The Contemporary Spanish Theater (1949–1972)* (New York: Twayne, 1975), p. 112.

24. *Tres maestros,* p. 41. See also an interview Buero gave in 1958, as quoted with comment by Nicholas, 'The Tragic Stages', pp. 54–5, n. 102.

25. Previous figures of this type include Christ *(Las palabras)*, Euriclea *(Tejedora)*, Oriana *(Casi)*, Doña Nieves *(Hoy)*.

26. 'Ibsen y Ehrlich', *Informaciones*, 4 June 1953.

27. This device was perhaps unconsciously inspired by Pirandello's *Ciascuno a suo modo*, a play Buero has long admired (see Nicholas, 'The Tragic Stages', pp. 76, 123; *Tres maestros*, pp. 18–22). At the Madrid performances in 1976 the two characters appeared at the interval in the foyer and provoked arguments with members of the audience; this seems perilously close to the 'physical' techniques of which Buero disapproves, but illustrates his acceptance that their carefully calculated use can be productive.

28. 'Es al público de nuestro tiempo . . . al que trato de sobrecoger sirviéndome de esos investigadores; y al emplear la palabra "sobrecoger" . . . quiero indicar también que no estoy intentando un efecto "brechtiano"; pues si los investigadores aclaran racionalmente algunas cosas, también tienen para mí una función, incluso superior a la de "aclarar racionalmente", emotiva y en este sentido no del todo acorde con la ortodoxia de Brecht. . . . Es, por lo tanto, esencial para mí el que se produzca una especie de sobrecogimiento histórico . . .' (It is the audience of our own day . . . which I am trying to shock by the use of those Researchers; and in using the word 'shock' . . . I mean to indicate too that I am not attempting a 'Brechtian' effect; for if the Researchers rationally clarify some things, they have also for me a function, superior even to that of 'rational clarification', which is emotive, and in this sense not wholly in accord with Brechtian orthodoxy. . . . For me it is essential, therefore, that a kind of historical shock should be produced.), etc. *Primer Acto*, 90 (November 1967), 10.

29. Compare the 'angels' seen by Silvano in *Aventura en lo gris* and Eloy's visitors from Mars in *Mito*.

30. In the lecture mentioned above (see note 21), Buero 'imagined' a play with a deaf protagonist whose audience was made to participate in his deafness in this way; but in *El sueño de la razón* the complementary visual participation I have mentioned should not be forgotten; we are 'led by the multimedia aspects of a performance into the very mind of the agonizing Goya'. Holt, *The Contemporary Spanish Theater*, p. 125.

31. 'Como en *El sueño de la razón*, pretendo nuevamente una interiorización del público en el drama mediante una técnica similar: cegar al público, pero haciéndoles ver las imaginaciones del protagonista, de la misma manera que en *El sueño* lo ensordecía, pero haciéndole oír las fantasías del protagonista.' (As in *El sueño de la razón*, I am attempting once more an involvement of the audience in the drama by means of a similar technique; making the audience blind, but forcing it to see the protagonist's imaginings, just as in *El sueño* I made it deaf, but forced it to hear the protagonist's fantasies.) *Primer Acto*, 138 (November 1971), 28.

32. As in *El sueño*, we enter the abnormal, private world of the painter-protagonist. The experience is very different, perhaps because those protagonists are different not only in their characters and circumstances but in what they represent. Goya is an historical personality whose tragedy, remoter from us, has more abstract implications. Julio is more specifically representative for Buero of many of the younger generation today; in some ways as deficient, as bourgeois, as guilty as

their parents, but capable *perhaps* (cf. esp. *Historia de una escalera, Las cartas boca abajo*), of confronting and correcting the errors of the past.

33. Doménech, *El teatro de Buero Vallejo*, p. 51.
34. F. Ruiz Ramón, *Historia del teatro español*, pp. 383–4.
35. For assistance in the preparation of this study, I must express my gratitude especially to my former colleague Derek Gagen, but also to Dr Philip Deacon, to Professor Patricia O'Connor, who generously supplied a copy of *La detonación* before its publication in *Estreno* (spring 1978), and to Antonio Buero Vallejo, for years now an admired and valued friend.

Word and image: aspects of mimesis in contemporary British theatre

MICHAEL ANDERSON

Bill. Oo's layin' ten bob next Saturday?
Ron. No thanks.
Bill. Come on, won't bet on yoor own side?
Lorry. I'll believe it when I see it. They thrashed us three times in the last four years.
Ron. We ent got no good bowlers. That's where we fall down.
Bill. We ent never 'ad a battin' side like we got this year afore. I reckon we could pull it off.
Joe. That's all a question of luck, anyroad.
Ron. Cricket ent luck. That's strength and skill and guts.[1]

[*Enter* Gary.]
Kev. Unlucky son, unlucky. Know what you did wrong?
Gary. Swung too hard.
Kev. You swung too hard.
Gary. Still, sixty-two ain't bad.
Kev. O, it isn't bad. I'll grant you that. In fact, a lot of people'd say it was very good. I mean, Bondy, put it this way, Bondy would have been bloody delighted to have got sixty-two. The only thing is . . .
Gary. What?
Kev. Well, it was all – look, you don't mind me giving you an analytical breakdown of where you went wrong, do you?
Gary. Well –
Kev. Frankly, your innings – well, it was distinctly lacking in, how shall I put it? Artistry . . .
Gary. Bullshit.[2]

Critics (especially academic ones), theorists and others with a professional interest in pronouncing upon the drama are often doubtful about embarking on a discussion of language in the theatre, for fear of being confused with or, worse, taunted by that species of *frère ennemi*, the critic of English literature. No actor or director can afford to imitate them in this: language is of the essence of theatre and, as will be argued later, attempts to displace it result in a coarsening of the dramatic effect and our response to it. The passages quoted above come from plays by two dramatists who cannot be accused of neglecting the non-verbal elements of drama. Cricket is the subject in both instances, and the way in which the game is linked to the main theme of the two plays can tell us something about their respective authors; we do not need the entire text of either play before us to see that very different linguistic means are at work. Although apparently much simpler, the first passage, from Edward Bond's *The Pope's Wedding*, is the more carefully put together. Many authors would have succumbed to the temptation to introduce a more articulate figure into the group: the terseness here is deliberate and disciplined. There is a careful ear for the non-literary quirks and rhythms of country speech; the characters are as thrifty with their language as physical labourers are with their actions. One of Bond's abilities, hinted at rather than fully revealed here, is to suggest the possession of great physical skills by characters minimally equipped with language (consider how Fred, almost monosyllabically, establishes his superiority over Len in the fishing scene of *Saved*);[3] and this, despite opinions to the contrary, must be described as a triumph of language in the theatre. The art in the first passage is of the kind concealing art, though we may concede that, in the last line quoted, Bond has not escaped a hint of old-fashioned rhetoric – 'strength and skill and guts' – which is avoided in the best of his later writing.

The second extract, from 'Getaway', the third part of Barrie Keeffe's *Gimme Shelter*, is more loosely written. It is wordier, but it communicates a good deal less: it is instructive to read the Bond passage, asking oneself how much one can learn about the opposing teams. Keeffe's dialogue is fluid, amusing and psychologically accurate (Kev's slow build-up to the criticism of his friend is partly for effect, and partly for fear of the response he knows it will get; and the phrase 'analytical breakdown' slips appropriately from the mouth of the trainee manager in an insurance company); nevertheless it takes time enough to make its simple contrast between the man of words and the man of action, and the joke continues in much the same vein for a further page of dialogue. In the passage quoted, everything depends on the correct delivery of that key word 'artistry': in Bond, there is no such simple climax, and all that spare, compressed speech must be handled with equal care and conviction by the actors.

Keeffe's trio of short plays undoubtedly forms a powerful piece of theatre, even if it is not easy to explain precisely why the trilogy makes the impact that it does. Partly, I suppose, it is the unusual form: only in the third of the plays do the two main characters meet, so that with a shock we realise that the up-and-coming young executive with his receding socialist ideals has struck the same pact with society as the institutionalised, anonymous Kid whose brief and violent protest against authority ended, inevitably, in defeat. The theme, although its general outlines are not unfamiliar to contemporary theatregoers, is distinctive in that it is haunted by a sharp and particular sense of what is new in the 1970s – the soul-destroying prospect of unemployment for some and radicalism in retreat for others. Visually, the play leaves its mark: there is the powerful spectacle of the Kid, a lighted cigarette poised over the open petrol tank of his motorbike, responding to the petty tyrants of his school with the ultimate logic of violence and, no less impressively, the moment in the final play when the blood from a cut finger causes old memories to stir in a Kid apparently cured of his violent tendencies, rendered a harmless and useful member of society (*Gimme Shelter*, pp. 90-1).

In an important way, *Gimme Shelter* is about the powerlessness of words: there is a crushing weight of conformity against which the glib tongue of Kev and the Kid's groping arguments are equally defenceless. Kev's repartee is witty and in effective contrast to his determination when, having been promoted, he is invited to play for the company. But the Kid's dialogue is handled less successfully. In scene i of 'Gotcha' Ton, the threatened schoolmaster, reminds him of the ultimate consequences of his action and the Kid, lighting a cigarette '*with hypnotising slowness*', launches into his reply:

> What after today for me . . . anyhow . . . I've been here, getting prepared for today for . . . five years. The great day. Stepping out into the wide world, an' that. One of . . . how many kids here? Twelve hundred, eh. What's going to happen to this one here – [*He points at himself.*] – after today? Hmmm? Mmmm? Fifty years of working life is . . . all spread out in front of me . . . they say when you drown, in the last seconds before you go under, the whole of your life passes before your eyes. . . . Well, this morning as we all stood there in the assembly[. . .] well, me life didn't pass in front of me eyes . . . but me future did. A great mist of nothing . . . (pp. 49-50)

Here Keeffe has let out all the stops. There is the subtle reinterpretation of Ton's demand; there is irony ('the great day'); there are rhetorical questions; and the final lines (from 'they say when you drown') are crammed with imagery. For all the Pinteresque dots, it is a highly coherent speech – so much so that the intensity of the dramatic situation ebbs away. Much better is this exchange in 'Getaway':

> *Kid.* Look, I don't wanna talk about it. It's over. Something that happened. I've served me time, repaid me debt to society and all that, right. I've started again. School, waste of bleeding time. Feltham though, showed me how to . . . give me a trade. [. . .] Got it made now. When I left, the governor, he said to me: 'You've achieved two things. Learned a trade. Gardener. And you've found respect in yourself.' [*Slight Pause*] I've got respect in meself now.
> *Kev.* For Christ's sake. You had more respect in your little toenail the day you –
> *Kid* [*leaps out of the chair*]. Shut up! Don't talk about it! (pp. 92-3)

The Kid finds pathetic comfort in repeating the phrases that do not belong to him ('repaid me debt to society'; 'got respect in meself'); and yet, ironically, there is a kind of passive dignity in the dulled Kid that we miss in Kev, the would-be revolutionary with one foot on the executive ladder. Not having gone so far either in rebellion or defeat he 'don't understand', as the

Kid puts it (p. 93). In this scene Keeffe has made his dialogue much more expressive and dramatically effective.

Returning to our comparison of Keeffe with the early Bond, we can now extend it. Instead of contrasting the articulate with the inarticulate and at times straining the dramatic structure to ensure that each side has its spokesman, Bond in *The Pope's Wedding* and *Saved* shows us a world without a *raisonneur*. In 'Gotcha' the School Head becomes one of the Kid's hostages: he is, rather predictably, a caricature of the bewildered liberal administrator: 'I presume this entire drama is some obscure attempt to draw attention to yourself ' (p. 67). Equally predictably, he shows which side he is really on at the end when the Kid is overcome. But at least he is there, the platitudinous representative of public values, however shopsoiled they may be. One of the moral shocks of *Saved*, aside from the physical violence, comes from the realisation that no one protests. After the death of the child one longs to hear a word, whether of conscious anger or remorse or even of reasoned exculpation: but it never comes. There is no easy identification that we can make with a conventional morality nor, just as significantly, is there any figure to whom we can feel superior – no harrassed official hopelessly out of his depth, no puzzled liberal trying to make sense of it all. That is what makes the play so bleak: the wry joke and the painful readjustment to life which conclude *Gimme Shelter* are disallowed in *Saved* and this could be shown to be implicit in the contrasting use of language by the two dramatists.

The language of drama can be analysed and evaluated without a blurring of the distinction between literature and drama, although there is bound to be some shared ground. The subject has been getting some attention recently. Gareth Lloyd Evans and Andrew Kennedy both begin their books[4] with Shaw and end with contemporary dramatists and both, in their different ways, are concerned to assert that what makes one dramatist different from another is, as much as anything, his approach to language. John Russell Brown's *Theatre Language* (London: Allen Lane/The Penguin Press, 1972) is more exclusively concerned with four contemporary dramatists and especially Pinter, the critics' favourite; and I quote from the opening chapter of John Elsom's survey *Post-War British Theatre* (London: Routledge & Kegan Paul, 1976):

> W. H. Auden once remarked that the prime duty of a poet was 'to maintain the purity of the language'. My instinct (hunch or prejudice – as you will) tells me that a similar duty rests on the shoulders of those who belong, even indirectly, like critics, to the theatrical profession. Their first task is to maintain the purity of the theatrical language.   (p. 1)

Two immediate comments are necessary. The first is, of course, that 'language' has almost as many meanings as critics using the word: it runs the full range from an equivalent of Aristotle's *lexis* – verbal expression as one of the six separate and necessary components of tragic drama – to a term covering every means of communication open to a theatre artist. Paraphrasing Cocteau, we may make a distinction between language in the theatre and language *of* the theatre. But the matter is not simple: much of the new 'language' of the theatre resides in the words put into the mouths of characters on the stage. Indeed, John Russell Brown's study, which is the most thoroughgoing attempt to explore the whole range of the dramatist's weaponry, opens with a detailed examination of Pinter's dialogue (admittedly on the premise that what is said reveals by concealing) and follows on logically from his earlier article 'Dialogue in Pinter and Others'.[5]

Second, it soon becomes obvious that this recent concern with language is, like Pinter's dialogue, concealing its own anxious sub-text: for all that we may speak of a continuing dramatic revival from the 1950s, there is a deep-rooted feeling among critics that all is not well. Arnold P. Hinchliffe opens his survey of recent English dramatists with a quotation from Kenneth Tynan: 'From a critic's point of view, the history of twentieth-century drama is the history of a collapsing vocabulary.'[6] 'The drama – the serious drama more than the trivial –' Graham Hough has written, 'is receding from literature towards a form where gesture, action and inarticulate half-utterance takes the place of self-subsistent dialogue';[7] and a simple statement of fact can soon become a value-judgement. Gareth Lloyd Evans is quick to sound the alarm: verbal drama, he declares, is 'in serious danger of being relegated to a minor position'; never before today 'has there been so much apparent evidence that verbal drama . . . is in jeopardy'.[8] Up to a point he is right: for every critic exploring language in the theatre there seem to be two or three asserting and even celebrating the overthrow of language.

The Edinburgh Festival of 1963 witnessed Britain's introduction to the Happening, in a carefully-planned disruption of the last day of a conference on the drama:

> Gradually one became aware of the low, throbbing sound of an organ and an electronic tape feeding back carefully edited excerpts from the week's discussions. Then a nude on a trolley was pulled across the balcony above the speaker's platform. Caroll Baker, who had been seated on the platform, took this as her cue to descend and begin clambering over the seats as if hypnotised by Allan Kaprow (the American director), who, Valentino-like, was spooking her from the other end of the hall. By this time a group of strangers had appeared at the windows overhead hollering: 'Me; Can you see me!' – and a mother ushered a baby across the stage pointing out the celebrities in the crowd. The final beat was when the curtains behind the speaker's platform suddenly tumbled down to reveal rows of shelves containing over 100 sculpted heads illuminated by footlights.[9]

Some delegates were angry, most of the public was confused, and the Lord Provost of Edinburgh called it 'a piece of pointless vulgarity'. The event was fairly trivial, in fact, and has not much affected the subsequent course of the British theatre. Nor was there anything new in the philosophy of the

Happening: the best of its exponents readily admit to the influence of Dada and Surrealism. It is mentioned here because it represents one of the extreme points in the assault upon conventional theatre.

That Happenings are in sharp contrast to the verbal theatre goes, one might put it, without saying. Happenings, explains Michael Kirby, 'are not *exclusively* visual'; but, 'while words are used, they are not used in the traditional way and are seldom of primary importance'. Happenings 'are essentially non-verbal, especially when compared to traditional theatre whose substance is vocal exchange between characters'.[10] Their non-verbal character is associated with a non-rational *modus operandi:*

> This does not mean that the concrete details [of Happenings] may not also function as symbols. They often do. But the symbols are of a private, non-rational, polyvalent character rather than intellectual. . . . Although they may, like everything else, be interpreted, they are intended to stir the observer on an unconscious, alogical level.[11]

Jean-Jacques Lebel, who also points to the non-verbal nature of Happenings, makes enthusiastic claims for the non-rational, non-representational form of the Happening: it

> interpolates actual experience directly into a mythical context. The Happening is not content merely with interpreting life; it takes part in its development within reality. This postulates a deep link between the actual and the hallucinatory, between real and imaginary . . .
>   It is *avant-garde* art that liberates latent myths; it transfigures us and changes our conception of life.[12]

This makes heady reading, but one detects a note of wishful thinking, confirmed when one looks at details of the Happenings themselves. In *Catastrophe*, we are told, Lebel 'opened the show by wheeling a toy baby carriage into the milling audience, a Tricolore draped across its top'; the tricolore was eventually snatched away, 'revealing a child's rubber mask of French President Charles de Gaulle'; the final scene saw the versatile Lebel 'slowly goosestepping out of the gallery shouting at the top of his voice "Heil Art, Heil Sex" '.[13] Admittedly other things were going on simultaneously (an Icelandic painter projected slides of his work on to a gyrating model, 'clad in the briefest of bikinis'),[14] but a distinctly programmatic bias, of a political nature, can be discerned as one element of the performance. The Edinburgh Happening was clearly an implicit comment on the nature of the conference in which it took place. At least some of the Happenings in Michael Kirby's anthology indicate an engagement with the technological culture of the U.S.A.: there is Jim Dine's *Car Crash* (1960) and Claes Oldenberg's *Autobodys* (1963). The engagement need not be an act of protest (one of the acknowledged influences upon the Happening was Futurism, whose leader Marinetti was enthusiastic enough about the technology of his day); but like much traditional drama, Happenings can invite their audiences to take a critical view of the social, political and intellectual world around them, and they do it by means of images, conjured up with careful precision before the spectators. This is a point to which we shall return.

In affirming the non-verbal nature of the Happening, its supporters are of course aligning themselves with a twentieth-century trend. The 'crisis of language' is a familiar phenomenon and has been well charted elsewhere:[15] it rests upon a pessimism about the ability of language to continue in its traditional role of expressing and clarifying the most profound areas of human experience. (One has sympathy with Lloyd Evans's attempt to blame the flight from the word on too much improvisation work in schools and colleges of education: but in so doing he is missing the wood for a very slender tree.) The English theatre in the early part of this century, as Kennedy notes, remained profoundly indifferent to the debate; in fact William Archer's *The Old Drama and the New* (1923) promoted a contrary doctrine that the theatre, shorn of artificiality and rhetoric, was entering upon a new era of expressiveness. So far as drama is concerned, it was Artaud who expressed the loss of faith in language in its most extreme form; and it was in the late 1950s, more or less contemporaneously with the advent of the Happening, that his influence was most keenly felt. The first English translation of *The Theatre and Its Double* appeared in 1958 and Kirby claims that 'the general theory propounded in the book is almost a text for Happenings'.[16] The influence of Artaud is obvious (and acknowledged) in the writing of Lebel. Artaud's opposition to a theatre 'which lives under the exclusive dictatorship of speech'[17] was unequivocal, but he gives us some visionary glimpses of what he wanted in its place and not a systematic programme. In 'The Theatre of Cruelty (First Manifesto)' he refers to an 'unique language half-way between gesture and thought', to 'a prodigious flight of forms which will constitute the whole spectacle', and to 'cries, groans, apparitions, surprises, theatricalities of all kinds'. And yet 'it is not a question of suppressing the spoken language, but of giving words approximately the importance they have in dreams'.[18] A blueprint for a Happening, perhaps, but now consider Lucky's speech in *Waiting for Godot*.[19] Lucky has wept, and danced, and now for the entertainment of the two tramps he is ordered by Pozzo to think: 'Think, pig!' There is one false start ('On the other hand with regard to –') and he is away:

> Given the existence as uttered forth in the public works of Puncher and Wattmann of a personal God quaquaquaqua with white beard quaquaquaqua outside time without extension Who from the heights of divine apathia divine athambia divine aphasia loves us dearly with some exceptions for reasons unknown but time will tell and suffers like the divine Miranda with those who for reasons unknown but time will tell are plunged in torment plunged in fire . . .

I doubt if the 'crisis of language' is presented anywhere so poignantly and this is because it is expressed, as it should be by an artist, from *within*, through the language itself. Lucky's speech is impregnated with literary and rhetorical devices, and their deliberate incoherence is carefully structured: if this is a rejection of language, it is as full of memory and painful detail as a lover's parting. My point is that while Happenings are usually contrasted with scripted drama, they can often be shown to be doing the same thing but more coarsely. The chance objects which appear in Happenings, with their random reference to the familiar world around us, have their counterpart in *Waiting for Godot* in the boots and bowler hats of the two tramps and in the concentration invested upon the stage properties, so sparse and yet so carefully introduced, in Pozzo's speech (pp. 23–4). Lucky's tirade moves on to its climax:

> in spite of the tennis on on the beard the flames the teams the stones so blue so calm alas alas on on the skull the skull the skull the skull in Connemara in spite of the tennis the labours abandoned left unfinished graver still abode of stones in a word I resume alas alas abandoned unfinished the skull the skull in Connemara in spite of the tennis the skull alas the stones Cunard (*Mêlée, final vociferations.*) tennis . . . the stones . . . so calm . . . Cunard . . . unfinished . . .
>
> (p. 44)

Using the full range of technical and allusive devices open to the literary artist, Beckett has achieved Lebel's object of 'liberating latent myths'. As Kennedy puts it, 'the idea of the failure of language has served Beckett as a myth *for* creation. . . . The whole texture of Beckett's language is created out of his ever renewed sense of the failure of language' (p. 135).

It might be objected that by picking on Lucky's speech, I am extracting a general principle from a unique case, but *Waiting for Godot* is unusual only in that it is so excellent and so close to the crucial issues of contemporary drama. It is the extreme example of a common tendency rather than something of a different order.

Kennedy remarks on the extent to which a *critical* element is found in the language of modern theatre: 'Much of contemporary theatricality amounts to parodistic montage – not necessarily satirical or "debunking" – but critically conscious: a play with or on received languages' (p. 33). He contrasts this 'conscious use of a language in quotation marks' with what he defines as the 'limited' language of naturalism:

> A limited dramatic language is no more than a first step towards that internalised, self-conscious limitation which may be called a critical dramatic language. The language of classical naturalism – above all the work of Ibsen and Chekhov – offers a clear idea of a limited language: it formally inhibits a gamut of expressive possibilities: verse, incantatory rhetoric, palpably stylised dialogue, and so on. (pp. 15–16)

One can see what is meant; but whatever may be said about its language considered in isolation, naturalism as a theatrical genre was conceived in a spirit of scientific, critical inquiry and it may be claimed that it has never abandoned it entirely. Its 'theatre language', in Russell Brown's sense of the term, is fully critical. Zola, who has been called 'the first of those who raised sociology to the dignity of art',[20] compared himself to the anatomist at work in a defence of naturalism whose sentiments have a Brechtian flavour: 'I am merely expressing my profound conviction – upon which I particularly insist – that the experimental and scientific spirit of the century will enter the domain of the drama, and that in it lies its only possible salvation.'[21]

It is not necessary to equate Zola's drama with Ibsen's or Chekhov's (nor indeed to minimise the great differences between the latter two) to see that they have something in common, and that what they share is a quality of interest in the observable surface of life – especially in its social aspects – which cannot exclude language. How far this interest is 'critical' is not really the point at issue, for the relation of Ibsen and Chekhov to the society portrayed in their plays is that of Beckett to language, where intimate knowledge makes the clinical detachment of the 'anatomist' impossible. The important point surely is the degree to which the audience is asked to observe the language, to infer from it, rather than to feel emotions in and through it (and it *is* a question of degree: there is not much dramatic language that does not have something of both qualities). When Ibsen referred to 'the very much more difficult art of writing the genuine, plain language spoken in real life'[22] he was concerned with the difficulty not solely of reproducing the nuances of everyday speech (although he certainly did not consider that an easy task), but also of combining the traditional aim of moving the spectator's emotions with the new exactitude of speech and action that the inquiring, 'scientific', spirit of naturalism implied.

The history of drama in our century is sometimes defined as a series of attempts to escape from the restrictions of naturalism, but in many significant respects all the rival 'isms' are lined up on the same side as naturalism, their battered but undefeated rival being the older view of drama as a representation of the passions of men and women in language simply calculated to articulate and communicate those passions. The dialogue, instead of being the main medium of the art, has become one of many. The setting, no longer there simply to indicate location or to create an atmosphere, carries 'meaning' in details of costume and furnishings. Imagery from nature, instead of colouring this or that speech, emerges from the spoken text to become the visual expression of a whole and complex idea (*The Wild Duck*, *The Seagull*, *Rhinoceros*). The supernatural, in an age of reason, can take on a similar function ('I am half inclined to think we are all ghosts, Mr Manders': and ghosts are everywhere in the plays of Edward Bond). Sentences (but never the generalised *sententiae* of rhetorical drama) carry an allusive burden far beyond their literal meaning: 'People don't do such things!' 'There's nowhere in the world better than Moscow.' 'How can I get down to Sidcup in these shoes?' The devices of rhetoric – irony, figurative allusion, the structured passion of a cogent argument – enjoy a continued, although muted, life within the speeches of particular characters, but their main importance is now within the whole economy of a play, outside language rather than within it. (I am talking of changes of emphasis rather than of a total transformation of the art: there are, of course, structured irony and the dominant theme of blindness in *Œdipus Rex* and *King Lear;* and comedy's concern with the way of the world has always sharpened its critical approach to language, setting and costume. But there *has* been a shift.)

There is significance in the importance given to the word 'image' throughout this century. '*L'image est une création pure de l'esprit*', wrote Pierre Reverdy,[23] and apart from giving its name to one of the major literary movements of modernism[24] it has, almost without anyone's noticing it, become a key term of dramatic as well as of literary criticism.[25] 'The dominant tendency of our own age', writes Martin Esslin, 'might be described as an aspiration of all the arts to attain the condition of *images*'.[26] Peter Brook refers to an 'acid test' in the theatre: when a play makes a lasting impression on the mind, 'it is the play's central image that remains, its silhouette will be its meaning, this shape will be the essence of what it has to say'.[27] In a recent interview Edward Bond has stated that he 'thinks in images': in *The Bundle,* for instance, 'the river is a simplifying image that enables one to see the structure of any human society that is based on an economy'.[28]

Like all critical terms the word 'image' lacks scientific precision, but what can be said about an image is that it is always greater than the sum of its parts. It takes its force from the juxtaposition of one idea with another, particular with general (Bond's river with 'the structure of any human society'). Within such an image, language, whether presented naturalistically or not, is so to speak a part of the picture. The film director with his camera and the choreographer with his *corps de ballet* can create dramatic images without the intervention of language, and so on occasion can the dramatist: it is certainly no part of my argument that the visual element in the theatre should be neglected. But language, by and large, remains the most fluent, complex and precise of the media through which a dramatist can work. T. S. Eliot has been called 'the invisible poet' and it may be that in an era when language is under constant suspicion and surveillance it can say most in disguise or (like those conversations carried out in embassy bathrooms) when it defeats our customary monitors. Inga-Stina Ewbank has suggested that Ibsen's 'extraordinary power, as a poet of the theatre, of creating in each play a subtext – a tissue of non-verbal interconnections – has sometimes unduly distracted our attention from the language of the text itself'.[29] And it is noticeable that the images which Brook records as 'engraved on my memory' are all from dramatists who are masters of the word – 'two tramps under a tree, an old woman dragging a cart, a sergeant dancing, three people on a sofa in hell'.[30]

Not many of the examples of language in the theatre cited in this discussion will find their way into literary anthologies: they derive their power from their context, and therein lies their strength as dramatic language and their difficulty for critics. An image works by implication and not by direct statement, and there is bound to be room for some variation of response to it. In criticism generally it has become too easy to evade a close and accurate reading of a work by referring to a 'dominant image', and thus to read what one wants into a play and force it along a route of one's own devising. A critic has every right (perhaps an obligation) to measure a play against the yardstick of his own moral and aesthetic judgement – and John Russell Brown's *Theatre Language* perhaps has a somewhat arid quality because this personal element is missing – but a critic's opinions must be anchored in the detail of the work to hand. And a focusing of attention upon the language of drama is to be welcomed as a concentration upon that detail.

Two of the studies of language in modern theatre, written from different points of view, throw light upon our argument. Gareth Lloyd Evans's contribution is calculated to have wide appeal, for it is not burdened with theoretical concepts and relies mostly on the author's own fresh and lively response to the dramatists who come under his scrutiny. This is the best possible approach, to the minds of many readers: but in *The Language of Modern Drama* it results in a series of hit-or-miss judgements. With some of them, naturally, one finds oneself in agreement, and there are many revealing insights. It is easy to be caught up in his enthusiasms, but his almost total lack of system makes it impossible to enter into debate. In the chapter on W. B. Yeats he admits, with typical generosity, that the plays 'haunt the memory and the imagination of anyone who reads them' (p. 118) but argues that the plays fail as drama because they 'cannot be reduced to that kind of simplicity by which the reader or audience is convinced of their human credibility. It is simply true that the best drama is, in a very significant way, capable of this kind of reduction' (p. 122). But what does that mean? At the level of dialogue there is enough spare and simple language in the best of Yeats's verse drama to make it as credible as any prose drama; at the level of character and situation Yeats, admittedly, was not aiming at simple realism, but that is a different issue, and one would have welcomed a deeper exploration of it. And it is difficult to see how Yeats's failings relate to those of Eliot, who after *Murder in the Cathedral* 'went on to write plays of progressively less dramatic credibility' (p. 161).

Lloyd Evans has a short and sensible chapter on Pinter (here his common sense is a valuable corrective to some of the academic theorisers); but it is strange, in a book concerned with theatrical language, that there should be nothing on Arden who, with Margaretta D'Arcy, has extended the range of both prose and verse within the contemporary theatre. His point is well taken that, in contrast to the kitchen-sink drama of the late 1950s, the 1960s produced a much more self-conscious genre, where the language

> is very much an invented thing. . . . It is very much nearer to being 'literary' than is the vernacular idiom. Some of the most distinguished plays of the contemporary period have employed a prose-literary idiom – *Rosencrantz and Guildenstern are Dead, Afore Night Come, Equus, Entertaining Mr Sloane, Narrow Road to the Deep North*, and a substantial number of others.   (p. 222)

This feature links diverse dramatists, he argues, 'because they either tacitly or consciously realise that the vernacular, widespread as it is in contemporary drama, just is not capable of carrying all that needs to be said – even about the very class from which it derives' (p. 222). But in general, he is pessimistic about the drama of the immediate present. Bond, especially in the early realism of *Saved*, is Lloyd Evans's *bête noir*, and enough has already been said to indicate that the main point at issue is the degree to which language can be taken out of its context and considered as a thing in itself.

Andrew Kennedy's *Six Dramatists in Search of a Language* began life as a dissertation, and bears the scholarly caution of that genre, without the customary tedium. For once, the bibliography is not a concession to pedantry but a gathering together of important and relevant material. Kennedy's Introduction perceptively sets out the range of possibilities within language available to the modern dramatist and the same thoughtful, critical awareness is deployed in the discussion of his six dramatists (Shaw, Eliot, Beckett, Pinter, Osborne and Arden). Kennedy has an ability, which the fevered, all-or-nothing world of the theatre does not always encourage, to point to the positive qualities of a particular dramatist without being blind to his weaknesses. After a generally appreciative chapter on Arden, for instance, he puts his finger on the principal difficulty inherent in his fondness for out-of-the-way regional and archaic speech:

> Technically, such exotic prose works through local heightening to achieve a local intensity in imagery and rhythm. It yields less interest in terms of interaction between characters, in the movement of dialogue from speech to speech. And it lacks the inner complexity, the nervous concentration or evasiveness, the ambiguity and stylistic many-sidedness, which does stamp much modern speech; features that have been exploited in some of the most interesting dialogue techniques of our time. In this respect Arden is – as he himself has implied – at the opposite pole from Pinter. We may value his achievement – the vigour and occasional beauty of his language – and still remain aware of a limitation.   (pp. 227–8)

The main question that presses itself upon me in reading Kennedy is how far, in the end, one can penetrate into a dramatist's world simply by studying his language. What he writes in comparison of Eliot with Beckett has admirable lucidity:

Eliot took pains to avoid, or to counterbalance, the pull towards subjectivity; his whole development as a dramatist might be seen as a conscious and progressive effort to 'objectify' his dramatic language, in terms of situation and character; he was prepared to sacrifice expressive power for the sake of deliverance from a private language and the attendant danger of *stasis*. . . . By contrast, Beckett starts from an acceptance of that solipsistic condition. For him language is irredeemably private: words germinate in the skull of the speaker, at an inestimable distance from things and other persons, motive and argument, local time and place.

(p. 131)

Better intelligent criticism like this, one might argue, than any amount of vapid theorising about the two authors' world-views; yet is there not something incomplete in a comparison of Eliot and Beckett that does not take into account their respective attitudes to religious faith? Lucky's speech, and the opening and closing scenes of *The Cocktail Party*, are exercises in language emptied of straightforward meaning: but the difference between them points a contrast whose analysis may begin in a study of language, but certainly cannot end there. For, whether we like it or not, most plays today have a *meaning*. This may not always have been so, at any rate in the same sense. Aristotle, it will be remembered, prescribed *dianoia*, 'thought', for the use of dramatic characters 'when proving or disproving some particular point, or enunciating some universal proposition':[31] there is no suggestion in the *Poetics* that the dramatist himself should show a point of view. In *De Copia* (1512), Erasmus stresses the importance of memory in rhetorical training: 'In reading authors you will carefully pick out any unusual word, archaism, or innovation, anything reasoned or invented unusually well, or aptly turned, any outstanding ornament of speech, any adage, exemplum, *sententia* worthy to be committed to memory.'[32] It is a different preparation for composition than anything to be found in an age which prizes originality of style and viewpoint above all. Doubtless a Shakespeare went beyond the mechanical procedures advocated by Erasmus: but John Russell Brown is probably right in arguing that Shakespeare was never meant to be 'interpreted' in the way that he is by critics and directors.[33] Unquestionably in the modern, image-laden drama a new tendentiousness has invaded the stage. *C'est une étrange enterprise que de faire rire les honnêtes gens* is the famous dictum put by Molière into the mouth of one of his characters: one could hardly imagine his making anyone say, with Trevor Griffiths's Mr Waters:

It's not the jokes. It's not the jokes. It's what lies behind 'em. It's the attitude. A real comedian – that's a daring man. He *dares* to see what his listeners shy away from, fear to express. And what he sees is a sort of truth, about people, about their situation, about what hurts or terrifies them, about what's hard, above all, about what they *want*. A joke releases the tension, says the unsayable, any joke, pretty well. But a true joke, a comedian's joke, has to do more than release tension, it has to *liberate* the will and the desire, it has to *change the situation*.[34]

Shall we ever return to the lost and no doubt deceptive innocence of an age when a true comedian could provide amusement for decent folk within the system, and uncritical (though not unstructured) abundance of language was the clear mark of a gifted dramatist? The appearance of the taciturn, guilt-ridden Shakespeare in *Bingo* suggests that Edward Bond does not think so; in the insistence with which he presses his considerable if errant gift for language into the service of dominant imagery, he has set off for the extremities of unspoken significance. And he has paid the penalty: for all his insistence on the rationality of art, audiences and critics alike have found difficulty in interpreting images so deliberately divorced from any explanatory text. But if Bond represents one polar extreme in the contemporary theatre, it may be that (with no Erasmus for mentor) a style wholly contrary to Bond's, in which the dialogue flows with a spontaneity which makes it impossible to separate communicated feeling from the language itself, has become equally characteristic of the contemporary theatre. The plays of John Osborne are rhetorical in a traditional sense, and it is easy to underestimate the influence of the great outburst of fluent, sharply-characterised dialogue in those early plays of his, since what has been transmitted is not a question of structure, of images, or even of 'meaning', but a much more personal matter in the detail of the dialogue itself. Not all contemporary playwrights of promise have fallen into the mode of sophisticated literacy described by Lloyd Evans: to list and evaluate the successors of Osborne would be the task of another article but if language, like democracy, needs eternal vigilance as the price of its preservation there is no lack of work for critics of language in the theatre, as well as of the language of the theatre.

NOTES

1. Edward Bond, *The Pope's Wedding* (London: Eyre Methuen, 1971), p. 22.
2. Barrie Keeffe, 'Getaway', in *Gimme Shelter* (London: Eyre Methuen, 1978), pp. 85–6.
3. Edward Bond, *Saved* (London: Eyre Methuen, 1969), pp. 47 ff.
4. Gareth Lloyd Evans, *The Language of Modern Drama* (London: J. M. Dent & Sons, 1977); Andrew Kennedy, *Six Dramatists in Search of a Language* (London: Cambridge University Press, 1975).
5. *The Critical Quarterly*, VII, 3 (1965), 225–43, reprinted in John Russell Brown, ed., *Modern British Dramatists* (Englewood Cliffs, N.J.: Prentice Hall, 1968), pp. 122–44.
6. Arnold P. Hinchliffe, *British Theatre 1950–70* (Oxford: Basil Blackwell, 1974).
7. Malcolm Bradbury and David Palmer, eds, *Stratford-Upon-Avon Studies*, 12: *Contemporary Criticism* (London: Edward Arnold, 1970), p. 45.
8. Lloyd Evans, *The Language of Modern Drama*, p. xii.
9. Charles Marowitz, 'Happenings at Edinburgh', in John Calder, ed., *New Writers IV: Plays and Happenings* (London: Calder & Boyars, 1967), pp. 59–60. See also Ken Dewey, 'Act of San Francisco at Edinburgh', *ibid.*, pp. 67–74. Both articles are reprinted from *Encore*, x, 6 (1963).

10. Michael Kirby, ed., *Happenings: An Illustrated Anthology* (New York: E. P. Dutton & Co., 1966), pp. 11–13.
11. *Ibid.*, p. 20.
12. Jean-Jacques Lebel, 'Theory and Practice', in *New Writers IV: Plays and Happenings*, pp. 20–1.
13. E. C. Nimmo, 'Catastrophe in Paris 1963: A Happening', in *New Writers IV: Plays and Happenings*, pp. 50–2.
14. *Ibid.* p. 51.
15. See George Steiner, *Language and Silence* (London: Faber & Faber, 1967); Richard Sheppard, 'The Crisis of Language', in Bradbury and McFarlane, eds, *Modernism 1890–1930* (Harmondsworth: Penguin Books, 1976), 323–36.
16. Kirby, ed., *Happenings: An Illustrated Anthology*, p. 34: Jill Johnston has suggested that the early authors of Happenings were influenced by work in progress on the American translation of Artaud: cf. Charles Marowitz, Tom Milne and Owen Hale, eds, *The Encore Reader: A Chronicle of the New Drama* (London: Methuen, 1965), p. 261.
17. Antonin Artaud, *The Theater and Its Double*, tr. Mary Caroline Richards (New York: Grove Press, 1958), p. 40.
18. *Ibid.*, pp. 89, 92, 93, 94.
19. Samuel Beckett, *Waiting for Godot* (London: Faber & Faber, 1956), p. 42.
20. F. W. J. Hemmings, *Emile Zola²* (Oxford: Oxford University Press, 1966), pp. 306, 37.
21. Emile Zola, 'Preface to *Thérèse Raquin*', (1873), tr. in Barrett H. Clark, ed., *European Theories of the Drama*, newly revised by Henry Popkin (New York: Crown Publishers, 1965), p. 378.
22. In a letter of 1883; see Kennedy's discussion of the passage, *Six Dramatists in Search of a Language*, pp. 16–17.
23. Pierre Reverdy, *Nord-Sud Revue Littéraire*, no. 13 (March 1918): I owe this reference to the Exhibition 'Dada and Surrealism reviewed' at the Hayward Gallery, London, 1978.
24. See Natan Zach, 'Imagism and Vorticism', in Bradbury and McFarlane, eds, *Modernism*, pp. 228–42.
25. For an account of its use in literary criticism, see René Wellek and Austin Warren, *Theory of Literature* (London: Peregrine Books, 1963), pp. 186 ff.
26. Günter Grass, *Four Plays* (London: Secker & Warburg, 1968), p. vii.
27. Peter Brook, *The Empty Space* (London: MacGibbon & Kee, 1968), p. 136.
28. Edward Bond, Interview with Peter Hulton, in *Theatre Papers, The Second Series: Number 1* (Dartington: Dartington College of Arts, 1978), p. 22.
29. Inga-Stina Ewbank, 'Ibsen and "The far more difficult art" of Prose', *Contemporary Approaches to Ibsen II* [= *Ibsen Yearbook 11*, 1970–71], p. 62.
30. Brook, *The Empty Space*, p. 136.
31. Aristotle, *Poetics*, 6.1450ᵇ (Bywater's translation).
32. Quoted in the author's translation by T. W. Baldwin, *William Shakspere's Small Latine & Lesse Greeke* (Urbana: University of Illinois Press, 1944), I, 83.
33. John Russell Brown, *Free Shakespeare* (London: Heinemann, 1974). Cf. Susan Sontag: 'In place of a hermeneutics we need an erotics of art', *Against Interpreta- and other Essays* (London: Eyre & Spottiswoode, 1967), p. 14.
34. Trevor Griffiths, *Comedians* (London: Faber & Faber, 1976), p. 20.

REVIEW SECTION

Peter Brook and Shakespeare

RICHARD PROUDFOOT

> ...Shakespeare is...not only of a different quality, he is also different in kind. And this is very little understood. So long as one thinks that Shakespeare is just Ionesco but better, Beckett but richer, Brecht but more human, Chekhov with crowds, and so on, one is not touching what it is about. ... what passed through this man called Shakespeare and came into existence on sheets of paper is something quite different from any other author's work. It's not Shakespeare's view of the world, it's something which actually resembles reality. A sign of this is that any single word, line, character or event has not only a large number of interpretations, but an unlimited number.
>
> (Peter Brook)[1]

Shakespeare has been central to the work of Peter Brook, who is reported, as a child, to have finished a solo performance of *Hamlet*, uncut, with the desire to start again at once and do it differently.[2] He has directed twelve of the plays – some more than once, one only in a French translation – since he emerged in the mid-1940s in the Birmingham Repertory Company and at Stratford as the 'boy wonder' of the English theatre.

Between 1945 and 1957 he rose to eminence as a producer, innovating boldly, especially with visual settings, which he liked to design himself, but within the existing traditions of English theatre. The outstanding Shakespearian successes of these years were *Love's Labour's Lost* (Stratford, 1946–7), *Measure for Measure* (Stratford, 1950–1), *The Winter's Tale* (Phoenix, London, 1951) and *Titus Andronicus* (Stratford, 1955). *Titus* later toured widely; *Hamlet* (1955) went to Moscow and played at the Art Theatre. Leading players in these productions included Paul Scofield (Don Armado, Lucio, Hamlet; also Faulconbridge in *King John* at Birmingham in 1945, and Mercutio in *Romeo and Juliet* in Stratford in 1947), Sir John Gielgud (Angelo, Leontes and Prospero in *The Tempest* at Stratford in 1957) and Alec Clunes (Claudius and Caliban). Sir Laurence Olivier played Titus Andronicus. *King Lear* (Stratford, 1962) was a turning point. With it Brook made the first of three returns to Stratford after long absence. *Lear* was his first production for the Royal Shakespeare Company, to be followed by *A Midsummer Night's Dream* (1970) and *Antony and Cleopatra* (1978), as well as by two encounters with *The Tempest*, as co-director in 1963 with Clifford Williams, and in 1969 when improvisations and exercises entitled '*Tempest* Exercises' were presented to audiences at the Round House.[3] In the 1960s and 1970s Brook's work on Shakespeare, while never losing touch with aims already apparent in his earlier work, involved increasingly radical experiment with theatrical means and progressive steps towards methods of direction and rehearsal far removed from those of the commercial theatre in which his reputation was established. Lectures delivered at four universities in 1965 were published in 1968 as *The Empty Space* and rapidly became a bible of experimental theatre in England. Also in 1968, he founded the International Centre for Theatrical Research in Paris and much of his work since then has been with this small international group of performers. He has directed them in productions (in French) of *Timon d'Athènes* (1973) and *Mesure pour Mesure* (1978) at the reopened and remodelled Théâtre des Bouffes du Nord.

A discussion of Brook's work as a director (to use the term appropriate to his later work, rather than the now old-fashioned 'producer') of Shakespeare, based on a few selected productions, may well begin with two opinions published in 1977, when the 1970 *Dream* remained his most recent English production. J. L. Styan, in *The Shakespeare Revolution*, found it easy, on the evidence of *Lear* and the *Dream*, to cast Brook in a near-Messianic role at the culmination of an optimistic history of the interrelation of Shakespearian production and Shakespearian criticism in our century, seeing him as the great exponent of 'non-illusion' in the theatre.[4] Kenneth Tynan,[5] more concerned with Brook's apparent loss of direction in the 1970s, looked back to earlier triumphs, speculating that 'he may go down in history as the last real master-director of the proscenium stage' and, as far as Shakespeare is concerned, 'a reclaimer of the secondary plays rather than interpreter of the major plays', thus preferring *Love's Labour's Lost*, *Titus* and *Measure for Measure* to *Lear* and the *Dream*. Of *Measure*, Tynan wrote: 'It was the first one for which he did the sets as well, and it still remains in my mind as the most unified Shakespeare I've seen – with every costume, every shoe, every side-effect, contributing to a total vision of the play. It gave Gielgud's career a second lease of life, because it was a much more restrained, realistic, unromantic performance than he had ever given before.' Tynan's main criticisms of Brook's work since *Lear* were that it was flawed by 'a rather shallow and factitious pessimism' (this points to *Lear* itself) and that an ingrowing preoccupation with the world of the theatre had produced three unhappy tendencies: towards the presentation of truism as revelation; towards a concern for rehearsal techniques that led to the production of shows revealing 'no specifically theatrical effect'; and towards nihilistic attack on words as 'bearers of rational thought'. Substantiation is easily to be found in accounts of Brook's experiments in Persia,[6] West Africa[7] and elsewhere in the early 1970s, and yet Tynan's attack seems as exaggerated in its disappointment with an apparently lost leader as does Styan's too tidy accolade.

Starting with *Measure for Measure*, rather than with the *Love's Labour's Lost* which launched Brook and revealed a then underrated play as fit meat for the war-weary tooth of the 1940s, and paying some attention to selected later productions, it may be possible to indicate some developments as well as some continuities in the work of our best director of Shakespeare.

In 1950 Brook returned to Stratford, from a brief flirtation with opera at Covent Garden, with *Measure for Measure*. John Gielgud also returned, after a longer absence, as Angelo; the Duke was Harry Andrews; Isabella, a young newcomer, Barbara Jefford. Brook controlled all aspects of the production, designing his own set and composing a tune for the song. Visually, the production was based on contrasts: between 'the opulent corruption of the court . . . and the beggarly vice and squalor of the streets, the stews and the prison house';[8] and between the bustle and seething life of a crowd of extras costumed and made-up to suggest Breughel or fifteenth-century Dances of Death and the quiet intensity of the many 'duet' scenes. Richard David described the set: 'This was a double range of lofty arches, receding from the centre of the stage on either side to the wings upstage. These arches might remain open to the sky . . . [for] – the convent at night, . . . Mariana's moated grange, and the street scene in which all odds are finally made even[see plate 9]; or in a moment, their spaces could be blanked out, with grey flats for the shabby decorum of the courtroom, with grilles for the prison cells. . . . The single permanent set gave coherence to the whole; its continuous shadowy presence held together the brilliant series of closet scenes played on a smaller section of the stage.'[9] This set both allowed of rapid transitions of scene and pushed the action downstage, thus helping to overcome the depth of the gap between stage and auditorium in the Stratford theatre. Even the orchestra pit was used, as a cell from which Barnardine was hauled up on a rope.

Reviewers praised the pace – 'approximating to what we take to be an Elizabethan rate of playing' – continuity and 'quiet fervour' of the performance. Most agreed that in such a production, 'swift, faithful to the text and spirit of the play, [and] imaginative . . . *Measure for Measure* gains on the stage a simplicity which it seems to lack in the study'.[10] It was not, in 1950, a universally admired play. Brook's production was applauded for its fidelity, both to a vision of life in the late Middle Ages (oddly, for a play written about 1604) and to the play's continuing meaning – though this was variously described. The argument of the play was what impressed: 'It is a play of ideas rather than of impressions and is concerned more with lines of conduct followed out to their logical conclusions than with the confusions and compromises of real life', wrote Richard David.[11] Such comments as 'Sympathy may not be stirred but interest is securely held'[12] were offered as praise of an unsentimental production which had avoided treating the play as a vehicle for Angelo and Isabella.

9 *Measure for Measure*, act v. Shakespeare Memorial Theatre, 1950. Escalus (Harold Kasket), Duke (Harry Andrews), Provost (Michael Gwynn), Mariana (Maxine Audley), Angelo (John Gielgud)

Some commentators noted infidelity in Brook's handling of the text. Though his invention of a prison scene in which his crowd represented the brothel-customers listed in Pompey's soliloquy met with approval, his handling of the last act raised more objections. 'It is odd that Barnardine's pardon should be omitted here, for it seals the mercy-theme with a proper finality. How could these three couples advance into their future of unimaginable things with Barnardine on the block?'[13] The pardon *was* granted, but in Barnardine's absence the lines granting it were addressed instead to Angelo! Brook faced squarely the crux of the Duke's proposal, indicating Isabella's silent acceptance of it, but made his own problem harder and caught some spectators off-balance by cutting all lines which in any way anticipate the proposal and leaving his Duke 'intractably incredible – how his final capers must dismay the Marriage Guidance Council!'[14] The major climax comes earlier, though, with Isabella's plea for pardon for Angelo: '. . . I asked Isabella, before kneeling for Angelo's life, to pause each night until she felt the audience could take it no longer – and this used to lead to a two-minute stopping of the play. The device became a voodoo pole – a silence in which all the invisible elements of the evening came together, a silence in which the abstract notion of mercy became concrete for that moment to those present.'[15] Independent observers testified to a pause of thirty-five seconds – already an eternity of stage time. This moment, and Brook's comment on it, define a great deal of his endeavour in directing Shakespeare: the sense of a meaning discovered and the intention of imposing that meaning on an audience by whatever means will combat their resistance or passivity (characteristics associated with what he categorises as 'Deadly Theatre'). In the same passage, he writes: 'If we follow the movement in *Measure for Measure* between the Rough and the Holy we will discover a play about justice, mercy, honesty, forgiveness, virtue, virginity, sex and death: kaleidoscopically one section of the play mirrors the other; it is in accepting the prism as a whole that its meanings emerge.'[16]

Shakespeare has always attracted Brook as a dramatist (indeed, apart from Chekhov, the only dramatist) whose work is of adequate range, variety and complexity to demand, and to provoke, the fullest resources of theatrical skill and imagination for its realisation in performance.

Measure for Measure lent itself (perhaps in retrospect) to Brook's classification of desirable forms of theatre as 'Holy' and 'Rough'. '[Shakespeare's] aim continually is holy, metaphysical, yet he never makes the mistake of staying too long on the highest plane. He knew how hard it is for us to keep company with the absolute – so he continually bumps us down to earth.'[17] The 'Holy' theatre he defines as the 'Theatre of the Invisible-Made-Visible',[18] whose goal is the clarifying simplicity of ritual and in which the actor becomes a sacrifice to his role. Brook's quest for the indefinable Grail of a specific quality of audience-response has offered his critics an easy target.

Not only are such responses hard to gauge but the means of evoking them easily become extreme, pretentious or exhibitionist. By employing striking means, like Isabella's pause, a director defines his attitude and that of his audience to a moment in the play, but at the risk of identifying the comment as his rather than the dramatist's or of restricting the meaning of the moment by the very act of definition. Meanings evidently excluded from *Measure for Measure* ranged from the association of the Duke with divine power and providence (this was done by cutting) to that concern with 'the confusions and compromises of real life' whose presence in the play critics were ready to deny. The Duke's lack of human involvement in the dénouement was a prime instance.

Brook's 'Rough Theatre' is the antithesis of his 'Holy Theatre': a makeshift theatre, seeking no unified style, using all available means, 'accepting inconsistencies of accent and dress', 'darting between mime and dialogue, realism and suggestion' in its appeal to 'a popular audience'.[19] It touches on his other positive category, 'Immediate Theatre', and can be seen as the ideal underlying much of his later experimentation with rehearsal and performance techniques. Brook has been conspicuously resourceful in style and invention in handling the low comics in Shakespeare, from the Stephano and Trinculo (Patrick Wymark and Clive Revill) who came near to stealing his 1957 *Tempest* to the overtly funny Clown in *Antony and Cleopatra*. Creative anachronism has ranged from a Pompey with a stock of address cards for the brothel in his capacious codpiece to the string-vested mechanicals of the *Dream,* with their toolbags, sandwiches and tendency to stage walkouts into the auditorium.

Brook has been called a cold director, an intellectual concerned with plays as mechanisms – not without reason – but there is also truth in the description of him as a pragmatic theatrical magpie, ready to draw on all sources for ideas, techniques, designs, concerned above all with *effect,* and ready to adapt his ideas even at the last moment. The 'Holy' and the 'Rough' may not have merged completely in *Measure for Measure* – the absence of Barnardine from the final scene suggests unease about his likely effect there. The 'Holy' strain reached its fullest expression with *Titus Andronicus*: later Shakespearian productions have drawn more strength from the 'Rough' and 'Immediate'.

Brook's *Titus Andronicus* was the first production of the play at the Stratford theatre: it was an outstanding success. A play suspected as of dubious authenticity, indubitable tastelessness and grotesque violence was revealed as, or transformed into, a tragedy which could without absurdity be mentioned in the same breath as *King Lear*. The triumph owed much to Olivier's playing of the leading role. 'We found ourselves', wrote J. C. Trewin, '(where we are so seldom) in the upper air of great acting. In quietness, the actor terrified; his voice seemed to cut out each word in flint. But it was the quietness at the core of a hurricane. In rage we felt the storm-wind of the equinox. . . . Titus's sudden laugh, slow to come, was like the menace of a tide on the turn. . . . This was acting that lashed to fear and could touch to pity: something none would have divined from the text.'[20]

The production which surrounded this tempestuous performance showed Brook's control at every point. He saw the play as 'not so much a piece of Grand Guignol as an austere and grim Roman tragedy; horrifying indeed but with a real primitive strength and achieving at times even a barbaric dignity . . . a tragedy cast in the Shakespearian mold'.[21] The production aimed at vindicating this vision. Brook cut the text severely, rearranging action to clarify the plot and removing any line or action which threatened provoke bathetic laughter.[22] The effect was to distance the horrors and to ritualise them into an action 'both full-blooded and bloodless'.[23] The vindictiveness of Titus was soft-pedalled, to retain sympathy for him in the later acts, and Marcus lost his rhetorical cadenzas over Lavinia after the rape. Brook designed both set and costumes. The set, comprising 'three great squared pillars, set angle-on to the audience, fluted and bronzy-grey in colour',[24] could change rapidly from forum to forest or interior by the resetting of an area within the central pillar, which could open. Colour was strong: the inner area was 'sombre and shadowy' as the tomb in act I; 'yellowish natural-wood colour' for domestic scenes; finally 'blood-red' for the cannibalistic banquet. 'The vivid green of the priests' robes and mushroom hats' and 'hangings of purple and green, richly suggest[ing] the civilized barbarity of late imperial Rome'[25] contrasted with the red ribbons used to suggest the blood streaming from the mutilations of Lavinia and Titus. Phantasmagoric barbarity was further evoked by the music. Brook created it by electronic manipulation of the sounds of a plastic toy trumpet, trombone, recorder, harp, piano and 'such things as ashtrays and pots and pans, pencils on Venetian glass phials, and wire baskets used as harps'.[26] Rarely, perhaps never, had a Shakespearian production so pervasively shown the impact of one man's imagination. Apart from Olivier, Antony Quayle (Aaron) and Maxine Audley (Tamora), the actors too were reduced to become 'puppets of the producer's conception.'

Amid the chorus of praise, a few critics expressed qualms. Richard David, conceding the power of 'one extended conjuring-trick, that held the spectator spell-bound', added 'spell-bound and yet quite unmoved. . . . In striving to make it more than [straightforward blood-and-thunder] Brook made it less than nothing. The blood was . . . turned to favours and to prettiness. . . . no amount of sand-papering can turn this old shocker into high tragedy à la Racine.'[27] The verdict may be endorsed by Brook's undoubted later concentration on major plays of Shakespeare, though both *King Lear* and *A Midsummer Night's Dream* also offer notorious challenges to the director – *Lear* haunted by the myth of its unactability, the *Dream* beset by the difficulty of finding an answering theatrical style for its fairy scenes.

Fresh from filming *Lord of the Flies* and already aware of Jan Kott's essay '*King Lear*, or *Endgame*' (to be published in England in 1964),[28] Brook might have been expected to bring a bleak vision to a tragedy increasingly accepted as apt to our time by virtue of its relentlessness. His many recorded statements about *Lear* indicate some main emphases: the play 'needs not only a capital performance in the part of Lear but equally illuminating acting all the way through'; *Lear* is 'the arch example of the theatre of the absurd' . . . 'The ferocity and horror of the play is destroyed if, as some unfortunate critics do, you try to tip it into Christianity or if you try to fit it into a Christian era'; 'the slightest effort to *impose* any unity on Shakespeare is tantamount to the destruction of Shakespeare'; 'You can only ask people questions, and open your ears to their questions';'*King Lear* is not a play about justice, but about movement'; 'The world of Lear, like Beckett's, is in a constant state of decomposition'.[29] Reference to the present time; awareness of complexity as the essential quality of Shakespeare; denial of didactic intent in the production – and of remote grandeur or religious consolation in the play; and concern with questions and with movement – these were among the defining considerations.

But of course Brook's view of the play was neither neutral nor impartial, nor did his care for the detail of physical setting stop short of imposing unity at least on the visual dimension of the production.

He insisted on five weeks of rehearsal (against a usual three); the rehearsals were chronicled by his assistant director, Charles Marowitz.[30] After several days reading the play with the company, Brook embarked on the job of 'looking for meaning and making it meaningful' – insisting that his role as director was to help actors to find their own performances and working always from a position of ignorance towards inquiry. Marowitz found the method 'relentlessly (and at times maddeningly) experimental. He believes that there is no such thing as the right way. . . . it is through the constant elimination of possiblities that Brook finally arrives at interpretation.' Im- provisation (a technique at that date still resisted by actors trained on the assumption – anathema to Brook – 'that if the verse can be made to work, proper interpretation will follow') was used to explore aspects of the charac- ters not defined by the text, the relationships, for instance, between Lear's three daughters, or Edgar and Edmund. Individual personalities were devised for Lear's knights, elaborately involved in the action of acts I and II. Here, as increasingly in his later work, Brook was in pursuit of an assumed 'hidden play', a sub-text which must be discovered and revealed by director and actors. Rehearsals also aimed at breaking down familiar styles of verse-speaking, in order to escape from the traditional heroic, pathetic, regal or cathartic tones of 'Shakespearian Tragedy'.

For all the *truly* experimental and corporate activity of the rehearsal period, Brook had in fact taken decisions crucial to the interpretation of *Lear* before rehearsals began. The casting of Paul Scofield as Lear at once precluded certain traditional readings of the role. What emerged was a Lear curiously close in quality, if not in physique, to William Poel's description of the character (quoted by J. C. Trewin): 'After the first scene Lear should appear in hunting costume, big leather boots, leather jerkin, leather cap. . . . He should be able to show that he has as much physical strength as the youngest and strongest man on the stage. . . . On no account should his figure stoop until he is broken down with grief. His manners are brusque, impulsive and dominating. When moved his outburst of passion is titanic and uncontrollable, causing him to form decisions opposed to his own interest and even to his own safety.'[31] Scofield's was a Lear more sinning than sinned against; the points of view of Goneril and Regan were presented with unusual force.

Cutting and stage business also determined interpretation. Lear's knights were presented as Goneril describes them, the climax of act I, iv being reached with their destruction of her hall furniture in a riot cued by Lear's own overturning of the dinner table. Though cuts were relatively few and short, they consistently removed comfort and virtue from the play, making a strong case for Goneril, Regan and Edmund, diminishing the cowardice of Oswald and turning the disguised Kent into an angry bully. Most often noted was the suppression of the pitying servants who help the blinded Gloucester from the stage at the end of act III. Placing his only interval here (after two hours), Brook had Gloucester, his head roughly covered with sacking and jostled by servants who are clearing the furniture, grope 'his way upstage, with the house lights going on, a broken figure long in view of a mesmerized audience sitting in full light'.[32] The same refusal of pity turned Kent's line over dead Lear, 'Vex not his ghost', into a cry of rage, and replaced Shakespeare's final stage picture of Lear dead surrounded by his three dead daughters with an exit for Edgar 'lug[ging] the body [of Edmund] into the wings like a slaughtered pig'[33] to the accompaniment of a low rumble of distant thunder.

Sets and properties evoked a primeval, pagan world in 'a rusting Iron Age'[34] and emphasised the steadily increasing size and emptiness of a stage on which small, vulnerable human figures appeared 'kneeling, grovelling, stumbling, squirming, wriggling about like worms, forced into graceless postures, slumped in the stocks, or shoved on their backs to be tortured'.[35]

Act IV, vi, with the grotesque morality-farce of blind Gloucester's attempt at suicide by leaping from a non-existent cliff and his subsequent encounter with mad Lear, was, Marowitz records, the 'germinal scene' in Brook's production. That scene, with Scofield's shattered but sonorous speeches, in which every rhythm caught a nuance of bitter meaning, and the suffering of Alan Webb's shrivelled Gloucester, remains my own most vivid memory of the film version. The pain of change and loss was savagely inflicted and no cathartic consolation was allowed – the purging of pity and terror being curiously spoken of by both Brook and Marowitz not as the *aim* of tragedy, but as a *risk* to be avoided, a problem to be tackled. On no account must the shaken audience be allowed any reassurance before leaving the theatre.

Critical comment, though necessarily divided on many points, was almost unanimous in praising the clarity with which the whole play (many reviewers, after four hours, supposed it to be uncut) had been allowed to unfold itself. Representative were the views of Philip Hope-Wallace, who noted a 'Wagnerian deliberation of speed, which pays off in that the hieratic preliminaries and the whole curve of the play – main subject and counter-subject – are wonderfully clear; and then how rich is the chord that is struck. I have seldom noticed so many points so intelligently taken.'[36] Others felt a sense that 'in seeking to find the heart of this most complex play Mr Brook somehow has taken the heart out of it'[37] or, defining more exactly the cost of success, 'if we have lost Lear the symbol, we have found Lear the man far more credible than usual. . . . This is an agnostic production which believes in the rights and duties of an earthly father, but ignores the powers and privileges of the gods in heaven and the king on his throne.'[38] The habitual cool voice of dissent, this time that of Frank Dibb, still conceded that the production was 'serviceable, reasonably quick in pace and happily devoid of gimmicks'.[39]

Like *Titus*, *Lear* went on tour, both in Europe and to the United States, before it reached some measure of permanence as a film, made in northern Denmark in 1969 and released in 1971. By then Brook's association with the Royal Shakespeare Company had become more intermittent than in the early 1960s. With the founding, in Paris in the spring of 1968, of his International Centre for Theatre Research, Brook moved into a new phase of his career, as theatrical researcher, directing not just a production but a living theatre-laboratory, in which a small international group of actors, designers, musicians and writers would explore all aspects of acting technique and styles and would search for a theatrical language capable of addressing audiences anywhere in the world. These preoccupations were to take Brook first to Persepolis in 1971 then, the next year, on a trek across North-West Africa. They also explain some features of his 1970 production of the *Dream* for the Royal Shakespeare Company which, at the time, took both audiences and critics by surprise.

Discussion of this celebrated production is complicated by the proliferation of published material about it. There are the usual reviews, including those for the world-wide tour, and interviews with Brook himself, but many of the company have also recorded their views and reminiscences. In 1974 the RSC even published, in conjunction with the Dramatic Publishing Company an 'Authorized Acting Edition' of 'Peter Brook's *Production* of *A Midsummer Night's Dream*'[40] – a dramatic document beside which 'Pyramus and Thisbe' and its prologues pale into theatrical insignificance. It is strange that Brook should have sanctioned a publication so plainly antithetical to his continued assertion that theatre is ephemeral and that a production of a play is *always* an answer to the play's questions appropriate to a particular time, place, company of actors and audience. However, much valuable comment on the production is included.

With the *Dream*, Brook met head-on the dilemma of the theatrical researcher who also directs for the commercial theatre: the life of the theatre resides in the spontaneous interplay of actor, text and audience, but the business of theatre depends on the performance being repeatable, a reliably marketable commodity. Brook's *Dream* endeavoured to make a peculiar kind of appeal to the imagination of its audiences, but one main source of its success, apart from its novelty, was the prestige of his own name, another the growing popularity of one of his leading players, Alan Howard.

The eight-week rehearsal period began with two weeks in which the text was hardly used at all: two weeks of questioning, of exploration of ideas and theatrical techniques. Then came a month of playing with the unusual properties used in the fairy scenes and of physical exercises to prepare the actors for the acrobatics and circus tricks which the ideas of director and designer required of them. Brook decided to double four pairs of roles, thus reducing the size of his cast and facilitating the chosen method of rehearsal. The doubles were Theseus/Oberon (Alan Howard), Hippolyta/Titania (Sara Kestelman), Puck/Philostrate (John Kane) and Egeus/Quince (Philip Locke). The four fairies demanded by the text also served as stage hands.

After the opening, Brook's ideas about the *Dream* were widely publicised. These were characteristic: the need to interweave the actions involving fairies, 'aristocrats' (the lovers apparently included) and mechanicals; the difficulty of finding stage techniques to create the play's magic for a materialistic modern audience; a determination that the play dealt covertly with dark sexual passions; and the propositions that 'the core of the *Dream* is the "Pyramus and Thisbe" play' and that 'It's a sort of celebration of the theatre arts.'[41]

A good general description was given by Rosemary Say, who also raised some of the points around which critical debate revolved.[42] 'Peter Brook . . . is more determined than ever to compel us to take a creative part in his production. This time we are to be bullied into getting our imaginations to work. His method, lively and inventive, just gets by – particularly when he allows Shakespeare to take some part in the proceedings from time to time. The stage is white-walled and empty. An iron gallery runs round the top where those members of the cast not immediately taking part stand to look down on the play in the manner of overseers supervising a factory floor. Two trapezes hang on black cords and a vast red plume is splashed across the back wall. The actors spill on the stage, a garish mixture dressed in King's

Road-type shirt and trousers, white silk cloaks and dresses of hard primary
colours. Last come the artisans, a gang of workmen carrying planks, sandwiches and mugs of tea.' For others, the set had different associations, among
them 'circus big top', 'squash court', 'polar bear pit at the zoo', gymnasium,
play-room – even the Elizabethan stage, with its tiring-house wall, two large
upstage doors and gallery above and behind the stage.[43]

A widely admired feature of the performances was, once more, clarity:
'Never have I heard the verse more beautifully spoken, every line comes
across as if the thought behind it had just been born in the actor's mind.'[44]
Even a tendency for verse, especially that of the lovers, to modulate into song
provoked little strong dissent. Clarity was also the key to the fairies and the
magic flower. No illusion was allowed, the means of the fairies' teasing of the
mortals were as visible as the devices of 'Pyramus and Thisbe'. The programme quoted from *The Empty Space:* 'It is up to us to capture [the
audience's] attention and compel its belief. To do so we must prove that
there will be no trickery, nothing hidden. We must open our empty hands
and show that really there is nothing up our sleeves. Only then can we begin'
(pp. 108–9). A circus trick represented the magic flower: a spinning plate
was passed from wand to wand by Puck and Oberon (and sometimes
dropped) as they swung on the trapezes. The nearly continuous musical
background was carefully orchestrated. The whole cubic space of the stage
was filled, by action on the trapezes; by the hoisting up of Titania's feather-
bed; by Puck on high stilts misleading Lysander and Demetrius; by the
metallic coil 'trees' dangled on fishing-rods from the gallery by the fairies;
and by the athletic running, jumping and climbing of the lovers. The lovers
were denied lyricism, almost becoming the knock-about comics of the play.
Hermia in particular was constantly in motion, being caught horizontally
across doorways or snatched up by trapeze, indignantly crying 'Puppet!'. A
still centre was afforded by the solemnity with which the mechanicals set
about rehearsing their play. In performance, its effect was to provoke in the
courtly audience not laughter but a hushed involvement. Titania's
encounter with Bottom, the climax before the interval, was remarkable for
the physicality of her lustful assault and culminated in a triumphant and
ithyphallic hymeneal procession, to the accompaniment of flying streamers
and Mendelssohn's wedding march, while Oberon swung wildly above on
his trapeze.

The allusion to Mendelssohn pinpointed the iconoclasm of the production. Not only was an older stage tradition left far behind but, for at least one
reviewer, Shakespeare's text too. John Russell Brown[45] spelt out, in acid
tones, the exact degree and detail of infidelity into which Brook's pursuit of
that 'hidden play' so 'very powerfully sexual' had led him, demolishing point
by point Brook's most extreme allegation about Oberon – that Shakespeare's King of Fairies is to be seen as 'a man taking the wife whom he loves

totally and having her fucked by the crudest sex machine he can find'.[46]

For the professional skill of the actors, no praise could be too high: they performed feats far beyond normal expectation (if hardly up to circus standard). They also succeeded remarkably in embodying Brook's idea of the play as having 'no set characters' and of each scene as being 'like a dream of a dream'. Reviewers frequently spoke of 'the actors' rather than 'the characters'. One crystallised the compelling quality of the performance with the words: 'The company seem not to act in it but to belong in it.'[47] Audiences left the theatre happy. So did most critics, though hindsight left some of them puzzled. The puzzles included the doubling. It undoubtedly contributed to the coherence of performance-style, but the conception of Oberon and Titania as subconscious projections of the unavowed desires of Theseus and Hippolyta found little to sustain it in the text and other doublings, notably that of Egeus and Quince, were even harder to rationalise. The mating of Titania and Bottom seems even further from the sense of this play, so much concerned with the power of imagination rather than of passion. The end of the play was another *tour de force* of production. For the final entry of Oberon and Titania, Alan Howard and Sara Kestelman had to change roles on stage, removing the cloaks which identified them as Theseus and Hippolyta. During their speeches, the other actors, 'whistling softly', also removed their coloured cloaks, to reveal white clothes beneath, and moved slowly downstage, led by Oberon, intoning his final speech on a solemn monotone. The ritual solemnity of the moment (of which the speech gives no hint) was followed by Puck's epilogue. After it, as the prompt-book has it, 'all off stage and into auditorium, shaking hands with audience'. This last action, cued by 'Give me your hands if we be friends,/And Robin shall restore amends', rejected the overt sense of requesting applause.

Audiences responded fairly well to the demand for reciprocity, though in doing so they were submitting to an intention imposed on them rather than expressing a spontaneous wish of their own. As the *Scotsman* reviewer drily put it, 'at times the players' easy chumminess with the audience throws up more barriers than it casts down'.[48] The solemnity of the ending, recognised as the touch of Brook, was an unsuccessful attempt to impose a meaning at odds with the obvious festivity suggested by the lines. This production, though verbally faithful to the complete text and clear in projecting it, ended by revealing that Brook's search for his 'hidden play' was proceeding not *through* Shakespeare's words, but *beside* or *beneath* them. Brook seemed to have grown tired of the constantly shifting suggestiveness of Shakespeare's language. Rejecting a style of 'Shakespearian acting' equated (perhaps unfairly) with the mouthing of verse in a 'poetry voice', he had reached an opposite extreme, where experiment and analysis led, not to renewed expressiveness but to rigid imposition of patterns of inflection and rhythm derived from rehearsal exercises rather than the spontaneous recreation of feeling in performance. Brook's choice of the *Dream* seemed, at last, to owe more to a preoccupation with acting technique than to a vital curiosity about Shakespeare's meanings. Its rejection of a sentimentalising stage tradition was dearly bought. By robbing it of human particularity, by reducing the fairies to subconscious projections of the humans, by rarifying the mechanicals into the Pirandellian heart of a mystery, Brook in his turn risked a sentimental reduction of the play, a confinement of its range and fantasy within a setting as modishly pretty and as thoroughly distracting as a whole forest of palpable-gross Beerbohm trees.[49]

Since *A Midsummer Night's Dream*, few of Brook's productions have been seen in England. In Paris, he has staged two French versions of Shakespeare at the International Centre's theatre, the Théâtre des Bouffes du Nord. *Timon d' Athènes*, performed in 1973, has been exhaustively described and analysed by Georges Baru and Richard Marienstras in *Les Voies de la Creation Theatrale*, v (1977). With *Mesure pour Mesure*, in November 1978, Brook returned to an early scene of triumph, directing it, to general critical acclaim, in the more chastened and severe manner of his recent years.

But English audiences had to wait eight years for his return to Stratford, where he directed a production of *Antony and Cleopatra* which opened at the Royal Shakespeare Theatre on 9 October 1978. The casting of Glenda Jackson as Cleopatra, as Brook has stated, fulfilled a long-standing ambition of the two to work together on the play. A necessary condition was to find the right Antony. Once Alan Howard was available, the ambition became a plan. Howard's presence in the cast, and the choice of Sally Jacobs and Richard Peaslee as designer and musical director, suggested continuities with the *Dream:* in the event, the production showed closer affinities with what Brook had been doing in Paris in the intervening years. The nature of the production stemmed from a number of clear and simple decisions, implemented with infinite pains and using to the full the outstanding joint resources of cast and director. The text was very lightly cut, losing only two very short scenes; a single set was used, modified in effect by simple large properties and by the occasional movement of hinged screens at its outer ends; costume, while generally suggestive of the Mediterranean world and of individual role and function, avoided both historical definition and visual splendour; music, though much used, rarely obtruded and was seldom introduced without invitation from the text or stage directions.

Brook (in sympathy with the views of Emrys Jones, whose New Penguin edition of the play[50] was used) saw the play as one of intimate action in a setting of threatening and intruding public events. Turning to advantage the fact that the action is made up of an unusually large number of short scenes, Brook used his setting to achieve very rapid continuity. With one interval, placed after III, vi (Octavia's return to Rome) and before Antony's reappearance in Egypt in III, vii, the play ran from 7.30 to 11.10. For so full a text, this was a rapid pace and it was achieved largely by superb continuity, as speaking was never rushed and often slowed down at moments of crisis. As with *Lear* and the *Dream*, Brook obtained a rehearsal period much longer than the season's norm: ten weeks for six principals, six for a further four actors and four to five weeks with the whole cast. As with the *Dream*, much rehearsal time was spent on exercises. The most apparent difference was in the approach to the text, which was read on the first day of rehearsals and towards which the cast were urged to direct each morning's exercises. The result was company playing of impressive strength and consistency: in this production there were no 'walk-ons', and many of the strong cast gave their best performances of the season.

The rapid succession of scenes which was integral to Brook's reading of the play was made possible by the set. Within the proscenium, four tall, translucent screens stood in a semi-circle, with wide gaps between them affording five entries. They enclosed the downstage area and the forestage, pushing most of the action well forward and counteracting the notorious lack of contact between stage and auditorium in this theatre. At the top, the screens were connected by further translucent sections, about half as long, which slanted inwards like the base of a polygonal dome. Behind the screens, the rest of the stage, a large bare area, could be seen stretching to back and sides neutrally hung with white. Outside the proscenium arch, some lower screens were hinged, three on each side. These were folded in towards the centre to afford a smaller, downstage space in front of them for the action of III, ii–vi. After the interval, they were open again, but were folded in once more for the final moments of the play, this time to enclose the dead Cleopatra and her women. At the base of the tall screens stood four benches. These were brought forward to set the stage for the Roman scenes. Until II, vii, the scene on Pompey's galley, the centre of the enclosure was occupied by a large rush mat, its weave emphasising its centre as the mid-point in the acting area. On it were four striped cushions, more being brought on for Pompey's banquet. The sudden flying of this large mat, dropping Antony to the stage from its upper edge, fused the one nautical image of the production – the rising carpet as a sail – with the scene's transition from polite to inspired drunkenness. The flying of this mat was the visual counterpart in the first half of the play to Cleopatra's monument, represented by another large carpet, of a vivid red. This descended slowly to serve as a backdrop for IV, xv, when the dying Antony is hauled up into the monument. After V, i, for which it remained hanging but only dimly lit, this carpet was laid out in the centre of the stage for the final scene. Only for the laying of this carpet and for the clearing up of the remains of the banquet after III, i were stage hands used: all other movements of props were done by the cast. A further carpet, pale with narrow dark stripes, was the main playing area from III, xii to IV, xv, being used at last for the dragging of the dead Antony upstage and out of sight at the end of IV, xv. A carpet, recalling the one used as playing-space by the company who accompanied Brook to West Africa in 1972, figured largely in the early weeks of rehearsal as the only playing-space. The other large properties were two round brass stools, standing each on a smaller brown carpet at the two downstage corners of the mat. In the first half, they were covered by kidney-bean-shaped cushions, black with red shadings: when they returned in the later stage of the second half, they were uncovered, and much use was made of the reflected yellow light from their tops during the sequence leading up to Antony's suicide. Their metallic gleam carried both hints of military action and a less defined threat of destruction. It was to one of these stools that Antony retreated to prepare for his suicide, sitting in profile to the audience, crossing his legs and loosening the least formal of his various tunics in a manner with Japanese overtones. Eros, having stabbed himself behind Antony, died slumped over the other stool. A third brass stool, taller than these two, was introduced as the throne when Cleopatra in turn prepared for her suicide.

While the carpets and large properties (which included two more of the dark kidney-bean cushions for the second half) provided the intimate and flexible setting for most of the play's many scenes, the arc of screens dominated the stage throughout. Not only did they allow for overlap between scenes, often of a startling kind when dialogue relating to a character about to enter was juxtaposed with the move of that character into position for the next scene (especially striking, for instance, at II, ii–iii, Antony and Octavia; II, vii–III, i, the breaking up of Pompey's banquet by the entry of Pacorus, knocking over benches before being struck down by the pursuing Ventidius; and IV, v–vi, where the entry of Enobarbus seemed almost to answer Antony's quiet, unheard call for his lost friend). Twice, scenes shared the stage: IV, x and xi were played with the two groups of characters side by side on the carpet; IV, xiii, where Cleopatra plans to escape to her monument and to send Mardian with false news of her death, was played upstage, behind the screens, while Antony remained downstage, prostrated in grief, his outstretched arms supported by the two brass stools. The depth of the stage was elsewhere used with striking effect for actions half-seen behind the screens. Enobarbus watched Actium far upstage, back to audience, while the lights faded three times nearly to blackout and disordered noise and music swelled and faded. At his entry in III, xi, Antony came forward to speak his first speech within the enclosure, behind which little light remained: throughout the scene, his followers remained in this obscure area behind the screens. Most startling of all was the moment, during Antony's last victorious battle, when blood-soaked sponges were suddenly thrown at the four screens from behind and slid down, leaving their stains as part of the setting for the final action.

Visually, the action was chiefly remarkable for its lucidity: each scene had been allowed to grow into its own shape, and each scene made its contribution to the unfolding action with such clarity that the loss of so small a section of text as III, v left a palpable gap in the narrative by leaving the fate of Pompey and Lepidus undefined. Attention was focused throughout on the actors: costume too aimed constantly at clarifying their relationships, functions, even moods. Cleopatra's variety, unusually well realised by the enormous vocal and emotional range displayed by Glenda Jackson, was reflected in a chameleon-like succession of robes, encompassing a wider variety of shape and colour than the rest of the costumes put together and transforming her by turns into an almost androgynous glamour, a hieroglyphic formality, a timeless North African grief and abasement and finally a subdued regal splendour. Apart from Antony's gift of a pearl, hung in a long necklace, she had no ornaments. Against her, in an opposition more powerfully realised than in most productions, stood Octavia, a slight, diffident figure, conspicuous in the only yellow gown on stage, but no icicle or mere political pawn. Affectionate with her brother, her response to Antony's 'I have not kept my square' mingled deprecating forgiveness with a hint of frank curiosity. Reds distinguished Antony's followers, blues, striping a basic white in various patterns, those of Caesar. Pompey's black was mixed with browns and greys for his men. Loose robes for the men combined dignity with grace and ease of movement. Antony's costumes reflected his movements from Egypt to Rome and from love to war by suggestive alteration rather than total transformation, the extremes being a striped 'dressing-gown' for act I and light leather armour with a Tartar helmet for the heroics of IV, iv–xiv.

Within the framework created by the design, interpretation took the form of a ceaseless search for exact meaning, in every scene and every speech. The emphasis was personal; characters were conceived in terms of the pursuit of personal fulfilment. The production was remarkable for its generous acceptance of the humanity of every character in the play. Though increasingly clear-sighted about political realities, even Caesar was neither cynic nor ambitious plotter. His love of Antony, especially after their reconciliation, and of Octavia was patently sincere, if as patently immature. As played by Jonathan Pryce, he was a slightly gawky shy smiler (with no knife beneath the cloak). Gained authority reduced the gawkiness, but the naiveté remained in his overt and enthusiastic curiosity on encountering Cleopatra and in the prolonged backward look at her before his final departure from the stage at the end of the play.

The heroic fatalism described by Plutarch in his account of the last days of Antony and Cleopatra may or may not have been in Brook's mind, but gaiety, even in defeat, was the mood of the production. Balancing the warmth of Caesar were an Antony and Cleopatra whose delight in each other was none the less confident and happy for their awareness that it was also fatal. Resilience was another quality much in evidence. Enobarbus greeted the news of Fulvia's death with an explosion of incredulous laughter and Antony, so far worried and shamed by the news, was surprised into honestly joining in. After defeat, each new blow, seeming at first to crush all hopes, only called forth new reserves of courage. Antony in defeat, 'valiant and dejected' by turns, ranted and swaggered through to a final recovery of dignity. Cleopatra, glazed into trance-like grief by the death of Antony, recovered to relish her defeat of Caesar's triumph with light-hearted and malicious ridicule and to accommodate a transition to and from a mood close to farce in her scene with Richard Griffiths's red-nosed, hieroglyphic comic-strip Clown. Joy had a more sombre tinge in Patrick Stewart's grey Enobarbus, a performance which had gained much in depth and sensitivity since he played the role in 1972. Risking a powerfully romantic response to the play, and especially to Cleopatra, Brook drew from the whole of his large cast performances of the clarity and conviction needed to safeguard such a response against sentimentalism. He had the good fortune to be able to cast powerful and experienced actors in many of the play's smallest parts. The search for inner conviction and for the full meaning of each scene was reflected in the force and significance of the speaking of lines throughout. Rehearsal activity aimed at breaking down theatrical cliché and actors' habits is among the most impressively fruitful of Brook's methods as a director. The text of *Antony and Cleopatra* can rarely, if ever, have been so fully and significantly played. The result was to be observed (on the second night) in an audience deeply involved with that experience of renewal of the known play so frequently recorded by writers on Brook's productions of Shakespeare.

Press response to *Antony and Cleopatra,* though appreciative, was also slightly baffled and gave mild hints of disappointment. Certainly there was no immediate invitation to controversy in the production. Yet with this production Brook seems to have come closer than with the *Dream,* or perhaps even *Lear,* to an impartial but deeply committed presentation of the whole play to the senses, intelligence and imagination of his audience. No axe-grinding cuts, no baseless fabrics of subtextual subterfuge, no self-indulgent (or didactic) importation of the activities of the rehearsal-room onto the stage distracted from the play and its richness of meaning. Nor was the production in any sense untheatrical. Rarely can the banquet on Pompey's galley have effected so refined a flight from intoxication into the wilder realms of imagination. Not many directors have the sheer confidence which can turn the mere pulling of Antony across the stage looped in the long head-dresses of Cleopatra and her women into a more powerful image of the difficult hauling of the dying man up into the monument than any more literal staging could hope to emulate.

In 1978 Peter Brook returned to England with a production that confirms his great distinction as a director of Shakespeare. In retrospect, this *Antony and Cleopatra* may come to seem, as any production must, to have stressed some aspects of the play at the expense of others. His rejection of visual elaboration may have endangered the play's military and imperial themes, but it was a healthy reaction against surviving mid-Victorian assumptions about staging and costuming Shakespeare. His projection of the play in no way inhibited the imaginative response of the audience; and topical concerns of the late 1970s did not distort the production – rather they informed it and brought conviction to what was, in every sense, a major *revival* of the play.

As this account of *Antony and Cleopatra* draws on information derived from interviews generously given by the designer, Sally Jacobs, and by Patrick Stewart, who played Enobarbus, on the day after the second performance (11 October 1978), and as the interviews contain much more detail about aspects of the production mentioned above, it seems proper to conclude with a very slightly abbreviated text of them.

INTERVIEW WITH SALLY JACOBS

R.P. This is something that came up already with the *Dream* a few years ago – when you were thinking about the set, were Elizabethan theatres in your mind?

S.J. Very much. We knew that you could perform any Shakespearian play without sets. It just started from that premiss – we didn't need anything. Everybody had got into a terrible sort of deadend, over-pictorialising everything, especially that particular play, which needed at that time a complete new broom. And that really is what led us to where we went.

R.P. But this set is very unlike the *Dream*.

S.J. Very unlike, but one actually started again with that over-made element of pictorialisation which is associated with Cleopatra. One was stuck with that in one's head. Somehow we had to get rid of that in order to release the play. So that, in that respect, I was trying to reinvent the play, for our production. But the solution is entirely different, because the play is entirely different – but again one was dealing with another form of degraded parrot.

R.P. It wasn't Mendelssohn you had to fight this time.

S.J. No. Liz Taylor and Richard Burton; Cecil B. de Mille and Claudette Colbert and the Victorians – and just sheer spectacle. The barge – and the treasures of Tutankhamen. . . . That was absolutely the only similarity, that one had to deal with that. And the way I did it was – I just went completely in the other direction.

R.P. The last production here did use that style of costume, quite a bit of Tutankhamen. [Trevor Nunn's production in 1972.]

S.J. Academically very accurate.

R.P. Which, after all, has nothing to do with Jacobean plays.

S.J. No, nothing at all.

R.P. Was it this theatre you had in mind from the beginning in planning this production? Was there no thought of its ever being done elsewhere?

S.J. No.

R.P. I wondered about that, because I thought that one of the most helpful things the set did was to reduce the size of the stage and to divide the areas of the stage in a most interesting way.

S.J. That again was a necessity: to create the right sort of intimate space for the play to happen against a background, an ambiguous background. A place where one could always be aware of the outside world affecting the domestic space – and to relate these. Which is why it's a half-seen world, semi-transparent, with many ways of coming and going in and out of it, anchored by the carpet area, which gives a focus to the main action.

R.P. All of that worked beautifully. There was a wonderful continuity too – the scenes coming in behind as others left the stage.

S.J. Well, that was Peter's commitment very early on. No obligation whatsoever to set the difference between Alexandria and Rome. That it should be a place in which everything can flow through, and the people come and bring their world with them and take it off with them, and that there was no commitment to showing location. This didn't seem necessary as you read the play. You didn't have to know.

R.P. At what point in the proceedings did you feel that the irrevocable decisions about the set had been made? Was there much change during the rehearsal period, or was it all pretty clear before then?

S.J. It was very clear right from the beginning. There were two opposite ways of using the space – which was *not* clear. Peter went on shifting one way and then the other for quite a while on that. That is, there was a way of arranging the enclosure which was more domestic, and then a way of arranging the enclosure which was more archetypal, noble, architectural: so that the one gave us the grandeur, and the other gave us the domesticity. Until he got well into rehearsal, he wasn't sure which way. Just by rearranging the parts that you saw there on the stage, one had still those two alternatives to play with, which he did go on being slightly ambivalent about until he'd got well into rehearsal, until he'd really worked the material through. Then he found, of course, that the domesticity is created by the carpet, and that it was perfectly all right to have it in the noble structure – and that if you domesticated the structure you could only play on one level. So, we got the best of both worlds, in a way, in the end – the way I hoped. But he felt overpowered by the set originally.

R.P. Was there ever any question of a raised level for the monument?

S.J. No, never.

R.P. I thought that it was the most wonderfully simple expedient for that scene [IV, xv]. It works beautifully, the pulling up of Antony.

S.J. He just knew, right from the beginning, that he would find a way of doing that which had nothing to do with levels. . . . We knew right from the beginning that we wanted a permanent setting, which could be used for everything, with variations just at the point where you'd saturated that use. You then overlay and bring in – like in music, you know – work the variations until you need a new theme. So we did that all the way through. But there was no place within that for structural set changes – and since there wasn't, he knew that he would find a way of pulling Antony up without there being another level.

R.P. Might I ask you to say a word or two about the costumes? Was there a very clear sense of the succession of Glenda Jackson's costumes as reflecting the different scenes in the play? She has what looks to be an enormous range and variety of costumes – maybe fewer than they seemed?

S.J. Actually, she had a lot more costumes than you saw. What I did was, I designed a wardrobe for her, and we found that if she wore everything for every purpose, she just had too many clothes. Some things seemed to pin her down and clarify the look better than others, so I began, at that point in dress rehearsal when you see everything for the first time, to eliminate certain things and to simplify. What we've come down to is just those changes which seem absolutely necessary for the playing of the play. I've eliminated quite a lot of other changes which seemed right psychologically – originally. But one always loses those things, because the actress or the actor, they do it without the need of costume eventually. Often it happens that you over-visualise the thing until the actors take it over and make it their own, and then they need very little, very little. It just has to be the right thing. So that with her clothes particularly it was almost impossible for me to pin down the right look until *she'd* got to the stage where she was herself – and I did that all through the dress rehearsal and preview period.

R.P. I didn't see the French production of *Timon* in Paris, but I wondered whether the costuming owed anything to what Peter Brook has been doing in Paris?

S.J. I think it owes a lot to what's happened since we did the *Dream*. Because what has happened is that so much good work now is done without costume or set. The line that the designer has to tread now is really minimal. So you can no longer go back to a production like this which, because it's on the stage in a conventional theatre, means that you have an obligation to set it and to costume it in the way that you can't do if you're setting up the carpet in the town hall, or out in the park somewhere. You actually have to dominate the space that you're in, which is a conventional stage. You've got to work against it and pull people into the world of the play. But you can't ignore what's happened in our vocabulary and our experience over the last ten or fifteen years, with all the superb work that's done in small groups with nothing. There are a lot of things which just seem terribly old-fashioned, seem over-designed now, which ten years ago would have been a treat. And that was very hard for me, to find that line between, where I know that if I just put an important big robe on an actor he becomes an important figure. But how far to go in the detailing of that towards historical truth, evocative romantic feeling, and all these things? I find now it's become very difficult to hit the right line. I struggled with these costumes, and I think I finally *got* it, with a minimum of what's necessary. . . . You never any more, I don't think, go into this highly pictorial, idiosyncratic, designers' world. It's meaningless now, it looks rococo.

R.P. What I got very strongly last night was an overall feeling from the costumes of a fairly timeless Mediterranean world – both the Roman and the Egyptian.

S.J. Oh, I'm so glad you said that! That's really what I based it on, more than anything.

R.P. They could have belonged to a distant period. They could be almost contemporary. In different scenes the different suggestions were there.

S.J. I'm very glad you got that.

R.P. I thought that was very strong – that scene [III, xi] when Cleopatra and her women come in after the first defeat, with suddenly their Arab head-dresses, and her prostration in front of Antony. The flexibility of some of the tunics and robes, the different ways they wore them, I found most powerful.

S.J. There was a long period where I thought I would just have to use togas for the Romans and battled with myself to get rid of the toga. In the end I went to the Middle Eastern big robe, with the stripes on it, which actually is a much more fresh way of looking at the world, but still had the stateliness of senators, important men in a hot climate – a cool, westernised world compared with the Egyptian.

R.P. I thought the Roman costumes wonderfully combined the different suggestions, and yet, as you say, got away from togas, which have nothing to do with Shakespeare anyway.

S.J. No. Also difficult to act in and restricting.

R.P. It fitted the performances beautifully to have the ease of movement.

R.P. [Of the production in general] . . . the play's revived by it, totally.

S.J. He [Brook] has that wonderful way of going fearlessly straight into that area where it is exposed – totally. And I go along with that, with him.

That's what he always does. The *play* always emerges, I think, in the most extraordinary way.

R.P. [Seeing a copy of Emrys Jones's New Penguin edition.] Is that the one you're using?

P.S. Emrys Jones? Yes. Very good.

R.P. There didn't seem to have been much cutting of it either. A very full text you're using.

P.S. I would think it is probably one of the fullest performances of the play that there have been. We've lost two complete scenes, which were lost the last time I did it. [Patrick Stewart played Enobarbus in Trevor Nunn's production which ran at Stratford and in London between August 1972 and March 1974.] They are a fragment – we could never quite understand why it was there – between Lepidus, Maecenas and Agrippa [II, iv]. And we've also lost the Eros, Enobarbus scene [III, v], which is quite an important little plot scene, in that it ties up the ends about Pompey.

R.P. And Lepidus.

P.S. I rehearsed that for six weeks too in 72, and it was cut at about exactly the same point that this was. . . . Other than that, there are no entire cuts, and very, very few internal ones. *I* am playing a much fuller text than I played for Trevor in 72 – which I'm pleased about!

R.P. I'm pleased about it too: it went very well. I got a curious experience, last night, of a performance which – because you were playing it again – had an element of familiarity in it, and yet it was a different person from last time.

P.S. Well, that's completely satisfying.

R.P. He seemed both more sombre, and happier.

P.S. Well! You couldn't have said a more pleasing thing to me. I've never thought of it in such simple terms, but I guess that's what has happened to Enobarbus as a result of this new production. At the very beginning, when I talked to Peter in Paris, his first remark was, 'Well, this is good. You can build on the previous work.' And then when we started work, I made a serious mistake. I tried to wipe out that past experience, denying myself access to all of that previous knowledge, richness, from rehearsal, and two years of performances. And this was an error. I think now it wasn't too damaging a one, because it meant that we seriously explored other aspects of Enobarbus and his relationship with Antony, and his major objectives and motives in the play, in a very, very new way. But latterly – in the last two or three weeks – I have been thinking much more about the old Enobarbus, and indeed the experience of playing the man has been pulling me more and more towards him. Also, in the meantime I've got

seven years older, which naturally changed things – and all the surroundings are quite, quite different. I would say that the major difference this
time is that the performance of the part is perhaps less sentimental than it
was before, and that he has become – I would hope – a *little* more complicated.

R.P. I had a feeling that he was less golden, that he'd got a bit greyer, and
that made him more interesting, in a way. It was a different tone, less
cynical than he was last time.

P.S. You thought me cynical last time?

R.P. Somewhat – at moments. It was an appreciative cynicism.

P.S. There was something of the old soldier who has seen it all and is not
really going to be impressed by anything any more. In this, he is – I
think – wiser. And in working with Alan and Brook, we've tried to tie in
Enobarbus's deepest desires with those of Antony. They are both, in their
way, looking for some richer fulfilment of their lives. Antony is making
that search very, very openly, and it explains many of his curious actions
in the middle part of the play. Less obviously, Enobarbus is too. And of
course I think they both find it too, for there is, in a curious way, a real
fulfilment in the deaths of both men. They do change themselves; there is
a – what does he call it? – 'transmigration'. [The reference here is to
Antony's description of the crocodile, a passage played with great
emphasis and comic brilliance by Alan Howard.]

R.P. I've never seen the death scene played before so as to make such total
sense. It was just the involvement of the audience in the simple question
whether or not Enobarbus is dead. You were dead, but the soldiers
expressed real doubt of it. Death is so beautiful in this play, isn't it?

P.S. It is. It is something to be embraced. I'm always immensely touched
by Cleopatra's line about Iras: 'If thus thou vanishest, thou tell'st the
world/It is not worth leave-taking.' It's one of those bits of Shakespeare
that one can carry with one for a very long time, and it brings a great
comfort. Yes indeed, death is a changing process. It does not mark dust
and a blank, but something much more than that. All of the people – the
major characters – are fulfilled in their deaths. Enobarbus is educated
during the process of his dying enormously. In the course of about the last
twelve hours of his life he learns a very great deal.

R.P. What very much struck me was the underlying sense of joy in this
performance of the play. The pleasure and the joy and the love are so real
this time. There is nothing forced, nothing superficial, nothing strained
about the passions. They all seem to be growing very, very powerfully out
of the people. I can never remember the first act seeming so genuinely,
unforcedly *happy*.

P.S. Oh, that's marvellous – because that's a word that has been used a lot in
the last three weeks. Joy and delight – the two key words for us. In trying

to create that Egyptian world – I think that Peter is absolutely right – it is not necessary to create in detail some magical or mysterious or semi-oriental world. No, it lies with the people and their attitude to life. And it's revealed in all kinds of curious ways. One of Enobarbus' lines – I think one of the key lines in the play – describes the Egyptian world and also Antony's and Enobarbus' feelings about living. When he says to Lepidus – they're arguing at the very beginning of the meeting scene [II, ii], and Lepidus is saying 'Now come on. Use your influence to calm him down', and Enobarbus says 'No. Quite the opposite. If there's any trouble, I shall encourage Antony to go in both fists flying', and Lepidus says 'Tis not a time For private stomaching'. Enobarbus says 'Every time Serves for the matter that is then born in't.' Living in the moment.

R.P. Yes! 'Some pleasure – *now*.'

P.S. That's right. It is not for the future, or in the past, but you enrich that very moment that you're living in and you suck it dry. You take everything from it. And what *is* at that moment is the most important, no matter *what* it is. This is one of the things that distinguishes the Roman and the Egyptian worlds, that Rome is very much a world where they are not living in that moment, but thinking of the future, and the past, and history.

R.P. There's a great sense also – in relation to what you said – of courage, and of courageous acceptance of defeat. The bit of the play I've always found most difficult is the middle, acts III and IV. In this production the general, overall shape of what happens is clarified in a way that I'd never seen before. The sense of courage and joy *past* despair, beyond defeat, in face of defeat, is very strong.

P.S. For Antony in particular this is a great question. Although he has to face up to the defeat at Actium, it must not be a destroying defeat, to him personally, because the energy and his own personal search has got to continue with the same sort of determination as it had before. The actor has to find a way of absorbing that defeat and making direct use of it in order to push himself further.

R.P. Has the experience of working with Peter Brook measured up to the kind of awe you expressed when you spoke to us at the Shakespeare Conference in August? [Patrick Stewart addressed the International Shakespeare Conference at Stratford in August 1978, answering questions mainly about his playing of Shylock in John Barton's production of *The Merchant of Venice* at the Other Place.]

P.S. There is less awe in me now in that sense of fear and the restrictiveness that that sort of awe can bring on you. Through these rehearsals I've learned to respect and love the man very deeply. I've also learned – which is an important lesson for all one's work – that to be made free and to be liberated from fear – as a performer – from habits, from inhibitions, is perhaps the most important search that we should make. And that is one of the things that he dedicates his life to. When I spoke of awe, I spoke of being a performer knowing that Peter Brook was in an audience, in a production that was not his. He came to see *The Merchant,* and his influence on that company that night was absolutely terrific. I don't think that can happen to me again now, because I know that for him there is never an expectation that anything is completed, that he would not expect to see a 'finished' piece of work. Work is always in progress and constantly changing and transforming itself and developing and growing. In fact, if one takes seriously to heart what Peter teaches – because he's a great teacher too, to all of us, the most experienced among us – he can reduce those elements of insecurity and fear, which can be such a limiting thing on an actor. So I don't think I would ever feel that same fear about him being at a performance again. Though, you see, I think tonight he may come to see our performance and he didn't last night, and his mere presence out there is going to add a kind of sharpness to the play.

R.P. I find it hard to imagine it being much better than it was last night – but it must feel different from your side.

P.S. Well, you are much relieved to get the first night over. Last night you were a wonderful audience. We had a disastrous audience the first night: hard to please, not prepared to make a move towards *us.* And so last night, with it all behind us, we could relax, and it was a warm audience.

R.P. It certainly felt like a very attentive audience.

R.P. The main thing that I would like to ask you about is just what happened during the rehearsal period, the progression of work on the play, the order of events. A lot has been written about Peter Brook's work on various productions and with his Paris group. Did the rehearsal period correspond to what you had expected, in the way of activity that went on during it?

P.S. I tried to go with as few expectations as possible, to be able to leave myself open to anything that came up. I would say the rehearsal period was divided very, very clearly into three quite distinct phases. Because he wanted to have a long rehearsal period and he wanted to begin before the last production (which was *Love's Labour's Lost*) had opened, he only had available to him six actors. They were Alan and Glenda, Jonathan Pryce and myself, Paola [Dionisotti] and Marjorie Bland. So you had the four principals, and Charmian and Octavia – important figures too. The six of us worked, with Peter, alone, for three weeks. I look back on those three weeks as being in many ways the most exciting and the richest time of rehearsal. The work was intensely concentrated. He makes demands on actors in rehearsal that are not made by many other directors. At any one moment, every person who is present in that rehearsal room has to be fully concentrated on the thing in hand. He frequently refers to others, who are not perhaps rehearsing the scene. He will frequently turn and say 'What did you think? Tell us.' – and so you can't switch off. In those three weeks, it meant very often eight hours of unremitting attention. But also with great relaxation. He seemed to be very happy during that time. I think working with a small group too was pleasant for him. We spent the first two days not in a rehearsal room but at his house – reading the play and talking about it, reading and talking, very, very slowly working through the play. We talked about language, and we did some exercises in language too. Then after the second day, we came into a rehearsal room, which had a square of carpet in the middle of it, and that carpet was to be our rehearsal space. Nothing but that for the next four or five weeks. We never moved off that carpet. Each day would begin with a period of exercise, warm up, which could take many, many forms. Physical integration, sound – but perhaps the dominant theme in all these exercises was the freeing and releasing of the imagination, coupled with an increased awareness and sensitivity to the things around you, your fellow actors. To develop a responsiveness that was lightning-sharp, and free of habit and cliché. We did many, many, many varied exercises – and improvisations. Some of them utterly demanding – where perhaps an actor had to hold on to two or three things – maybe a rhythm and a bodily movement, and a conversation, and another conversation, with someone else. Three or four things having to go on at the same time, all of which he had to keep in the air – very much like a juggler. I found those sessions – thrilling. They would last usually an hour and a half, sometimes a little longer, sometimes half a day. But, they were always geared to move from the exercise into the work on the play, in such a way that the exercise would reflect directly into the text work we would then go on to do – always. Peter constantly asked us to 'make the connections.' This was *not* isolated exercising followed by conventional rehearsal. We had to carry over *that* experience into our work on the text.

R.P. Was much of what appears in the production devised during rehearsals in this way? I'm thinking particularly of the scene on Pompey's galley, the song and dance passage there. I thought it worked quite superbly well and had a range of meaning and effect that I hadn't seen in it before. Is that something that was worked out at rehearsal?

P.S. There's almost nothing that is 'worked out'. It *is* the one scene which was built up out of pure improvisation. It is not his way to take any scene and to place the actors and to ask them to move here and there, so that at rehearsal things would change constantly, every rehearsal, in a search to find the happiest solution to a particular problem. That scene was given no formal shape until a very few days before we appeared in front of an audience. He knew that he wanted it to have initially, not a sort of

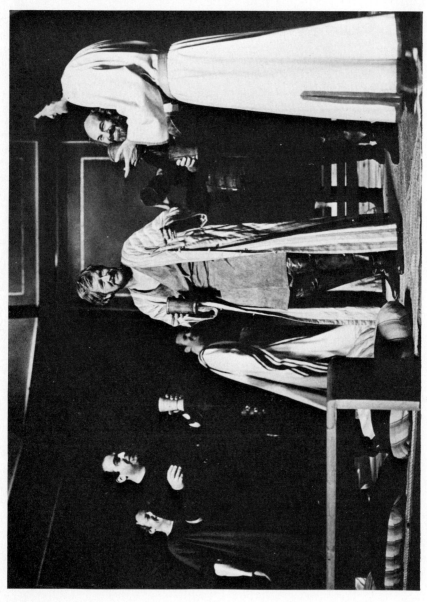

10 *Antony and Cleopatra*, II, vii. Royal Shakespeare Theatre, 1978. Demetrius (David Lyon), Pompey (David Suchet), Agrippa (Paul Webster), Antony (Alan Howard), Enobarbus (Patrick Stewart), Octavius (Jonathan Pryce)

boisterous rugby-club feeling, but something which was to do with liquor and food, which had not brought men into a beery, boisterous state, but rather to something which was elevated and very refined – where wits were sharpened. A little bit like – I suppose – being slightly stoned. This was the way we rehearsed it one time, and out of that, delicately, the Egyptian bacchanal would begin to grow. And what happens there is entirely improvised – and indeed is every night: it never repeats itself.

R.P. The singer isn't necessarily picked up by the same people?

P.S. That, finally, was worked out. What happens to the singer is plotted, and when he passes from one character to the other. But all the things that happen on the fringe, the moving around, the wildness, the tumbling onto the carpet, when the carpet goes up – all that, that is improvised.

R.P. Your business with the bench? [At the climax of the dance, Enobarbus falls off a bench, pulling it on top of him and embracing it.]

P.S. That is now fixed. I had to look for something that would feed Jonathan's 'strong Enobarb is weaker than the wine', and so that was found. And it was thought to be good, so it was kept in. It is interesting, because many people refer to that scene. In rehearsal, I was eager to get it set, to get something firm about it. I always felt it was a bit of a mess whenever we did it. It bothered me that Peter seemed to be perfectly happy. At the end of maybe two hours spent on the scene, with many of us feeling that we had achieved nothing, and that we still had the same sort of confusion we'd had two hours before, he seemed to be utterly untroubled by that. Well, his way proved to be the right way, because it marks a change in the rhythm of the play.

R.P. It was satisfying and exciting to see it also followed, and broken into, by the Parthian scene (which is usually cut) rather than by the interval. It so often is made the climax before the interval.

P.S. It was last time.

R.P. The placing of the interval too was very satisfying indeed. [It came after III, vi.] That strong opening to the second half – your entrance in collision with Cleopatra, the opposition that's so strongly projected at the beginning. You get the play moving tremendously.

P.S. Yes, it's completely satisfying. It is for me, because putting the division there marks the great change in *my* story – I think even the major story of the play. It puts us on the edge of Actium, and nothing is the same again after that.

R.P. It curiously harks back to the beginning of the play as well. It almost has a second movement feeling to it.

P.S. We played around an awful lot with intervals. We've had three or four different ones. We actually had two intervals at one time. I mean, we played it with an audience with two intervals. But everyone knew that it

was not possible to make a second break in the play, between Antony's
death and Cleopatra's. The two must be linked.

R.P. It made more sense than any other placing of the interval I've seen in
other productions.

R.P. I was very interested to hear you speak of having started rehearsal with
a reading of the play. One has heard that sometimes the text of the play
entered Peter Brook rehearsals rather later.

P.S. We met those words on the first day. We began to read them to one
another – but only six of us. It's not the same as a whole company sitting
around. I was talking about the shape of rehearsals. For the first three
weeks, we had just six of us. When the other productions were on, we were
joined by four more actors – David Suchet [Pompey], Allan Rickman
[Alexas, Thidias], Paul Brooke [Lepidus], Richard Griffiths [Messenger,
Clown]. They were with us for about ten days. It was only in the last four
or five weeks that we had all the twenty-six actors. When we *all* met on the
first day, after a morning of exercising with the whole company, we sat in a
circle, and we all read the play from beginning to end. But there was only
one copy of it, and that copy was passed from hand to hand. I mean, there
was in a sense only one copy, in that no one read their own role, but
somebody said: 'All right. Start with "Nay, but this dotage of our general" – there.' And at the entrance of each new character, or the beginning
of each new scene or development, it would be picked up by the next
person round the circle. And so it was read around, and it went round the
circle three or four times. That was the way that this company first read
the whole of *Antony and Cleopatra*.

R.P. What you say about the whole company having come in later is very
surprising, One would never have guessed. The sense of focus in the
performances is tremendous. I can't remember when – if ever – I last
heard the whole of a Shakespeare play spoken so intelligibly as last night,
and so devoid of any kind of theatrical cliché. It seemed quite wonderful as
a rendering of the text to listen to.

P.S. Isn't that marvellous! From a man about whom usually one
thinks – well – improvisation, movement, great stage effects, and so on.

R.P. Initially, I was rather puzzled by one thing about Cleopatra, which
could be related to Enobarbus. When you got to the bit about 'hopping
through the public street', my credulity stretched to breaking point. This
seems to imply in Cleopatra a degree of fragility somewhere, which was
nowhere apparent in Glenda Jackson's powerful performance of the role.

P.S. Peter and I think it's a very important passage. It's actually marked by
my taking two or three steps forward – in a sense, almost out of the
scene – it is isolated. That's an attempt for the audience to be put in touch

with something about this personality which is deeper, more profound, than someone who is a behaviourist. There is something about her which cannot be explained, a power, indeed a perfection. It's a thing which occurs so much in the play – the contrast of opposites: that at a time when she would appear to be most vulnerable, most human – she has been running through the streets and she was out of breath – her very disorder displayed itself as a kind of perfection, a sort of magic. I don't think that that suggests there is any particular fragility in her, but that it's to do with an inner quality, a completeness at the centre of the person, which expresses itself *at all times*. When I was playing the part before, I often used to want to cut those last few lines of Enobarbus' speech – 'for vilest things Become themselves in her, that the holy priests Bless her when she is riggish'. Those lines always seemed to me to be an anticlimax after what had just gone before. But not so: because it's right at the heart of the whole barge speech, that it is *when* she *is* at her coarsest and crudest – apparently so – that she expresses something that is almost religious in its nature. I feel they must be very important.

P.S. The week when we did our first previews, Monday was a day of technical work, with a full dress rehearsal at night. Tuesday was to have been a similar day, and Wednesday was our first public preview. So, we were breathlessly within hours of going in front of an audience. Having done the dress rehearsal on the Monday night, all of Tuesday – the entire day – was given over to the company, and Peter, and at times the designer and the composer, sitting, in a circle, talking about the performance of the previous night. The whole *day* was given over to it – when in any other experience I've had – you know – last-minute desperate adjustments will be made here, and the director will be working on this point, and on that point. No! We sat down quietly, and yet again every member of this group was encouraged – indeed it was insisted upon – to make his contribution. We were all invited to be out in the audience whenever we could that night, watching scenes we were not involved in, so that we could then come back and talk about them. And nothing was held back. Now, to do that – to have the courage to do that! Of course it's not courage, it's actually common sense, when you see it work. To do that had a wonderful effect on this group. It's a case of what you feel your priorities are. You reach a point when you *can* spend every spare moment perfecting. But to do that would suggest that finally there is going to be something which will be complete. You will add the last piece – and that is it. As though you would say, 'Hold it! Let's take a picture of it! Because that's what we've been working towards for eight weeks.' It's not like that with him. Nor is it really like that with any of our directors. Now, nobody believes that. But Peter takes it very much further. It is 'work in progress'. And the first night was just simply one moment, a very important moment, for all of us. But it was important because we were performing the play, and in that sense no more important than last night, or tonight. And that's in another way one of the reasons why the actors were so calm on that first night.

R.P. Obviously it's to do with his extraordinary personality and gifts and experience, but how much do you think the extended rehearsal-time is a necessity for achieving a result like this? Presumably you had much shorter rehearsal for *The Merchant?*

P.S. Oh, yes. Actually – no, we didn't. We had eight weeks on that production. Yes, we were very, very lucky. Though it was much broken into, because people were rehearsing other shows as well. There were people who were in *The Tempest* and *The Merchant.* With *Antony* we needed all of those ten weeks. If we had only had five weeks, or six weeks, it would have been difficult to have spent the amount of time exercising that we did. You couldn't give over half of every morning – or perhaps a day – to talking. But with a play as complicated as this, as structurally difficult, with creatures who are so complex, I would say that time was necessary.

NOTES

1. In Ralph Berry, *On Directing Shakespeare: Interviews with Contemporary Directors* (London: Croom Helm, 1977), pp. 114–15.
2. Biographical information is derived from J. C. Trewin, *Peter Brook: a Biography* (London: Macdonald & Co., 1971).
3. Reviewed by, among others, Irving Wardle, *The Times* (19 July 1968); Ronald Bryden, *The Observer* (21 July 1968); Jeremy Kingston, *Punch* (31 July 1968); Ronald Hayman interviewed Brook, *The Times* (29 August 1968).
4. J. L. Styan, *The Shakespeare Revolution* (Cambridge University Press, 1977); ch. 11, 'Shakespeare, Peter Brook and non-illusion.'
5. 'The Director as Misanthropist: on the Moral Neutrality of Peter Brook', *Theatre Quarterly*, VII, no. 25 (1977), 20–8.
6. See A. H. C. Smith, *Orghast at Persepolis* (London: Eyre Methuen, 1972).
7. See J. Heilpern, *Conference of the Birds* (London: Faber & Faber, 1977).
8. *Birmingham Mail.* Newspaper reviews quoted in this article were consulted in the scrapbooks housed at the Shakespeare Centre, Stratford-upon-Avon: not all are identified or dated. *Measure for Measure* opened on 9 March 1950.
9. 'Shakespeare's Comedies and the Modern Stage', *Shakespeare Survey 4* (Cambridge University Press, 1951), p. 136.
10. *The Times.*
11. *Shakespeare Survey 4*, p. 135.
12. *Manchester Guardian.*
13. Richard Findlater, *The Tribune* (17 March 1950).
14. *Time and Tide.*
15. Peter Brook, *The Empty Space* (London: McGibbon & Kee, 1968; Harmondsworth: Penguin Books, 1972), p. 100.

16. *Ibid.*, p. 100.

17. *Ibid.*, p. 69.

18. *Ibid.*, p. 47.

19. *Ibid.*, p. 75.

20. J. C. Trewin, *The Night Has Been Unruly* (London: Robert Hale, 1957), p. 273.

21. *Titus Andronicus* opened on 16 August 1955.

22. See D. Scuro, '*Titus Andronicus:* A Crimson-flushed Stage', *The Ohio State University Theatre College Bulletin*, 17 (1970), 40–8.

23. Interview with Brook, August 1955.

24. R. David, 'Drams of Eale', *Shakespeare Survey 10* (Cambridge University Press, 1957), p. 126.

25. *Ibid.*, p. 126.

26. Trewin, *Peter Brook*, p. 87.

27. *Shakespeare Survey 10*, p. 128.

28. In *Shakespeare Our Contemporary*, tr. B. Taborski (London: Methuen, 1964).

29. Interview in *Plays and Players*, December 1962; '*Lear* Log' (see note 30). *King Lear* opened on 6 November 1962.

30. '*Lear* Log', *Encore*, no. 41, vol. 10 (1963), 20–32; reprinted in S. Trussler and C. Marowitz, *Theatre at Work* (London: Methuen, 1967), 133–47.

31. *Peter Brook*, p. 127.

32. Tom Stoppard, *Scene* (15 November 1962).

33. Trewin, *Peter Brook*, p. 130.

34. J. C. Trewin, *Birmingham Post*.

35. K. Tynan, *Right and Left* (London: Longman, 1967), p. 132.

36. *The Guardian*.

37. *Daily Express*.

38. Alan Brien, *Sunday Telegraph*.

39. *Oxford Times*.

40. Editing and interviews by Glenn Loney, City University of New York.

41. See interviews for *The Times* (29 August 1970); *Plays and Players* (October 1970). *A Midsummer Night's Dream* opened on 27 August 1970.

42. *Financial Times* (28 August 1970).

43. *Birmingham Sunday Mercury; Sunday Times*.

44. *Jewish Chronicle* (4 September 1970).

45. 'Free Shakespeare', *Shakespeare Survey 24* (Cambridge University Press, 1971), pp. 133–4.

46. *Plays and Players* (October 1970).

47. *South Wales Evening Argus* (31 August 1970).

48. 29 August 1970.

49. See Benedict Nightingale, *New Statesman* (4 September 1970).

50. (Harmondsworth: Penguin Books, 1977).

BOOKS

The Revels History of Drama in English
volume v, *1660–1750*
reviewed by BRIAN GIBBONS

The endpapers of this, the most recent history of drama after the Restoration,[1] display an architectural sketch of a classical interior – a set design of
a state bedroom, attributed to James Thornhill (see plate 11). It unmistaka-
bly recalls the masque designs of Inigo Jones, although the fact that it is a
*bed*chamber may lightly indicate certain changes in emphasis and direction
in the drama after 1660. Prominent among these new directions was the
regular use of scenery in public theatres, first in Lisle's Tennis Court in
Lincoln's Inn Fields, the first English playhouse equipped to present, regularly, shows with scenery to the general public, then in Dorset Garden and
Drury Lane, the first two buildings made for the purpose. Emphasis is given
to this development by the presentation in the very centre of the *Revels History*
of Thornhill's sets for Clayton's opera *Arsinoe* (1705, see plate 12) and all five
engravings of sets for Settle's horror tragedy *The Empress of Morocco* (1673).
In a detailed commentary Richard Southern reconstructs the staging of
these two works, after considering the inaugural event in public scenic
theatre in England, the performances of Davenant's and Webb's *Siege of
Rhodes* at Lisle's Tennis Court.

Questions of staging and theatre history are important in their own right,
of course, but it can happen that they are also important in the critical study
of drama. Perhaps because of the organisation of this particular volume,
Southern is not concerned to defend these works on artistic grounds: for him
they are historically significant and technically exemplary; but a more
important point needs to be made about them. Any account of Webb's work
for *The Siege of Rhodes* must of course emphasise how he and his collaborator
Davenant endeavoured to revive the techniques of court masque staging
developed by Inigo Jones (both of them had worked with him); but here
surely is the germ of an alternative to the approach which keeps rigidly
within the period and tells its tired platitudes, of how comedy declines into
sentiment and heroic tragedy gutters after its fierce yet frigid outburst,
leaving Gay and Lillo to bury the dead.

It is now possible to get a stimulating and scholarly idea of theatre
between 1660 and 1750, taking in its various, disorderly, and ephemeral life,

11 Design for a state bedroom, attributed to Sir James Thornhill

12 Design of a garden by moonlight for act I, scene i of Clayton's *Arsinoe*, by Sir
James Thornhill

recognising that evolution, where it can be discerned at all, may be broken and discontinuous. Room may be made for Christopher Fishbourne's *Sodom* and Howard's *The Committee*; Dryden may command more attention than he has been wont to receive; Rich's career may be soberly inspected, dog imitations and all;[2] but there remain the central critical issues live and kicking, and the wide perspective requires adjustment of the critical focus.

I think it is right to look back to the Jacobean and Caroline masque at the outset of a discussion of drama after 1660 because it keeps the mind in touch with Shakespeare, Jonson and Milton; whereas *The Empress of Morocco* tempts one to join only a line of expostulators stretching from Jonson to Shadwell: 'Then came Machines brought from a neighbour Nation,/Oh! how we suffered under decoration!'[3] and from Shadwell to Clifford Leech: 'in the accoutrements of their work they had debased the tragic style'.[4] Though Southern's running commentary seeks to bring Settle's drama alive, it cannot mask the awkward interruptions and clumsy articulation to which the scene changes bear witness; it does not matter if the dramatic narrative loses its rhythm, or the scenic effects are distracting. They are not coherently related to one another, or to the dramatic poetry or design; each element exists disconnected from the others. So act II begins: '*The scene opened, is represented the Prospect of a large River, with a glorious Fleet of Ships, supposed to be the Navy of* Muly Hamet, *after the Sound of Trumpets and the Discharge of Guns.*'[5] (See plate 13.) Made up no doubt in relief, with side scenes, hanging borders and ground rows before a backscene, this remains during the section in which Muly Hamet is celebrated. Flats then close and Crimalhaz is left alone on stage to deliver a soliloquy, after which the stage direction reads 'The Scene opened. *A* State *is presented, the King, Queen and* Mariamne *seated,* Muly-Hamet Abdelcador *and Attendants, a Moorish Dance is presented by* Moors *in several Habits, who bring in an artificial Palmtree, about which they dance to several antick Instruments of Musick; in the intervals of the Dance, this Song is sung by a Moorish Priest and two Moorish Women: the Chorus of it being performed by all the Moors.*'

The scenic theatre which Ben Jonson and Inigo Jones created in collaboration had as its ideal the *integration* of dance, music, poetry, scenery and action; *The Empress of Morocco* shows clearly enough that machinery is no substitute for imagination, but it also reveals how little the ideal of integration seems to have been recognised, or sought after, at this early stage of post-Restoration experiment. The handling of perspective, the very key to the much vaunted 'realism' of the scenes, seems wholly banal, literal-minded, and it is interesting that when Settle presents his Hell '*in which* Pluto, Proserpine *and other Women-Spirits appeared seated, attended by Furies*' it is merely as a masque put on by some of the characters (its conclusion borrows, and devalues, a device deployed with potent irony in the catastrophe of *Women Beware Women*): '*Here a dance is perform'd, by several infernal Spirits, who ascend*

13 Act II, scene i of *The Empress of Morocco*

from under the Stage; the Dance ended, the King Offers to snatch the Young Queen from the Company, who instantly draws her Dagger, and stabs him' with the words 'Take that Ravisher'. Settle seems unable to use the scene with any conviction. Even the famous final set scene (see plate 14) in which Crimalhaz '*appears cast down on the Gaunches, being hung on a Wall set with Spikes of Iron*', though perhaps making use of three-dimensional waxwork for bodies, dismembered limbs and odd bones, has no integrated function, is quite meaningless compared to Webster's use of the tableau of horror. The life in Settle's play is in what happens on the forestage, the unparticularised acting area, brightly lit by large candle hoops, sharing the same kind of lighting with the auditorium, to which it was linked architecturally; thus the episode in which Mariamne appears at the balcony above one of the stage doors, and her lover looks up dazzled at the surprise, has at least human and dramatic immediacy.

The designs for *The Empress of Morocco* are uninteresting because they are not metaphorical; they are at the mercy of such a wit as Addison. It was not for this that the art of perspective was introduced into the seventeenth-century English theatre, and there is nothing necessarily anti-metaphysical in that art, of course.[6] Thornhill's designs for *Arsinoe* are a most instructive contrast: these sets are spaces in which emotional life is free to develop; they contribute an elevated tone and imply an idea of the world, and in this they are properly dramatic. This point is crucial.

Every great dramatist since the invention of the scenic theatre has had to struggle until he has endowed its properties with his own imaginative truth. For Ibsen the real green lampshades in the softly lit study in act I of *The Wild Duck* contribute to a large metaphor, and though at first the spectator may only recognise it subliminally, when he has fully experienced the play he will see the ambivalent meanings lurking in that scene, with its ironic suggestion of the sub-aqueous. Irony indeed controls Ibsen's whole view of the 'photographic realism' of the stagecraft, as it does of the acting style, of his day. Shaw admired Ibsen's dark revolution in both areas, 'to substitute the incidents and catastrophes of spiritual history for the swoons, surprises, murders, duels, assassinations, and intrigues which are the commonplaces of the theatre at present'.[7] In that perspective Shaw himself may be numbered with Strindberg and Chekhov as dramatists who, despite Ibsen, had each of them to forge their own original kind of theatre. In the case of Synge we can point to *The Playboy* as a work in which the dramatist's objectivity transforms stereotypes of Stage Ireland and the Stage Irishman to expose raw social fact. Through his 'gallous story' Synge offers analogies to national political life, with its mixture of sentimental rhetoric and actual callousness, its inner paralysis. Indeed Synge's diagnosis of his people was more offensive than the first audience seem to have realised, for all their uproar. At the same time, the fact that Synge chose so rudimentary a set, a country shebeen, allows barriers of time and nationality to dissolve, and through the cruel modern

14 The final scene of *The Empress of Morocco*

Irish farce emerges the daemon of an ancient and primitive dramatic rite.

The scenic theatre of Restoration heroic tragedy, on the other hand, may be compared with the Shakespearian productions of Kean and Daly in Victorian England. Processions, panoramas, palaces, epiphanies clutter the place up. What Kean did to *The Winter's Tale* is typical in its gross obfuscation of the actual dramatic meaning, though it is best known for its astonishing archaeologically correct settings. For the statue scene Kean has a vast crowd in torchlight procession, who then witness with well-lit and extravagant emotion an episode which in Shakespeare is tender and intimate and quiet. As to the careful settings, Kean adopted Hanmer's suggested solution of the problem that Bohemia has no sea coast, by using the setting of Bithynia. A further question, of the presence of bears in Bithynia, was solved by reference to the Bible, II *Kings* 2, xxiii–xxiv: 'And he went up from thence unto Bethel . . . and there came forth two she-bears out of the wood.' Generously, *The Times* reviewer granted that the bear 'is a masterpiece of zoological art'.[8]

Shaw, reviewing a Daly production of *A Midsummer Night's Dream*, takes us to the heart of the matter:[9]

> In my last article I was rash enough to hint that [Daly] had not quite realised what could be done with electric lighting on the stage. He triumphantly answers me by fitting up all his fairies with portable batteries and incandescent lights, which they switch on and off from time to time. . . . Another stroke of his is to make Oberon a woman. It must not be supposed that he does this solely because it is wrong, though there is no other reason apparent. He does it partly because he was brought up to do such things, and partly because they seem to him to be a tribute to Shakespeare's greatness which, being uncommon, ought not to be interpreted according to the dictates of common sense. . . . Verse, music, the beauties of dress, gesture, and movement are to him interesting aberrations instead of being the natural expression which human feeling seeks at a certain degree of delicacy and intensity. He regards art as a quaint and costly ring in the nose of Nature. . . . Mr Daly is, I should say, one of those people who are unable to conceive that there could have been any illusion at all about the play before scenery was introduced. He certainly has no suspicion of the fact that every accessory he employs is brought in at the deadliest risk of destroying the magic spell woven by the poet. He swings Puck away on a clumsy trapeze with a ridiculous clash of cymbals in the orchestra, in the fullest belief that he is thereby completing instead of destroying Puck's lines. His 'panoramic illusion of the passage of Theseus's barge to Athens' is more absurd than anything that occurs in the tragedy of Pyramus and Thisbe in the last act.

Evidently there were many productions of Shakespeare in the theatre between 1660 and 1750 which deserved the same treatment that Shaw gives Daly in this passage. Dryden, commending his own collaborative adaptation of *The Tempest* in 1667, complacently explained that 'Davenant, as he was a Man of quick and piercing imagination, soon found that somewhat might be added to the design of Shakespeare'; Gildon adapted *Measure for Measure* in

1700, inserting Purcell's *Dido and Aeneas* act by act, ostensibly for the entertainment of Angelo. In the 1750s Rich was to ascribe the success of his production of *Romeo and Juliet* to the funeral procession, with music by Thomas Arne, devised by himself. Yet what needs to be stressed is that the pattern is not as consistent as such a selection of instances might suggest. Tate may deserve ridicule for his adaptation of *King Lear*; but he also collaborated with Purcell in one of the great tragic masterpieces of the age; Dryden shared in some triumphs of scenic theatre. There is much to be said, in identifying the nature of these successes, for a glance back at the Jacobean and Caroline masque, and for some emphasis on the principles which the great artists saw as governing the form.

In *A Midsummer Night's Dream*, as in *The Tempest*, elements of the masque suggest themselves naturally to Shakespeare as a means of presenting questions of the possibility of human fulfilment and its reflection of divine concord, since the masque traditionally expresses, through mythology and ceremonial music and dance, the double sense of self-delight and subordination to higher laws:

> Concord's true picture shineth in this art,
> Where divers men and women ranked be,
> And every one doth dance a several part,
> Yet all as one in measure do agree,
> Observing perfect uniformity. . . .[10]

The possibility that there was a performance of *A Midsummer Night's Dream* as part of the wedding celebrations in a noble family only emphasises how deeply Shakespeare responded to the idea of masque, a form in which a myth is created to express the relation between communal and individual piety and licence, limitation and fulfilment, and which invites feelings of irony and affirmation naturally to co-exist. In Spenser's *Epithalamium*[11] stress is placed on the particular time and on the particular real place in which the couple will live; their night of love is frankly welcomed as sensual fulfilment, though caught in the dance of art and music in the poetry, and compared to the night

> when Ioue with fayre Alcmena lay,
> When he begot the great Tirynthian groome.   (lines 328–9)

Prayers are sung to ward off evil spirits, deluding dreams, dreadful sights, though there is humour in the familiar tone which prays disarmingly

> Ne let th'unpleasant Quyre of Frogs still croking
> Make us to wish theyr choking.   (lines 349–50)

The real wedding is placed in a rich tradition, pagan as well as Christian, rustic as well as learned and noble; and particular emphasis is put on the importance of increasing the family and the pleasure and value of the estate, 'the earth which they may long possess'.

It is a way of seeing which welcomes multivalence, as a challenge to the art and to the spirit; it is imaginatively heroic. The powers of darkness, the energies of the subconscious (which may appear, in feeble examples of the form, as merely thin caricatures) attract the deepest imaginative response from both Shakespeare and Milton; and though this is a truth which calls for more attention, it should be recognised that the powers of light, of delicacy, exquisite sensation, wit and grace are no less integral to the form. Jonson's non-dramatic ode *To Penshurst* is a superb example of the masque-poet's art, achieving perfect balance between emblematic symbolism and realistic depiction in this version of scenic theatre,[12] where plants and animals perform their parts, dance their measures, yet have value as themselves:

> Each banke doth yeeld thee coneyes; and the topps
> Fertile of wood, *Ashore*, and *Sydney's* copp's,
> To crowne thy open table, doth provide
> The purpled pheasant, with the speckled side:
> The painted partrich lyes in every field,
> And, for thy messe, is willing to be kill'd.
> And if the high-swolne *Medway* faile thy dish,
> Thou hast thy ponds, that pay thee tribute fish,
> Fat, aged carps, that runne into thy net.
> And pikes, now weary their owne kinde to eat,
> As loth, the second draught, or cast to stay,
> Officiously, at first, themselves betray.
> Bright eeles, that emulate them, and leape on land,
> Before the fisher, or into his hand.   (lines 25–38)

After this dance, enter the fruits, augury in their freshness, roundness and blush of the daughters of farmers and peasants bearing capons, cakes, cheeses, or 'An embleme of themselves, in plum, or peare'. These anti-masque figures are presented with direct commendation; they whet the appetite for the next scene, a feast in the hall. The point is significant as compliment to Sidney, for there is normally an element of ridicule in the brilliant fantasies of the anti-masque, as in *Neptune's Triumph,* where Jonson's Poet is disdainful of the dance of ingredients (including partridges, a turkey, and an artichoke) who emerge from the cook's pot.

The first scene in *Penshurst* offers a dazzling Inigo Jones palace with a row of polished pillars, a roof of gold and a lantern: but then the whole palace opens to discover an ancient English pile in a fair landscape of fields, woods and water. It is a witty device to surprise the Court, discreetly adjusting their perspective in accord with satiric as well as Serlian principle. The final scene in the masque is of domestic piety, the children taught to pray 'Each morne, and even', seen for a moment like a family group on a Jacobean tomb monument, before the poet brings us down to earth and the virtue of practical action in the real world of 'manners, armes, and arts'. With this unmasking we are in the present tense and active voice.

In contrast, Jonson collaborated with Inigo Jones in the masque *Pleasure Reconciled to Virtue* to make a drama of consciousness: the heroism of Hercules here is not in outward action but the inner drama of the will, and the art of dramatist and designer is deployed in expressing, through the medium of scenic theatre, a spiritual action. In this sense Jonson's masque looks back to *The Tempest* but also forward to *Comus*, and to *Samson*. Here the drama of consciousness requires music to perform key dramatic actions: the chorus is intuitively sympathetic to Hercules' mind and, mysteriously, is prompted by the will of Atlas, who silently presides over the fulfilment of his prophecy. In the opening scene the awesomely gigantic mountain creates a sense of mystery increased, rather than dissolved, by his 'huge head at the peak, right under the very roof of the hall' which 'rolled its eyes and moved itself with wonderful cunning'.[13] He may have his head and beard all hoary with frost, but he is truly, if unfathomably, genial. The arts of emblem and perspectival illusionism wonderfully combine in the scenery. Hercules encounters a dionysiac revel of an anti-masque of men turned by Comus into bottles and a barrel; his heroic virtue effortlessly and scornfully dismisses it:

> Can this be pleasure, to extinguish man?
> Or so quite change him in his figure? Can
> The belly love his pain, and be content
> With no delight but what's a punishment?
> These monsters plague themselves, and fitly, too.[14]

The chorus invite Hercules to sleep; but Jonson shows us that the sleep of reason breeds monsters; as if from his unconscious, a capering anti-masque of pygmies floods the stage. It is at this point that the chorus sing out a warning to the hero; his waking releases an active virtue so potent that the nightmare creatures are instantly driven from the scene; the chorus turn to charm the mountain with song, and the power of music releases the masquers from the rock to begin the revels. Busino, an eye-witness at the performance in the Banqueting House, tells how: 'The mountain then opened by the turning of two doors, and from behind the low hills of a distant landscape one saw day break, some gilded columns being placed along the sides to make the distance seem greater.'[15] Here perspective scenery symbolically portrays spiritual experience. What links this masque particularly with *The Tempest* and with *Comus* is the concluding figure of the maze, forming the pattern danced in the revels by direction of Daedalus:

> as all actions of mankind
> Are but a labyrinth or maze,
> So let your dances be entwined,
> Yet not perplex men unto gaze;   (lines 249–52)

there may be a hint of humour in needing Daedalus himself to interweave this supremely 'curious knot', but the concluding song gravely returns to the

truth that the virtuous life is strenuous, the path through the maze perplex-
ing: the chorus sing of how Virtue will have us know that though 'Her sports
be soft, her way is hard'; and so, gesturing to the mountain, they advise

> You must return unto the hill,
> And there advance
> With labour, and inhabit still
> That height and crown
> From whence you ever may look down
> Upon triumphed Chance.
> She, she it is, in darkness shines.
> 'Tis she that still herself refines
> By her own light. . . .   (lines 320–28)

In the masque Jonson's collaboration with Inigo Jones perfectly integrates
scenery, action and idea, and the myth expresses itself through the metaphor
of music. Of course, this presentation of conflict is ideal rather than actual;
whereas the fascination of *Comus* is in Milton's development of dramatic
conflict, reshaping the masque form towards the idea of opera. Sixteen years
had passed since *Pleasure Reconciled to Virtue* had been performed at the
Banqueting House in Whitehall, and the illusionism of Inigo Jones's scenes
and machines had grown steadily more sophisticated. Andrew Marvell's
sense of the intoxicating but darkly disconcerting effect of this baseless fabric
informs his poem *Upon Appleton House*; for Marvell the transformation scenes
of the Caroline masque express an intuition of a world dangerously unstable,
in which a pleasant landscape can so easily turn into a scene of massacre:

> No scene that turns with Engines strange
> Does oftner than these Meadows change.
> For when the Sun the Grass hath vext,
> The tawny Mowers enter next;
> Who seem like Israelites to be
> Walking on foot through a green sea.
> To them the Grassy Deeps divide,
> And crowd a Lane to either Side.
>
> With whistling Sithe, and Elbow strong,
> These Massacre the Grass along.[16]

In *Comus* Milton, like Jonson, presents a world in which virtue can achieve
stability and concord: but unlike Jonson, Milton concedes much to darkness;
the immense power of his art goes to create the dionysiac energy which
brings Comus and his rout dramatically alive. Only a profound and heroic
imaginative effort can redirect, transform and redeem such forces. The inner
requirements of Milton's design call for powerful simplicity in staging; so
powerful is the conflict that only a god in a machine can resolve it; and no
better proof of Milton's full acceptance of the art of theatre need be sought
than the moment when, after the tense silence that follows the song of
invocation, '*Sabrina rises attended by water Nimphes and sings*'.

In the masque as a whole there are just three scenes: the wood, the palace, and the prospect of Ludlow. They represent successive stages in the moral drama, and for this reason are fully and richly symbolic. This point is important because there is every likelihood that in the original performance, at Ludlow Castle in 1634, Milton was expecting to use scenery borrowed from the Revels storeroom in Whitehall, sets by Inigo Jones in his mature style for *Albion's Triumph* or *Tempe Restored,* a year or so earlier.[17] Perspective scenery is integrated in the imaginative vision: Milton uses it with conscious restraint, as he uses music; but he certainly intends that both shall produce intense dramatic experience.

Comus reveals Milton the dramatist; the small scale of his work enables him to keep control of all the elements of the theatre, and seems to augur well for the future: but the Civil War intervened, and there is magnificent defiance, as well as critical judgement, in the decision to write *Samson* according to the most strict and restrained tragic decorum. Performances in our own day have established its power on the stage: it was never performed in the Restoration. The theatre was unworthy.

Comus, it could be said, aspires to the condition of opera; but it would require a composer of genius to match Milton's emotional power and dramatic poetry. The adaptation by Thomas Arne and John Dalton for Drury Lane in 1738 was an attempt to turn it, formally, into a Restoration dramatic opera, retaining the spoken dialogue for the principals, though making omissions and additions (to the taste of the times) and providing extended episodes in music. The music is not in itself dramatic, and so the work is rather an entertainment than an opera. Arne fights shy of setting the debate between Comus and the Lady, and the dionysiac energies become mere salacity. It is an irony that such a piece's popular success drew Handel's interest towards Milton, leading via the masque-like *L'Allegro ed Il Penseroso* to the overwhelming triumph of the opera *Samson*: perhaps *Comus* could have been successfully interpreted by the composer of *Acis and Galatea.* Yet had there been a composer of true genius in the English theatre during the first two decades after 1660, it may well be that the depraved philistinism of the Restoration audiences, and the financial dependence of the theatrical companies on them, would in any case have inhibited the development of true music drama. In England, then, music drama consisted of gallimaufreys of spoken dialogue, song-and-dance numbers interpolated, and unconnected spectacular scenes; Shakespeare was adapted to provide escapist fantasies. Shadwell, who had collaborated with Locke on such an adaptation of *The Tempest,* explained complacently of its successor *Psyche,* that it had as its 'great design' to 'entertain the Town with variety of Musick, curious Dancing, splendid Scenes and Machines'.[18] By contrast, in France, the economic situation of the theatre, the enlightened patrons and audiences, and prevailing critical theory, all favoured the creation of true music drama.

Lully had a close collaborator in his librettist, Quinault; and it is significant that the first substantial English dramatic opera, *King Arthur*, involved a
real act of collaboration between Dryden and Henry Purcell. Dryden had
already written the libretto but explains in the Preface that at Purcell's
request he had made many alterations, and 'in Reason my Art, on this
occasion, ought to be subservient to his'. Temperamentally Purcell and
Dryden share certain artistic qualities, and Purcell is able to match in his
music the poet's gift for wit and humour, while endowing the patriotic myth
with solemn and grave choric emotion. Although the work remains a series of
exotic and marvellous episodes, Purcell's music gives dramatic unity to
individual sequences; it seems clear from Gray's description of a revival in
1735[19] that Purcell and Dryden achieved at least in the frost scene a perfect
triumph in fusion of all the elements, and pointed towards the ideal:

> ... the inchanted part of the play, is not Machinery, but actual magick: the
> second scene is a British temple enough to make one go back a thousand years,
> & really be in ancient Britain: ... the Frost Scene is excefsive fine; the first
> Scene of it is only a Cascade, that seems frozen; with the Genius of Winter
> asleep & wrapt in furs, who upon the approach of Cupid, after much quiver-
> ing, & shaking sings the finest song in the Play; just after, the Scene opens, &
> shows a view of arched rocks covered with Ice & Snow to ye end of ye Stage,
> between the arches are upon pedestals of Snow eight images of old men &
> women, that seem frozen into Statues, with icicles hanging about them, &
> almost hid in frost, & from ye end come Singers, viz.: Mrs Chambers, &c:
> & Dancers all rubbing their hands & chattering with cold with fur gowns &
> worsted gloves in abundance.

In *Dido and Aeneas*, of course, the limitations imposed by the fact that the
work was composed for performance by a girls' school induced a restrained
use of scenery, spectacular action and singing technique; there is a striking
analogy here with the *Athalie* of Racine as well as the *Comus* of Milton.
Purcell's art is unified and intense in *Dido*. Tate's libretto is an abbreviation
by two-thirds of the heroic tragedy on which it is based; under Purcell's
authoritative control the dramatic design is fulfilled in the music, composed
with a subtle, ironic and mercurial intelligence which reveals a rich response
to dramatic tradition, as Wilfrid Mellers's analysis[20] of the handling of the
anti-masque shows:

> sometimes they sing straight ceremonial music, like a masque or chorus, the
> irony being in the situation, not the music. Two witches invoke the storm in a
> canon two in one, there being a kind of blasphemy in the echo chorus 'In our
> deep vaulted cell': the blasphemy being inherent in the singing of such nobly
> ceremonial masque-music by such low types. The echoes split up the words,
> literally destroying meaning ... the masque chorus is followed by another
> echo piece, a dance of furies, in which the texture is riddled with *false* relations
> and the echoes are a deceit. This illusory quality is the more pointed because
> the Sorceress's dark F minor has changed to a pastoral F major. Moreover, the
> echo-ritual and dance of furies are most cunningly placed. They immediately

precede the idyll wherein Dido and Aeneas consummate their love: and so hint
at the element of illusion with the idyll itself.

Here, certainly, is a work that reveals Purcell's supremely dramatic gift.
With Purcell's early death in 1695 there was a severe interruption in the
development of opera in England, though there was in fact to be a great
triumph, with the English works of Handel. In this evolution there is one
notable link which perhaps receives less emphasis than it deserves. For the
opening of Vanbrugh's new theatre in the Haymarket, the Queen's, it was
planned that a new opera should be created by Congreve and Eccles. Had
this work, *Semele*, been performed in 1705, as was originally intended, much
might have resulted; but for reasons which perhaps remain conjectural, it
was withdrawn and an Italian work substituted. It may be characteristic of
Congreve's conservative talent, or of his respect for his old friends Dryden
and Betterton, that he combined elements of English dramatic opera with
Italian, basing the extremely elaborate staging on that provided by Betterton for Shadwell's *Psyche*.[21] But, disastrously, possible evolution was
blocked, and *Semele* remained unperformed in the crucial period. However,
when at last in 1743 Handel began work on the sensitive libretto he had had
prepared from Congreve's *Semele*, not only did he respond imaginatively to
the Greek feeling of the work, he also retained many of the details of
Congreve's intended staging in his autograph.[22] This is a particular indication of what is generally obvious from the music itself, the deeply dramatic
nature of Handel's opera, and reveals that he actually composed with scenic
theatre, rather than oratorio performance, in mind; his *Semele* is, as oratorio,
a powerful and intense spiritual action, but had it appeared as scenic drama
originally, this notable consummation in the evolution of English music
drama would have been seen for what it is. Even as it was, the creative
encounter of Handel with the greatest tragic writer of the Restoration,
Milton, and with its greatest comic writer, Congreve, resulted in *Samson* and
Semele, two masterpieces.

The history of English theatre between 1660 and 1750, considered in this
way, might justifiably give more prominence to music drama, a form in
which the most grave and lofty as well as the most fantastic and brilliant
works appeared.[23] From 1660 onwards the great achievements in comedy
are satiric in mode and make very limited use of scenery and music; the
apparently popular genre of heroic tragedy is finally unserious as art,
yielding no masterpieces. Farce and burlesque blunder along, and the
volume and degree of attention given in histories to a work as fundamentally
philistine as *The Beggar's Opera* seems disproportionate. English dramatic
operas by lesser artists may have their weaknesses; but our view of theatre in
this age ought to bring Purcell and Handel into focus, and we shall then
recognise that continuity was maintained, at the profoundest levels, with
'the Gyant Race before the Flood'.

NOTES

1. John Loftis, Richard Southern, Marion Jones and A. H. Scouten, *The Revels History of Drama in English*, vol. v, *1660–1750* (London: Methuen, 1976).
2. See Paul Sawyer, 'John Rich's Contribution to the Eighteenth-century London Stage' in *The Eighteenth-century English Stage*, ed. Kenneth Richards and Peter Thomson (London: Methuen, 1972).
3. Cited by Allardyce Nicoll, *A History of English Drama 1660–1900* (London: Cambridge University Press, 1952), I, 34.
4. Clifford Leech, 'Restoration Tragedy: A Reconsideration' reprinted in *Restoration Drama*, ed. John Loftis (New York: Oxford University Press, 1966), p. 157.
5. Elkanah Settle, *The Empress of Morocco* (London, 1673).
6. See especially D. J. Gordon, 'Poet and Architect: the Intellectual Setting of the Quarrel between Ben Jonson and Inigo Jones', *Journal of the Warburg and Courtauld Institutes*, XII (1949). John Summerson, *Inigo Jones* (Harmondsworth: Penguin Books, 1966) discusses the philosophical basis of Jones's work and remarks: 'Behind Jones the architect there is always Jones the philosopher' (p. 73). This is echoed by R. Wittkower, *Architectural Principles in the Age of Humanism* (London: Warburg Institute, 1967); see also Harris, Orgel and Strong, *The King's Arcadia* (London: Arts Council of Great Britain, 1973), especially pp. 61–3.
7. Bernard Shaw, appendix to *The Quintessence of Ibsenism*.
8. Cited by W. Moelwyn Merchant, *Shakespeare and the Artist* (London: Oxford University Press, 1959), p. 216.
9. *Our Theatre in the Nineties* (London: Constable, 1932), I, 178–9.
10. Sir John Davies, *Orchestra*, stanza 110.
11. Spenser, *Epithalamium* in *The Poetical Works*, ed. J. C. Smith and E. de Selincourt (London: Clarendon Press, 1912).
12. *To Penshurst* in *The Complete Poetry of Ben Jonson*, ed. William B. Hunter Jr (New York: W. W. Norton Inc., 1968), pp. 78–9.
13. English version of a report by Orazio Busino in the archives of St Mark's Venice, by Stephen Orgel and Roy Strong, *Inigo Jones, the Theatre of the Stuart Court* (London: Sotheby Parke Burnet, 1973), I, 281–4.
14. Jonson, *Pleasure Reconciled to Virtue* in Orgel and Strong, *Inigo Jones*, I, 285–8.
15. *Ibid.*, p. 283.
16. Andrew Marvell, *Upon Appleton House*, stanzas 49–50, in *Complete Poetry*, ed. George de F. Lord (New York: Random House Inc., 1968).
17. See John G. Demeray, *Milton and the Masque Tradition* (Cambridge, Mass.: Harvard University Press, 1968) p. 103.
18. *The Works of Thomas Shadwell*, ed. Montague Summers (London: The Fortune Press, 1927), vol. II.
19. Thomas Gray, letter to Walpole dated 3 January 1736.
20. Wilfrid Mellers, *Harmonious Meeting* (London: Dobson, 1965), pp. 209–10.
21. Shadwell remarked in the Preface to *Psyche:* 'In those things that concern the ornament or Decoration of the Play, the great industry and care of Mr Betterton ought to be remembered, at whose desire I wrote upon this subject.' Dryden makes a similar gesture in the Preface to *Albion and Albanus*.

22. Winton Dean, *Handel's Dramatic Oratorios and Masques* (London: Oxford University Press, 1959), p. 379.
23. Neither *Semele* nor Handel's *Samson* are mentioned in *The Revels History*: Milton's *Samson* appears in a Chronological Table as 'a non-dramatic literary work'. Seven pages at the end of a 295-page text discuss opera.

The Oxford Ibsen, volume VIII,
translated and edited by James Walter McFarlane

reviewed by CHARLES LELAND

English-speaking Ibsen students and devotees, ever-increasing in number, have been waiting impatiently for the publication of the eighth and final volume of the *Oxford Ibsen*.[1] At last, in 1977, five years after the appearance of the previous volume in the series and seventeen years after the first volume, *The Oxford Ibsen, Volume VIII: Little Eyolf, John Gabriel Borkman, When We Dead Awaken*, has appeared. Our patience has been amply rewarded since volume VIII has all the distinctive literary and scholarly features which have already made the previous seven volumes the authoritative 'Ibsen' of the English-speaking world. Professor James W. McFarlane, general editor of the whole series and translator of most of the plays has explained in his 'Preface' to this final volume a major reason for the slackened pace in the publication of the last four volumes: his own involvement for eight years in the administration of the University of East Anglia, first as Dean of its School of European Studies and then as Pro-Vice-Chancellor. We can only marvel that through it all Professor McFarlane retained his enthusiasm, taste for scholarship, critical acumen, and soul!

His edition, containing all twenty-six of the plays, is the first complete English edition of Ibsen's dramatic work, since five early plays were not included in William Archer's historically important edition (1906–12). McFarlane also provides a valuable critical 'Introduction' to each volume together with an 'Appendix' for each play. Each 'Appendix' recounts the literary history of the play and always contains the following:(1) 'Dates of Composition' or 'Genesis of the Play', (2) 'Draft Manuscripts', (3) 'Some Pronouncements of the Author', and (4) 'Contemporary Reception'. The appendices to certain plays have even more parts, for example, the one on *Peer Gynt* includes 'The Folk-tale of Peer Gynt and the Bøyg' and 'Collaboration with Grieg'. A study of the draft material, much of which appears for the first time in English, is particularly enthralling. Here we find preliminary notes, scenarios, 'visions and revisions', drafts which finally grew into Ibsen's final version. The student enjoys not only an invaluable insight into the genesis of a particular play but also a glimpse into the mind and method of the dramatist. What better essay topic for students of modern drama,

graduate or undergraduate, than a comparative study of Ibsen's drafts and
the final version of a play! McFarlane does not – and he admits it – provide
us with *all* the draft material. For this one would need more volumes. The
French edition, which attempts to include all the draft material – the *Oeuvres
Complètes* (1914–45) by P. G. La Chesnais – runs to sixteen volumes. But
McFarlane, with an unerring instinct for the significant, gives us all the
really important draft material in only eight. For many, I suspect, these
drafts, now available in English, will be the most valuable aspect of McFarlane's edition. Here, indeed, is God's plenty!

'Some Pronouncements of the Author' can also be fascinating. Here we
get not only letters by Ibsen relevant to the play, but also critical essays (for
example, 'On the Heroic Ballad and its Significance for Literature'), unpub-
lished papers of various sorts, and poems. In the final volume, for example,
'Bergmanden' is given us, both in the original and in a literal translation. I
might just mention here that the 'epic Brand', in a good prose translation,
precedes the dramatic version of *Brand* in volume II of the series. With so
much, it is almost ungrateful to wish for more, yet another volume, containing all of Ibsen's poetry, would have been welcome. 'Terje Viken', 'På
viddene' and the many haunting shorter lyrics like 'Borte' are known to very
few English-speaking readers. Ibsen's lyric and narrative poetry is an important aspect of his work.

In the last part of each appendix, 'Contemporary Reception', we are, for
example, treated to letters by Henry James regarding *Little Eyolf* and *John
Gabriel Borkman*, Joyce (of course) on *When We Dead Awaken*, one of Alexander Kielland's letters, certainly not published in English before, regarding
Little Eyolf, clusters of references to reviews in various Scandinavian, English
and American journals and newspapers. The fascinating material McFarlane gathers to document the contemporary reception of any one play could
easily be developed into a short thesis or monograph.

This final volume of *The Oxford Ibsen* also includes an appendix of 'Ibsen
Productions in English': (1) Principal London productions, (2) BBC radio
productions, and (3) Television productions in Britain. Fair enough,
although the trans-Atlantic and trans-Pacific students, might have appreciated some reference to productions in the United States, Canada and
Australia.

Each volume in the series concludes with a bibliographical appendix,
valuable for the specialist and the general student alike. There are items
which one might just have missed; one example being 'F. Anstey, *Mr Punch's
Pocket Ibsen*. A collection of some of the master's best-known dramas. Con-
densed, revised and slightly arranged for the benefit of the earnest student
(London, 1893).' Studies in English of particular plays are noted, as well as
studies in other languages, especially Norwegian. The Norwegian bibliography is particularly helpful, of course, to the growing number of serious Ibsen

students who have learned Norwegian. Inevitably there are omissions, especially of the most recent work; so I might mention here a fine article on *Little Eyolf*, 'The Crutch is Floating' by Arne Røed, which appeared in the *Ibsenårbok 1976*. Professor McFarlane brings to his edition a most discriminating and exact scholarship. There is nary a slip-up, nary a mistaken reference, as far as I checked. In the appendices all is laid out in a wonderfully clear and orderly way.

I would now like to turn to the critical introductions to the three plays in the final volume and also to say something about the translations. The thirty-four page 'Introduction' to the volume gives us what we have come to expect from McFarlane's pen: a critical essay formidable in the variety and depth of its insights and in the sensitive awareness of the complexity of Ibsen's dramaturgy, written in a style reflecting in itself the complexity of its subject matter. McFarlane's medium is certainly an important aspect of his message. Even the structure of the 'Introduction' is not easy to perceive. Towards the end the plays are discussed in order, but much happens before then. The essay begins with a glance at *When We Dead Awaken* as a 'dramatic epilogue'. But even Ibsen's sub-title is not univocal. A culmination the play most certainly is, but a culmination of what? the four last plays, written between 1892 and 1899? the eleven or twelve 'contemporary plays' (depending on whether *Pillars of Society* is included or not), extending back over a quarter of a century? or the totality of Ibsen's life-work, extending back to the publication of *Catilina* in 1850?

'In obedience to the first of these three recognitions', McFarlane moves back through the last three plays to *The Master Builder* and the 'crucially significant' short poem, 'There they sat, those two' ('De sad der, de to . . .'). The poem is quoted in Norwegian together with a line-by-line English translation in accordance with the practice in earlier volumes. It is then located as being first written for *The Master Builder*, rejected, and then transferred to the draft version of *Little Eyolf*. Its relevance to the latter play is noted, as is the fact that it is again rejected in the final draft. Finally the poem is analysed in itself and shown to articulate 'in severely abstracted form' a constant preoccupation in Ibsen's later years:

> The world of Ibsen's last plays is the creation of a mind haunted by problems of personal relations in conditions of stress, and by the way these things bear on individual happiness and faith. With the same compulsive anguish that Alfred brings to his poem – 'I had [he exclaims] to give expression to something which I cannot bear in silence any longer' – these dramas explore the complex interactions, the interdependencies, the shifts and dislocations, the endless conjoining and disjoining of multiple relationships which, though individually often deceptively simple and linear, combine into chains and patterns of daunting elaboration and subtlety.   (p. 4)

I quote this, not only for its own value in understanding McFarlane's thinking on Ibsen, but also as an example of his style. He is not given to the short, pithy sentence. Rather, sentences are flung further and further out in order to catch every nuance, every contour of Ibsen's mind as it plays around its dramatic subject. There is a sense of victory achieved when we come to the end of a sentence and are still able to hold it all together in our minds.

An interesting discussion of the various and complex kinship links in *Little Eyolf* and *John Gabriel Borkman* follows. In these plays one is confronted with 'ties parental and filial, of sibling and other blood relationships, of affiliate and affinal connections of astonishing variety' (p. 4). Simply to take the idea of motherhood, we have 'natural motherhood, step-motherhood, foster-motherhood, adoptive motherhood, usurpative or surrogate motherhood, and of course metaphorical motherhood' (p.5). All these function, as McFar-McFarlane rightly observes, as 'subtle determinants of individual conduct', to which Ibsen gave 'earnest and athletic attention' (p. 7). (One wonders a bit about 'athletic'.) One good example of this is the way Ibsen in *Little Eyolf* modified 'the relational pattern as one draft of the play succeeded another' (p. 8).

> The reiterated Asta-Eyolf transferences, the reported transvestite practices of the earlier days, the association of Alfred's betrayal to Rita of these childhood secrets (as well as of Eyolf's crippling accident) with a moment of highly charged sexual passion – all these and more were late additions or adjustments to the play and must have post-dated the decision to eliminate any blood relationship between Alfred and Asta. Such factors, by their deliberate and pondered introduction, draw attention to the weight of symbolic significance which Ibsen attached to the meta-relationship between kinship obligations and sexual compulsions in the business of daily living.   (pp. 9 and 10)

With this, the discussion of the redactions of *Little Eyolf* is dropped for the time being, to be picked up again towards the end of the essay, when the plays are treated one by one.

Professor McFarlane now turns to the 'sexual nexus running obliquely across kinship links and casual encounters' (p. 10). Again we are treated to a list of sexual relationships to be found in the plays which one might venture to call exhaustive: 'marital, pre-marital, and extra-marital, consummated and unconsummated, promiscuous and abstinent, invited and withheld, sensualised and sublimated, overt and suppressed, deviant and incipiently incestuous' (p. 10). Amusing as this list may seem, reference to the plays reveals that it is entirely accurate: each item can be justified. In this way, time and time again, McFarlane confronts us with the complexity of Ibsen's genius. I think he simplifies a bit, however, when he observes that it is 'the women who are destined to take the sexual initiative', while 'the men . . . are for the most part conspicuously deficient in libido' (p. 10). 'Suppression of sexuality is seen by these men [Allmers, Borkman and Rubek] as a kind of victory, a triumph of self-control, a defeat for those darker, disruptive forces which would otherwise subvert life's greater, nobler purposes' (p. 11). It is too simple to equate voluntary 'suppression of sexuality' with 'deficiency in libido'. I think it is an open question just how 'deficient' Borkman and Rubek are, although they both, at some cost, suppress their sexuality, one ostensibly for the social good, one for the achievement of art. Misguided they may be, but not necessarily impotent. It is a different matter, probably, with Allmers.

Professor McFarlane then moves from the consideration of familial and sexual relationships, the horizontal plane, as it were, to the vertical plane, 'the deeper and less rationally accessible level' where 'there is to be seen at work a pervasive influence from mystic or quasi-mystic (or even mock-mystic) forces, a system of "pulls" and "currents" and "undertows" of will and suggestion' (p. 14). Alas, these dimensions are treated simply as psychological, rather than relating to other dimensions of reality which Ibsen might be suggesting. For McFarlane they are simply 'deeper and less rationally accessible levels of *this* world'. They are also associated 'with the power of mind over mind and the influence of mind over matter'. So 'the subterranean spirits' calling to Borkman are merely aspects of his disturbed psyche. This is certainly one reasonable assumption, an assumption which to some extent determines Professor McFarlane's view of the play. But it is not, I suggest, the only reasonable assumption. McFarlane does refer, in a typically suggestive sentence, to 'a reverberant universe of motivation' which compliments 'the surface forces of these last plays' (p. 14). No attempt is made, however, to explore the dimensions of this 'reverberant universe'. Borkman's 'higher motives' for action must be 'shamefacedly but unconvincingly' corrected to read 'other motives' (p. 12). I don't think Borkman *is* correcting himself, but he realises that his 'higher motives' will appear to be simply 'other motives' to Ella. Consideration for Ella, then, is the reason why he corrects his statement; the motives remain 'higher' as far as he himself is concerned.

Deceit, self-deception, dissimulation are currently seen to be endemic in Ibsen's world. Readers and viewers are cautioned to 'beware of accepting the characters and their version of events at face value' (p. 14). McFarlane and most orthodox Ibsen critics today accept this principle without question or qualification. Borkman is deceived about his calling, as Foldal is deceived in his. They voluntarily practise mutual deception in order to sustain and support one another. Their encounter is seen 'as a double melodic line, a two-part harmony' (p. 15) – a rather unhappy conjunction of metaphors, since a 'double melodic line' is not the same as 'two-part harmony'. In any case, the famous lines are quoted:

> *Borkman.* So all this time you've lied to me.
> *Foldal* [*shakes his head*]. Never lied, John Gabriel.
> *Borkman.* Have you not sat there feeding my hopes and beliefs and confidence with lies?

> *Foldal.* They weren't lies as long as *you* believed in *my* calling. As long as you
>   believed in me, I believed in you.
> *Borkman.* Then it's just been mutual deception. And perhaps self-deception too
>   – on both sides.
> *Foldal.* But isn't that what friendship really is, John Gabriel?   (p. 15)

McFarlane and most other critics take Foldal's final, Swiftian reply at face
value, making him, in some way, the *raisonneur* of the piece. But might it not
be that the deception lies in believing that the calling can be realised in *this*
world by one's own efforts alone? There may have been no deception about
the calling in itself: Foldal may have been called to be poet quite as much as
Borkman may have been called to be captain of industry and creator of light
and warmth in the world. For McFarlane, I think, these 'calls' are nothing
other than rationalisations attempting to cover up weakness or sordid and
dishonest behaviour. This is certainly a possible reading of the text. But it is
also possible that neither Foldal nor Borkman is deceived concerning his
initial calling.

Ibsen was certainly convinced of the reality of *his* calling! In the famous
letter to Carl XV of Sweden (15 April 1866) he asks for a yearly grant 'so that
I can live for my calling as poet' ('at kunne leve for mit Kald som Digter').
Despite the inflated rhetoric of Ibsen's letter, we would hesitate to call him
deceived!

The case of Allmers is different. As Rita is not deceived by his noble words
about obligations towards Eyolf to whom his career as a writer must be
sacrificed, so neither are we. I think McFarlane is at his best as a critic in his
analysis of *Little Eyolf*, an analysis which involves a fascinating study of the
modifications brought to bear on the draft material. *Little Eyolf* is seen in
terms of Ibsen's changing conception of the play as he wrote and rewrote it. I
shall leave the reader to ponder McFarlane's masterful and exciting portrayal of this process. A full experience of art involves an appreciation of
means as well as ends. James McFarlane has given us a chance to appreciate
Ibsen's means as no other editor has done.

With the discussion of *Little Eyolf*, we come to the final part of the
'Introduction', which considers each of the three plays from a different
perspective. We have noted the perspectives given to *Little Eyolf*. *John Gabriel
Borkman* is seen in terms of 'the dynamics of obsession and self-delusion within
what is now a recognisably Ibsenist area of complex interlocking personal
relationships'. Borkman 'designs a comprehensive personal myth, within
which he casts himself for the central role' (p. 24), the myth of a Napoleon of
industry, great liberator of the wealth of the earth. He is a Nietzschean
Ausnahmemensch to whom the ordinary norms of human conduct do not
apply. Driven by Faustean ambition and lust for power, he creates his own
norms, single-mindedly pursues his own course, regardless of the human

destruction he spreads around the shoddy act of embezzlement he commits. From all guilt he exonerates himself. The so-called heroic end justifies the squalid and treacherous means. His actions are in 'obedience to the call of mystic mineral powers'. McFarlane also maintains that the actions have 'their source in a Gynt-like pursuit of his [Borkman's] deeper self'. Even worse, Borkman is seen as recategorising 'essentially personal ambition' as an unselfish 'agency of social enrichment: "I wanted to build myself an empire, and thereby create prosperity for thousands upon thousands of others."' Like Bernick in the play written almost two decades before, Borkman gilds 'motives of crude commercial gain' (p. 25) and ambition with heroic, salvific utterance about bringing the greatest good to the greatest number. 'This is not heroic; it is only heroics' (p. 26), McFarlane maintains. This is certainly the generally accepted interpretation of *John Gabriel Borkman*, brilliantly articulated. But it is also interesting, it seems to me, to consider the possibility of Borkman as hero after all! This would indeed be the final ironic twist. He might, indeed, have received a mystical call and be acting in obedience to it. His own evaluation of himself is, after all, not precisely as a Napoleon of industry despite his stance at the entrance of Foldal. He considers himself, essentially, as a man chosen ('utvalgt') for an exceptional calling, an exceptional saving mission. Such men are, of course, often deceived. But are they *always* deceived? Borkman, with what might be termed rare metaphysical insight, seems to have a profound sense of the uniqueness of his being. In trying to explain himself to his wife early in act III, Borkman says, 'People don't understand that I *had* to do it because I am as I am – because I am John Gabriel Borkman, and not anybody else' (p. 207) ('Menneskene skjønner ikke at jeg måtte det fordi jeg var meg selv, – fordi jeg var John Gabriel Borkman – og ikke noen annen'). To have this sense of the uniqueness of one's being and the modalities with which this uniqueness is to be realised in action is not *ipso facto* to be deceived. Finally, there is the saving mission to be realised through the steamships he is to build: 'They create a world-wide sense of community. They bring light and warmth to the hearts of men in many thousands of homes. That was what I dreamed of achieving' (p. 230). (The translation fails to convey all the force and beauty of the original: 'De bringer forbundsliv hele jorden rundt. De skaper lys og varme over sjelene i mange tusen hjem. Det var det jeg drømte om å skape.' 'Forbundsliv' is much stronger than 'sense of community'. Borkman's mission is to create [note the strong verb repeated in two forms: 'skaper' and 'å skape'] a new kind of *life* in the world: 'forbundsliv lys og varme over sjelene'. There are the echoing rhythmical patterns: 'hele jorden rundt . . . mange tusen hjem'.) Borkman's words on the heights in the final act can be heard as pretentious and insincere, can be heard as the ravings of a madman, but they can also have the effect of exalted, inspired poetry, born (dare one say?) of a kind of mystical vision, a vision of the 'levendegjorte skygger . . . livkrevende verdier' ('shades brought to life . . . life-seeking values'). This interpretation flies in the face of critical orthodoxy, most ably represented by Professor McFarlane, by considering evidence which either is not recognised by the orthodox or is evaluated from another perspective.

As mentioned above, McFarlane also used Nietzschean terms in his analysis of Borkman, who casts himself as *Übermensch* in his 'comprehensive personal myth' and as an *Ausnahmemensch* 'living by standards different from those that apply to his more "average" fellow men' (pp. 24 and 25). Borkman, indeed, includes himself among the 'unntagelsesmennesker' in the course of his argument with Foldal in the second act:

> *Foldal.* Det er ikke noe prejudikat for slikt.
> *Borkman.* Behøves ikke for unntagelsesmennesker.
> *Foldal.* Loven kjenner ikke den slags hensyn.
>
> *Foldal.* There's no precedent for it.
> *Borkman.* Only ordinary people need precedents.
> *Foldal.* The law doesn't recognise such distinctions.   (p. 190)

Strange that McFarlane's own translation should obscure the Nietzschean reference! Why not translate literally: 'Not necessary for exceptional people'? Or, a little more freely, 'Exceptional people don't need precedents'?

There can be little doubt that Ibsen had read Georg Brandes's monograph: *Frederick Nietzsche: En Afhandling om aristokratisk Radikalisme* (1889), the work which introduced the German philosopher to the Scandinavian reading public. But we also have Ibsen's own word (in the famous letter to Bjørnson about the composition of *Brand*, quoted below) that he was an inveterate Bible reader. Another word which Borkman uses about himself in his discussion with Foldal in act III, 'utvalgate', not mentioned by McFarlane, is, I think, just as significant as 'unntagelsesmennesker': 'vi utvalgte mennesker' ('we chosen individuals') (p. 183). The overtones of Isaiah, St Paul and the liturgy cannot be gainsaid. The chosen ones are always the chosen of God, the elect. The words can sound pompous, condescending, incredibly proud. But we know that Ibsen had a profound sympathy for those men who, because of a deep sense of vocation, feel called upon to stand alone in their efforts to realise a vision. Ibsen, significantly, uses the word 'utvalgt' of Brand too. As Gerd says in her vision of him as Christ at the end of the play:

> . . . du går jo først
> I din hand er naglehullet;
> du er utvalgt, du er størst.
>
> You are above us all!
> In your hands are the holes of the nails . . .
> You are the Chosen One . . . the Greatest.[2]

Also it can be no accident that Ibsen gave Borkman the name Gabriel, the angel sent to explain to Daniel the meaning of his visions, visions which Daniel alone sees: 'I Daniel alone saw the vision: for the men that were with me saw not the vision' (Daniel 10.7). 'And I heard a man's voice . . . which called and said, "Gabriel, make this man to understand the vision" ' (Daniel 8.16). Ibsen conflates Daniel and the angel in having Borkman stress the uniqueness of his vision as well as interpreting it to Ella. It is interesting also simply to think of the play as having some relation to the most apocalyptic book of the Old Testament. Turning to Luke's Gospel we find that it is Gabriel who brings to Zachary and Mary the news of a marvellous new order of things to be realised through the births of John the Baptist and Jesus. Finally, Gabrî-ēl means 'hero of God'. Hebrew was not one of the subjects Ibsen presented for his *examen artium*, but, considering the attention given to the names of his characters, he might well have known the derivation of the name he chose for the eponymous hero of his play.

I think John Gabriel Borkman is an authentic Ibsenian hero – flawed, complex, suffering, defeated from one point of view, but a hero none the less with the three virtues of Ibsen's heroic world recognised by Daniel Haakonsen: 'erkjennelse, ansvar, og troskap mot den ideale inspirasjon i ens liv'[3] ('recognition, responsibility, and fidelity to the ideal inspiration in one's life'). He recognised his exceptional calling, took responsibility for it, and remained faithful to it until death.

When We Dead Awaken is seen in terms of a fall from innocence, or a 'progression from innocence to experience, from simplicity to complexity' as symbolised by or embodied in a work of art which has 'demanded human sacrifice. . . . Art functions here as a life-destructive force' (p. 28). McFarlane's analysis is, again, fascinating and merits careful study. I think, however, he has not finished plotting the curve. There is, certainly, a 'shift in the artist's view of life: from an earlier confident belief in simple pieties and a faith in his own capacity to communicate them through art, to a seriously uncertain, ambivalent, and complex view of things in which truth is elusive and where guilt and remorse and a sense of forfeited opportunity and wasted life occupy the central place'. All this is embodied in or symbolised by 'the re-working of the sculpture' (p. 28). So there is a movement from life to death certainly, a vision of living art which demands a sacrificial dedication ultimately destructive of purely human happiness. But Ibsen called his play *When We Dead Awaken*: it has something to do with resurrection. The Resurrection Day in art has something to say about a Resurrection Day in life. But for this final resurrection to take place, there must obviously be a *death*. No resurrection without death! There is, indeed, 'human sacrifice . . . - sacrificial dedication destructive of human happiness' (pp. 28 and 29), but all this is a necessary prelude to new union, giving promise of new life. Consider some of the final lines of the play in McFarlane's translation, which here convey almost perfectly the depth and beauty of the original:

> *Irene* [*rapturously*]. . . . Up into the glory and splendour of the light. Up to the
> promised peak!
> *Rubek*. Up there will we celebrate our wedding feast, Irene – my beloved!
> *Irene* [*proudly*]. Then the sun can look down upon us, Arnold.
> *Rubek*. All the power of light can look down upon us. And of the darkness, too.
> [*Takes her hand.*] Will you come with me now, my bride of grace?
> *Irene* [*as though transfigured*]. Gladly and willingly, my lord and master.
> *Rubek* [*drawing her along*]. First through the mists, Irene, and then . . .
> *Irene*. Yes, through the mists. Then right up to the very top of the tower, lit by
> the rising sun. (pp. 296–7)

They have a foretaste of the resurrection before the avalanche overtakes them. They must go through the mists and the darkness before they reach 'the top of the tower, lit by the rising sun'. Irene moves in a few moments from sadness and skepticism to a kind of transfiguration. Ibsen uses the biblical word 'forklaret', hinting at a new and glorified existence:

> *Irene* [*smiles and shakes her head*]. As the young woman of your resurrection looks
> down, she can see all life laid out on its funeral straw. (p. 296)

Then, in answer to Rubek's invitation to come with him as his bride of grace,

> *Irene* [*as though transfigured*]. Gladly and willingly, my lord and master.

Here the rhythmic Norwegian, with its indication of transfiguration and the eager following the Master, must be quoted:

> *Irene* [*som forklaret*]. Jeg følger villig og gjerne min hersker og herre.

And Irene is then given the final, optimistic words of their exchange, quoted above.

The play ends with the Nun spreading her arms out towards the fallen (*'stretches out her arms to them as they fall'*) in the liturgical gesture of benediction. She then says three words: 'Irene' (a name obviously chosen for its Greek meaning) and '*Pax vobiscum!*' The '*pax vobiscum*' is the greeting of the priest as he enters the room of the dying with the Viaticum. It is also the greeting of Christ as he, in his glorified body, walked through the door into the room where his disciples were assembled. I think that the curve of the play, then, should end with an upward swing, not with human happiness and life destroyed, but with new life hinted at, a new and transfigured life, 'som lyser i soloppgangen'. The play ends, not with a *nedgang* but with an *oppgang*. Ibsen's 'Dramatic Epilogue' is a great comedy – dare we even say a divine one? And if the 'Dramatic Epilogue' is meant to include other plays as well: the last four or the last eleven or twelve or his whole dramatic work from *Catalina* on . . .?

Professor McFarlane finds little 'positive asseveration' in Ibsen's final plays. They 'establish a gallery of deeply flawed lives. . . . Crippled, guilt-ridden, bankrupt, mortally sick, frigid, impotent, ineffectual, mentally disturbed, these characters exemplify a wide variety of inauthentic living' (p. 31). (As usual, he itemises exhaustively.) Whatever seems positive is either

> naïvely superficial or ironically undermined: Erhart's escape from the 'stuffy air' of the parental home to what he claims will be the 'great, glorious, living happiness' of life in the arms of Mrs Wilton; Maja's escape from the 'cold damp cage' of her existence with Rubek for the 'free and unafraid' life, the sensual satisfactions, which Ulfheim can bring her; Foldal, finding exquisite joy in his daughter's abandonment of him, and wholly content in those circumstances to be 'run over' by life; and Borghejm who, despite the self-evident fulfilment which his road-building brings, still cannot think of life as anything other than 'a kind of game'.   (p. 31)

It is significant, I think, that characters who might be considered the peculiarly Ibsenesque 'heroes' of the plays are not mentioned: Rita and Allmers, Borkman and Ella, Irene and Rubek. It could be argued that each of these, by the end of the play, achieves a positive balance, even in their worldly defeat or death. There are surely, besides the 'unexpected shallows' in these characters, unexpected depths too! And the plays convey to me something more than inauthenticity, defeat, and self-deception. At the end of each play irony gives way to a positive, if at times somewhat obscure, vision – a vision of another mode of living, of a new and exalted life. Consider the beautiful ending of *Little Eyolf* after Allmers has hoisted the flag to the top of the pole:

> *Allmers.* We have a strenuous working day ahead of us, Rita.
> *Rita.* You will see. A Sunday calm will come over us now and then.
> *Allmers* [*quietly, moved*]. Then we may perhaps sense the presence of spirits.
> *Rita* [*whispers*]. Spirits?
> *Allmers* [*as before*]. Yes. Perhaps they may visit us – those we have lost.
> *Rita* [*nods slowly*]. Our little Eyolf. And your big Eyolf too.
> *Allmers* [*staring straight ahead*]. Perhaps now and then, on life's way, we might catch a glimpse of them.
> *Rita.* Where shall we look, Alfred?
> *Allmers* [*gazes at her*]. Upwards.
> *Rita* [*nods in agreement*]. Yes, upwards.
> *Allmers.* Up . . . towards the mountains. Towards the stars. Towards the vast silence.
> *Rita* [*nods in agreement*]. Yes, upwards.   (pp. 105–6)

At the end of *John Gabriel Borkman* there is Ella's 'It is best so, John Borkman. Best for you' (p. 232). These simple, peaceful words in the face of death remind me, perhaps because of the repeated 'bests', of the final chorus of *Samson Agonistes:*

> All is best, though we oft doubt
> What th' unsearchable dispose
> Of highest wisdom brings about,
> And ever best found in the close.

One cannot help sensing the calm after storm at the end of *Borkman*, nor can one avoid seeing something positive in the reconciliation of the twin-sisters as they reach out their hands towards each other. Through his death John Gabriel is beginning to establish some peace and unity and community – 'forbundsliv'.

Finally, there are the unforgettable final lines of *When We Dead Awaken*, quoted above. Ultimately and in the profoundest sense, these so-called losers (Allmers, Borkman and Rubek) are seen not to be losers after all.

At the end of his 'Introduction' McFarlane finds Ibsen judging himself as 'poet' in the last plays and thus condemning himself:

> The bitterest term of abuse which Irene can find for Rubek is 'poet'. A poet is doubly culpable: not only does he (in common with all artists) mercilessly exploit the human situation for his artistic ends, taking young human life and 'ripping the soul out of it'; but also when finally the enormity of his conduct is borne in on him, he offers merely *poetic* expiation, makes the stirrings of his conscience into the very stuff of art, and by condemning his created *alter ego* to an infinity of guilt and remorse, thinks thereby to win exoneration for himself. 'Why poet?' Rubek asks in astonishment at this mode of rebuke. 'Because you are soft and spineless and full of excuses for everything you've ever done or thought', Irene replies. 'You killed my soul – then you go and model yourself as a figure of regret and remorse and penitence . . . and you think you've settled your account.'   (p. 33)

But surely the act of creating a work of art is in itself something not to be condemned. I am probably not following the argument very well at the end, however. As William Archer remarked in a lecture on Ibsen delivered at University College, London: 'To this day there are many people who understand Ibsen better than I do – and sometimes, I suspect, even better than Henrik Ibsen did.'[4] I am quite sure that Professor McFarlane understands Ibsen better than I do. It could be even that he understands him better than Ibsen did.

Nevertheless, Professor McFarlane can only be placed in the very forefront of genuinely stimulating and original Ibsen critics. At times, obviously, I simply disagree with his reading of the text. However, Ibsen, like Shakespeare, is great enough to invite many different readings. Disagreements cannot alter my profound gratitude to McFarlane for casting so much light on a great dramatist.

And now let us turn to the translation, 'a labor of love', as John Northam put it, 'begotten by despair upon impossibility'.[5] By and large McFarlane has gracefully managed to cope with this impossibility. The lines are sayable; they do not sound like a translation. At the same time, those 'familiar with the original' will be 'reminded of it at every stage' ('Preface', p. x). Further, McFarlane's rendering is honest, true to the text, in that he does not cut, alter, or change anything radically, as other recent translators have done. For this we can be very grateful.

No two translators, of course, would render Ibsen's text in exactly the same way. I have gone through the translation line by line, comparing it at every stage with the original, and naturally there are many places where I would have rendered a word or phrase or sentence differently. There are, however, very few instances of what I would consider infelicity in translation, even fewer instances of apparent or real errors. Also since I am not a native Norwegian speaker, I am certainly not sure of all the nuances Ibsen's language is meant to convey.

Ibsen's Norwegian abounds in alliterative, assonant, or rhyming doublets. At times McFarlane is remarkably successful in rendering them. The Rat Wife speaks of the little beasts 'creeping and crawling ('kribbet og krab-bet'). . . . Over the floors, scratching and scraping ('hvislet og rislet') in all the corners' (p. 47). Later on Rita suggests various ways of coping with life: she and Allmers could entertain many guests, 'Throw ourselves into some-thing which might deaden and dull ('døve og dulme') . . .' (p. 83). Sometimes the doublets are not, perhaps cannot, be rendered. Erhart, in explaining his sudden departure with Mrs Wilton, simply says, 'Everything was arranged' (p. 219). This is a rather bland rendering of 'all ting var jo klappet og klart'. Reasonably successful is Ulfheim's 'anything that's got life and vigor and warm blood' for 'bare det er frisk og frodig og blodrikt'. It is clear enough, however, that the alliteration and assonance in the Norwegian gives strength and colour to the original lacking in the translation.

A small problem is the occasional use of a colloquialism unfamiliar to the non-British English speaker. The Rat Wife speaks of her dealings with the vermin: 'Between us we put paid to them' (p. 47). The Norwegian has the simple and (I am told) not particularly colloquial 'alle sammen fikk vi to has på'. I doubt if many Americans or Canadians are familiar with the expression 'put paid to'. Why not simply 'between us we disposed of the rats'? Or, if a colloquialism seems to be called for, one familiar to most English speakers might be used: 'Between us we sent the rats packing.'

Occasionally there are translations which tend to obscure a clear Nor-wegian text. In the stage directions at the beginning of act II of *John Gabriel Borkman* 'lenger foran' is translated 'forward of this', rather than simply and idiomatically 'further downstage'. We also have a 'tapestry-covered door without surround' for 'en tapetdør uten innfatning'. 'Uten innfatning' implies, surely, a door set flush with the wall and thus having no frame. Finally, 'møblene er holdt i stiv empirestil' becomes 'the furniture is res-tricted to a severely Empire style' (p. 179). Would not 'stiff' or 'formal' be a better rendering of 'stiv' than 'severely'? It is remarkable how often a literal translation of Ibsen's words turns out to be the best translation.

Sometimes, indeed, a translation which is not quite literal obscures the significance of what Ibsen surely wants to convey. In *Little Eyolf*, for exam-ple, Rita and Allmers must come to feel themselves as true husband and wife, as one flesh; hence the pronouns *vi* (we) and *oss* (us) are significant when used by them. Hence I think it is a mistake to translate 'bare for oss to' as 'only to you and me' (p. 97); the disjunction of 'you and me' separates what is united in 'oss to'. Also, as we read through the play, we gradually come to realise the significance of the simple vertical concept 'up and down' *(opp og ned)*. Great care must be taken in the translation of these words whenever they appear, since they reflect the tension between heaven and earth. Rita and Allmers agree that they are 'earthbound':

> *Allmers.* Så jordbundne er vi begge to, Rita . . .
>
> *Rita.* Å, vi er jordmennesker, du.
>
> *Almers.* So completely earthbound, are we, Rita, you and I . . .   (p. 102)
>
> *Rita.* Ah, we are but earthbound creatures, Alfred.   (p. 104)

So it is important, I think, when Asta hurries 'nedover' and Allmers stares 'nedover', as indicated in a stage direction in act III (p. 96 in the translation) that the two 'nedover's be translated literally, 'down'. Instead we have Asta hurrying 'away', while Allmers is, quite properly, staring 'down'. At the end, however, both Rita and Allmers realise that they must aspire upwards. *Opp* is incorporated into three strong verbs: 'Så får jeg oppdra meg til det. Opplære meg. Oppøve meg' says Rita. I think it is impossible to get into English the upward thrust of these three verbs. McFarlane tries to overcome the problem by adding a sentence with the proper upward motion in it: 'Then I shall have to rise to it. Teach myself to do it. Instruct myself. Train myself' (p. 104). The beautiful conclusion of the play, quoted earlier, with the thrice repeated *oppad*'s, is rendered perfectly by McFarlane. Earlier in the play, however, the *opp* or *oppe* is sometimes dropped. Asta speaks of Rita: 'Hun går litt omkring oppe i haven.' This is rendered, 'Walking in the garden, I think' (p. 69). Later on Asta pleads with Allmers: 'Gå opp til Rita.' The English has her saying, 'Go to Rita, I beg you' (p. 74). In both cases, I think, something is lost in the failure to translate literally.

Ibsen, always a poet, loves the verbal echo: single, significant words are often repeated, sometimes once in a specific context, sometimes more than once, sometimes many times throughout a play, thus forming the rich verbal harmonies, which can be heard in many plays. The Norwegian language does not have the rich vocabulary of English, and I think there can be justification for translating the same word in different ways according to the context. But the translator should be very conscious of what he is doing when he decides to render differently the same word in the same play. At the end of *Little Eyolf*, for example, 'søndagsstillhet' and 'den store stillhet' are surely meant to echo each other. But one is rendered 'the Sunday calm' and the other 'the vast silence' (pp. 105 and 106). Since the words come so close together, the translator must have decided deliberately to suppress the echo. I wonder why.

Yet another example reflects Ibsen's concern with individuals' differing perceptions of the world, confirming their isolation. Borkman sees the steamships and hears the wheels of industry turning. Ella sees only the snowy landscape and the dead tree. Rita in *Little Eyolf*, act III, hears the rhythmical 'the crutch is floating'. Allmers responds: 'I hear nothing. There *is* nothing' (p. 98). ('Jeg hører ingenting. Det er ingenting heller.') Allmers thus insists that Ella is deceived by repeating the *ingenting* twice and immediately after echoing the final phrase. 'Du skal ikke stå og lytte efter noe som ingenting er.' This is translated as 'You mustn't stand here listening to something that doesn't exist' (p. 98). I submit that a literal translation, giving us a third *ingenting* in an emphatically echoing and paradoxical phrase is preferable: 'You mustn't stand here listening to something that is nothing.'

Allusions, inevitably, are sometimes lost in the translation, but sometimes they seem to be added. In act III of the play John Gabriel Borkman attempts to justify himself to his wife. He explains he had to do what he did 'because I am as I am' (p. 207) ('fordi jeg var meg selv'). The original suggests Borkman's Gynt-like pursuit of his deeper self, to which McFarlane alludes in his 'Introduction' (p. 25), or, as I see it, Borkman's insight into the uniqueness of his own being. But the translation seems to suggest an allusion to the words of God from the burning bush to Moses in Exodus 3.14: 'God said unto Moses, I am that I am.' This allusion, if it really *is* an allusion, is not in the Norwegian.

Borkman's plea for understanding goes unheeded. Gunhild only shakes her head saying: 'Nytter ikke noe. Tilskyndelser frikjenner ingen. Innsky-telser heller ikke.' This is translated – 'No use! Motives are no excuse. They don't acquit you' (p. 207). The single word 'motives' is used to cover both 'tilskyndelser' and 'innskytelser'. Admittedly, the words are as close in meaning as in sound. But the syntax of the sentences indicates that Ibsen wants them carefully distinguished as well as compared. Translation is certainly not easy. However, Inga-Stina Ewbank's rendering is faithful to the meaning and syntax of the original: 'It's useless. A man's not acquitted because of his character. Nor because of his instincts.'[6] 'Character' may seem to be an inaccurate translation of 'tilskyndelser', but 'character' does seem to relate to the 'self' to which Borkman had just been referring in self-justifica-tion: 'Jeg var meg selv' ('I was myself'), a theme to which Borkman twice returns in the following speech (also on p. 207). Indeed, 'meg selv' is mentioned three times in two of Borkman's speeches on this page. The phrase is translated in three different ways. 'Fordi jeg var meg selv' becomes, as we have seen, 'because I am as I am'. 'For meg selv' becomes 'in my own mind'. 'Det er meg selv' becomes 'is myself'. Surely in each case the concept 'meg selv' is the same and should thus be translated in the same way.

Also in this same important scene Borkman mentions another reason for doing what he did: 'Jeg hadde makten! Og så den ubetvingelige kallelse inneni meg da' ('I had the power! And the indomitable sense of ambition!', p. 207). Here surely it is easy and quite proper to translate literally as Inga-Stina Ewbank does: 'I had power. And an irresistible calling inside me.'[7] Borkman insists that his activity is an answer to an irresistible call. I think 'calling' or 'call' is used here, as in *The Pretenders* and *Brand*, with the full weight of Biblical connotation. The 'call' is, in a sense, a 'divine call'. Now Borkman may be deceived: he hears things, for example the wheels of the factories, which others don't hear. Or his inflated talk about an 'irresistible calling' may be simply a device to mask his 'indomitable sense of ambition'. But I wonder whether it is the business of a translator to provide a rendering which is so obviously an interpretation and in no way reminds us of the original. 'An indomitable sense of ambition' is not the same as 'den ubetvingelige kallelse'.

In general, Ibsen's indebtedness to Biblical language should be noted. In the famous letter to Bjørnsen (12 September 1865) in which he mentions, among other things, where he got the inspiration for the new, dramatic form of *Brand* (St Peter's in Rome), Ibsen writes that here, in the peaceful surroundings of Ariccia, he 'reads nothing but the Bible – it is powerful and strong'. ('Herude er velsignet fredeligt . . . jeg laeser ikke andet end Bibelen – den er kraftig og staerk.') This must have been a bit of an exaggeration. But there can be no doubt that the Bible provided one important subtextual basis for his language. John Northam has shown how this works at the end of *Rosmersholm* in a recent essay.[8] On re-reading the last three plays carefully, as I have been forced to do in connection with this review, I have found countless Biblical allusions – explicit, oblique, submerged, unconscious. Sometimes these allusions are deftly caught in the English. 'So God created man in his own image, in the image of God created he him' ('Og Gud skapte mennesket i sitt billede, i Guds billede skapte han det') – so runs the famous text in Genesis. Rubek creates his vision of the Resurrection Day in Irene's image. 'That's how I created her. Created her in your image, Irene' (p. 259). 'I ditt bilde skapte jeg henne, Irene.'

At times, however, an allusion is almost lost, or completely lost, in a translation which is not quite literal. Speaking of his son, Allmers insists that 'somebody will follow me and do it much better' (p. 43). Ibsen's words are these: 'Det kommer en bakefter som vil gjøre det bedre.' ('There is one coming after who will do it better.') Here the words clearly echo Matthew 3.11: 'Den som kommer efter mig er sterkere end jeg.' ('He that cometh after me is mightier than I.') In the literal translation the allusion is clearly caught; it is much less clear in the translation in *The Oxford Ibsen*. We find another example of this in *When We Dead Awaken*. Rubek is talking to Irene, his disciple (as it were), in act I: 'You left your family and your home . . . to go with me' (p. 259). Instead of 'to go with me' the original has 'og fulgte meg', thus making the references to Christ's calling the Apostles and their leaving everything to follow him quite clear. Perhaps the most famous of these is in Matthew 4.19 and 20: 'Follow me and I will make you fishers of men. And they straightway left their nets and followed him.' ('Følger efter mig, saa vil jeg gjøre eder til menneske-fiskere. Men de forlode strax garnene og fulgte ham.') In act II of the same play a less obvious, but perhaps more important, Biblical reference is also lost. Irene compares herself with Christ at the Transfiguration, an event which, in traditional exegesis, anticipates and gives earnest of the Resurrection and Glorification: 'Men lysgledens forklarelse stråler over mitt ansikt fremedeles?' This is rendered, 'But my face is still radiant with the light of joy?' (p. 278). The key word, of course, is 'forklarelse', defined as 'transfiguration' in Einar Haugen's *Norwegian–English Dictionary*. A dictionary published in Copenhagen in 1802 has this definition:

> *forklarelse* – Bruges meest i theologisk Forstand til at betegne: Forherligelse, Herliggiørelse. Christi Forklarelse paa Bierget.

> *transfiguration* – used most frequently in the theological sense to indicate transfiguration, sanctification, as in Christ's transfiguration on the mountain.

The verb form is used in two of the three accounts of the Transfiguration – Matthew 17.2 and Mark 9.2: 'Og han blev forklaret for deres øine.' So, in order to catch the allusion, the translation might easily have been, 'But my face is still transfigured with the light of joy?' The past-participial form used in the Bible *is* translated literally at the beginning of the same dialogue between Irene and Rubek:

> *Rubek*. The day will dawn and all will grow bright for the two of us. You'll see.
> *Irene*. Never believe that!
> *Rubek* [*urgently*]. I do believe it. I know it will! Now that I've found you again. . . .
> *Irene*. Risen.
> *Rubek*. Transfigured!
> *Irene*. Only risen, Arnold. But not transfigured.   (p. 274)

> *Rubek*. Du skal se det vil dages og lysne for oss begge.
> *Irene*. Tro aldri det.
> *Rubek*. Det tror jeg! Og det vet jeg! Nu, da jeg har funnet deg igjen –
> *Irene*. Oppstanden.
> *Rubek*. Forklaret!
> *Irene*. Bare oppstanden, Arnold. Men ikke forklaret.

Here the translation is literal and the Biblical allusion caught. Surely we are meant to be reminded of it when Irene refers to 'lysgledens forklarelse' a few minutes later. While her physical being is not yet transfigured, she hopes that her being as it exists in her child, the work of art, *is* transfigured.

Finally, a small, but perhaps significant, point. It is obvious to anyone that there is much about art, the artist, and artistic creation in *When We Dead Awaken*: *kunst, kunstner,* and *å skape* in various forms come up frequently. Of course the words are concerned with a central issue in the play, and they occur most frequently in the marvellous dialogue between Irene and Rubek quoted from above. It is a pity that the first reference to *kunst* and the first use of *å skape* in the dialogue are obscured in the translation. Irene is talking of the *diakonisse* (translated as 'nun' rather than 'deaconess'): 'Hun går og øver trolldomskunster. Tenk deg, Arnold, hun har skapt seg om til min skygge' (p. 587). This is rendered, 'she practises witchcraft. [*confidentially*] Do you know, Arnold . . . she has changed herself into my shadow!' (p. 274). That the first reference to art is to the black arts ('trolldomskunster') and that the first reference to creation is to a kind of alteration to a non-human and sinister form might be seen as casting an ironic shadow over the positive words used so often in the ensuing dialogue.

Inga-Stina Ewbank has recently reminded us of the difficulty in speaking 'about Ibsen in a discursive way' and that we are beginning more and more to see 'his meaning as tied up with tone and attitude, and all these in their turn as closely bound up in his choice of words, his syntax, his rhythms, his speech-patterns'. Therefore the translation should try 'to mirror in English the lexical, syntactical, and rhythmic qualities of the original'.[9] For the most part Professor McFarlane has been eminently successful in doing just this. In concentrating on a few problems with the translation, I have been unfair in not pointing out the innumerable admirable renderings of the tone and style of the original. The fact is that the reader can pick up the English text at almost any point and become absorbed. This has happened to me often in the course of writing this review. Certainly a good sign! We can only be grateful to the many years' hard work Professor McFarlane has devoted to his task. The work has born fruit in a worthy English edition of Ibsen's plays. Professor McFarlane may well sing now with Maja at the end of *When We Dead Awaken:*

> Jeg er fri! Jeg er fri! jeg er fri!
> Mit fangenskaps liv er forbi!

Yet I think that there must be some regret too at leaving a work with which he has lived for so many years.

To Professor McFarlane for his edition: *Hjertelig takk!*

NOTES

1. All quotations from this volume will be followed immediately by the appropriate page number in round brackets. Occasionally there will be a series of quotations from a single page, which will be indicated only after the final quotation in the

series. Page numbers do not follow quotations from Ibsen's Norwegian. These are all located closely enough in the text of the essay itself, and I did not want to clutter the page with more numbers. The Norwegian text used was *Ibsen: Nutidsdramer 1877–99* (Stavanger, 1968), the edition owned by most Ibsenites unable to afford the *Hundreårsutgave*.

2. *The Oxford Ibsen*, II, 248.
3. 'Fins det en moral i Ibsens skuespill', *Festshrift til Jeus Kruuse* (Aarhus, 1968), p. 182.
4. 'The True Greatness of Ibsen', *Edda, Bind XII* (Kristiania, 1919–20), p. 188.
5. 'On a Firm Foundation – the Translation of Ibsen's Prose', *Ibsenårbok 1977* (Oslo), p. 79.
6. Henrik Ibsen, *John Gabriel Borkman*, English Version and Introduction by Inga-Stina Ewbank and Peter Hall (London: The Athlone, Press 1975), p. 70.
7. *Ibid.*
8. 'A Note on the Language of *Rosmersholm*', *Ibsenårbok 1977* (Oslo), pp. 209–15.
9. 'Translating Ibsen for the Contemporary Stage', *Theatre Research International* (October 1976), p. 45.

The Revels History of Drama in English
volume VIII, *American Drama*

reviewed by MICHAEL J. SIDNELL

The anomalous fact is that the theater, so called, can flourish in barbarism, but that any *drama* worth speaking of can develop but in the air of civilization.

(Henry James)

In Spanish America the colonists used drama as a medium of religious celebration and propaganda. The actors included aboriginals whose own dramatic forms survived the shock of the new culture. In the English colonies, by contrast, drama arrived later and as the offshoot of the vigorous commercial theatre of England, and it was brought not *by* but *to* the colonists. From the application of business principles to the rapid growth of the new states this drama derived its praxis. Unlike that of Athens, Rome, medieval Europe, Elizabethan England, nineteenth-century Germany or Ireland at the turn of the century, in which other impulses and determinants were operative, drama in America began and developed as a form of business. It was very deliberately not religious, not festive, not patriotic, not even academic – though there were early stirrings in the colleges and, ultimately, an exceptionally important academic theatre – not these, but commercial.

It may have been unfortunate that, in the economy of the colonies, a professional theatre was able to pay its way and, before long, become very profitable indeed for actors with outstanding talents, and some without. It is certainly essential to recognise a strong reaction against the commercial theatre in America. For the historian, however, the first requirement would seem to be the description and analysis of a theatre originating and developing as a commercial venture. Such a phenomenon might be no less interesting than that of the transmutation of ritual into drama, and perhaps there is no intrinsic inferiority in a theatre operated on business principles; or, if there is, its character and history might indicate a more general social failing and be well worth attention for that reason. It is fair to say, I believe, that in the *Revels History*[1] Travis Bogard and Walter J. Meserve take the view that drama in America emerged out of the struggle with, and partly through the defeat of, theatre as business; that there was a period of transition in which 'theatre art' and 'meaningful' content managed to assert themselves by opposing the weakening force of commercial motives in the theatre. Not that they conduct such an argument. The reader is left to find his own way of understanding a rich assemblage of material, strongly coloured by attitudes and dissociated points of view but not articulated as a continuous discussion.

In colonial America the theatre was scarcely accorded the dignity of being commercial. The first continental congress of 1774, enunciating a crude economic theory, distinguished productive transactions from dissipations. It regarded performances of plays as belonging to the latter category, and, amidst much vital business, found the time to pass a resolution (which Walter Meserve incorrectly calls an 'interdict') discountenancing them. An outright prohibition was beyond the power of the congress and would, in any case, have been ill-advised, since the response to theatrical ventures in the colonies ranged from sheer intolerance to active encouragement, with many gradations and equivocations in between. At the intolerant end of the scale were, as ever, the city fathers of Boston, who passed an ordinance against plays in 1750. Charleston, at the other extreme, had enjoyed the theatre for many years. Less than a year before the congress passed its resolution, Douglass had replaced the existing theatre there with a new home for his American Company. In Philadelphia, despite continuing opposition and a brief period of prohibition, Douglass's Southwark Theatre had been in operation for many years; while in partly anti-theatrical New York, yet another Douglass foundation, the John Street Theatre, appeared to be a permanent amenity of the colony.

What the first congress was discountenancing was the institution established in the colonies primarily by the Hallam–Douglass companies, the pattern of which not only survived Independence but is still discernible (in the one-way traffic in touring actors, plays and productions from England and in devotion to Shakespeare) even today. A major initiative had been taken in 1752 by William Hallam, a London manager fallen on hard times. He sent his brother Lewis, with wife, three children and a small company, to Williamsburg, where they opened with *The Merchant of Venice*. At the time they were the most substantial professional company, though not the first, to play in Williamsburg's theatre, from which they made forays into other parts of the colonies. After the death of her husband in Jamaica, Mrs Hallam joined David Douglass, who was playing there, in a matrimonial and professional alliance. In 1758, Douglass, Mrs Hallam, Lewis Hallam Jr and a reconstituted company launched the enterprise that, with energy, guile and very little serious competition, provided plays and playhouses in the American colonies until the rumblings of Revolution sent the company back to Jamaica once more.

In the early days, Douglass and the Hallams offered themselves to the public as 'The London Company' but, in the course of the sixties, decided that 'The American Company' was a more politic and ingratiating title to play under, and they billed themselves thus until the appearance of new competition inspired them to call themselves 'Old American'. Perhaps they really felt some inclination to go native since Douglass produced, in 1767, Thomas Godfrey's *The Prince of Parthia*, the first play by a native-born American to receive a professional production, though not in any other sense an American play. But Douglass's line of business, the title of his company notwithstanding, was to supply English drama performed by English actors. In this he received a good deal of support from English governors and officials and, moreover, he achieved most success in establishing the theatre in the colonies in which the Church of England was already established. If many of the colonists were not content to have it thus, it was not because they resented English dominance in this particular form but because they were opposed to the theatre itself. As a choice of evils, indeed, it was better that there should be an English professional theatre than that the ungodly occupation should take root.

In a culture dominated by the Puritans, says Travis Bogard, 'there was little hope that even amateur theatre could prosper'. But it was amateur theatre especially that was inhibited by Puritan opposition, which thus helped to sustain the supremacy of the English professionals. The professional companies, being self-contained communities and mobile, managed to avoid, evade and even defeat Puritan antagonism. One of their main tactics was to make quick sorties from safe bases into Puritan territory; another was to counter Puritan antipathy by making large claims for the moral utility of drama. Thus a culturally dependent, commercial and moral drama was, in part, a Puritan legacy to modern America. 'Something worth the name of American drama' would have been a contradiction in terms for the Puritan colonists. Their descendants, in wanting an American theatre without the profanity of the theatre were less clear-headed; and it might be said that the real profanity of the stage is something that America, particularly, is disinclined to recognise, despite such outright provocations as *Dionysus 69* and *Hair*.

The first congress did not object overtly to the theatre as an institution English and profane. It did not need to. It was enough that the performing of plays lay outside a pragmatic and comprehensive social morality of 'frugality, economy and industry'. Playing, like gaming, was a dissipation. Far from contributing to the colonial economy, the theatre diverted human and material resources from manufacturing, agriculture and the (productive) arts. In 1774, the economic argument could be made to subsume the rest. But time hath its revenges. One hundred and sixty years later the economic argument was reversed when the Roosevelt administration, recognising that the theatre was a very important part of the depressed national economy, took steps to support it. Of course the theoretical underpinning of the Works Progress Administration was much more sophisticated than eighteenth-century economics, and the theatre had not only vastly increased its business but also its status. Still there is some significance in the fact that the official attitude to the theatre was expressed first (though by no means only) in economic terms. As might have been expected, government funding attracted political interference. As something other than a business venture, the theatre was revealed, not least to itself, as a not-easily comprehensible and possibly dangerous social force, rocking who knew what monsters in their cradles.

There was also something of a revelation of the nature of theatre when the professional companies left the colonies for the duration of the Revolutionary War. Amateur groups sprang up in the garrisons and they presented not only classical but also new plays. The British were more active but the American soldiery was sufficiently diverted by play-production for congress (acting now with authority) to put a stop to it. No doubt it was fortuitous that General Burgoyne, as dramatist, pasted his opponents on the boards but not on the field, and that, in general, military success and theatrical license were inversely apportioned; but it is significant that, in the absence of a theatre business and in the context of strong feelings of community, theatre germinated.

After Independence, the Old American Company returned and, by internal fission, gave rise to new troupes; most notably that of the comedian who created the role of Jonathan in *The Contrast*, Thomas Wignell. Wignell's own comic talent and his skill in recruiting actors from England made his company a surpassing rival of the old firm. The Old American Company, in its turn, strengthened itself by new infusions of English talent. The rivalries were played out in terms of managerial deals, partnerships made and dissolved, theatres controlled and, above all performers retained or lost. The talents and drawing-power of actors were used somewhat as in professional team sports at present, though in a more fluid situation, performers could, and frequently did, become managers on the strength of their talents. When Wignell opened the Chestnut Street Theatre in 1794, he introduced Philadelphians – indeed America – to new standards of production, physical and artistic. This large, well-equipped playhouse accommodated such outstanding performers as Eliza Kemble, John Bernard and Thomas Abthorpe Cooper and some two thousand spectators. The competition from Chestnut Street was altogether too much for the Old American Company, which was forced to vacate the Southwark Theatre. But the company itself was far from finished. John Hodgkinson, a relatively recent recruit, displaced the manager who had hired him and went into partnership with Lewis Hallam Jr. Hallam and Hodgkinson later sought to resolve professional and personal difficulties by making a triumvirate with William Dunlap. Dunlap's career as manager, prolific adaptor of plays and historian of the theatre was one of the great *American* careers, for which he was to be appropriately honoured as 'father of the American theatre'. His original play *André*, written in 1798, was a very early example of an attempt to use drama as a means of questioning the political integrity of the new nation, dealing as it did with the unjust hanging of the British officer, Major John André. This theme from recent history was apparently somewhat too advanced for Dunlap's audiences and, man of the theatre as he was, he repented of his desire 'to excite interest in the breasts of an American audience' with the dramatisation of an event not very much to the credit of the nation. He did penance with the much more popular *The Glory of Columbia* in which André is portrayed more as spy, less as British patriot and the pretensions of verse tragedy are abandoned. The career of Dunlap is embedded in a complex of theatrical events and personalities from which the history of drama as playwriting cannot be sensibly abstracted. Text and theatrical context in eighteenth- and nineteenth-century America are inseparable, though it is perhaps more feasible to give an account of the theatre without dwelling on the plays than to isolate the latter.

In the middle, and most satisfactory, section of *American Drama*, Richard Moody expertly and, for the most part, lucidly surveys the shifting patterns of the theatrical scene, from the beginnings of theatre in America to the present. As he approaches the twentieth century, however, the difficulty of incorporating all the necessary credits in a continuous narrative becomes overwhelming. Continuity degenerates into syntactical ingenuity by which names have the appearance of being linked. At this point it might have been more straightforward and useful to have cleared the text by appending a list. As it is, the latter part of this section is bedevilled, as theatre 'history' so often is, by a mass of miscellaneous memorabilia unleavened by thought. This section of the volume is one long, but severely compressed, chapter. The third section, on 'The Dramatists and their Plays' by Walter J. Meserve, is by contrast made up of fourteen very short chapters; and the two sections are organised on quite different principles; Moody's being traditionally, and usefully, chronological; Meserve's being a grid of chronology and theme which, in itself, tends to evade the problems in relating diverse contemporaneous works and, in relation to Moody's section, unnecessarily isolates the drama from its theatre. Very important topics fall through the gaps, moreover; one of them being what Meserve calls 'one of the American theatre's major contributions to world theatre', musical comedy. 'What it contributes to American drama is another question', adds Meserve, and as far as this book is concerned, it remains one.

Indeed, the incoherence of the structure of *American Drama* overall makes the book inferior, in this important respect, to such works as G. B. Wilson's unpretentious survey, *Three Hundred Years of American Drama and Theatre* or, in a quite different style, the collection of essays, edited by H. B. Williams, which manages to live up to the title, *The American Theatre: a Sum of its Parts* or, different again, Barnard Hewitt's largely documentary *Theatre U.S.A.*; all of which have a clarity of purpose that *American Drama* notably lacks. For this deficiency the General Editor must bear chief responsibility. In a very brief preface he rather disingenuously claims that 'the effort has been made to achieve coherence and avoid mere duplication', but in fact there is little of the first and (infuriatingly) much of the second. Information is very often repeated where it might have been developed. A bizarre Chronological Table is symptomatic, excluding as it does items presented with great emphasis in the text (as, for instance, the founding of the Chicago Little Theatre and *Theatre Arts Magazine* and the first performances of *Uncle Tom's Cabin* and *Showboat*), and including such remote matter as the publication of *Howards End*, *The Rainbow* and Yeats's *Poems* of 1895. Otherwise conceived and executed the table might have mitigated the disconnectedness of the volume. It is a pity, too, that the table was not used, as it might very simply have been, to indicate the demographic facts that are so distinctive and important in the American context.

In the first decades of the nineteenth century, the growth of theatre in America was measured by the proliferation of companies, the opening of theatres and, most of all perhaps, the magnitude of the visiting stars: George Frederick Cooke, who on two tours demonstrated the audiences' appetite for, and the attractive financial possibilities of, such visitations; Edmund Kean, who came in 1820, ten years after Cooke, and also opened his campaign with Richard Crookback; Junius Brutus Booth, who came in the year after Kean's first visit, also played Richard in New York, and staying on in America sired the nation's most renowned actor as well as one of its most infamous; William Charles Macready, who made three tours, the last of which raised the rivalry of stars and their fans to the pitch of intensity that occasioned the Astor Place Riots. These and lesser lights contributed to a theatrical development so rapid and luxuriant that it all but stifled native plays. 'English managers, English actors, and English plays (we say it in no spirit of national antipathy, a feeling of hate) must be allowed to die away among us, as usurpers of our stage. The drama of this country *can* be the mouth-piece of freedom, refinement, liberal philanthropy . . .' – thus Walt Whitman in 1847, interestingly proceeding from English dominance of the stage not to an American theatrical take-over, but to the development of a new drama of moral significance.

It was with the emergence of native-born actors that America began to take possession of its theatre, though non-American theatre sometimes took possession of them. John Howard Payne was one of the latter group, and a big disappointment from the American point of view. His first play was produced at the Park Theatre when he was a prodigy of fourteen with the highest ambitions for American drama. He made his début as an actor three years later, and for several years flourished as an 'American Roscius' before he moved to England. He made a success there as both actor and playwright, his *Brutus* being staged at Drury Lane and only later in the United States. Payne's main contribution to the theatre, however, issued from France where he settled and became a prolific adaptor of French plays for the English stage. He was borne by the strongest theatrical currents of the time and these flowed through, not from, the United States.

Another significant loss to the American stage was Ira Aldridge. He spent twenty-five years on the English stage and received his greatest tributes on the Continent. It is inconceivable that Aldridge could have had a comparable career in his native country. The experiment of the African Theatre in New York failed, or was aborted, a year or two before Aldridge made his début in London. The American theatre had a very limited and very special place for black performers and none for a black tragedian like Aldridge. This is as much as to say, seeing by hindsight, that for social reasons the American theatre and drama could not be fully American; or, to put it another way, the forces of market and morality kept the theatre from blatant profanations, diverted them, with respect to the inevitable absorption and reflection of black culture, into the fantastic guise of black-face. Black-face, it should be observed, is something that occurred not only in the theatre but in the drama too. George Harris is every inch a white man. He speaks white, acts white, and feels whiter than white. His blackness is much less than skin-deep. Some black-face roles came to be played by black actors, but in Aldridge's time America was certainly not ready for a *black* Othello.

If Ira Aldridge was too obviously American for the American stage, two native performers of mid-century were supremely suited for it. Charlotte Cushman and Edwin Forrest both possessed not only superior abilities but what could be thought of as distinctively American qualities. The tall, broad-shouldered, deep-voiced Charlotte Cushman was especially suited for female parts that called for a commanding energy, and for breeches parts. With Macready's encouragement and help she went to London as a promising actress, somewhat rough-hewn, and returned to America several years later as a star. Forrest, by contrast, was already America's foremost actor when he showed that an American star could illuminate the theatre at least as brightly as any English rivals; a demonstration that culminated in 1849 with a comparison of Macbeths, Forrest's and Macready's, and the fury of a mob roused by Macready's temerity in challenging Forrest on his own ground. Thirty-one lives were spent in the satisfaction of American theatrical pride. Could such a riot have occurred had the rivals been both American or both English? Probably not *such* a riot as that at Astor Place. Forrest was a very patriotic American, made much of his Americanness and exploited his fans' identification with it. Edwin Booth was to excel his namesake as an interpreter of great roles but not in American quality.

Forrest had learned from the best English actors in America, including Thomas Abthorpe Cooper and Edmund Kean. In the latter, particularly, he found an assimilable example of passionate and very physical acting. Forrest was well equipped for such a style and became a tragedian of tremendous emotional power, with voice and body to match. But not content with the great Shakespearian roles, Forrest wanted American parts that would demand equal abilities, and, through him, drama made its response to the needs of the theatre.

By the simple device of playwriting competitions, Forrest acquired the kind of plays he wanted, and for very little money; such plays as Stone's *Metamora, or the Last of the Wampanoags*, Bird's *The Gladiator* and *Oralloossa, Son of the Incas* and Conrad's *Jack Cade*. These are clear instances of the dependence of American drama on the theatre of the time, a condition that has produced the world's great drama. These plays are not that. They served primarily, though not entirely, as vehicles for virtuoso acting and spectacular scenic effects. The playwrights' dependence is touchingly evident, also, in the arrangement which gave Forrest total ownership of highly profitable commodities that he could market over and over again. And for all one's sympathy with the efforts of later playwrights, led by Boucicault, to secure the rights in their own works, there was *some* fairness in Forrest's dealings. Metamora was as much an occasion for Forrest as a role. It was his person and voice, not Stone's pen, that incarnated the theatrical figment. Stone's play was not only not available to readers but probably of little interest to them either. It would, of course, have interested other *players* and Forrest, if he was artistically supreme in the role, did not have to prove that supremacy since he monopolised it. That was one of the advantages of American plays. They were in private domain.

When adequate copyright protection was achieved in the nineties, the balance had already shifted in the playwrights' favour. The theatre had already become more attentive to plays and their themes, less doting on the glories of performance. With copyright, also, playwrights could afford to be more independent of the theatre, and some of the worst of them were. The right symbiotic balance between the claims of the theatre on the one hand and plays on the other has rarely been achieved. The relatively short history of the American theatre and drama is a divided history, poised over a period of antagonism between playwriting and performance. This antagonism, strong in Europe, was reflected in America with an intensity heightened by the colonial traditions of the theatre and the immense pecuniary interests involved. The antagonism still persists as theatrical commerce versus dramatic cult – Simon versus Shepard – but with a strong third force of civic and academic theatres.

To draw out the connection between American theatrical tradition and modern American drama seems to be an obvious task confronting historians. *American Drama*, as indicated above, evades it. Travis Bogard and Walter Meserve are obviously on the side of the artistic angels. Bogard, in an excellent chapter on the rise of little, independent and art theatres makes good sense of the twentieth-century reaction against monolithic theatrical business. Here the Chicago Little Theatre, the Washington Square Players, the Provincetown Players, the Theatre Guild, the New Playwrights' Theatre and other groups, including *the* Group Theatre, are admirably placed in context with each other and with the work of the directors, designers and playwrights associated with them. The chapter is a first-rate essay curiously placed in the book. (With some co-ordination it could have been used to alleviate the problems of compression in Moody's section on the theatre.) This chapter, called 'Art and Politics', is one of four that constitute the first section. The other three are: 'Actors in the Land', which gives highpoints of the theatrical history that Moody surveys in a compressed but more extended form later; 'The Central Reflector', which touches on highpoints in American drama and discerns such important themes in it as preoccupation with the land; and 'O'Neill versus Shaw', a summary of O'Neill's achievement presented under the pretext of a comparison, which scarcely begins (and why should it?) with Shaw. The design of the four-chapter section overall remains obscure and the purpose of the essay on O'Neill particularly so. Why not compare O'Neill with Goethe or Yeats, Shakespeare or Aeschylus? These would be more sensible comparisons in a history – though not to be entertained lightly! And, more practically speaking, why place an essay on O'Neill towards the beginning of the book? I suppose this has something to do with the honorific place of O'Neill in American drama; probably, too, with the historical difficulty that O'Neill presents, a difficulty inextricably associated with that of establishing links between America's theatrical tradition and its modern drama.

The short way with O'Neill is to call his work a beginning and proceed to his achievement, but that will not do in a history. In *American Drama*, however, O'Neill remains as the authors found him, unaccommodated historically, isolated by his stature – a beacon from which American drama takes the message of self-respect but no direction.

One of the links between O'Neill and the theatre of the previous century was, of course, his father's career. O'Neill was uncommonly well placed to observe, criticise and absorb the tradition of which James O'Neill was an embodiment. The perception of men as actors of roles, the dynamics of the relation between soul and role, the processes of differentiation and identification between player and part, are brought into the field of consciousness in O'Neill's plays partly from the rich sub-conscious life of the theatre his father knew, as well, no doubt, as from Jung.

If plays in James O'Neill's time tended to be overshadowed by their actors, plays also entrapped them. The identification of actor with role often imbued the role with a liveliness not in the writing, but it could also impose a servitude by which actors such as Jefferson, Mayo and O'Neill were possessed, not always unwillingly, by a character: Rip Van Winkle, Davy Crockett, the Count of Monte Cristo. The requisite conditions for such life sentences were a long circuit of theatres in centres of population and affluence, connected by adequate means of transportation. In the course of the nineteenth century these conditions became ever more favourable and towards its end a population of some eighty-five million had recourse to some three thousand theatres. These magnitudes made it possible for an actor – a 'tommer', for instance – to spend the better part of a career in one production (something that the age of tourism was to make possible in London). Under irresistible financial stimulus, local stock companies gave way before 'combinations', actors received steady employment at the price of shrunken repertoires, and syndicates, by means of 'vertical integration' gained control of theatres and productions. The vastness of its hinterland made New York a different kind of theatrical capital from London and the economics of production costs and returns gave the entrepreneurs an unparalleled importance. The system was vigorously opposed by such intrepid spirits as Mrs Fiske, Sarah Bernhardt and David Belasco and it was broken, but not destroyed, by legal action. The new drama also undermined the old theatre business; and, more effectively, moving pictures cut into it, absorbing audiences, money and, eventually, performers.

In the Depression the spectre of a large business enterprise in ruins, with thousands of employees out of work, led the government to extend the shelter of the Works Progress Administration to the theatre. But the WPA's instrument, the Federal Theatre Project, created by Harry Hopkins and directed by Hallie Flanagan, conceived larger objectives than the support of an ailing business. The FTP aimed to develop regional theatres, native plays and original methods of production. It was, in fact, an attempt to re-found the American theatre and drama and perhaps its greatest strength was the clear perception that drama, theatrical form and theatre economics were a single complex. The regionalism promoted by the FTP, a force long suppressed or inhibited in the American theatre, has grown stronger. The radical approach to theatrical form died, however, with the FTP.

If the Americanness of American drama has been much less a matter of form than of content one might propose a number of reasons for this being so. First, dramatic forms were imposed by the English companies and the models they presented, the strongest counter-influence coming not from America itself but from the melodrama of France and Germany; secondly, the apologists for drama in America took, or were driven to, moral ground, defending drama for its moral content; thirdly, and most important, the advent of realism gave American playwrights a form which immediately took on a local colour since, axiomatically, it demanded a local content. If we overlook musical comedy, some important playwrights experimenting with expressionistic and related forms between the wars, and O'Neill's search for form, then realism can be seen as the manifestly destined form of American drama in this century. If we do not overlook these phenomena then we might say that contemporary playwrights in America still confront the task that O'Neill addressed himself to, of creating dramatic forms that are peculiarly appropriate to America and its traditions.

Douglass's playbill of 1761 advertising a 'Series of Moral Dialogues in five parts Depicting the evil effects of Jealousy and other Bad Passions and Proving that Happiness can only Spring from the Pursuit of Virtue' is justly renowned as a delicious tongue-in-cheek way of putting over *Othello*. For six shillings, the citizen of Newport, Rhode Island was promised 'improvement of the mind and manners' and that he 'might go home at a sober hour and reflect . . .'. Doubtless Douglass himself had in mind something other than moral improvement, and even other than money, in playing Othello; but whatever it was he could not for practical, and possibly intellectual, reasons formulate it. There was no conventional place for drama as a recreation, entertainment, distraction, indulgence, purgation of demons, or whatever. In the nineteenth century the moral justification of drama was, if anything, more strongly emphasised in America than in England. The profane excitements of melodrama in particular called for a heavy moral overlay. And from Herne to Rabe, realism on the stage has been used with exceptional vigour in America as a moral instrument designed to stir outrage at sexual, financial, commercial, military and any number of other hypocrisies and vices by their representation on the stage.

In his survey of American drama, Walter J. Meserve tends to write as one engaged with its development as a moral force. So he observes, at one point, that the rude stereotyping of immigrants on the stage

> was to work to the disadvantage of a national unity by leading Americans to basic misconceptions about people from foreign countries. As time passed, the unfortunate character of these ignorant and innocent impressions would have a serious effect upon society. By mid-twentieth century, for example, the nineteenth-century stereotypes of the American Indian, the Negro, the Chinese and East European minority groups were beginning to explode in the faces of a passive majority as they began to exercise political, social and economic power. Just as the drama had been a force in creating these stereotypes, it later became a force in breaking them.   (p. 178)

The notion that national unity is fostered more by true than by false images of minorities seems at least doubtful. One might better suppose that the effect of ridicule and distortion would be to encourage conformity to new ways and so develop, for what it is worth, national unity. But there is probably a confusion of civic virtue with theatrical effects in Meserve's observation; and it is one to be resisted in these days when censorship lobbies can be so energetic (as I know from encountering one at a Shakespeare Festival at which *The Merchant of Venice* was being presented) and also effective. In his own day, Edward Harrigan was accused of misrepresenting American society by dealing in stereotypes of black-, German-, Italian- and, especially, Irish-Americans. He replied, as well he could, that he was guided by the theatrical virtues of power, interest, humour and beauty. And Harrigan has the right of it. Drunken, brawling Irishmen (with or without kind hearts and high ideals), dull Germans, childish blacks, hypocritical Englishmen, sexless whiteys and so on, are part of a profane theatre language which has little (though something) to do with the counterparts of such figures in life. They are more like the stuff that dreams are made on and, though brought temporarily into the service of ephemeral moral notions, no more to be suppressed than dreams – or, at least, not without equivalent danger.

One of the native notes in the emergent American drama was, naturally, the moral (and often physical) superiority of native Americans; their frankness and directness being contrasted with the superficiality, deviousness and vacillation of mannered Europeans or Americans aping them. In the theatre there was something self-defeating in the theme, as the nicely ambivalent epilogue to Anna Cora Mowatt's *Fashion* indicates. The folly of following the fashion is the slight theme of the piece and this folly the audience, in attending the theatre, may be guilty of:

> Here let it see portrayed its ruling passion,
> And learn to prize at its just value – *Fashion*.

In *The Contrast*, an earlier treatment of a similar theme by Royall Tyler, theatregoing is presented unequivocally as a prime instance of fashion-mongering. Colonel Manly attempts to correct his susceptible sister's love of fashion, which is most evident in her long and elaborate description of what goes on in 'a side-box at the play'. He himself possesses a native candour to which the theatre and all fashionable behaviour is alien. As a character he is not much fun on the stage, lacking the vitality and interest that comes from role-playing. His 'waiter' Jonathan is a much livelier character. He is as incapable of putting on an act as his master is contemptuous of so doing. Jonathan, outdoing Partridge, even manages to go to the theatre, and be shocked by it, without realising that he is in a theatre at all. Jonathan is a comical Yankee devised for the stage, a new stereotype forged for theatrical service in the new society, and the instrument of the theatre's good-natured revenge on that society's contempt for theatrical virtues.

In Walter J. Meserve's account, American drama progressed towards a 'meaningful' (his too frequent adjective) realism of which James A. Herne was the first harbinger, and, beyond that, to a more fundamental concern with Man.

> The most distinctive development in American drama from the period of the Civil War up to the end of the First World War was the increasing interest shown in the problems of man. In 1865 man was still primarily a caricature in American drama – either romantically conceived, or burlesqued or a stereo-

type, but hardly a man, that 'poor, bare, forked animal' struggling to cope with the daily problems of this world and his fears of the next. By 1920 both the United States and man in it had changed drastically, while drama as a faithful reflection of a culture responded in kind. (p. 203)

It later becomes clear that Meserve has particularly in mind O'Neill's attempts ('Man! How d'yuh spell it?') at a modern, and inevitably pessimistic, humanism. It was only with O'Neill, says Meserve, 'that the concept of a modern drama, first presented by James Herne, was realized in the theatre'.

It is certainly tempting to see realism as the inevitable form of American drama. It brought American dramatists into their own in terms of content and, moreover, it displaced the emphasis on the actor with an emphasis on the character as the source of perception and emotion, having no use for the kind of theatrical role-playing that America had accepted, enjoyed, paid for and distrusted. James A. Herne, William Vaughn Moody, Edward Sheldon, Clyde Fitch and other playwrights were able to present fundamental human conflicts in specifically American terms. In Moody's *The Great Divide*, for instance, the conflict of sex and morality, male aggression and female inhibition, is melded with that of Western hustling against Eastern respectability. The subliminal theme of the play is American self-sufficiency in all varieties of human character, behaviour, suffering and conflict. When it comes to these, the play seems to say, America is just as rich in examples as the old world. Contemporary dramatists such as Lillian Hellman, Arthur Miller and Tennessee Williams picked up the thread of realism, after a period of experimentation in the American theatre, in such a way as to make realism seem the solid sub-stratum of American drama and amongst the youngest group of writers to achieve prominence (Rabe, Shepard, Mammet and Babe, for instance) realism still holds sway in variously intensified, or 'super', forms.

But to see the antecedents of modern American drama (the American antecedents that is to say), from the perspective of modern realism may be too restrictive; likely to lead to a too quick dismissal of nineteenth-century drama and even to limit our view of the modern playwright in whom the continuity from the nineteenth century is most apparent – Eugene O'Neill.

Consider the greatest American play, by certain standards, of all time, *Uncle Tom's Cabin*. In it we find an American hero of comparable stature in the gallery of types with Shylock or Tartuffe and as distinctively American, as a product of the imagination, as Falstaff is English. The play held the stage for fifty years and, at the turn of the century, was being played by five hundred companies. It was still going strong after the Great War. As late as 1945 a theatre conference thought it worthwhile to 'banish' the play by manifesto. Now the play is apparently dead, a phenomenon of theatrical history entombed in time.

Amongst other things, *Uncle Tom's Cabin* seems to be an example of a work once esteemed for its moral excellence and utility and now seen as the product of a vision distorted or perverted by moral ignorance – it being the way of morality for the new to spurn the old. In this case the moral transvaluation is so complete that the hero's name has passed into common speech (where 'Shylock' used to be found) as a term of contempt. The example is altogether sufficient to make one distrustful of right-thinking as a theatrical virtue and even distrustful that audiences inclined to profess pleasure in it really know what they are about. Of course it is obvious why *Uncle Tom's Cabin* should appear to be a relic, though an unforgettable and embarrassing one. But will it be so forever? Is it conceivable that audiences may come to care as little about the unreality of Tom's blackness as about the monstrousness of Shakespeare's Richard Crookback? It is possible that with this play, and others of its period, we are in a kind of chronological no man's land: too far from the actual conditions that animated the work and obscured its false view of them; too involved in present conditions that make the falsity offensive to us. In the particular case we are dealing with one of the most extraordinary and original products of the American imagination – black-face. If Tom, George Harris and Topsy could be accepted, as once they were, as not black but black-face characters, then one could imagine a revival of a play which is a powerful and profane conjuration of cruelty, love and pathos.

Harriet Beecher Stowe was at pains to demonstrate that her novel was based on reality, but she knew much more about slavery than about the transforming power of the imagination. She was, however, sufficiently alert to the seductiveness of the stage to refuse permission for any dramatic adaptation of her novel. In this she made a sensible, though not sophisticated, distinction between forms. With the elimination of a narrator both immediacy of effect *and* distance from objective reality tend to increase. The economy of the stage forces the stage characters to know and declare themselves – to play roles. So Topsy, in George Aikens's version of *Uncle Tom*, knowing too much, becomes a rather Ariel-like spirit of amoral beauty and vitality instead of the example of natural goodness deprived of moral enlightenment that the moral machinery requires. The saintliness of Tom and the nobility of George Harris are similarly the products of refinement in the crucible of the theatrical imagination.

In this respect, *Uncle Tom's Cabin* bears a relation to Negro minstrelsy, which has been described (elsewhere) by Richard Moody as America's only indigenous form and accorded the dignity of comparison with *commedia dell'arte*. What minstrelsy and *Uncle Tom's Cabin* have in common is not only burnt cork but the fantastication of a sub-culture which could not be expressed in an authentic form on the stage. But minstrelsy was an original form, arising rather mysteriously from some real contact with black models and developing in the context of purely theatrical imagination unvexed by morality.

As to authentic black forms, a moment of potential development was apparently missed with the extinction of the African Theatre in New York in 1823 after two years of existence. *The Drama of King Shotaway*, which was produced there, sounds from its proto-Shavian title as though it might have been of intrinsic interest as well as historical. But in drama black forms, as opposed to black themes and acting, have scarcely emerged. Despite the efforts of Langston Hughes, Leroi Jones and other recent playwrights, *The Emperor Jones* remains the most far-reaching attempt at a distinctive Afro-American form.

Consider another of the great antecedents, *Metamora*; a play taking for its theme another submerged American culture. The virtues of Metamora himself are plain-spoken truthfulness, unflinching courage, domestic tenderness and spiritual purity, and these are enhanced, on the stage, by a thrilling (though merely verbalised) fondness for the application of tortures. As an American hero he is the counterpart of Tom. Black-face is Christian and pathetic; red-face is pagan and tragic. Metamora is so spiritually absolute that he and his tribe end as the only good Indians proverbially do, conveniently dead. For forty odd years this noble aboriginal was embodied by Forrest as a quintessential American. The virtues of the 'dead' race ('that never existed', as Mark Twain said) became, by an act of sympathy by and with Forrest, ancestral. The genocidal colonists in the play are unimportant emotionally, though there is some significance in the fact that the worst of them is a regicide.

In *Metamora* the theatrical transmutation of the Indian is more obvious than the equivalent process in *Uncle Tom's Cabin*, and this is what makes it less offensive to modern sensibilities; not that genocide was less real than slavery. The style and form of *Metamora*, the high rhetoric of its verse and its approximation to English tragedy, declare its theatricality; while *Uncle Tom's Cabin.* being stylistically much closer to realism invites correction from the objective reality. But nevertheless the latter is a richer product of the theatrical imagination.

One of O'Neill's ambitions was to overcome 'the discordant, broken, faithless rhythm' of his time through the creation of dramatic forms which would be faithful to a modern perception of reality yet capable of bearing 'great language'. In *Long Day's Journey* it is the old nineteenth-century actor, playing a variety of life-enhancing and also destructive off-stage roles, who is the apologist for great language while the son (in whom a touch of the Gregers Werle is surely not accidental) attempts to tear off the masks. The best language available to Edmund is the morbid poetry of the nineties and his refuge from reality is not role-playing but alcohol. The dissensions and miseries of the Tyrones are accompanied, even produced by, cultural and social disorders, specifically those connected with the theatre: the domestic and artistic consequences of touring; the effects of a theatrical vocation on personality; above all the incomprehension on both sides of a break in the tradition.

In his work O'Neill attempted to establish a continuity between the drama and theatre of the past (not just the American past, of course) and that of modern America. *Long Day's Journey* reports, in a highly personal and moving way, his sense of failure. The challenge remains an artistic and historical one. *American Drama* may well stimulate the historical inquiry, partly as a source of information based on extensive research and partly as a work which fails to clarify many aspects of the history of drama in America.

NOTE

1. Travis Bogard, Richard Woody and Walter J. Meserve, *The Revels History of Drama in English*, volume VIII, *American Drama* (London: Methuen, 1977).

Samuel Beckett: The Critical Heritage
edited by Lawrence Graver and Raymond Federman

reviewed by JOHN PILLING

The success of Routledge's Critical Heritage series is dramatically illustrated in the endpapers of this latest addition,[1] which list over eighty volumes published or forthcoming, including such very useful items as the two-volume *Joyce*, the five-volume *Shakespeare*, and the *Jane Austen* that began it all. It has seen off its only serious rival, the Penguin Critical Anthologies, which were cheaper, less cumbersome and (in comparable cases) more enterprising, and is now left virtually alone in its chosen field. There are many who have had reservations about the series, from those who have muttered that students are being spoon-fed to those who have questioned whether from the immediately contemporary reception of an author we do in fact 'learn a great deal about the state of criticism at large and in particular' (as the General Editor claims in his preface). It is, indeed, obvious that some volumes in the series are very much more useful and imaginative than others. But on balance anything which reduces the present proliferation of published materials and renders it more manageable must obviously be welcomed. And so, albeit with some reservations, must the present volume. There has certainly been more ink spilt on Beckett than on any other post-war writer, and some of it has not so much clarified as obscured the nature of Beckett's enterprise. The editors of a volume of this kind are in the difficult position of being both passive reflectors of 'what oft was thought' and active custodians of what was 'ne'er so well expressed' at one and the same time. In so far as much of 'what oft was thought' is in the process of being rethought, their book will doubtless provide a stimulus to later critics. But precisely because their selection is less discriminating than it might have been, they have missed an opportunity to put subsequent Beckett criticism on more secure foundations.

Not that the history of the reception of Beckett does not call in question the concept of a 'heritage', for it does. There is a large lacuna between the 1930s and the 1950s in this volume, during which period Beckett was of course mainly occupied in writing the prose and drama on which his present fame rests, and when he may scarcely be said to have had any critical reputation at all, except with those who knew him personally in the Paris of the war and post-war years. There is also an unavoidable lack of chronology in the book's structure, the result of the delayed publication of *Watt* (written 1942–5, published 1953), the suppression of *Mercier and Camier* (written 1946, published 1970) and the gap between Beckett writing in English or in French and then translating from one language to the other. Clearly this is something that the historian of contemporary reception cannot allow himself to be worried by, although it is bound to make for a rather unbalanced profile of the writer's career, which in the case of Beckett is especially unfortunate, since many if not most of his works have been written in reaction to what preceded them. The tangled unfolding of the Beckett bibliography (which even the editors of the standard study, *Samuel Beckett: His Works and His Critics*,[2] could not entirely clarify) is not significantly improved by a compilation of this kind.

Given the paucity of early criticism of Beckett, it is surprising that the editors do not reprint all the 1930 reviews, however ephemeral or brief, in order that, for those few who may read this volume consecutively, the 1930s might be allowed their full say before the deluge of the last twenty years swamps them without trace. No doubt Graver and Federman were guided by the General Editor's remarks about 'intrinsic critical worth' and 'representative quality', for it is obvious that even Kate O'Brien's excellent review of *Murphy* (the best of the early reviews, from the *Spectator* of 1938) has long been superseded by book-length studies of the novel and the full panoply of academic overkill. Here the editors must also have faced the problem of whether or not to include extracts from the Beckett industry, and decided (rightly or wrongly) that anything already in book form would have to be omitted, to make more room for reviews and theatre notices. But with such a large amount of important criticism omitted, the collection's claim to provide us with an accurate image of the contemporary reception of Beckett is inevitably weakened. The Penguin Critical Anthologies are much more sensible here, and do not fight shy of the business of excerpting a chapter or a paragraph from a work of scholarship that has decisively affected all subsequent criticism. It might be objected that this would compromise the contemporaneity of the response, but in so far as we are all (as the preface puts it) 'near-contemporaries' of Beckett, it would surely have been legitimate to include something of the kind, if only as a representative example.

No one could quibble about the fact that Graver and Federman have devoted six of their eighty-three extracts to *Molloy*, nine to *Waiting for Godot*, four to *Watt*, five to *Endgame* and six to *How It Is*, although four on *The Lost Ones* and three on *Mercier and Camier* may seem like rather too much of a good thing. By and large they have kept a good balance between English, French and American reactions, although they have neglected the recent German interest in Beckett and seriously scanted the reaction of the Irish to their own product. The forty-page introduction gives the editors the chance to refer to

items that they have elected to omit and to impose a shape that is inevitably
lacking in the anthology they have chosen. But the anthologist is, more than
most, on a hiding to nothing, and there are a number of pieces here that one
would willingly have sacrificed in favour of some that may never see the light
of day again. Why, for example, was Richard Seaver's serviceable but
superficial 1952 'introduction' to Beckett preferred to Niall Montgomery's
self-indulgent but exciting overview of 1954?[23] Why have they reprinted
Alan Schneider's 'Working with Beckett' (already available in *Beckett at
Sixty*)[24] and E. M. Cioran's 'Encounters with Beckett' (already available in
the *Cahiers de L'Herne*)?[25] Both are extremely interesting but neither, strictly
speaking, is part of the contemporary *reception* of Beckett. Why is there no
entry at all for *Embers*, Beckett's most underrated play, when there is a
surprisingly imaginative review of the first radio broadcast in *The Times*?[26]
Likewise, whilst it might not be desirable for all the extracts to possess the
verbal fireworks of Montgomery (or John Updike or Kenneth Tynan or
Nigel Dennis or Dylan Thomas, all of whom are included), why could not
space have been found for Roy Walker's excellent *Listener* review of *All That
Fall*,[7] John Berger's stringent Marxist critique of *Waiting for Godot* (if the
author and the *Daily Worker* had been willing),[8] and any of B. S. Johnson's
pieces on Beckett (of which a *Spectator* review of 1964 is perhaps the best)?[9]
Johnson's own novels were much influenced by Beckett and are part of a
'creative' heritage that may well prove more important than any 'critical'
one. All three of these items actually offend less against the suppressed
premiss of omitting scholarly articles than do the two essays from the
American magazine *Spectrum* (one by Donald Davie, the other by Hugh
Kenner) or David Lodge's attempt at 'Some *Ping* Understood' from
Encounter. There are other strange omissions: the anonymous review (in the
Irish Times) of Beckett's first dramatic venture *Le Kid*;[10] the anonymous
Dublin Magazine review of *Murphy*;[11] A. J. Leventhal on *Godot* (also in the
Dublin Magazine);[12] The *Irish Times* review of *More Pricks than Kicks*.[13] But it
is not only the Irish who have some reason to feel slighted; space might also
have been found for Beckett's one-time collaborator Georges Pelorson on
Beckett's 'classicisme retrouvé',[14] Alain Bosquet (on *Fin de Partie*),[15] Ludo-
vic Janvier's review articles on *Watt* and on the residua for *Critique*;[16] and at
least one (and preferably both) of Edith Fournier's excellent accounts of *Sans*
and *Comment c'est*.[17] One of the great successes of the volume, by contrast, is
the reprinting of three interviews that Beckett, more or less willingly, granted
to Israel Shenker, Gabriel d'Aubarède, and Tom F. Driver. (A fourth, the
John Gruen interview in *Vogue*, is neither included nor referred to.)[18] These
are not easily available and deserve a more permanent existence than they
have previously enjoyed. But even here one wonders whether they may truly
be said to have much to do with 'the contemporary reception' of Beckett.

   The editors are to be congratulated upon the way they have selected intelligent negative responses to Beckett, although here too they might have found space for one prize piece of inveterate silliness that lacked the redeeming panache of Tynan and Updike.[19] It would have added more drama to the book to have had one example of recantation (Mailer's, from *Advertisements for Myself*, for example)[20] and one instance of a critic finding Beckett gradually less and less *simpatico* (*The Village Voice*, where Mailer's 'advertisements' first appeared, could have provided several examples). Of those who appear more than once in this collection (Donald Davie, Harold Hobson, Kenneth Tynan, Christopher Ricks, A. Alvarez, Federman himself, and Robert Brustein) only Brustein seems to oscillate between extremes of attraction and repulsion in an interesting and inquiring way.

It is disturbing to observe how, in this collection, the quality of Beckett criticism declines quite dramatically after Federman's essay on *Film*, admittedly one of the highspots of the volume. The immediate response to Beckett's 'ends and odds' in prose and drama has been much less sensitive than that accorded *Molloy* or *Krapp's Last Tape*.

Anyone who thinks highly of Beckett's 'late' period will be dismayed at the way the editors treat the 'critical heritage' of the last decade, ignoring the intelligent and informed response to *Lessness*, *Still*, the *Fizzles* and the recent stage and television plays – as 'contemporary' as one could wish for – in such journals as *Critique*, *Poétique* and the *Journal of Beckett Studies*, and settling instead for the puzzled and paraphrastic response of more or less stilted newspaper reviewers. This has the unfortunate effect of making the end of the 'heritage' look strangely like the beginning, and prompts one to wonder whether even Beckett's 'middle' period has been properly understood. It is salutary to be reminded that a heritage can come into existence in so short a time as a quarter of a century; but not much can be done with a 'heritage' that leaves Beckett criticism precisely where it was, in a stage of muddle and misapprehension. In offering us a partial portrait of this heritage, the editors awaken in us a desire that they themselves could have done more to satisfy: to see the Beckett critics criticised. One is loath to recommend that there should be any further barriers placed between the reader and Beckett's text; but it is clear that, unless someone soon undertakes this onerous and unattractive task, the text is in danger of becoming little more than the sum total of commentaries upon it. It may be, as some Structuralists would claim, that this is the fate of any text whatever, and it may already be too late to arrest the process. But there may never be a better opportunity to see whether it can be done, now that one version of the heritage has been given a permanent form. For 'heritage', it should be remembered, denotes not only what has been handed down to us, but also what may be handed down to others in the future.

NOTES

1. *Samuel Beckett: The Critical Heritage*, ed. Lawrence Graver and Raymond Federman (London: Routledge & Kegan Paul, 1979).

2. Raymond Federman and John Fletcher, *Samuel Beckett: His Works and His Critics* (Los Angeles and London: University of California Press, 1970).

3. Richard Seaver, 'Samuel Beckett: An Introduction', *Merlin* (autumn 1952); Niall Montgomery, 'No Symbols Where None Intended', *New World Writing*, no. 5 (April 1954).

4. *Beckett at Sixty* (London: Calder & Boyars, 1967).

5. Tom Bishop and Raymond Federman (eds), *Cahiers de L'Herne: Beckett* (Paris: Editions de L'Herne, 1976).

6. *The Times* (25 June 1959).

7. *The Listener* (24 January 1957).

8. *Daily Worker* (22 March 1956).

9. *Spectator* (June 1964).

10. *The Irish Times* (20 February 1931).

11. *Dublin Magazine* (April–June 1939).

12. *Dublin Magazine* (January–March 1956).

13. *The Irish Times* (23 June 1934).

14. *Table ronde* (February 1953).

15. *Combat* (21 February 1957).

16. 'Le difficultés d'un séjour', *Critique* (April 1969); 'La lien du retrait de la blancheur de l'echo', *Critique* (1967).

17. 'Sans: cantate et fugue pour une réfuge', *Lettres Nouvelles* (September–October 1970); 'Pour que la boue me soit contée', *Critique* (May 1961).

18. *Vogue* (December 1969).

19. Kenneth Tynan in *The Observer* (2 November 1958); John Updike in *New Yorker* (19 December 1964).

20. Norman Mailer, *Advertisements for Myself* (New York: Putnam's, 1959).

FORUM

Ibsen: a reply to James Walter McFarlane

RONALD GRAY

There was a time when Congreve's *Mourning Bride* was taken as the high peak of tragedy – it was the time that never saw Shakespeare except in Nahum Tate's or Davenant's rewriting, and is a mark of how ephemeral a dramatist's reputation can be. Ibsen's has been among the highest now for over a hundred years, and may yet suffer the same eclipse as Congreve's, so far as tragedy is concerned.

So it was frustrating to find the first large-scale and authoritative review[1] of my *Ibsen. A Dissenting View* confined so much to what Professor McFarlane admits might be 'aberrations . . . defensible as momentary slips of attention' (McFarlane, p. 308), rather than the larger issues, the comparisons with Sophocles and Chekhov, the question whether all Ibsen's plays are poetry, of whether there is so much triviality in so respected a playwright. It was even more frustrating to find such an aberration as my curious insistence on calling Torvald Helmer Helmer Torvald – inexplicable to me myself – described as a *dangerous* indication of inattention (McFarlane, p. 303). But then McFarlane has a 'fear', more than a fear, a theory, that the errors he finds are the result of an impatience giving rise to prejudiced readings and even deliberate hostility, deliberate calculation to obfuscate the meaning, wilful myopia. If he is right, and I deliberately put Torvald's name back to front in the interest of some preconceived reading of my own, I am more than dangerous, and ought to be locked up. But McFarlane brings no evidence of my deliberate intentions, only taxes me with what he takes for errors, which then loom up with so much the more portentousness.

His first critical point is an error itself, as to fact. I have, he says, 'easy fun' by remarking that Ibsen must have wanted to introduce Irene, in *When We Dead Awaken*, as humorously as possible 'by making Rubek imagine that the figure he saw walking about the grounds at night was wearing a bathing-costume' (Gray, p. 188). It is 'feigned innocence' in me that lets me see Irene as though she were some Miss World contestant. *Badedragt* (which is literally nothing else but a swimming-costume) 'in this context *must* of course be thought of as some kind of enveloping "bathing-wrap" in order to match the actual appearance of Irene a few moments later "dressed in a fine creamy

white cashmere . . . her dress floorlength . . ." ' (McFarlane, p. 302). But
McFarlane has confused two occasions. The time when Rubek saw Irene in
her *badedragt* was the previous night; it is on the following morning that he
tells Maja about it. She is amused at the idea, putting Rubek on the
defensive, which suggests some incongruity. And it is a few moments after
this conversation, not a few moments after Rubek first saw her, that Irene
appears in her perfectly respectable floorlength dress, having had plenty of
time to put it on as normal daytime wear – it does not sound at all like a
bathing-wrap. So my case stands: Ibsen's introduction of Irene is oddly
humorous, like his dressing of Ellida's Stranger in a tam-o'-shanter and a
ginger beard. But Irene becomes yet more odd later on (Gray, p. 192).

Fortunately, the discussion does not remain at this trivial level, and
McFarlane scores a direct hit with his next thrust, aimed at my account of
The Wild Duck. My criticism of Ibsen's time-scheme, which seemed to allow
only a few months for Hjalmar to be bamboozled into marrying Gina, was
seriously at fault, and I can only withdraw it, together with the suggestion
that it shows up Hjalmar for a fool. On the other hand, it was not my only
reason for describing Hjalmar in uncomplimentary terms. On the following
pages I add many more indications of Ibsen's heavy hand in portraying
Hjalmar's fatuity (Gray, pp. 102–3). My view of this caricature of a character is unaffected by the mistake.[2]

With Krogstad, we are on more disputable ground. McFarlane finds me
grotesquely insensitive here. ' "Bad" he may be, but essentially like one of
those "méchants animaux" of the standard phrase: "Quand on les attaque,
ils se défendent".' Krogstad has not charged exorbitant interest, or used
blackmail against Nora before. Only when he is quite outrageously sacked
from his job at the whim of a new manager, 'and thus finds his entire career,
his children's future, his family's existence destroyed at one cruel and
arbitrary stroke does he vigorously react to defend himself and his position'
(McFarlane, p. 306). There is some truth in that. Yet I am not alone in
finding Krogstad what Raymond Williams calls 'the villain' in a play typical
of intrigue drama. Self-defence exonerates only up to a point, and Krogstad
not only shows signs of having bided his time, he wrings every ounce of
advantage out of his knowledge of Nora's forgery. He has kept Nora's now
worthless security – worthless ever since her father died – without asking for
any replacement of it, though he knows the father's signature on it is forged.
Now that an occasion offers itself when he can use it, he is implacably
ruthless. He operates through the distress of Nora, rather than go straight to
Torvald, though he knows from his own experience that such threats as he
uses may drive her to suicide. He looks for more than a mere reinstatement in
his position at the bank, and plans to use his knowledge of Nora's guilt to
become, in effect, bank-manager in Torvald's place. McFarlane, in defending him, is driven to belittling any forgery Krogstad may have made (though

it was nearly the cause of his own suicide), and even to arguing that his 'wild talk' of ousting Torvald from the managership is based on an assessment of Torvald's character which is 'legitimised' by the entire subsequent course of the play (McFarlane, p. 306). I do not understand that 'legitimised' – does it mean that because Torvald is a bad husband he can properly be pushed out of his job? – any more than I understand the admission that Krogstad is 'ruthless perhaps', or the omission of any reference to his cruel tormenting of Nora.

Krogstad, in the blackmailing scenes, is ruthless full stop. That is what links him with the villain of melodrama, while the swiftness of his withdrawal when Mrs Linde offers him the prospect of a happier life brings home how much of a puppet in Ibsen's hands he is. The man who so promptly accepts domestic content, and who evidently sees what that content could really mean, is not the man to give way to such tooth-and-claw tactics as Krogstad uses, even in self-defence: his scruples would show more clearly. But as Eric Bentley says – and I quoted him – 'Krogstad . . . is a mere pawn of the plot. When convenient to Ibsen, he is a blackmailer. When inconvenient, he is converted.'[3] What Ibsen needed for his plot was a character vicious enough to plant the dynamite letter in the letter-box, yet decent enough to pop in a free pardon for Torvald and Nora the moment after the dynamite had exploded. For the purposes of such a rapid *volte-face* Krogstad was born.

It was the first *volte-face* I came to. Others (Gray, p. 227) included Mrs Alving's sudden conversion to the beneficial value of incest, Stockmann's rapid change from euphoria to a desire to exterminate the civilised world, Rosmer's abrupt abandonment of his whole life's mission after a single conversation, Løvborg's fall from high idealism to total despair and suicide at the temporary loss of a MS, Ulfheim's transformation from swashbuckling Superman to lady's lapdog, and others besides. Krogstad is merely one instance of Ibsen's manipulations of character in the interest of plot.

McFarlane misrepresents me when he says that it is central to my view of *John Gabriel Borkman* that the Erhart element is arbitrary. Far from being central, the point he takes up is an aside. It was that, whereas Earl Skule's son Peter attempts to carry on in his place (and, I might have mentioned, the memory of their son Eyolf is an inspiration to the Allmers, while Stockmann's daughter is to become a missionary for his cause), Erhart's departure is totally remote from any concern with his father John Gabriel. My central concern was with the vagueness of Erhart's own purposes as part of the vagueness of the whole play.

My drawing attention to this in relation to Borkman's betrayal by Hinkel seems to McFarlane a piece of mystification, deliberately introduced by me in my efforts to darken what is perfectly clear. Yet there is a mystery about the whole crime for which Borkman has suffered so long. First, there is the extraordinary pact between Borkman and Hinkel, whereby Borkman renounced his interest in Ella Rentheim (as though she were a parcel of shares) in exchange for the control of a bank. 'You made me', she says, 'part of your cheap bargain. . . . Traded your love with another man. Sold my love for . . . a bank directorship!' (*The Oxford Ibsen*, VIII, 196). This seemed to me both a strange charge for Ella to bring, and strange conduct in any man: how could any of them imagine a woman's love could be switched from one man to another as part of a deal? Does Ella herself take her own accusation seriously? That McFarlane can see 'the complex interplay of business ethics, power seeking, love and marriage at work here' (McFarlane, p. 307) suggests that he does take it seriously. He has been steeped so long in Ibsen that such manipulations of the passions no longer seem unusual: in fact he supplies a whole pattern of events not mentioned in but 'implied' by the play – and thus dramatically inert – which rests on the assumption that both men, at least, perhaps Ella as well (as her own quoted words seem to show) believed in their ability to direct her affections at will.

The other obscurity concerned Borkman's complaint that Hinkel sold him down the river by publishing his private and confidential correspondence, precipitating his downfall. This McFarlane finds clear: the letters 'obviously revealed to the world Borkman's fraudulent business plans', and in his now published translation that seems confirmed, since he makes Borkman say: 'There was no aspect of my affairs I ever felt I couldn't reveal to him.' But the original is not so clear-cut. Borkman speaks not of 'affairs' – if by that is meant business affairs – but of not concealing 'hele min vandel', which could refer to his whole life. There is in fact much to suggest that Borkman is not complaining merely that his business secrets alone had been divulged. He would scarcely persist with his accusation against Hinkel of having committed 'the most infamous crime a man can be guilty of', or describe him as 'infected and poisoned in every fibre with the morals of the higher rascality' if Hinkel had done no more than reveal his double-dealing. (As for 'higher rascality', or *Überschurkenmoral*, explained by McFarlane with reference to Nietzsche, its aptness is still obscure, in this particular situation.) Borkman seems to have something peculiarly monstrous in mind, something far more evil than commercial trickery. What Hinkel published were things confided to him and to him alone, 'like a whisper in a dark, empty, locked room' – it sounds as though the very secrets of Borkman's soul were involved. Far from wanting to rewrite the play 'so that some simple stock-market slump sends Borkman to prison', I was drawing attention to a dimension which McFarlane quite fails to recognise, a concern of Ibsen's which for some reason he could not bring fully into the open, but of which I offered a possible explanation (Gray, p. 178). My puzzlement at the disproportion of Borkman's accusations in comparison with any everyday businessman's likely protest at being cheated led me to the hypothesis that, as so often, a mythical element was at the roots.

However, seeing that at one point Borkman decides after many years' deliberation that he is entirely innocent of the whole affair for which he was imprisoned, something more definite than we are offered would have been a help to understanding.

Vagueness about the past is surprisingly common in Ibsen. McFarlane quotes my parenthetical question about Alving's nose turning red as though it were rather vulgar of me, but it is part of a long string of questions designed to show how impossible the story of the Captain's past life is (Gray, p. 68). And this is merely one instance among many. Rosmer could never, in nineteenth-century Norway, have been unaware that the long evenings spent alone with the beautiful, unmarried Rebecca were grieving his wife. Stockmann, after so many years in the North, could not have acquired so much evidence of local corruption as he is said to have done within a day or two of arriving. A timid scholar like Tesman could never have proposed to spend evening after evening with Thea Elvsted while his wife was being entertained at home by Judge Brack. Such improbabilities matter more in Ibsen than they do in Shakespeare, who has no reputation as a realist and relies heavily on the conventions of romance and legend. If Ibsen's basic situations are unreal, his whole plays begin to fall apart.

I can accept, therefore, only a small part of Professor McFarlane's strictures. What disappoints me most is that he should have paid so little attention to what I wrote about Ibsen's language – the supreme test for any writer, dramatist or not. To take me to task for a whole page, one-tenth of the review, on whether I needed to raise the question of the meaning of 'at digte' (McFarlane, p. 309) looks rather like a postponement of the admission that in my chapter on 'The poetry and the prose' I had successfully shown up the currently common mistake of trying to find poetry where there is none. Where did the mistake arise? How was it that critics have found it possible to speak of 'hidden poetry', 'latent poetry', to maintain that 'all of Ibsen's books, early or late, in verse or in modern prose, are a form of poetry'? Perhaps some were misled by a misreading of 'digte' – not necessarily in any translation; perhaps there has been a sense that if Ibsen's honour were to be saved, after his reputation as a social dramatist had waned, the rank of poet must be claimed for him. The causes are not the main thing. What I looked for was an acknowledgement of the kind McFarlane begins to make when he writes: 'There is no doubt that the choice of the term "poetry" for the enriched meaning that informs the dramatic mode – whether "realistic", "symbolic" or whatever – bedevils the debate' (McFarlane, pp. 309–10). As that argument develops into a more and more involved attempt at admitting what I claim to have proved, while using a language more and more unlike McFarlane's usual straightforward style, a whiff of Bernick at confession floats on the air:

> If – to adapt an older and in these days wholly non-trendy definition from I. A.
> Richards – one were to postulate that drama is a mode of communication, and
> that *what* it communicates and *how* this is communicated and the value of what
> is communicated is then the legitimate business of criticism, provision is made
> for a suitable framework of reference for such elements inherent in drama as
> visual imagery, physical movement and gesture and the semantics of situation;
> but to take all which is extra to the sum of the referential meanings of the verbal
> utterances and call it 'poetry' is, though legitimate enough, nevertheless at the
> risk of inviting a set of stock responses to the term which are obstructive of true
> understanding.   (McFarlane, p. 310)

We shall none of us be better critics for reading that, and I am sorry that it
should have got in the way of a discussion of the actual instances I quoted.

What is most at fault in *Pillars of Society*, for instance, is not that Bernick
only appears to have made a clean breast of it, though Edmund Gosse and
several of his generation supposed he had. The play ends badly, as McFarlane himself comes near to saying (*The Oxford Ibsen*, v, 11–12), because
Bernick's language becomes so 'unpromisingly ponderous . . . monumen-
tally rhetorical . . . prolix, verbose' that no audience could fairly be asked to
say whether his partial concealment of his misdoings is consciously ironical
or not. (It is not enough to allow him, as happened in John Barton's
production, to invite the audience to enjoy the joke by means of one single,
final wink: the whole point of his speech is to wrap up the truth so well that
neither the audience on stage nor the one in the stalls can take it in at one go.)
Rosmersholm ends badly for the opposite reason, that the language signifying
the union of Rosmer and Rebecca is so bald, so arithmetically calculating,
and so pretentious at the same time (Gray, p. 122). *Little Eyolf* ends with
words which I called 'orotund melodrama' (Gray, p. 173) – a phrase which
McFarlane quotes as though in surprise. But is there not, whether in
Norwegian or English, an inflated solemnity in the lines which conclude:

> *Rita.* You'll see. A Sabbath stillness will fall on us now and again.
> *Alfred* [*quietly, moved*]. Then perhaps we shall be aware of the visit of the spirits.
> *Rita* [*whispers*]. The spirits?
> *Alfred.* Yes. Perhaps they are about us – those we have lost.
> *Rita* [*slowly nodding*]. Our little Eyolf. And your big Eyolf too.
> *Alfred* [*Staring ahead*]. Perhaps we will still, along life's way, catch a glimpse of
> them.
> *Rita.* Where shall we look for them, Alfred?
> *Alfred* [*fixing his eyes upon her*]. Upwards.
> *Rita* [*nods in approval*]. Yes, yes – upwards.
> *Alfred.* Upwards – towards the peaks. Towards the stars. And towards the
> great silence.
> *Rita* [*giving him her hand*]. Thanks!
>   (translation Ronald Gray. See also *The Oxford Ibsen*, VIII, 105–67)

This, helped by the Norwegian flag that moment hoisted by Alfred, has a
portentousness that is as much in the stage instructions as in the words

spoken: the whispering, the staring ahead, the fixed gaze of Alfred's eyes on Rita, as well as the unmeaningful general gesture at Higher Things, none of which have had any mention hitherto, all contribute to the sense that, as I wrote, they love themselves in this new role. Much virtue in 'upwards'.

It is on points like these that I would have welcomed debate. Is it not a cliché, in both languages, that Hedda uses when she speaks of Løvborg's having had the will to take leave of life's feast? Do Rubek and Irene not speak in clichés – do their words undergo some miraculous degeneration in translation – when they say 'Both in us and around us life is fermenting and throbbing', 'Up in the light and all the glittering glory', 'All the powers of light may look upon us. And all the powers of darkness too' (Gray, p. 196)? Is Ulfheim's language meant to be comical, or is his swagger meant to sound impressive? Are Irene's cheerful inanities about the death of her husband the mark of the tragic heroine or the penny dreadful? These are questions more important than whether she is wearing a swimming-costume or whether Krogstad may be partly exonerated. They go to the heart of the play, its whole tone and feeling and sense, and criticism which takes no account of them will always be inadequate.

I am obliged to Professor McFarlane for his courteous review. Perhaps it does not matter too much that a whole year must pass before this reply is published. If I am right on the whole, it is absurd to expect quick conversions, and the process of revaluing is bound to be slow at the level at which we are moving. But I fear that the essential nature of my dissent has still not received attention, or even been properly understood.

NOTES

1. *Themes in Drama*, vol. 1, *Drama and Society* (Cambridge University Press, 1979), pp. 299–311.
2. This and other errors will be corrected in the forthcoming paperback edition.
3. Eric Bentley, *In Search of Theater* (New York: Vintage Books, 1957), p. 345.

Index